Mirror Image

By Michele Pariza Wacek

This book may be purchased for educational, business, or sales promotional use. For information, please email
info@michelepw.com.

ISBN–10: 0-9968260-6-8
ISBN–13: 978-0-9968260-6-8

Library of Congress Control Number: 2016937893

DEDICATION

To Paul, for believing in me (and kicking my you-know-what) to get this book out there.

Chapter 1

Silver eyes, sharp as blades, tearing through him, leaving his body shredded and bloody.

He blinked. Where the hell did that come from?

Joe took another look at the girl who accompanied him to his apartment. The harsh lights of the hallway made her look more pale and tired than she had appeared in the bar, but she smiled at him nonetheless, and he felt reassured. He grinned back, realizing it likely looked more like a lopsided, drunken leer than a smile. He lightly pressed his hand on her back, bumping into her slightly, alcohol blurring his brain.

"Your eyes are gray," he said, his voice slurred.

The girl looked at him, surprised. "What color should they be?"

Joe laughed, thick and hoarse. "Silver. I thought they were silver."

"Oh," the girl smiled at him. "That happens a lot. Reflections."

Yeah, reflections, that was it. Her eyes were such a pure gray — no hint of green, brown or blue. The color seemed to reflect more light than other gray combinations, making them appear silver.

Joe stumbled, banging his knee into the wall. He felt nothing, his legs heavy and numb. She laughed slightly, putting an arm around his waist to help him walk, her purse bouncing off his leg.

He nuzzled her hair, her neck. She smelled of sweat, beer, cigarettes and perfume — very strongly of perfume. In fact, he realized her perfume all but obliterated those other scents. He usually didn't like it when women used so much, but at this point it made no difference.

"Why won't you tell me your name?" he asked again.

For an answer, she turned her face toward him and gently bit his lip. He felt a sting and tasted blood, which excited him even more. Rough. He'd never had it that way before. He could feel himself getting hard.

Everything about the woman was different. First off, he hadn't had to convince her, cajole her, like all the other women. "Of course, I really like you. Of course, this is special for me. I've never met a woman like you before. I don't normally do this either." The gray-eyed woman seemed to want it as much as he did, and she needed no promises or lines. They both knew exactly what tonight represented — a good fuck and nothing more. When he picked her up in the bar, she seemed a dream come true.

They reached his door. He fell heavily against the frame while fishing for his keys. She tightened her grip, steadying and surprising him. When he had first looked at her, under the lights in that little white dress, he had thought her delicate. Insubstantial. But now, he knew he had been incorrect. There was clearly more to her than he originally thought.

Joe struggled briefly with the key. The keyhole kept eluding his drunken, trembling hands, but he was finally able to slide the key in. He unlocked the door with a click.

"Gee," she said. "I hope you don't have that much trouble tonight."

Moving toward her, he answered by kissing her on the mouth. She tasted sour — of beer and something else, something he couldn't identify. As her tongue slid into his mouth, he quit trying to figure it out. The door creaked open when they leaned against it, and they quite literally fell into his apartment.

She got to her feet first, pushing his clumsy hands from her body. "Where's the bathroom?" she asked.

"Down the hall — first door to your left," he said, fighting to get up. The room whirled and dipped beneath him. Alcohol churned unpleasantly in his stomach. He couldn't be sick. Not now. Slowly he hoisted himself to his feet, hanging on to the doorpost, blinking his eyes to focus.

"I guess I'm drunker than I thought," he said out loud, pulling the door shut and locking it. Then he remembered the joint he had smoked before hitting the bars, and figured that probably had something to do with it, too. He didn't usually smoke pot, but tonight he had allowed his roommate to talk him into it.

Joe took a couple of deep breaths, still hanging onto the door. The room settled, ceasing to spin. He let go of the door, stumbling across the living room and into the hallway.

He saw his bedroom door open, the light on. She was sitting on the bed, her coat off. "I hope you don't mind," she said. "I decided to make myself at home."

Joe shook his head, shed his coat and crossed the room to sit on the bed next to her. The little white dress clung to her large breasts. He leaned over to kiss her, his hand creeping onto her lap. She let him, but barely responded. He stopped and looked at her. "What's wrong?"

Her eyes were that weird color again. Silver. He couldn't keep her face in focus. Her features kept blurring, melting together into one indistinguishable mess. Had he totally misread her after all?

"I want to do something different," she said, and he started getting excited again. She pushed him down on the bed. "Lie down."

Joe obeyed, instantly hard despite the alcohol and drugs in his body. She stood up, running her hands up her body and across her breasts, slowly and sensually. Her silver eyes never left his face when she dropped her hands to her waist, untied the scarf around her waist, and unwound it.

She held it up over her head, the end fluttering down softly beside her. She trailed it across his body, tickling his face with it, then got up on the bed and straddled his chest.

Gently, she picked up his right hand and wrapped one end of the scarf around it. She tied it to the bedpost, her speed slowly increasing, then swiftly tied his left hand up.

Her hair, thick with perfume, brushed his cheek while she worked. The scent surrounded him, suffocated him. Musky. He couldn't quite identify it.

"Did you ever see *Basic Instinct*?" she purred, her hands on his chest, unbuttoning his shirt. "I love that movie."

Her hair swung in front of her face, obscuring it. He began to feel slightly uneasy. Why would she bring up *that* movie? He faintly recalled a few scenes — images mostly — something about men being tied to beds and stabbed. Carefully, he tested the knots. Very tight. "Just as long as you don't stab me with an ice pick," he joked weakly.

She lifted her head, her silver eyes burning into his. She smiled. "I promise I won't stab you with an ice pick."

He tried the knots again.

She began unbuttoning his shirt, removing his shoes, pants, underwear, creatively using her mouth and tongue in ways Joe had never before experienced. He groaned.

He reassured himself that he had nothing to be paranoid about. She liked to play it rough, and he wanted to enjoy it. God knew this wasn't something he found every day.

Her nails scratched his chest, his thighs. Deep scratches, drawing blood, as her mouth worked him over. He groaned again, thrashing slightly, the pain mingling with pleasure in the most unanticipated ways.

She licked the scratches, gently nibbling, tearing his flesh even more. He thrashed harder, moaning constantly now.

The room seemed to tilt and sway, his mind overwhelmed by the alcohol and what she was doing to him. She lifted her head. A tiny drop of blood dotted the corner of her mouth. She licked her lips and smiled, her teeth smeared pink. She looked like a wild cat who had just devoured its prey or, worse yet, a vampire. He shuddered lightly, the contents in his stomach churning together unpleasantly, making him fight the urge to vomit.

"I like you," she said, her voice rough and thick. "So I won't make you suffer too long."

She leaped off him and began dancing wildly around the room, her movements jerky and wooden. She looked like some sort of macabre puppet, whirling around and around. He stared at her in disbelief.

Then she began to laugh. A horrible, high-pitched laugh. It almost resembled a scream.

He fought against the knots in earnest, but they wouldn't give. He tried to use his upper body, kicking with his feet and throwing his body forward, but he felt so weak, so numb. He could barely feel his legs anymore. He cursed himself for drinking so much, for the pot he had smoked.

He suddenly became aware that she had stopped dancing. She stood perfectly still, watching him. *Watching him.* Her silver eyes gleamed.

"You won't get away," she said in a very flat voice. "You're too drunk and too stupid to get away."

He stared at her, terrified. The silence, the stillness was more frightening than her dancing and laughter had been. "Why?" he managed to choke out. "Why?"

She cocked her head and smiled at him, showing her bloodstained teeth. His blood. And he had goddamned enjoyed it, too.

Oh God … he was going to die.

She laughed, her high-pitched, screaming laugh, and raised her hand, her purse dropping to the floor with a "thunk." He could see the glint of the blade she clutched in her hand.

"See, I told you it wouldn't be an ice pick," she sneered. The silver of the blade matched the silver of her eyes.

He stared at her, too shocked to scream, in utter disbelief. This had to be a dream. Some stupid, drug- and alcohol-induced dream. A horrible hallucination. Except he suddenly had never felt more sober in his life.

Then she was on him, on his chest, pressing the knife against his cheek. It was as cold as ice, burning through his skin.

He tried to buck her off, but she laughed and rode him effortlessly.

"I told you I liked you, and you won't suffer. Now don't make me take that back." She tightened her thighs and calves around his chest, squeezing him, suffocating him … no longer the least bit delicate. He felt his ribs cracking.

"Who the hell are you?" he managed, his breathing thick and choppy. His heart pounded so hard, it echoed in his ears. She squeezed harder. The room darkened, spun, along with her face, the features merging and melting together.

Except for those eyes. Those horrible, inhuman, silver eyes.

And then he saw — saw exactly what he had invited home to his apartment.

Joe's mind snapped shut, unable to deal with the horror straddling his chest. He opened his mouth to scream, but it was too late. He couldn't suck in enough air.

He watched as she raised the knife above her head, pausing for a second, before slowly, slowly, beginning its descent. He tried to scream again.

The knife tore into him, cutting off his anguished cry.

He felt no pain at first. Just blood, everywhere — gushing out of his neck, onto the sheets, onto that thing, the monster who straddled him.

Then the pain hit. It seared him, burned him. His body was co-cooned in agony, writhing uncontrollably. He could no longer breathe at all.

She watched him die, a small smile on her distorted, twisting, melting face. Curtains of blackness hovered at the edge of his vision. He could feel himself fading away, his life force draining out of him, and he struggled to hold on.

Watching his battle, she leaned closer still, her face nearly touching his, and opened her mouth.

"My name," she whispered, her mouth huge and black, her tongue purple and forked, like a serpent, "is Elizabeth."

Joe closed his eyes and fell into a sea of fire, pain and blackness.

CHAPTER 2

Someone else is dead.

Linda paused, her hand reaching for *The Riverview Times*. The words echoed strangely in her head, bouncing around like some demented ping-pong ball.

Someone else is dead.

Where had that come from? What did it mean?

She stretched her hand forward again to take the paper, but found herself unable to make actual contact with it. Instead, her hand hung there, motionless. Uneasiness crept through her body, as thick as black ink oozing across a table.

All right, now she was being ridiculous. Where on earth was any of this coming from? She shook her head and snatched up the newspaper. Tucking it under her arm, she hurried to her car, refusing to think about why she had such a curious reluctance to touch it.

She deliberately turned the radio off in her car, not wanting to hear any news. Instead, she drummed her fingers on the steering wheel and watched the clouds scuttle across the dull gray sky. Another beautiful November day in Wisconsin. For the millionth time, she wondered if it would kill the sun, to show its face a little more.

Turning into the parking lot of Bay Mutual Insurance, she thought again of how much she hated her job. And again, she reminded herself that she didn't have a whole lot of options to choose from.

Linda parked and entered the building, passing the company's mission statement in the lobby. Bay Mutual offered auto, home, business, health and life insurance to its customers. *And squat to its employees,* Linda added to herself, as she did every day.

She hung up her coat and headed to the cramped break room for coffee. Carla was already there, pouring herself a cup.

"So, how was your date last night?" Linda greeted her, taking a mug out of the drying rack.

Carla rolled her dark blue eyes, filling Linda's mug with steaming, black liquid. "Don't even ask."

"That good?"

"It started there. Then, it went downhill." Carla put down the coffee pot, fluffed her short, curly brown hair and opened up the refrigerator for cream. "My mistake was thinking it couldn't get any worse. Then, I heard the radio this morning. Another dead single man. It's already nearly impossible to get a decent date in this town. Now, some crazy person is killing the few eligible men out there!"

Someone else is dead. It hit her like a slap in the face, and Linda put her coffee down without drinking it, instinctively knowing she could never force the liquid past the thick sludge that now filled her throat.

She watched Carla as she doctored her coffee with cream. Forever on a diet that never seemed to work, she perpetually remained on the short, plump side. Pretty, she looked a little like a perky-nosed cheerleader who had graduated from high school and promptly lost the "battle of the bulge." Her personality matched that persona. Carla dealt with the perils and problems of human existence with a strong dose of sarcasm and bad jokes. Linda suspected real tragedy had never touched Carla, allowing her to float through life without bumps, scratches or bruises.

Linda herself looked exactly opposite of Carla. Frizzy, dark brown hair, plain brown eyes and a plain oval-shaped face with dull features. Just … plain.

Carla tasted her coffee. "They think it was someone he picked up. Like the others."

"So he was picking up women in a sleazy bar. You should take heart in that. He was probably a jerk. Or gay."

"Or both." Carla sighed. "But the Green Room is a meat market, not a gay bar. Do you really think a woman could be doing this?"

"How should I know? Ask the police." Linda started walking toward her desk. Carla followed. Both of them worked in clerical support for the underwriting department along with Rachel, who was pregnant with her third child. She was already at her desk, diligently working as usual.

Carla kept talking, but Linda tuned her out. She didn't want to think about the murders. Better to focus on something neutral, like the pile of work in front of her. That was safe, familiar.

Thankfully, it kept her busy until noon. Over the last six months, she had acquired the incredibly useful skill of focusing completely on even the most mundane tasks. She had learned well, and prided herself on her efficiency.

Carla stretched and yawned and asked if Linda wanted to get some lunch.

Linda started straightening piles on her desk. "I don't know. I'm not really hungry."

Carla shook her head. "Linda, you've got to eat. You're practically wasting away."

"Carla's right," Rachel said. "You must have lost over 20 pounds these last six months. You're thin enough."

"I'm not trying to lose weight," Linda protested. "I'm simply not hungry."

"Well, you should eat anyway," Carla said. "I mean, you look great and all. But, your clothes don't even fit anymore."

Linda looked down at herself. Funny, it had never occurred to her just how loose her outfits had become. That morning, she had forgotten to put on a belt so her beige straight skirt kept falling around her hips and untucking her white blouse. Although her coworkers had brought this subject up before, she had always dismissed it. She wasn't trying to lose it, and she wished they'd let it go.

"You need a shopping spree, big time," Carla said. "Why not buy some stuff at Marshall Fields? I'm sure you get an employee discount."

"Yeah, I do," Linda said. "But the money I make there is going into my school fund."

"You're going to have to do something," Carla said. "Your clothes are practically falling off you."

Linda was saved from answering when the telephone rang.

"Yes."

"Hi, Linda," the receptionist said. "There's a police officer here to see you."

"A police officer? To see me?"

"A Detective Steve Anderson. He says he knows you."

Linda frowned, instantly nervous. It couldn't be. "Steve Anderson? From high school?"

"I'm not sure. Do you want me to ask?"

"No, no, that's okay. Send him up." She hung up the phone.

Both Rachel and Carla stared at her.

"What's the police doing here?" Rachel asked.

"Have you been involved in some illegal activity we're not aware of?" Carla joked.

Linda stood and tucked her blouse in. "No, no, of course not. I think it's someone I knew in high school. Although why he would look me up here is beyond me."

"Hello, Linda."

Linda whirled around and took a deep breath. He stood in the doorway, looking exactly the way she remembered him, all those years ago. "Hello, Steve."

Steve came several steps forward into the office bay. "It's been a while, hasn't it?"

Linda took a deep breath, suddenly all too conscious of her ill-fitting skirt, her frumpy blouse, her hastily applied make-up, her uncombed hair, her lipstick that had long worn off. "Yes, it has."

Now that they were closer, she saw that the years had left their mark on him. His thick black hair sported a shorter cut, and stubble dotted his chin. Instead of jeans and a tee shirt — his daily uniform in high school — he wore a button-down white shirt and a striped tie beneath his overcoat. His green eyes, however, were exactly the way she remembered them.

He came forward, bringing with him a breath of cold air that grazed her cheek. He reached out, as if to touch her, but then at the last moment rubbed his hands together instead. "It's really great to see you again."

She licked her lips, suddenly finding her mouth filled with sand. "Same here."

His eyes swept over the cubicles, taking in every detail. She found it an oddly calculating move. "I'd like to talk with you. Could I take you to lunch? I know it's last minute; I was up all night on a case." He shrugged and half-smiled at her.

Linda turned away. Out of the corner of her eye, she could see Carla and Rachel pretending to work while hanging on every word.

She didn't think she was ready to face Steve and the demons he would bring from her past, but suddenly, that option seemed more appealing than enduring the inquisition Carla and Rachel surely had in store for her.

"All right. I guess," Linda said, eyes glancing up, but not quite meeting his face.

CHAPTER 3

Steve took her to a little deli not far from the insurance company. It was a cheery, "homey" place, sporting red and white curtains, sparkling white tables and bright red napkins and napkin holders.

So far, Steve had only made a few remarks about the weather. Linda answered in monosyllables, all the while cursing herself for agreeing to such a ridiculous farce of a "reunion." After all the years that had passed, and their history, whatever he wanted now couldn't possibly be any good.

He kept her in suspense until after the waitress took their order — a club sandwich for him, a bowl of soup for Linda.

"Now that I'm here, I'm not sure where to begin," Steve said, looking down at the table and playing with his napkin. "I guess I thought this would be easier."

"What would be easier?"

He didn't answer immediately, just kept folding and refolding his napkin. Finally, he looked up. "I guess I'd like to start by expressing my deepest sympathy over the death of your sister."

Linda went instantly cold. Elizabeth. Of course it would be about Elizabeth. What else would it be?

She sat up a little straighter. "Thank you."

"I know it's been several months ..."

Six months, she thought.

"And I'm sorry about that. You probably don't know this but I was at the funeral."

Linda looked at him a little sharply. "Were you? I don't remember seeing you." Not that she would have remembered much of anything during that nightmarish joke of a funeral.

Steve looked uncomfortable. "I didn't stay long. Just long enough to — well, I didn't think your family really wanted to see me."

Linda gave a short bark of laughter that reflected no actual humor whatsoever. "I can't imagine why not. Maybe dating Elizabeth wasn't the smartest move after all."

He dropped his napkin and stared directly at her. "What exactly did you want me to do? Your brother tried to beat me up several times in high school. I figured if he saw me there, it would just make an already tense situation worse."

He had a point. She tilted her head sideways. "Touché."

Suddenly he smiled — a real smile. "You always were impossible, you know that?"

"And you always were a righteous son-of-a-bitch."

He laughed at that. She could feel her insides thaw ever so slightly.

"Anyway, down to business," he took out a notebook and flipped through the pages. She picked up her glass of water to take a drink as he glanced at her above the notebook. "About Elizabeth," he began.

Linda could feel the glass start to slip through her fingers. She firmly set it on the table, refusing to look at him. Already she could feel a coldness rolling through her again. When would she ever learn? For a moment, she was thrust back into high school, brimming over with insecurity, hurt and raging jealously. He'd made his choice. Steve chose Elizabeth. He couldn't have them both.

He was looking at his notebook, oblivious to her plight. "Well, indirectly, it's about Elizabeth. I want to talk to you about the murders."

Now Linda stared at him. "Murders? What murders? The ones in the paper? The serial killer?"

Steve opened his mouth to answer, but before he could, the waitress appeared with their food. Linda glanced at her soup and looked quickly away. Just the smell of it, wafting up to her nostrils, made her stomach lurch. She covered it with her napkin.

He picked up a fry. "Yes, those murders."

"But those murders are happening now. What could they possibly have to do with Elizabeth?"

"Give me a second, and I'll tell you," he grinned.

She studied the other diners while he chewed his food: all well-dressed professionals busy conducting business over salads and sandwiches. How she envied them. None of them were stuck talking to a cop who had chosen their dead sister back in high school.

Steve wiped his mouth with a napkin. "You've probably read about it in the papers. Two men, in their early twenties. White. Both had a history of picking up women in bars. Both were found dead in their beds, naked, tied to the bedposts, throats slit.

"We're still looking into the details surrounding the first victim. But we've already made some interesting discoveries about the second man, the one who died last night. He went to The Green Room with his roommate – a good friend of his for years. They separated, both looking to pick up a woman. Around eleven, the victim approached his roommate, letting him know he "got himself a 'hot one," and to not come home that night. The roommate agreed, the victim left, and that's the last time he was seen alive."

Something deep inside Linda stirred. A vague feeling, an uncomfortable knowledge began to surface in her, like a serpent uncoiling its tail during a restless sleeping. "What was the name of the victim?" she interrupted.

Steve paused, took a bite of his sandwich, and paged through his notebook. "Joe Maytu," he said.

The name echoed in her head, as her mind searched for the familiarity … a reason for the discomfort she was feeling. She found none.

Steve finished chewing and continued his story. "The roommate did get a quick look at the woman he had seen talking to Joe – the one he thought Joe was picking up. She was halfway across the bar and her face was turned away, so he couldn't see much. He's not even a hundred percent certain that who he saw was the same woman Joe left with.

"But the one he saw — she wore white — either a white dress or a white shirt and skirt. And she had pale blond hair, almost white. He also said that she must have been standing underneath a light because it looked like there was a halo around her. Almost like she was an angel. That's a direct quote; he thought she 'looked like an angel.' Some angel, huh?"

"The angel of death," Linda murmured through stiff, cold lips. She had a terrible feeling about where this was leading.

Elizabeth had pale blond hair … Elizabeth used to wear a lot of white … Father used to call her his "little angel."

Steve looked directly at her for the first time since they had sat down to lunch. "Yes, exactly. The angel of death. But there's more.

"Remember, the roommate couldn't describe her face, because he really didn't see her clearly. But of course Joe did. According to the roommate, Joe's exact words were ..." Steve leafed through a couple of pages. "'Find somewhere else to sleep tonight. That one over there, she's so hot. And her eyes. She has silver eyes!'" Steve shut the notebook and looked at Linda.

She closed her eyes. This couldn't be happening.

"They never found her body, did they, Linda?" Steve's voice floated over to her, disembodied, tearing at her.

Linda shook her head, eyes still closed. Whispers of pain crackled along her temples, darted down her neck. Bright red and yellow flowers blossomed in the corners of her vision. The monster headache that had lain dormant for months began to stir again, to roll over. Pretty soon, it would open its mouth and roar, fully awake and angry at the disturbance. She rubbed her temples, wishing with all her might she had stayed at Bay Mutual.

She felt his hand on hers, and it nearly burned against the coldness of her flesh. "Linda, look at me."

Linda squeezed her eyes tighter for a second, trying unsuccessfully to force back the waves of pain. She opened her eyes.

"You're as cold as ice. Are you all right?"

"Yes," Linda said, pulling her hand away. "It's cold in here. Don't you think it's cold in here?"

Steve cocked his head. "I'm comfortable."

"Maybe I'm sitting in a draft." She studied the fat drops of condensation sliding down the graceful curves of her water glass, glistening under the lights, until they landed with a "plop" on the table.

She could feel Steve's gaze boring into her. "Elizabeth is dead," Linda said flatly, refusing to look up, to do anything but stare at her glass. "She killed herself."

Steve said nothing, but watched her, his eyes shiny and bright, almost predatory, she thought. She squared her shoulders and looked him right in the eye. "What exactly are you insinuating? That she faked her own death, in Massachusetts of all places, simply to return to Wisconsin so she could murder innocent men?"

"It IS quite a coincidence, don't you think?" His voice sounded faintly accusatory.

"She died six months ago. This hardly sounds like a coincidence to me."

Steve leaned forward, his expression both tense and alert. "What it sounds like to me is just about the perfect amount of time for someone to leave her old life behind, and start fresh."

Linda could only sit there, struggling to keep her expression neutral, feeling like she had just walked right into one of her awful nightmares. "You can't be serious. This is Elizabeth we're talking about. Elizabeth. Are you listening to yourself?"

Some of the tension drained from his face. He sat back, the movement sudden and jerky, running his hands through his hair. "I don't know what I think anymore. I read the police report on Elizabeth's death, and though I do think she's dead, there's something that just doesn't feel right about all of this."

Pain raked across her temples, the monster sharpening its claws. She opened her purse to fish out her box of aspirin. If she couldn't get this headache under control in the next few minutes, she might stab herself with her butter knife.

Steve didn't say anything, just watched her swallow a handful of aspirin. Finally, she set her water glass back down with a "thunk." "Steve, what do you want me to say? No, Elizabeth has not been in contact with me or with anyone I know since her death. I don't know why someone who resembles her was seen with the man who was killed last night. And, I certainly don't know anything about her sexual preferences, whether she liked to tie people up or not. You'd know more about that than me."

He tapped his fork against the table. "Well that was a bitchy thing to say. But, I suppose it wasn't entirely unjustified."

Linda snorted. "Entirely unjustified? Gee, I wish I had your conscience – or lack thereof. I'd sleep like a baby at night, I'm sure."

"You mean you don't?" There was that tone again, that hint of accusation.

Linda pushed back her chair and stood. "My sleep habits are not your concern. I have to get back to work. Thanks for the lovely lunch."

Steve got up as well. "I guess I'll go pay," he said reaching for the check. "Although," he looked pointedly at her napkin-covered soup, "It seems you weren't very hungry."

Linda didn't bother to dignify that with an answer. Instead, she turned and marched out of the restaurant.

She couldn't believe what she had just heard. Elizabeth, alive and killing men? How absurd! She was dead.

Dead.

Linda pressed her fingers against her forehead, her temples. She imagined the scene, blood soaking into the white sheets, slashes in his body. She dropped her hands and found Steve had joined her outside, and was looking at her intently. "Was there anything else ... done to the body?" she asked suddenly, the question popping out of her mouth, taking her entirely by surprise. Why would she ask such a thing?

Apparently Steve wondered the same. "Why do you ask?" His eyes flickered over her, his expression strange and unreadable.

She looked away. "No reason."

She felt his gaze boring into her again.

She studied the side of the restaurant, built solidly of red brick. What would possess her to ask about the bodies?

He touched her arm lightly. "Let's go." Dutifully, she followed him to his car.

Neither spoke on the way back to the insurance company. Linda watched Steve as he drove, his hands on the wheel, looking relaxed and comfortable. She envied him then; she couldn't even remember the last time she felt that kind of peace.

He pulled up next to the front door and stopped. Linda collected her purse and unbuckled her seatbelt, making a point to avoid looking at him.

"Thank you for lunch." She reached for the door.

His voice stopped her. "I may need to get in touch with you again," he said, his voice cool and professional. "About the case. Here's my card. If you think of anything or see anything suspicious, give me a call. My home number is on the back."

She took it gingerly. "Thank you." She studied his profile, the hard set of his mouth, and felt as if she needed to say something more, but nothing came. She turned and got out of the car.

CHAPTER 4

Bypassing her office for the restroom, Linda splashed cold water on her face. He hadn't come there for her. Of course he hadn't. She needed to refocus. What she had to concentrate on right then was formulating a plausible reason for his coming to see her in the first place, so she had an answer to her coworkers' inevitable questions. Her entire body ached; the monsters hadn't finished toying with her yet. Whispers of pain darted through her head while her stomach painfully churned. She desperately wanted to go home and sleep, but she knew she couldn't. Even if she was actually able to, which she doubted, it would mean she wouldn't be able to sleep that night. The thought of being awake all those long hours, staring at the ceiling, watching the moonlight shift along her bedroom floor convinced her to tough it out at work.

She dried her face, then rummaged through her purse to find her comb so she could at least try and make sense of her brown, frizzy hair. Her make-up had smeared, so she tore off some toilet paper, and set to work repairing the damage.

Finally, she surveyed her refection. Blood-shot brown eyes stared back at a blotchy and nearly make-up-free face. "I look like hell," she said aloud. What on earth would she tell Carla?

She straightened her clothes, hitched up her skirt again, picked up her purse and coat, left the restroom and headed toward her desk.

Carla and Rachel were at theirs — Rachel working, Carla pretending to, her eyes nearly popping with curiosity.

"So, how was lunch?" she asked, a little smile on her lips. Her smile drooped when she got a closer look at Linda. "Oh, my God, Linda. What's wrong?"

Linda managed a smile at her and Rachel, who also looked at her with a mixture of concern and curiosity.

"I'm okay," she said, sliding behind her desk.

"But ..." Carla began. Linda cut her off, the half-lie, half-truth rolling smoothly off her tongue. She hadn't known what she was going to say until she found herself saying it.

"I knew Steve in high school. He dated Elizabeth. He just wanted to express his condolences. " She was amazed at how calm she sounded, and inwardly congratulated herself.

It pleased her even more to see Rachel's and Carla's expressions. She knew they wouldn't question her too closely now, since they both thought she was still grieving Elizabeth. She still grieved all right, but not the way they thought.

"Why'd he wait 'til now?" Rachel asked gently.

"He's been out of town," Linda said. "He missed the funeral, and he's been traveling so much these past months that he hasn't had an opportunity to pay his respects."

"Oh," Rachel said, and turned back to her work.

Carla did the same.

Linda breathed a sigh of relief.

The afternoon, though quiet and uneventful, flew by. No one said much to Linda, which worked out just fine; she had enough to keep her mind occupied. Her head even started to feel better, thanks to regular doses of aspirin.

She stayed a little later than usual, finishing up work that didn't really need to be completed as of yet. On her way home, she stopped at a little deli for take-out — a grilled cheese sandwich and a bowl of tomato soup. Next, she stopped at the drugstore for aspirin and sleeping pills.

She carried her purchases into her tiny one-bedroom apartment, just as she had done so many other evenings. It was practically routine, at this point. In the months following her sister's funeral, she must have gone through a dozen bottles of aspirin and sleeping pills, her evenings almost always comprised of half-eaten take-out and partially-watched Netflix movies. It had taken nearly three months to wean herself from that ritual, to get to the point where she could stand even her own company again.

So much for progress. She was right back where she started.

She found herself hoping it wouldn't take as long to get back on track again, this time around … to get back to the point of allowing herself to think again.

Right then, the thought came, despite her best efforts to avoid it: it was her fault Elizabeth was dead.

She squeezed her eyes closed and, with extreme effort, willfully forced the ugliness back.

She was surprised by everything she was feeling around her sister's death. After all, she didn't even miss her. In fact, there had been times Linda had even wished Elizabeth dead.

Still, how could she not be sorry her own sister was dead? Suicide, at 24. *What kind of person wouldn't be sorry,* Linda wondered, admitting to herself in the same moment that only a truly terrible person could be *that* cold.

Guilt and blame, not regret, were her personal, terrible demons – much worse than regret or sadness. Their teeth were sharper, their claws longer. They taunted her, laughed at her, humiliated her, because she knew, deep down in her heart, that if people understood how she really felt about Elizabeth, how she really felt about her death, they would shun and despise her, just as her own family had.

Felix, her black-and-white cat, strolled up to Linda and meowed. Grateful for the distraction, she placed her purchases on the table and bent to pick him up. "I know you're hungry, but it's not time to feed you yet." Not that it really mattered. He only ate when she wasn't anywhere near him. He could be starving, but he wouldn't eat if she stayed in the kitchen. *Stubborn cat,* she thought.

She sighed and looked around her apartment. A closet for a kitchen, a cramped living room that held her couch, chair, bookcases and kitchen table, and one bedroom crammed with a desk, drawing table, dresser, bed and nightstand. The few pieces of furniture couldn't hold all her belongings, and they seemed to spill out everywhere, overflowing into every available inch of space, amassing into a giant, chaotic mess.

She hated her home, but she couldn't afford anything else.

She picked up the television remote to select a movie. Time to stop thinking, she thought, and mindless, action-adventure movies were a perfect alternative. She had enough setbacks today. She didn't need anymore.

It was my fault.

There it was again.

The demons kept her prisoner, chained in steel forged by her own hand, each link formed by her own anger and guilt.

She never knew guilt could become such a complex emotion. That guilt could have nuances – lots of them. She wished she could just feel grief, instead – so simple, in comparison.

She shook her head to clear her thoughts, and pushed "play" on the remote, turning the sound up deliberately loud.

She fed Felix, and then managed to eat most of her soup and part of her sandwich while half-heartedly watching the movie. Her mind kept wandering, though, so she finally poured a glass of milk and took a couple sleeping pills, with more aspirin. She stayed put on the couch until her eyes stopped focusing, and her eyelids drooped heavily.

Finally, she clicked off the movie and stumbled into bed. Felix, who had curled up on the couch with her during the movie, crept in with her. Most of the time, he didn't like to be touched, only allowing her to pet him when *he* felt like it — and even then, he didn't tolerate it for long. But occasionally, very occasionally, like tonight, he seemed to somehow understand that she desperately needed a living creature near her for comfort, and there he would be. Those times made her eternally grateful, relieved she had chosen him over a dog.

She fell asleep, and landed in a chilling nightmare.

She could hear Elizabeth calling her, faintly: "Linda. Linda." Over and over again. She seemed to be saying more, but Linda could only decipher her name.

She was lost in some huge building. A mansion perhaps. Very poorly-designed, it had low ceilings, dim lighting, and narrow, twisty halls lined with doors. Some stood ajar, some shut tight. She kept bumping into things — doorframes, walls, doorknobs, hinges.

Still the voice called her. "Linda, Linda." Haunted her. Goaded her. She began throwing open doors, searching rooms, finding nothing but cobwebs, old furniture and shadows. So many shadows. They were everywhere. Shifting, growing longer and blacker, twisting, taunting. Linda tried not to look at them, to focus on finding the source of the voice that relentlessly called her name.

It had to be Elizabeth. But it couldn't be Elizabeth. Elizabeth was dead. Dead. Suicide. Six months ago. It couldn't be Elizabeth. She could not have come back to life. She could not be killing those men.

She awoke, drenched in sweat, her breathing harsh and violent, the blankets twisted around her. Felix was gone.

She lay there for a long moment trying to get hold of herself. The moonlight filtered into her room, the shadows it created darker than normal. Her breathing, raspy and uncertain, echoed loudly in the stillness. The shadows, black and long, stretched out against the wall and floor. They seemed to be growing even as she watched, hysteria beginning to bubble in her chest. Darker. Longer.

She flipped on her bedroom light a split second before true panic set in. The warm glow filled the bedroom, chasing the shadows away to whatever hell they had come from. She slowly calmed down.

She had never remembered her dreams before, and immediately considered her recollection of the one that had just occurred as a definite bad sign.

Even in the beginning, after learning of Elizabeth's death – hell, even after that nightmare masquerading as a funeral – she had never remembered her dreams. Without fail, the moment she opened her eyes in the morning, the memory vanished.

Her nightmares left her "gifts," however ... psychotic Santa Claus type gifts, not the Sandman type: a body sticky with sweat, a thrashed bed, pillows tossed everywhere, dry mouth, a sickness in her stomach. But despite all of that, the content of her nightmares always remained a mystery, once she had woken up. For that, she felt indebted to her demented Santa.

But as of tonight, it seemed even that reprieve was being taken away.

She got up, untangling herself from the covers. She glanced at the clock. Three-fourteen. No more sleep tonight.

Turning on all the lights as she walked, she went to the kitchen and drank a big glass of water, then turned on the television.

At five-fifteen she went back to her bedroom, threw on some clothes, and went for a walk.

This was another ritual — early morning walks when sleep abandoned her in the middle of the night. The fresh cold air stung her face. She breathed deeply, filling her lungs. The icy air numbed her throat and burned her chest. Still, it felt good. It cleansed her, purified her, ridding her body of shadows and cobwebs.

She walked briskly to keep warm, the light brightening with every step. The trees stood stiffly, stark against the sky, their naked branches bare, exposed. Darkened windows in the other rundown apartment buildings and duplexes seemed to mock her — only she suffered from sleep problems, while everyone else rested peacefully.

The frozen ground, with its brown grass and cracked mud looked so hard, so unforgiving. She wished it would snow, really hard, and cover all the blemishes, soften the lines of trees, turning the world into a winter paradise. Without snow, winter became dreary and lifeless.

She made it back to her apartment by six and began the rest of her morning routine. Throwing herself into her every day, monotonous chores, she forced herself to forget, to black out the memories, to harden, as she brushed her teeth and showered. These "auto" tasks, the ones most people never even gave a thought to, took every ounce of her energy and concentration. They kept her sane, and she loved them for it.

***

Linda maintained her grueling schedule: no days off meant no time to think. She worked Friday night, all day Saturday and all day Sunday at Marshall Fields. She stayed late every night at Bay Mutual. At home, she watched movies until she fell asleep.

Her nightmares continued, but she had stopped remembering them again. The headache monster returned to its slumber, the serpent loosened its grip on her stomach. By Thursday, she began to think she just might be all right, that she might even make it through the holidays *without* cracking. Perhaps she truly would be fine.

Until she went to sleep that night.

It began as the same awful dream — trapped in that mansion, hearing Elizabeth call her name, over and over again. This time, her voice seemed slightly louder, but Linda still couldn't make out any words except her own name. The shadows were back too, black and horrid, stretching their way across the hall, the floor, the ceiling.

She threw open the doors again, searching for Elizabeth. The same rooms greeted her, empty save for the black shadows. Again and again she struggled, flinging doors open wildly, uncontrollably. Until one door refused to open.

She heard noises coming from inside. A shuffling. Mumbling.

"Elizabeth?" Linda asked, frantically.

She grasped the doorknob, trying to turn it, but it stayed firmly locked. She flung herself against the door, pounding on it, screaming Elizabeth's name over and over.

Without warning, the door opened. She fell into the room, landing on her hands and knees.

The harsh, bright light nearly blinded her. She tried to block it with her hand, but her palm felt wet … stuck to the floor. She looked down to see why, but the room tipped and swayed. Suddenly, Linda was desperate to get out.

She attempted to stand, but her limbs felt thick and heavy. She moved torturously slowly, as if underwater. A thick, sticky substance seemed to pull at her, keeping her stuck in perpetual slow motion. Oh God, she was moving way too slowly.

Finally, she made it to her knees, slowly raising her body, and then at last, she stood. She instinctively avoided looking forward. She tried to back away, but couldn't. Something *compelled* her to look. Something, either herself or some outside force, refused to let her turn away, so she could continue her search for Elizabeth. She knew she didn't want to be in that room; she knew Elizabeth wasn't there.

But she found herself unable to resist the force that pushed her to look straight ahead. At the light. At the bed in the light.

It was a normal bed, a cheap bed, not even much of a headboard — really, it was just a piece of wood. Stains covered the rumpled sheets. Big, black stains.

She saw something else, too. Something else on the bed.

Although she struggled against it, Linda found herself moving forward, floating almost, toward the bed. She did *not* want to see.

But there it was — a figure, laying in the bed. A figure with its arms stretched and bound to the corners of the bed. A figure that had its throat cut, its body slashed. Blood dripped everywhere, staining the sheets and pooling on the ground.

As she drew closer, she saw it was a man. A young man. He appeared to be quite dead, his face turned away from her, his eyes closed.

She continued floating, closer still, until she practically hovered above him, near enough to reach out and touch him, had she wanted. She stared at the man, his pale face, his bloodless lips, his skin so shockingly white against the red blood.

The figure moved.

The face turned toward her. The eyes opened. Silver.

Linda screamed.

Instantly, she was in her own bed, sitting straight up, her hand clasped to her mouth. She nearly screamed again when Felix darted off the pillow, a black shadow swiftly disappearing under the bed.

Along with terrifying herself, she had just managed to do the same to the cat. *What would be next,* she wondered? The entire apartment complex? The neighborhood?

She briefly considered the possibility that one of her neighbors had heard her scream, and was about to call the police. Maybe Steve Anderson would be the one to answer the call.

Oh God, just the thought of that made her want to crawl under the bed with Felix. Instead, she forced herself to get up, to turn on all the lights in the apartment, to drink milk in front of the television set, to patiently wait until the newspaper arrived. Even though she knew newspapers were old-fashioned and she could get the same news online, much faster, she disliked reading on her computer, or the itty bitty screen of her outdated iPhone. And there was something about the smell and feel of the paper that was comforting to her.

She found herself staring out the window, waiting. She told herself that, even if another man *had* been murdered, it certainly wouldn't be in this morning's paper already. How could it?

All her careful reasoning didn't stop her from running down to get it, the moment she saw it delivered. Her hands shook as she reached for it, neatly rolled up in the slot next to her mailbox. She could barely open it, her hands trembled so hard, and she nearly dropped it more than once. The newspaper unfurled.

"SERIAL KILLER STRIKES AGAIN" the headline blared. In smaller letters, "Body found just moments after killer leaves."

Her eyes traveled quickly over the words, her mind numb, barely able to register them — until she saw the photograph.

She didn't scream, though for a second, her panic threatened one. Instead, she crumpled to the ground, her knees buckling, her eyes unable to tear themselves away from the picture staring back at her.

The young man smiled at her from the depths of the grainy newsprint, trapped forever in newspaper hell. Dressed in a suit and tie, the photograph appeared to be some sort of graduation picture.

She had seen him before. Last night. The figure in the bed, in her nightmare. He had looked right at her ... and now, he was dead.

CHAPTER 5 — ELIZABETH

When Elizabeth was born, her mother knew beyond a shadow of a doubt that the hospital had made a mistake.

It had been a difficult pregnancy. Marie spent most of it in bed, nauseated, uncomfortable, exhausted. She barely kept anything down, subsisting mostly on tea and saltine crackers. When the time came to deliver, the doctors performed an emergency Caesarean section, so she wasn't able to actually watch the birth.

She couldn't explain it, but the first time the nurses presented her with Elizabeth, she refused to even hold the baby. "There must be some mistake," she insisted.

"There's no mistake," the nurses said, their approach firm and no-nonsense.

Blond and pale, Elizabeth looked nothing like the other dark-haired members of the family. But it was more than that. Elizabeth *felt* wrong. Marie sensed it every single time she looked at Elizabeth, touched Elizabeth, smelled Elizabeth. The baby was alien to her. Elizabeth was *not* her baby.

But she could do nothing about it. Her husband hadn't seen the birth. He had refused to attend any of his children's births. The nurses kept assuring her that no one had made, could possibly have made, a mistake. So Marie had little choice but to bring her home.

Elizabeth was different, always — strange. Marie hated to use that word about any of her children, especially her youngest, but she could find no other word to describe her. Elizabeth was strange. Period.

From birth, the baby kept quiet. Rarely fussed. Hardly cried. She started talking at six months, much earlier than the rest of her children, and started forming full sentences at just over a year old.

She spent most of her time alone or, once she learned how, reading. In fact, Elizabeth remained such a quiet child, Marie could easily forget about her. It made her nervous. Elizabeth was *too* quiet.

Even her scent was all wrong. Babies smelled warm and sweet, of milk and talcum powder. Elizabeth's scent reminded her of meat just beginning to spoil: thick and rotten.

But there was something else wrong with Elizabeth, something more serious than her near silence, her behavior, her scent. Even more serious than that alien feeling, which Marie had tried to dismiss as simple post-partum depression, although it never did go away entirely. When Marie was really being honest with herself, which didn't happen often, she could admit what really disturbed her most about her daughter.

Her eyes. Elizabeth had silver eyes.

Not always. Most of the time they looked gray. But sometimes, they changed to silver. Occasionally, Marie even thought she could see them glowing, like a cat's. Especially at night. There Elizabeth would be, lying on her back, perfectly quiet in her crib, her eyes strangely open, shining faintly in the darkness. Marie would tell herself that Elizabeth's eyes merely reflected the nightlight in a bizarre fashion. After all, none of her other children's eyes ever glowed. But it still didn't make her any easier to face, late at night, as silver eyes stared at her from the darkness. They seemed so old, so ancient. Eyes that had seen thousands of years and hundreds of lifetimes. Those eyes peered out from her newborn's face, watching her every move, strangely calculating, full of adult understanding and knowledge. She felt afraid, if she were being honest … all alone in the room with those peculiar silver eyes watching, watching, always watching.

Nonsense, she reassured herself. Surely, she could not be afraid of her own infant daughter! What would her husband say? Plenty probably, and most of it with his fists.

Still, she found herself checking on Elizabeth less and less. She argued with herself: Elizabeth didn't fuss much anyway. Marie didn't need to check on her so often — not like she did with her other, noisy, "normal" babies.

Her other children. Such a joy they were, her four boys and other girl — Peter, Mark, Mike, Chad and Linda. All healthy, regular children, with coarse dark hair, brown eyes and a little bit of baby fat on their bones. They looked the way children should look, the way *her* children should look, like their parents. But more importantly, they acted the way children should act — loud, boisterous, rough, needy. Marie loved them for it, loved how she couldn't get a moment's peace when they played together. Even when their play turned to fighting, she still preferred it to Elizabeth's silent, eerie presence.

But Marie loved Elizabeth, too. Loved her fiercely, with the same passion she felt for her other children. Marie knew she did. She told herself she did, time and time again. The fact that she felt relief when Elizabeth wasn't around meant nothing. She just needed time away from her children, after all. Almost all mothers welcomed the time they had away from their constant, children-related responsibilities. It didn't mean she loved them any less. It didn't mean anything at all.

CHAPTER 6

Linda had no idea how long she lay sprawled on the floor, dressed in her limp sweatpants and ratty sweatshirt, eyes fixed on that picture, that terrible picture, in the paper. She wasn't even sure if anyone had walked by, while she lay there. Her first conscious thought was, *I'd better get ready or I'm going to be late for work*, and it jolted her back to reality with a burst of the commonplace, the mundane, the everyday.

The words ripped through her head, so loud in their absolute normalcy that they shattered her thoughts and finally brought her to her feet. She slowly slunk back to her apartment, meeting no one in the halls and praying every moment she wouldn't.

It was a little after six when she returned. She couldn't have been in the lobby too long. Or could she? What time had she gone down there? She couldn't remember. Perhaps it just felt as if days had passed. Her legs had even cramped, as though she had been frozen in that position for eons. But wouldn't someone have noticed her, if she had been?

Confused, she quickly stripped off her clothes and started her shower, the water so hot, her skin turned bright red.

She threw herself into the ritual, moving as fast as she could, not allowing herself a moment to think. She even drove to work fast, borderline recklessly, pulling in front of cars and switching lanes with barely a glance.

She made it to work twenty minutes early. The receptionist hadn't even arrived yet. Immediately, she started brewing a pot of coffee. As soon as it was ready, she poured a cup, drinking it black and scalding. She was on her third when Carla arrived.

"What a cold, awful, gray day," Carla said, filling a cup for herself. "Did you see the papers?"

Linda winced slightly. "I know. A third murder."

Carla shook her head. "This is absolutely out of control. Who could be doing it?"

Linda swallowed. "Some psychopath, I imagine."

Carla opened the refrigerator and pulled out some cream. "It's just inconceivable."

Linda stood up. She could feel all that coffee bubbling up inside her. Any second now, it would spew out of her, black and thick. She had to get out. She knew having something other than coffee in her stomach would probably help, if she could force it. "I'm going to run to the cafeteria. I ran out of bread this morning so I didn't have breakfast. Want anything?"

"Nope," Carla said, pouring more coffee and adding cream.

She hurried out of the break room, deposited her cup on her desk, and went to the cafeteria to buy two pieces of toast. She successfully choked one down.

Although she had mountains of work piled on her desk, she couldn't concentrate on any of it. Her usual focus had disappeared. She realized she had probably lost it while lying on the apartment lobby floor, her focus seeping out of her like water through a crack.

Maybe she should talk to someone about her predicament. Steve? Yeah, right. Let's tell the detective in charge of the murder investigation that she dreamed about the victim the night he died. Brilliant.

But if not Steve, who? She knew the answer before she even finished the question. Terri. Her old friend from high school. The only person who would completely understand.

Of course, there was a slight glitch. She had barely spoken to Terri since the funeral, over six months ago. She couldn't. She had channeled all her energy into trying to keep her sanity. She had nothing left over for anyone else.

Well, she might as well give Terri a call. It didn't look as if she had much choice. At this point, Terri seemed her only hope.

She pulled out her cell phone and found Terri's number. What's the worst that could happen, she reasoned while she listened to the phone ring. Terri could hang up on her. Then she'd be right back where she started.

"Linda Rossini?" The familiar voice on the other end of the line almost immediately began to loosen the tight knot in Linda's chest. "As I live and breathe! I was sure you'd dropped off the face of the earth."

"I know. I'm sorry I didn't call, but it's been pretty rough. I haven't talked to anyone."

Terri's voice softened. "It's okay. I'm sure it's been a complete nightmare."

It had, Linda wanted to say. But what it was then didn't even come close to what it was turning into now. Instead, she asked Terri if she wanted to get together that evening.

Terri immediately agreed and offered to come pick Linda up after work. "I get off before you so I'll come get you," she said.

Replacing the receiver, Linda felt a lightness fill her body. For a moment, she couldn't figure out just what it was she was feeling, but then she realized it was relief. It had been so long, she had practically forgotten that emotion completely.

Linda settled back into work, finally feeling as though she could concentrate, when Carla appeared in a flurry of paper and files.

"Meetings," she said, her voice disgusted. "I swear they were invented to waste time. And the fact I have to sit there and take dictation when nothing is accomplished anyway is simply ridiculous. Why on God's green earth do they want a record of these staff meetings anyway? So their total inefficiency can be captured on paper?"

"Lighten up," Linda said. "It's great job security. We need more busy work. Maybe that should be our slogan."

"So when I go in for my next job review, I should proclaim I deserve a raise and more busy work?"

"Sure. You can tell them that the more busy work they create for us, the more valuable our jobs become to them, so therefore we deserve a raise."

"And stock options, too, I suppose."

"I'd hold out for a company car."

They both started laughing. "I think I'd be holding out for a long time," Carla said.

"Think so? I can't imagine why."

They both went back to work, still laughing. Linda suddenly realized how long it had been since she'd laughed, really laughed. It felt good. Maybe she'd still be able to salvage something out of this mess after all.

***

Going home, Linda had just reached the lobby when Terri breezed through the revolving door. She brought the wintery air in with her, smelling like snow, although none had fallen yet. Her brownish-blondish hair curled around her face; her dark brown eyes virtually sparkled. No one had looked so good to Linda in a very long time.

"I am so glad to see you!" Terri exclaimed, holding her arms out for a hug. "I've really missed you," she said, squeezing her.

"I've missed you, too," Linda said, and realized when she said it how much she meant it. Terri smelled like raspberries and honey, the same scent she had been wearing since high school. It was so familiar, so reassuring to Linda. It brought back a flood of emotion, and she had to step away from Terri to get it under control.

Under her coat, Terri wore a navy blue suit, an off-white blouse and a strand of pearls. Her hair, against the dark blue, looked more blond than brown. As usual, Terri exuded elegance. "You've lost weight."

"You can tell?"

"Honey, you're practically falling out of those clothes. And you feel like a pile of bones. Haven't you been eating, or have you finally found a diet that works?"

"Both, I guess."

Terri shook her head. "I know you always thought you were fat. But you weren't. Not even in high school. This is too much."

Linda bent to pick up her jacket she had dropped to give Terri a hug. With Terri, she could be honest; she was the only person in the world who made her feel that way. "I know I'm too thin. I just can't eat."

"Well, you'll eat tonight," Terri said briskly. "But first, we go shopping."

"Shopping?"

"Well, you need to work up an appetite for all the food you're going to stuff yourself with. But, even more importantly, you really need new clothes. Let's go. I'm driving."

"But, Terri," Linda protested, following her out the door. "I don't have the money for new clothes."

"Linda, you're at the point where you can't afford not to have new clothes. Do you really want your skirts falling down around your ankles when you get up from your desk?"

Linda opened the car door. "I suppose not."

Terri settled in the driver's seat. "All right then. Where to?"

"Marshall Fields. I work there part time so I can get an employee discount."

Terri paused and raised an eyebrow. "You work at Marshall Fields and you don't think you can afford new clothes?"

"It's my school money. Oh never mind. Drive."

Terri started the car. "You did get my messages, didn't you?"

Linda stared hard at the road. "I didn't mean ... I just couldn't ..."

Terri touched her hand. "It's okay. I wasn't trying to blame. I know it's been rough. Hell, it's been rough for me and she wasn't even my sister. Having someone you know kill herself. Horrible. I left you messages just so you'd know I was there for you. I didn't really expect a call back. Especially after that funeral. I mean God, your crazy family. And Peter." Terri pounded on the steering wheel. "God. That brother of yours. Hitting you like that. Christ, I nearly punched him myself."

Linda turned toward Terri, remembering. *You bitch. It's your fault she's dead.*

"It wouldn't have done any good. He's stronger than you and he would have hit you back. Only harder."

"Yeah, but —"

"Besides, I got off lucky. He didn't break my nose again, thank goodness. Just a few bruises that healed pretty quickly."

Terri glanced at her sideways. "You have a very interesting definition of 'lucky.'"

Linda shrugged. "I *was* lucky."

Terri pulled into the mall parking lot. Located in a large mall on the outskirts of town surrounded by trendy chain restaurants and bars, Marshall Fields was just one of several dozen shops they could choose from. After parking, they got out of the car and walked into the store, their shoes making a dull clumping noise on the asphalt. Terri immediately breezed over to the career section, and began flipping through a selection of jackets.

"You always wear such dark things. How many times do I have to tell you to wear jewel colors? Red, purple, green. None of these browns and beiges. With your coloring, you'd look smashing in jewel tones." Terri pulled a couple of jackets off the rack.

Linda trailed after her. It wasn't that she didn't listen to Terri — she knew she looked better in brighter clothes than neutrals. But she felt safer in browns and beiges, as if they helped her fade into the background. When she wore brighter colors, she felt like she might as well spend the entire day shouting, "Here I am!"

A woman shopped near them, wearing a neat black-and-white business suit, her hair pulled back nicely, her make-up carefully applied. But what really stood out about her was her scent — she smelled horrendous. Apparently, she had bathed in perfume that day. "I did have something else to talk to you about," Linda said to her friend.

Terri rummaged through more racks of clothes. "So talk."

Linda moved away from the woman with the strong perfume. "Actually, it has to do with Elizabeth, though indirectly. Remember Steve Anderson?"

"Remember him? How could I forget him?"

"Well, he's a detective now."

"Really? And how do you know this?"

"Because he came to see me."

Terri quit piling clothes in her arms and stared at Linda. "He came to see you?"

"It's not what you think."

"It doesn't matter what I think. What were you wearing when you saw him? Not that awful brown I hope. Next time wear red. What did he look like? Is he still gorgeous?"

Linda nodded.

"Really? That's encouraging. Or is he married?" Terri's face fell.

Linda shook her head. "I have no idea. We didn't get to that. You know the murders?"

"You mean those men killed in their beds? The ones they think picked up the suspect?"

"Yes, that's right. Well, Steve stumbled upon a pretty surprising link."

Terri frowned. "A link? To you?"

"Not to me directly. But indirectly, I guess it concerns me. It's about Elizabeth."

"Elizabeth? But she's dead. What could she possibly have to do with the murders?"

Terri herded her friend into the carpeted dressing rooms, tastefully decorated in gold tones, while Linda repeated her conversation with

Steve. Even in there, she could still smell that woman's perfume. Maybe she had sprayed herself while trying on clothes, too, Linda mused.

Terri stood outside Linda's cubicle, occasionally peering over the door to see what Linda was wearing, and to hear Linda's story better. Her height, coupled with the short door, made it easy for her to see over it. She started shaking her head even before Linda finished her story.

"So there's someone out there who has an uncanny resemblance to Elizabeth. I don't see what that has to do with anything. Elizabeth is still dead. No eyewitness description is going to change that. Put that red jacket on with that blouse. See, look what it does to your coloring."

Linda obeyed. "But, they never found her body."

"So what are you saying? Elizabeth pretended to drown herself in the ocean so she could come back here and become a serial killer?"

"That's almost exactly what I said to Steve."

"And Steve's response?"

"He agreed it was a long shot, but ..."

"But, what?"

"Well," Linda slid a black skirt over her hips. "You have to agree that Elizabeth has a pretty remarkable physical description."

Terri rolled her eyes. "So? Try on that green suit next. See what a difference it makes when you wear clothes that fit? I agree Elizabeth was unique-looking. And you're right, I've never seen anyone her color eyes. But, that's the end of it. Her eyes are different. Other than that, she looks as much like someone else as you do. She was still human, after all."

"What are you saying?"

"I'm saying that if you take away the gray-silver eyes, she looks just like other blond women. That's all."

"You have a point. But we can't dismiss her eyes. The victim said she had silver eyes, Terri."

Terri threw her arms up. "So what? Maybe the light in the club hit them just right. Maybe she was wearing colored contact lenses. Maybe the witness misheard the guy. After all, he never saw them for himself, right? And those bars are noisy, and I'm sure they both had had alcohol in their systems. Or, maybe it was Elizabeth's twin. We all have one."

Linda adjusted the green suit. "Maybe."

"No maybes about it." Terri nodded at the suit. "See that looks wonderful on you. Besides, even if she did fake her suicide to come back and kill people, why on earth would she target men?"

Linda had never thought about that. "You have a point."

"I mean, Elizabeth could always, always manipulate a man. It was the women she didn't get along with. If she were going to kill anyone, she would be killing women, I bet."

"But maybe men are easier for her to trap because she can manipulate them. Women would immediately mistrust her, and be on their guard."

"I'm sure Elizabeth would have found a way around that. Elizabeth wasn't anything if she wasn't resourceful. But why kill *anyone*? Why would she?"

Linda started removing the green suit. She had to admit, it did look nice on her. Terri had spectacular taste.

Terri handed her a scarf over the door. "Put this on with that bluish-purple suit. Elizabeth wasn't a nice person. I would never argue that she was. She was a con artist and a manipulator and she seemed to enjoy causing other people grief. I think she may even have been capable of murder, under the right circumstances. But to fake her own death to become a serial murder —" Terri shook her head. "That simply wasn't her style."

Linda hung up green suit. "Her style?"

"She was a bitch, not a killer. But, this is all beside the point anyway. She's dead. She can't hurt anyone anymore."

"Oh yes she can." Linda told her about the dreams, about seeing the third victim's face the night he was murdered.

While she spoke, the woman with the heavy perfume sauntered through the dressing room, obviously listening to their conversation.

Terri glared at her. "Some people have no manners," she looked pointedly at the woman, who sniffed and strutted out.

Terri turned back to Linda as she finished her story. "Overactive imagination," she said, dismissing it.

"It has to be more than overactive imagination."

Terri leaned over the door, meeting her eyes in the mirror. "Linda, listen to yourself. You've gone through a very difficult six months. And now, someone comes along and suggests that your own sister has somehow defied death, something even Houdini couldn't do, and is hacking apart men in their beds. This is morbid at best, and downright spooky at worst. No wonder you're having nightmares. I'd be surprised if you weren't. I'm probably going to have nightmares myself, now."

To have Terri say it like that sounded so reassuring, so comforting. But, she still couldn't shake the uneasy feeling she had in the pit of her stomach.

"But the victim? I saw his face in my dream."

"Maybe you've seen him before, and it was just a coincidence that you happened to dream about him the night he was killed. Maybe it was a bit of a psychic impression. Maybe your own state of mind opened yourself up to this murderer, and when he killed, you somehow sensed it and saw the victim's face. It still doesn't mean that Elizabeth is the one doing the killing. Although, if you really want to be helpful to the police, you should dream about the murderer next time, instead of the victim."

Linda made a sour face. "Gee, thanks."

"Just trying to be helpful. Or maybe you really didn't dream about the victim, but you were so emotional about everything that when you saw the newspaper, you convinced yourself it was the man you saw in your dream."

Linda thought about it, twisting the decorative scarf around her neck "No. It was him." Yet she somehow didn't feel as sure of herself as she had before.

"Look, there could be a million other explanations that I'm not thinking of right now. The point is, Steve gave you a good scare when you were emotionally vulnerable. And I think that's at the core of whatever's happening to you."

Linda stared at herself in the mirror. The outfit added color to her face, brightening her otherwise sickly complexion. She glanced at Terri, watching her in the mirror. Terri's eyes were still, her silky hair that now appeared more brown than blond hung over the stall.

"You're right," Linda said. "It is nothing."

Terri nodded. "Of course I'm right. And I'm right about the clothes, too. I think you should buy all of them."

Linda groaned. Maybe she shouldn't even look at the price tags, just hand over her credit card and forget it. It would probably be easier than arguing with Terri.

***

After shopping, they had dinner — Terri's treat. She insisted. And she insisted that Linda stuff herself. Luckily, Linda had finally started to feel faint hunger pangs while shopping, so she was able to eat enough to satisfy her friend.

For the first time in months, Linda felt relaxed: really relaxed. Seeing Terri was so good for her. She shouldn't have waited so long to call.

***

As she drove home to her apartment, humming to the radio, she realized she hadn't done that either, since Elizabeth died. Oddly comforting, she let herself consider that perhaps everything would finally work itself out, after all.

She turned the corner, coasting down the street to where her mud-colored apartment building stood, dwarfing a turquoise-blue duplex and a fourplex building nearby, built with dull red brick. Lights shone from a multitude of windows, like beacons in the night. She felt as if she were being welcomed home.

Just then, out of the corner of her eye, Linda spotted a figure. She turned her head to get a better look. He or she stood motionless, barely visible under a streetlight, shrouded in darkness. In fact, if it weren't for the little bit of light, he would have blended into the darkness almost completely, practically indistinguishable from the night itself.

Linda found herself easing off the gas, slowing down, to get a better look at the figure. As far as she could tell, the figure was alone, standing there half in light, half in darkness. But something nagged at her — a feeling of familiarity. She felt that she somehow knew this solitary, isolated person.

The figure raised its head then, light cascading against pale hair that spilled across the black coat, reflecting almost as a halo.

Linda gasped. It was Elizabeth standing there in the darkness. Elizabeth staring at her with curiously flat, gray eyes.

Good God. She *was* alive! Linda slammed on the brakes, glancing at the road in front of her before turning back to the streetlight. But Elizabeth, or whoever it was, had disappeared.

She threw her car into park, her engine jerking to a stop and making a thumping noise that normally would have worried her, but at the moment, she gave it barely a thought. Not bothering to pull over to the curb, she fumbled with the door handle, finally locating the release and rushing out of her car.

Linda stumbled to the sidewalk, straining her eyes to make out a figure, any figure, in the darkness. But she saw nothing. The street was completely deserted.

Had it all been in her head?

Linda slowly made her way back to her car, continually searching the darkness, although she knew it was a futile exercise. She *couldn't* have seen her. There was no way it was possible.

She's dead. Dead. Dead. Dead.

But what about the funeral? A smug-sounding, annoying little voice piped in her subconscious. *You thought you saw Elizabeth at the funeral, too.* Linda quashed the little voice flat, refusing to answer, refusing even to acknowledge it.

It was just the strain of everything. The power of suggestion. That was all.

She forced herself to get back in her car and finish driving home. The power of suggestion. There was a reason why that had become a cliché — because there really *was* power in suggestion. Steve suggested Elizabeth may be alive. A few days later, she sees Elizabeth. Bingo. Power of suggestion.

Linda drove the rest of the way to her apartment, trying feverishly to recapture the good feeling she had before seeing that figure. It was all in her head. It meant nothing.

She parked her car, took her purchases out of the trunk and slowly walked up the steps to her apartment. Her legs felt heavy, swollen, and she could feel twinges that signaled the beginning of a headache in the back of her head. Her stomach felt bloated. Probably from too much food.

She opened the door to her apartment. A very loud meow greeted her. "Felix?" she said, snapping the light on. Felix rarely meowed when she arrived home.

Felix looked at her, tail twitching, from where he was elegantly poised on the back of the couch. He immediately leaped from his perch and hurried over to her, meowing the entire time.

"Felix, what's gotten into you?" He arched his back and rubbed his body against her legs.

Linda draped her purchases across a chair and scooped him up. He began purring. "You're a strange cat," Linda said, closing and locking the front door. "This is certainly a treat, to hear you purring!"

Felix rubbed his face against hers, leaving a cold wet streak across her cheek, his green eyes staring solemnly into hers. She was touched; he so seldom showed affection that intensely.

She carried him into the bathroom with her to get aspirin and sleeping pills. Then she headed back into the kitchen, rubbing Felix under the chin, her eyes trailing across the living room.

Something was bothering her, teasing her behind her subconscious, but she couldn't pinpoint it. She put Felix on the floor, dumped food in his food dish and pulled the milk out of the refrigerator.

Carefully, she studied her apartment while she poured milk into a glass and slowly drank it, swallowing her pills. Something *wasn't* right. But for the life of her, she couldn't figure out what.

An icy coldness began prickling at the base of her spine. Had someone been here? Had someone been in her apartment?

No, surely not. That was silly. No one has been there. No one at all, she reassured herself.

How can you be so sure?, a smug-sounding voice in her head countered. *You just saw Elizabeth outside. Why else would she be here, except to visit ... YOU?!*

It took every ounce of her willpower not to drop the glass, not to scream, not to let her knees buckle beneath her. Carefully, deliberately, she lowered her arm to the counter and forced her fingers to release their death grip on the glass. The glass slipped through, landing with a "thunk." Apparently, her hand hadn't been that close to the counter, after all.

She turned her head, forcing her body to swivel around, her movements sluggish, slow. She carefully surveyed her apartment, moving cautiously from room to room. She found nothing: nothing at all that seemed out of place. She saw no evidence whatsoever that someone had been in her apartment.

Nothing, besides that teasing sensation at the back of her neck, and the uncharacteristic affection from her cat.

It wasn't until she was in bed, drifting off to sleep, when it hit her. It wasn't something she should have been *looking* for — a sight. It was a *smell*. A rich, dark, musky odor. Very faint, but unmistakable.

Elizabeth's perfume.

CHAPTER 7

Linda switched off her computer, sat back and sighed. Another day, done. Another night to face.

The previous night, after realizing it was Elizabeth's perfume that was tormenting her, she had jumped out of bed, fully awake, and thrown open the windows, despite the icy wind howling outside. The cold air swept in, smelling fresh and clean. For a moment, she had just stood there, breathing deeply, feeling the cold plunge into her lungs. It bordered on painful, but she welcomed the pain. It made her feel cleansed.

She thought of Terri. What would she think of Linda standing there in her nightgown, the windows thrown open on a frigid November night? What would she have to say about what Linda saw, what she had smelled?

The idea that she could finally tell someone comforted her. Finally, she had someone to talk with, to share her worries, her nightmares, her fears. She wasn't alone anymore, struggling to get through each and every day without breaking down, without letting others know about her secret terrors. Most people wouldn't understand — definitely not the way Terri would — because they didn't know Elizabeth.

Afterward, with the window still open a crack, she had fallen asleep. A deep sleep. No dreams, no nightmares. She had awakened feeling fresh, almost as if she had been reborn. She wondered how that could possibly be, when she had been surrounded by so much eerie strangeness. But she firmly shut the door on those kinds of questions. She had seen nothing. She left it at that.

Linda shook her head, bringing herself back to the present. Enough about that. Time to go home.

She had just stepped onto the sidewalk leading to the parking lot when she heard a voice behind her.

"Hello, Linda. Got a minute?"

Linda jumped, dropping her keys in the process, and whirled around to see Steve standing there.

"So, is this what you cops do? Sneak up on unsuspecting people?"

Steve half-smiled, then bent to retrieve her keys. "Sorry. Didn't know you startled so easily."

There was that tone again. That hint of accusation. What was he getting after now?

"Sorry. Didn't know you could be such an ass," Linda retorted.

He stood up and held out her keys. "Gee, are we a little testy today?"

Linda took her keys. "Gee, I don't know, Steve. Maybe it's because every time I see you, I feel like I should have a lawyer present."

He stepped back and held his hands out, palms facing out. "Okay, seriously. I'm a cop. I don't mean to sound like I'm interrogating you. In my line of work, it's pretty hard to trust anyone."

She tapped her keys against her thigh. "So, does that mean I *should* have a lawyer present?"

His eyes narrowed ever so slightly. "Only if you have something to hide."

A jolt of ice shot through her, freezing the very marrow of her bones, nearly taking her breath away. Did he somehow know about her dreams? She took a deep breath. She had to stop being foolish.

"Of course not," she said, clearly and firmly.

He shrugged. "Then there's no problem. Have a drink with me?"

"Oh, that sounds lovely. So we can continue this line of questioning?"

He laughed and touched her arm. "Come on. For old time's sake."

The last thing she wanted to do was have a drink for "old time's sake." Still, she found herself being escorted to his car.

She jerked herself out of his grasp. "I'd rather drive myself, thank you very much."

"Oh, but then you might not actually make it to the bar, and then I would miss the pleasure of your company. It's not far and I promise, I'll bring you right back." Steve held the door open for her.

For the second time in a little over a week, she found herself in Steve's car, allowing him to push her around. Again.

She fumed at herself. She was a grown woman; it was ridiculous for her to let him have such an influence over her. She was too old for a school girl's crush. She turned away when Steve got in, and refused to speak as he drove to a nearby bar.

Once inside, he bought drinks while Linda seated herself at one of the booths at the back. Although early, just a little after five, the bar was already filling up with people stopping in for a quick one after work. Smells of smoke and beer mixed with the sounds of chatter and laughter, making Linda realize that despite the good night's sleep she had last night, she was still exhausted. She sank into the ripped, vinyl cushion and rubbed her suddenly throbbing head.

Steve slid into the booth across from her and pushed over a glass of wine. Red wine. Linda looked at its color, almost black in the dim bar lightening. The color of old blood.

Where the hell did that thought come from? She was going to make herself nuts. She deliberately reached over, grasped it and took a sip. Of course, it tasted exactly as it should. What had she expected? She quashed the little voice before it could answer.

He took a sip of his beer, watching her over the rim of the mug. She set her glass down.

"Are you going to tell me what this is really about, or do you want to play twenty questions?"

He smiled. "Always impatient. I told you, I wanted to have a drink for old time's sake."

Linda tapped her fingers on the painted wooden table. "Steve, when was the last time we saw each other?"

He raised his eyebrow at her. "High school."

"And how long have we been out of high school?"

"Almost ten years. Our reunion is coming up."

That's exactly what she needed. Her high school reunion to remind her of how much of a loser she was. She shook off that train of thought and continued her questions.

"And how many times have you looked me up for old time's sake in that decade since we last saw each other?"

For the first time that night, Steve looked uncomfortable. "Your point is …?"

"Obvious. You want something. So, out with it."

He laughed. "I've missed you, Linda. I always enjoyed our discussions."

Linda refused to acknowledge his comment.

He sighed. "Okay, it's about the last murder."

Linda nodded and drank some more wine. "That's what I thought. What about it?"

"Like the others, the victim was at a bar, The Starr, which is another well-known pick-up joint, as you probably know. He went there with a big group of friends. All college students. He was to graduate in December," Steve paused to drink some beer and wipe the foam off his mouth. "Hell of a time to pick up the wrong person. According to his friends, he was all about playing the field. No steady girlfriend. So, it wasn't a surprise to anyone when he told his roommate and a couple of other friends he was leaving. No one remembers exactly what he said. In fact, they can't even be sure he left with a woman. They just assumed that's what he was doing. No one saw him leave with anyone, and no one saw him talking to anyone."

"That doesn't sound like much."

"No. It isn't. All of his friends were pretty hung over today. I suspect they don't remember much of the evening.

"We questioned all of them about the people they saw in the bar. And this is the part that gets interesting. Two of his friends saw a blond-haired woman with remarkable eyes wearing white in that bar."

Linda closed her eyes. Not again. She could almost see Elizabeth's face laughing at her. The monster in her head uncoiled and hissed.

She opened her eyes and tried to sound normal. "Why were the eyes remarkable?"

Steve played with his beer glass. "They didn't say. When I asked them point blank, they both sort of shrugged. One of them said her eyes were light-colored. The other just repeated what he had said."

"What are you saying? That the police are drawing a connection to Elizabeth now?"

"No, not the police."

"Are you?"

The question hung there, like a black cloud, hovering over the table, pregnant with old blame, old guilt, old hurts. Steve swallowed some beer, never taking his eyes from Linda.

"It's hard for me to believe Elizabeth is responsible."

Pain twisted inside her, the wound suddenly fresh and new. How on earth did she manage to do to this to herself — get herself into impossible situations like this with the man who had chosen her sister over her ten years ago? "Why?" she sneered. "Because she's dead or because she was just too sweet to ever do such horrible things?"

"Linda ..."

She banged her wine on the table. "I've had enough. Take me back to my car."

"Why are you being this way?"

"Why do you think?"

They glared at each other, eyes locked, both refusing to give an inch. Then Steve sat back, his eyes narrowing, turning cold. "I still have some questions for you."

"Maybe you should take me to the police station instead," Linda said.

"Would you feel more comfortable there?"

"Dammit, Steve. Are you accusing me of something or not? You certainly sound like you are. I'm sick of these games. The least you can do is be straight with me."

He turned away, finally breaking the gaze that was heating to the point of boiling between them. "No. I don't think you're involved."

Linda sagged in her seat. Until Steve had said that, she didn't realize how tense she had become, virtually squeezing her insides together. Now, with the release, she could barely hold herself upright.

"But," he added, his eyes narrowing again.

Linda felt the knots inside her tighten up once more.

"I do have a feeling you know something."

Memories — of her dream, Elizabeth on the street corner, smelling her perfume — danced before her eyes. She had to fight to keep her face composed, so her expression, her eyes, wouldn't betray her. "Why do you say that?" Her lips felt numb. She could hardly move them.

He sat back, the tension draining from his body. "Well, isn't it obvious? If the killings are done by someone who looks like Elizabeth and Elizabeth is dead, wouldn't it make sense that that person would have known Elizabeth in life? And if that's the case, don't you think you might know him or her, too?"

She stared at her wine again. Old blood, blood that had been exposed to the environment a long time. "I guess I hadn't thought of it that way." She couldn't pull her eyes away from the glass.

He leaned forward. "I was hoping that by talking to you, you might remember something, anything at all, that could help me. Even if it doesn't seem very important, it might be enough to break the case."

She forced her gaze away from her glass, forced herself to look at him. She didn't think she would ever be able to drink red wine again.

"I'm sorry, I don't think I can help you."

"Are you sure? Think about it. Anyone ever threaten Elizabeth? Or stalk her? Maybe a jilted lover?"

Linda almost laughed. Steve might as well get out a phone book if he wanted a list of men who had obsessed over Elizabeth. And he could put his own name right at the top.

"Or, did anyone hang around her who maybe didn't seem quite right?"

Linda shook her head. "I can't think of anyone offhand."

He studied her for a moment, then leaned back in his seat, settling in. It looked too practiced a move to be spontaneous. Linda immediately mistrusted it.

"Do you know why she chose Massachusetts to kill herself?"

Linda closed her eyes. He would have to ask that. "No."

"No?"

Linda opened her eyes. "Not really."

He leaned forward. "Yes, you do. You know something."

Linda ran her hand through her hair. "I don't. Not really."

"Anything could help. Anything at all. No matter how small or insignificant you think it is."

Linda sighed. "When we were kids, we went to Massachusetts for a family vacation. While we were there, we took a boat ride. Elizabeth fell out of the boat, into the ocean."

Steve raised an eyebrow at her. "And?"

Linda shrugged. "And, a crewmember rescued her. That's it."

Steve's eyes narrowed. "Really? She fell off a boat. Into the ocean?"

"Yes."

He was silent. She could almost see his brain turning, the wheels clicking, trying to fit this new piece of the puzzle in with the rest of his information.

He cocked his head. "Then what happened?"

Linda turned away. Across the bar, an older, balding man dressed in a limp suit anxiously tried to buy an attractive younger woman a drink. Even from here, Linda could see he reeked of desperation.

"Linda?"

Why couldn't Steve leave this alone? Wasn't it obvious that what happened in the past had nothing to do with the here and now? She turned and looked him square in the eye. "Look, she got sick afterwards. Pneumonia. She almost died. I honestly don't see the connection here and I would rather not discuss it."

She could see that she had startled him. He picked up his beer, fighting to put a neutral expression on his face. "I'm sorry."

The red wine glinted at her from the table. She could almost swear it winked at her. "There's nothing to be sorry about. It happened long ago. I just don't like talking about it." Not to mention thinking about it. Especially about what happened after Elizabeth recovered. That was most definitely the worst part of the story. She sat up and began to fuss with her jacket. "Are we done now?"

Steve finished his beer. "For now. But, would you think about what we talked about? About anyone 'different,' hanging around Elizabeth? Maybe you'll remember something. You have my numbers." He put his jacket on and started to get up, but then sat back down again. "Just … one more thing. There was something else about this last murder. Something even stranger."

Linda had started putting on her coat, relief flooding over her that their conversation was finally coming to an end, but something in his voice stopped her. It was too casual, too offhand. She didn't like the sound of it one bit.

"We questioned as many people as we could find who were in the bar about the same time as the victim. One of the women we found had a bizarre story to tell. She was acting strangely, fidgeting, all the time. We questioned her. She finally told us."

Steve paused and pulled his keys out, jingling them in his hand while he talked. "She told us she saw a man standing in the corner of the bar. He was dressed all in black; his face was in the shadows. She was staring at him, trying to see what he looked like. She thought he seemed a little peculiar. Suddenly, he turned toward her and looked her straight in the face. She said his eyes were bright red. She was so startled, she looked away. When she looked again, he was gone. That night she had nightmares about it. Said there was something about him, something so evil. She was sure the only explanation was that it had to have been the devil himself."

Linda deliberately finished putting her coat on, then crossed her arms across her chest. "And, you're telling me this story for what reason?"

He shrugged. "No reason. Kind of spooky, isn't it? Maybe the devil was out that night."

"Or maybe she had a few too many pills mixed with a few too many beers," Linda said, smiling crookedly.

Steve half-smiled back. "That's what we thought, too. Come on, let me take you to your car."

Linda slid out of the booth. How had she ever managed to get herself in the middle of such an extremely odd situation? She must have a talent for attracting that sort of eeriness to herself — that could be the only sensible explanation.

Steve dropped her off at her car and she drove home. No surprises, although she found herself jumping every time she saw a shrouded figure under the street lights.

Elizabeth is dead. That meant she never saw her. So, she had to quit looking for her.

She pulled into the apartment garage and made her way up to her place. Exhaustion, made more intense by the wine and the pointed conversation, dogged her every step. When she finally did make it inside her crummy little apartment, she draped herself on one of her kitchen chairs, feeling as if she had just used up every bit of energy she had.

It was her fault Elizabeth was dead.

She closed her eyes and tried to fight the memories, but they swept through her defenses, weakened as they were by alcohol and sleeplessness, and demanded to be heard.

***

There was no body.

At the memorial service, her family, shocked by grief, had grouped near a huge photo of Elizabeth. The muffled voices of friends and family who had come to pay their respects blended with the solemn organ music droning in the background.

Linda was struck by the change in her parents. Her mother, always a meticulous, neat, elegant woman, now looked sloppy. Her typically carefully applied make-up was uneven and blotchy, as if she had put it on that day without a mirror — eye shadow smeared, blush streaked, lipstick uneven. Foundation leaked into the corners of a new crop of wrinkles that heavily lined her face. Her hair hung in long, greasy strands.

Even her behavior had changed. Gone was any sense of calm. Her hands constantly fidgeted and pulled at her dress. The worst change of all, though, was in her eyes. More than simple grief, her eyes were almost completely blank, like those of the shell-shocked soldier who had seen battle, and suffering, and death, and fought desperately to hold onto his sanity.

Her father seemed to be turning into a pale, blurry shadow of the person he used to be. Although dressed as impeccably as always, his clothes hung on him, like he had shrunk overnight. No longer an imposing, powerful figure, he looked small and old.

Her parents stood close together, almost touching, yet millions of miles apart in their grief. In fact, each member of her entire family seemed to suffer alone, drawing no strength or comfort from one another.

The air was heavy and rich with the perfume of dozens and dozens of flowers — roses, carnations, lilies, flowers she couldn't even name — baskets and baskets of them, piled everywhere. Their cloying scent began to make her sick. Thick, suffocating, she could almost see the clouds of floral perfume floating among the guests. The air felt way too dense, close. Without warning, the room began to tilt and sway, and she found herself gasping for air and falling, falling, falling into one of the numerous displays of lilies. She was covered with flowers, with petals, their sickening scent enveloping her and she couldn't get them off, couldn't escape.

"How could you?" Peter screamed in her face. He grabbed her by the arm, yanking her to her feet. "Have you no respect? It's not enough that you hated her while she was alive. Now you have to insult her memory, too?!"

She tried to answer, but there wasn't enough air in her lungs.

Chad put his hand on Peter's arm. "Peter, come on, she fainted for God's sake."

Peter whirled on Chad. "And you. Always taking her side. Where's your loyalty? Your sister is dead. Dead. Do you understand?"

"And your other sister is alive." Chad took a step closer to him.

Peter turned to look at her, his eyes filled with contempt. "I have no other sisters," he said, roughly dropping her arm and turning away.

"Thank god — that must mean I'm not related to you after all," Linda spat.

It was a childish taunt, but Peter took the bait anyway. Linda was an expert at pushing the right buttons. He whirled back, pulling his lips into a grimace. "Bitch. How dare you. It's your fault she's dead! Do you hear me? It's all your fault!" He slapped her, hard, across the face.

Bright, tingling pain cut across her cheek and nose. Hot blood poured into her mouth, and her eyes filled with tears.

Peter kept screaming at her, his voice rising with each word. "If you had been a real sister, a true sister, you would have known something was wrong! You could have helped her, you could have —"

"Stop it," Chad yelled, as he barreled into Peter. The two crashed to the floor, knocking over a vase of roses. The display smashed against the ground, splashing water and rose petals everywhere. Mike and Mark, her other brothers, jumped in then, trying to pull them off each other.

Linda backed away from the chaos, her hand over her nose, trying not to slip on the broken glass and remains of the flowers. The funeral director pushed past her, knocking her into a pew, while he hurried to assist in stopping the brawl. She clutched at her nose, trying to stem the bleeding. She tilted her head back, her eyes still watering.

Her gaze fell to the window. Outside, bushes of lilac and crab apple trees feverishly bloomed. The sky was cloudy and gray ... typical Wisconsin. The scene wavered in front of her, blurred by watery eyes.

Standing by the trees white with flowers, a figure turned. Linda blinked, trying to clear her vision. White-blond hair blowing in the breeze, she seemed incongruous against the flowering tree and the clouds scudding overhead.

It was Elizabeth. She looked directly at Linda and smiled her sardonic smile, her eyes flashing silver. Linda's stomach slammed to the floor, the force of it dizzying her.

"Linda, let me help you." It was Terri's voice, standing behind her, holding a cloth against her face. Linda clawed against it, pushing it aside, pointing to the window.

"Terri, look out there —" But then, there was nothing. Nothing at all, except crab apple trees, lilac bushes and scudding clouds.

"Look at what?" Terri asked, peering out the window. "What is it?"

Of course, there wasn't anything there. If it had been her, did she really think Elizabeth would let herself be seen by anyone else?

Madness.

Linda closed her eyes and pressed the cloth against her face. "Nothing," she said, her voice thick and heavy in her chest. "Nothing at all."

She hadn't seen anything. Elizabeth was dead. How could there be anything to see? It was Linda's imagination, a trick her mind played on her, brought on by too much stress and being hit in the face. She briefly wondered if maybe she had suffered a mild concussion when she had fainted.

***

Nearly six months later, here she was, seeing her sister again. There had been no injury this time. No fainting.

"I'm so tired. I just need to get some sleep," Linda said aloud to her empty apartment. Enough of this trip down memory lane. What she needed was a deep, dreamless sleep — emphasis on "dreamless."

There was one bright spot, though: she didn't have to face Bay Mutual the next day. Instead, she looked forward to the pleasure of battling the multitudes of shoppers at Marshall Fields. She told herself not to knock it when she went into the bathroom to collect her sleeping pills. It was better than spending the weekend with nobody but her thoughts and her cat for company.

That, she decided after she settled down for the night, was a truly scary idea.

Linda swallowed her sleeping pills, and waited for the sweet relief she hoped sleep would bring.

CHAPTER 8 — ELIZABETH

When Elizabeth was six, her odd behavior began to become apparent to *everyone* — even the neighbors.

Mrs. Jensen lived across the street from the Rossinis, in a neat, white two-story house. Her husband had passed away several years before, and her children, busy with their own children, had all moved away. Nevertheless, Mrs. Jensen kept herself busy: no one could ever call her lazy. She focused on needlework, sewing, gardening and house-cleaning, even squeezing in time to bake cookies or cakes to share with the children of the neighborhood.

But, not the Rossini children.

"There is something wrong with that family," Mrs. Jensen said, often and firmly. "Something is just not right." She'd nod her head when she said it, her gray hair pulled tightly back into a bun, her eyes shrouded by thick glasses. Their other neighbors would nod right back, in agreement.

Of course, there was no concrete proof of anything being wrong. No one ever actually *saw* anything. Still, the Rossini household bothered Mrs. Jensen all the same. Although she knew she couldn't do anything about it – couldn't even actually place what she felt was "off" – she continued to wonder if perhaps she should dig deeper.

She invited Chad and Linda, the two middle children, over several times. Sometimes, they'd accepted. They'd sit at her table, their eyes downcast, eating no more than two cookies between them, or one piece of cake each. Such quiet children — never chattering, never giggling or trying to steal another treat behind her back — always so well-behaved. And so beautiful — Linda with her brown eyes peering out behind a mass of wild hair, Chad with a sensitive, wounded expression on his face. They looked very much alike.

Most of the time, though, when she asked them in, they would simply scurry away, fear in their eyes, yet always polite: "No, I'm sorry, Mrs. Jensen, I can't. My parents are 'specting me home."

That fear she saw in them always got to her. It haunted her, the terror in those children's eyes. Sometimes she even saw them in her dreams late at night, watching her, pleading for her help.

What bothered her even more, however, was the *lack* of fear in the other children's eyes, especially the youngest.

The three older boys, Peter and the twins, had the same look in their eyes as their father: flat and cold. It reminded her of stones — bright, hard stones. Especially Peter. He resembled his father most: shorter than the others, brown hair carefully combed back, clothes always neat and tidy.

Violence lurked behind those eyes. The father's. The sons's. Terrible violence. Even if she hadn't seen the bruises, the casts on broken arms and legs, and the swollen noses, she would have sensed the violence that had taken up permanent residence in the Rossini house.

A strange and elusive mistress, fear marked each of the children differently. Chad and Linda grew more frightened, quieter, drawing deeper into themselves. The three older boys, however, became colder and colder, internalizing the violence, giving it life inside them, suckling it, allowing it to grow and fester, until one day it would become something so huge and ravenous, they'd not be able to contain it.

Pure and simple, the three older boys frightened her. The father frightened her. But the one who truly terrified her was the youngest: the one they called Elizabeth.

She was a monster.

This child never sported casts and bruises, like the other children. Her father and brothers never touched her. On the contrary, they treated her gently, as if she was made of delicate porcelain and might break if handled roughly.

"How are you today, Elizabeth?"

"Is my angel having a good day?"

"Is there anything I can get for you, my precious little girl?"

Elizabeth would simply smile back at them … yet her smile never reached her eyes. Hers was almost predatory, and she answered in a sweet, little voice that nearly dripped with sugar. So sweet, in fact, that it almost (but not completely) disguised the unmistakable venom that practically poured out from inside her.

Mrs. Jensen hated that voice. Hated watching her sit on the porch, never playing or running around, never acting like a six-year-old. She seemed practically void of emotion. She never got angry, never cried, never even raised her voice.

Nor did she ever, ever laugh.

She did nothing but sit on the front porch and read. And the books she read were not picture books.

What six-year-old could read books like that?

For that matter, what six-year-old never laughed or cried?

Mrs. Jensen knew something really needed to be done, when it came to Elizabeth, but she had no idea what. It was disarming, to say the least, to see how boys — even men — treated her. They would go out of their way, husbands, sons, grandfathers, two or eighty, it didn't matter, to "court" Elizabeth. At least, that was what it looked like to Mrs. Jensen. Elizabeth would sit on the porch, her hair the color of bleached old bones, brushed and shiny, her dress neat and tidy, and males of all ages would gather around to talk to her, touch her, be near her. She looked like a little queen, attending her subjects. It wasn't right. Especially when it came to the adults. *They certainly should know better*, Mrs. Jensen thought.

Her brothers were especially doting. Particularly Peter. He would follow Elizabeth around, talking to her, touching her. Mrs. Jensen thought it very unhealthy. She had even seen him attack Linda, screaming at her about hurting Elizabeth, although Mrs. Jensen had never once seen Linda so much as bother her sister.

Elizabeth watched those violent encounters with eyes gleaming, a small smile, almost a smirk, on her face, appearing to enjoy the conflict. Sometimes, she would even lick her lips. It made Mrs. Jensen shiver, that hungry expression on Elizabeth's face.

Women, on the other hand, avoided her at all costs.

Even the animals had more sense than the men; they kept their distance from her, too.

Dogs, friendly dogs, like the Albertson's lab who wouldn't hurt a soul, always wagging his tail for everyone in the neighborhood, couldn't stand Elizabeth. He would growl and bark at her. Once he actually snapped at her. But he never hurt her, at least not that Mrs. Jensen could see.

Cats were the same way. They hissed and snarled at Elizabeth. Once in a while, Mrs. Jensen saw one or another of them actually launch itself at Elizabeth, fur puffed up, yowling, making that growly cat noise. Elizabeth would always fling it away, her face contorted in an awful, terrible expression, one of the few times Mrs. Jensen ever saw any emotion at all reflected on her face. It was like watching a monster – the one hidden deep beneath that cold, calculating face – emerge.

If the animals didn't trust her, friendly animals, people's pets, who lived their lives by instinct … why on earth should Mrs. Jensen?

Not to mention Elizabeth's flat, empty gray eyes that sometimes turned silver — a bright, hard silver.

Of course, Mrs. Jensen was practical, and not given to flights of fancy. She knew it was ridiculous, even when she saw Elizabeth's eyes turn, herself. Eyes couldn't turn *silver*. Not human eyes. She convinced herself that it must have been a trick of the light.

Still, she was cautious.

Perhaps the animals should have been a bit more cautious, as well. One-by-one, they disappeared.

Mrs. Jensen would watch as the father, or Peter, or one of the twins, walked outside of the neighborhood, carrying a rifle, as Elizabeth sat on the porch, or peered through a window at them, smiling her sharp, empty little smile. Then, she would hear the gunshots, at odd times of day and night.

And each time she heard it, an animal wouldn't come home.

The other children in the neighborhood would make themselves sick, hunting everywhere for their pets. Fewer and fewer animals lived in the neighborhood. And those who did bring home a pet kept it inside — far from the Rossini house, and the creature within.

Of course, nobody came right out and actually accused the Rossinis. In fact, no one said much of anything to them.

But what really tore at Mrs. Jensen's heart was those two poor Rossini children who seemed normal, living in that hell of a house. Each time a gunshot was heard in the neighborhood, Linda and Chad dropped their eyes, and huddled together. They loved animals. Mrs. Jensen would see them playing with the neighbors' dogs and cats. That is, until too many animals disappeared.

Those two children kept to themselves more and more, avoiding the rest of the neighborhood, the other children and their pets. They isolated themselves inside the Rossini house, trapped in the hatred and violence.

And Mrs. Jensen knew who was really in control. Not the father with his clipped manners and pressed suit, but the *creature*. She was the one watching over them all, orchestrating the pain. The six year-old. She was the one who manipulated them all. Elizabeth.

CHAPTER 9

"Are you feeling okay?"

The question startled Linda. She had been leaning against the cash register counter, drinking coffee, not paying attention to the scene around her. It was a very slow day, at Marshall Fields.

She turned and saw Mary, one of her coworkers, standing in front of her. Mary worked in cosmetics, looking hardly old enough to drive, much less have a job with her petit frame, long blond hair and round face. The concern in her eyes seemed genuine enough, and Linda forced herself to smile.

"Yeah, I'm fine."

Mary didn't look convinced. "Are you sure? You look like you have that flu bug going around."

"No, I'm fine, really. Just a little tired. Stress, you know, with the holidays." Linda tried on another smile, feeling like a fraud. Sure, aside from having seen her dead sister and dreaming about murder victims, she was fine.

"You're probably working too much," Mary continued. "Maybe you should take a break."

Linda put down her coffee cup. Why wouldn't the girl give it a rest? "The plague of our society, working too much. It's everywhere, we can't escape." She tried to make it a joke, but felt like she was failing miserably.

"If you say so," Mary said and wandered away.

She picked up her mug again, but instead of drinking it, she twirled it in her hands, watching the coffee slosh on the sides. Why was Mary so interested in her health and work habits? Did she really look that bad?

She made her way to the bathroom and stood in front of a mirror. A puffy face stared back at her, pale and strained, with grayish-black circles forming under her eyes. No wonder Mary was concerned. Now that she saw herself, she was surprised more people hadn't asked. She looked like hell. She definitely needed to get some sleep. That, or start using a lot more make-up.

The afternoon dragged. Linda had no idea time could move so slowly. She finished folding the towels, priced a few other items, and rearranged two displays. No customers appeared. Tanya, the other salesperson in the linen department, had long since deserted her responsibilities, chatting instead with a friend in the shoe section. Linda found herself leaning against a display, eyes glazing over. It was actually painful to stay awake. She felt so thick and foggy, as if she was peering at the world through a distorted glass that made everything hazy and misshapen. Her eyelids were incredibly heavy — she struggled to keep them propped open. Maybe she'd just close her eyes for a second, well, maybe a few seconds. Just rest them a bit. After all, there weren't any customers in her department; there seemed to be hardly any in the entire store. She just needed a few seconds to rejuvenate herself, to wake herself up ...

When she opened her eyes again, she found herself in her apartment, the television on, Felix curled up on the couch next to her.

She blinked several times. The scene didn't change. The television continued droning. She put her hand on the couch, feeling the rough scratchy material beneath her hand. It certainly felt like her couch. She reached over to stroke Felix. Warm and soft. He purred, his tiny body vibrating under her palm. Yes, this was her cat.

The faint odor of rotting food — she really needed to take the garbage out, she realized — mingled with the scent of fish someone in the building was cooking hit her hard. She hated it when the neighbors made fish — that greasy smell infiltrating her apartment like a black fog.

No, this definitely didn't smell like the department store. No scent of overheated bodies, too much perfume, mixed with the sharp odors of new products, materials, and different types of cloth.

She *must* be home. The question was — how the hell had she gotten there?

She must have fallen asleep at Marshall Fields. That could be the only plausible explanation. Exhaustion finally caught up with her.
She settled back against the couch, desperately attempting to ignore the little voice that hammered in her head. *How* had she gotten home? She didn't remember driving.

She focused her eyes on the television set, watching the crime drama for a few minutes, concentrating much harder than necessary. It was during a commercial that the little voice began screaming again, a little louder this time.

This show doesn't come on until nine o'clock. The store closes at 5:30. Four hours unaccounted for. What happened? Where have you been?

Linda felt a coldness creeping up her spine, prickling her skin and causing her hair to stand on end. She rose unsteadily from the couch and tottered over to her purse and cell phone. Nine-thirty-two.

Four hours, two minutes, unaccounted for.

"That can't be," she said aloud, needing to hear her own voice. There had to be some explanation.

She stumbled into the kitchen to read the clock on the microwave. That one said nine-thirty-four. She nearly ran into the bedroom, knocking over a stack of books and tripping over a pile of clothes. Nine-forty-five, that clock said. She always set that one ahead, on purpose.

The coldness crept in again, draping over her entire body, numbing her with its iciness. Even her fingers stiffened. She moved clumsily, on legs that felt so brittle she thought they would snap in two and topple her to the ground. All the while, her brain kept repeating the same question, over and over again: *where had those four hours gone?*

She staggered back to the kitchen, opened the fridge, and took out the gallon of milk. Milk was calming, soothing. She set it on the table, went to the cupboard to take out a glass, her movements wooden but familiar. She could do it. She'd poured milk thousands of times.

When she turned back to the table, her eyes focused on a sack sitting next to the gallon of milk. It was brown, with the words "Pick N' Save" scrawled across it. It sat there, quietly on the table, minding its own business.

The glass slipped out of her hand and crashed on the floor. She took a step, and her foot crushed and ground the broken pieces into the linoleum. She felt no pain, and looked down. She still wore her shoes.

But, of course, she would still be wearing shoes. She had just walked in the door, hadn't she?

Just walked in the door. She refused to follow that line of thought any further. Instead, she reached the table, and leaned over to get a closer look at the bag.

Yes, it certainly looked like the kind of bag the deli at Pick N' Save would use. She often stopped there for something different to eat, or when her usual deli was closed. But she had no recollection of going there that night, and she had no memory of driving home.

Her fingers, trembling so much she could barely control them, slowly opened the bag. A white Styrofoam container of food sat inside. She pulled it out, feeling the warmth travel up her cold hands. Although the heat was not even close to unbearable, she nearly dropped the container, the shock against her freezing fingers almost too intense to handle.

She opened it. A gust of steam greeted her, warming her face with little droplets of moisture, filling her nostrils with the scent of fried chicken and potatoes.

She stared at the food. It was still hot. Still hot.

Hot.

Oh, dear God, she *had* just gotten home. It was nine-thirty, four hours after she would have left work, and she had just now gotten home.

Where in God's name had she gone? Had she been with anyone, or was she alone the entire time?

She ran out of the kitchen, knocking over a chair in her haste. She swept up her keys from the floor and dashed out of the apartment, closing the door behind her.

She took the stairs instead of the elevator, running all the way down to the garage where her car was parked in its spot. She could still hear the faint ticking noise of the engine, and when she pressed her hand against the hood, it was warm. She jerked her hand back.

Shivering, she stood there in the unheated garage, listening to her car ticking. She could see her breath in the frigid air. She must have just gotten home, walked into her apartment, put the food on the table, taken her coat off and turned on the television.

She remembered *none* of it.

Finally, she gathered her strength, and looked through the window at the gas gauge. Half full. Wasn't that exactly how much there had been earlier in the day, when she had checked it? She couldn't remember. But, unless she stopped for gas somewhere, more likely than not she hadn't been driving around much during those four missing hours.

But if she hadn't been driving, where had she gone? What had she done?

Slowly, she turned away from the car and walked back up to her apartment. It seemed to take forever. She examined the hallways while literally pulling herself up the steps, her feet leaden. She lived in a total dump. It amazed her that somehow she was just seeing it now for all its deteriorating glory — matted brown carpet, three different shades of brown paint peeling off the cinder block walls. Somehow, that obvious fact had simply never registered before. It was falling apart before her very eyes. She thought it terribly ironic, that a woman who wanted more than anything to design beautiful buildings lived in such a dump, and had never even realized it, before right then. It suddenly appalled her. She had moved so far from her chosen field that she could live here, without cringing every time she walked in to the building.

Linda the architect. What a joke. Perhaps she should take her college savings and invest in some serious therapy, so she could learn how to spend the rest of her life in a job she couldn't stand, without one day snapping and blowing up a post office.

She leaned against the banister, dragging each foot up to the next step, berating herself with every movement. At least this train of thought was better than thinking about the lost four hours.

Her legs had stopped responding again, and she felt the urge to use her hands to make them move. When she reached her apartment, she felt completely drained.

She fetched a second glass from the cupboard and this time successfully filled it with milk. She collapsed in one of the chairs, her legs finally giving out completely. Sipping the milk with one hand, she rubbed her face with the other.

"Think, Linda," she said aloud. "Don't fall apart here. You have to figure this out."

Start with the facts, she reasoned. First, she had to admit that she had lost at least four hours of time. The last thing she remembered was closing her eyes at Marshall Fields. She couldn't recall the exact time, but it certainly couldn't have been close to closing. The store closed at five o'clock, but employees stayed until five-thirty, cleaning up and preparing for the following day.

She made a mental note to look at her time card the next day, to see when she had punched out — if she had punched out. For now, she would assume she had left at five-thirty.

Then, at some point, she had obviously stopped at Pick N' Save, since the evidence still glared at her from the table. That meant she could account for at least a half hour, probably closer to forty-five minutes.

That left more than three hours. What else would she have done?

She shook her head and swallowed more milk. She didn't have a clue.

Maybe she had been kidnapped by aliens. Hadn't she read somewhere? That people who claimed to have been abducted lost time? Minutes, hours, sometimes even days? Or perhaps she had a seizure: another explanation for the lost time.

Or maybe there's an even simpler explanation, the little voice whispered in her head, a very evil little voice. *Maybe you're going mad.*

She banged the milk down on the table and got up, pointedly ignoring the food. She went into the bathroom to collect her pills. Perhaps she was having a reaction to the combination of Benadryl and sleeping pills she had been taking together. Or maybe it was just stress, or an anxiety attack. Lord knows she was under a great deal of stress.

What if there was another explanation? Something completely different. Like a brain tumor. That could be it. It would explain everything that had been happening to her. Yes — she had a brain tumor.

She was probably the only person in the world relieved at the idea of having a brain tumor. But somehow, it seemed a lot less frightening than losing her mind.

Even if she didn't have a brain tumor, it still might be something physical. Something the doctor could diagnose. And hopefully cure. Maybe she could get some sort of treatment, some medication, and it would all go away. Maybe she would need an operation and the doctor could cut something out. Then, she'd be all right.

She liked that idea a lot. An operation. Cutting out whatever had turned bad in her brain. Like throwing out rotten fruit from the fridge.

And once the blackness had been cut out of her head, then she'd be fine. She'd be cured.

It was such a clean thought. Not like the alternative. Not like falling into the void, into the blackness that would consume her and never let her go.

It was something physical. She knew it now. Monday she would make an appointment to see the doctor.

She smiled to herself. She felt better already. Rising from the floor, she left the bathroom and settled herself on the couch. Now she would try to sleep. That would make everything better. Just one good night's sleep.

She refused to acknowledge the nightmares looming above her, laughing at her. She needed sleep. Everything would be all right if she could just get some sleep. She repeated it to herself again: Monday she'd go to the doctor and everything would be fine.

She had to keep believing that. She had no other choice.

CHAPTER 10

Linda stood outside of Antonio's Pizzeria waiting for her brother Chad. In a week, they'd celebrate Thanksgiving with their family. Time to fortify their defenses.

She tried not to think about the past week, about how she had checked her time card on Sunday to find that she *had* punched out of work at five-thirty. Nobody treated her any differently, since that day when she had lost a four-hour block of time, which didn't really relieve her. Apparently, she could function quite well, even if she was experiencing totally memory loss and confusion.

Linda stamped her feet and rubbed her hands together. On nights like this, she swore she could feel the cold settling in her bones, freezing the very blood in her veins. Still, she didn't go inside. To go inside would mean having a glass of wine, which with Chad would turn into having two, then three, and she was too exhausted to drink. Normally, she didn't have much of a problem controlling her alcohol intake. Chad, however, sometimes influenced her a bit, in that area. She glanced at her watch. It wasn't like her brother to be late, especially to his favorite restaurant. He *loved* Antonio's stuffed pizzas. Fortunately, Linda liked them too, and she had eaten many of them over the years.

Plus, some of her fondest memories had taken place in this restaurant. After spending the day with Chad driving around, looking at and sometimes sketching old intriguing barns or houses, they would go to Antonio's for dinner, starving because they had skipped lunch.

But the restaurant held its share of bad memories, too. Like the time she spent talking Chad out of committing suicide. The waitress had literally thrown them out that night, long after closing time.

Linda shook her head and stamped her feet some more. Not a particularly good time to dwell on *that* memory.

A couple of college students walked past her, laughing at some joke only the two of them knew. The girl wore a bright red ski jacket that set off her long blond hair, and the cold made her eyes sparkle. After they passed, Linda saw him gently push a lock of blond hair out of the girl's face.

Linda turned away, trying to ignore the sharp pains of envy and jealously that knotted her stomach. They looked like members of a fraternity or a sorority, with rich parents and a bright future, not to mention the fact they had each other — most likely madly in love.

"You're a dried-up, jealous old witch," she said out loud to herself. "You had your chance at having all that, and you threw it away. You have no one to blame but yourself."

And Elizabeth, the little voice inside added. *Elizabeth made sure you threw away your future.*

A group of people emerged from Antonio's Pizzeria, breaking her train of thought with a blast of light and heat. Moist air kissed her cheek, and she could smell the thick scent of tomatoes, onions and garlic.

It only took one whiff to convince Linda that she would have a hell of a time trying to make it through dinner. The smell of food nauseated her. It seemed her appetite had drained away again, leaving room in her abdomen for the heavy, sick feeling to fester in its place.

Not only that, but her eyes felt grainy and dry. Exhaustion toyed with her like a giant ruthless cat, lazily pawing at her, letting her know it could pounce at any moment, and she'd be helpless to defend herself against it.

Five straight nights of broken sleep. Five straight nights of nightmares.

Going to sleep now terrified her. She wondered how long she would be able to function without *any* sleep at all. She was about ready to try and find out – to avoid it, at all costs …

She spotted Chad hurrying toward her, shrouded by his black overcoat. Because of his dark hair, black earmuffs, black scarf and coat, he seemed to materialize out of the night, like some dark creature from old legends. She shook her head slightly, trying to clear it, wondering where that thought had been born. She must be tired beyond belief to link Chad to some kind of vampire legend. Other members of her family maybe, but never Chad.

"Sorry I'm late," Chad said, bending down to kiss her quickly on the cheek. She welcomed the diversion. Now maybe she could stop thinking.

"Are you very hungry?" he asked.

Linda shrugged. "Why?"

"Because I thought we could take a walk before dinner. I know it's a cold night, but ..." he let the sentence hang while he smiled at her, that crooked, self-conscious smile she knew so well.

She couldn't help but smile back, although she was so cold she thought her teeth would freeze together. Chad always did love to walk, no matter what the weather was like. "Sure. If we walk fast we can warm up," she answered, relieved that he didn't want to eat at that moment.

He shook his head at her, his smile changing to one of exasperation. He reached over, his hands clothed in black gloves, and tenderly pulled her hood over her head and wrapped her scarf around her neck.

"It isn't that cold," he said, zipping her jacket up to her neck. "If you just dressed for the weather, you wouldn't shiver the way you are. How many times have I told you that most of your body heat escapes from your head, and to keep it covered?"

"Yeah, yeah, yeah. Sorry, 'Mom.' I know I don't listen well." Linda said, deciding against telling him that of all of her body parts, her feet were what felt like icicles, and she didn't think that wearing her hood would have any effect on that.

He turned and started walking at a brisk pace down the street. Linda had to hurry to keep up, even though she had changed into jeans and tennis shoes (and thin socks) before meeting him. If she had still been wearing her work clothes, she never would have stood a chance.

They walked for a while without speaking. Despite the cold, they had plenty of company — many other people, mostly college students, shared the sidewalk with them. The crisp, clear air easily carried the sounds of their voices and laughter toward them, and Linda envied their happiness. It had such an *innocent* quality to it. They had their entire future, with all its infinite possibilities, laid out before them, without a hint of the heartbreak it could all lead to.

She and Chad passed beneath the white halo of a streetlight. She felt (more than saw) Chad's head turn, his eyes studying her. She refused to acknowledge his stare, knowing what was coming next.

Ever since Elizabeth died, Chad had been harping on her lack of appetite. She hoped he couldn't see how thin she had become with her jacket on. At least her jeans fit.

"I've noticed you've lost more weight," Chad said, breaking the silence along with her hopes that her dwindling body fat would remain unnoticed.

Linda closed her eyes briefly. *Here we go again.* "I'm trying to eat."

Chad didn't respond. Linda turned her head to peer into the darkened store windows. The windows refused to reveal their secrets. Instead, they simply reflected shapes back at Linda, distorting them, along with the twisted limbs of the trees and streetlights. She turned away, faintly disturbed by the images. They reminded her of something, something she had tried very hard to forget.

"Why do you do it, Linda?" Chad's voice was low and broken. Linda turned to look at him.

"I told you I'm trying to eat."

"You're not trying hard enough."

"How would you know that? That's not true. I'm just not hungry."

"Look how much weight you've lost. How can you simply not be hungry?"

Linda raised her voice slightly. "People respond differently to grief. You've gone to therapy. I haven't been hungry."

"At least mine has taken a healthy outlet."

"I didn't say I stopped eating. I haven't. I've eaten something every day no matter how I've felt."

Chad, in his agitation, swung his arms up and shook them. The movement pulled the black overcoat away from his wrists and Linda caught the faint gleam of the dead white, jagged scar against the delicate skin. She dropped her eyes quickly, not wanting to see the vivid, broken reminder of the time he almost succeeded in committing suicide.

He caught her movement, faint as it was, and lowered his arms.

"Look, I'm sorry," he said. "I didn't come here to antagonize you."

"That's good," Linda said, "because we both get enough of that from the rest of our family."

"It's just that I worry about you."

"Well, I worry about you too."

"I really think you should get some therapy."

"Christ, Chad. Not again."

"I'm serious. My therapist has done wonders for me."

"That's great. Really it is. I'm happy for you."

Chad gently touched her shoulder with his. "Linda. I really wish you would listen to me. I know you've repressed a lot that's happened to us as children. Besides that, you're so bitter. Even if you can't see it, I can. And you need to let go of that bitterness, if you hope to ever have a better life."

"Thank you, Billy Graham. The next time I want a sermon, I'll ask you for it."

Chad looked away from her. "You don't have to be sarcastic. Why are you resisting me?"

Linda sighed. "I'm not trying to resist you. I just don't like the idea of talking about my problems with a stranger. And, besides, I can't afford it."

"I'll pay for them."

Linda rolled her eyes. "With what money? You're not doing much better than I am."

"I passed the test. I got a raise. And a promotion. I'm no longer an assistant. You're talking to a full-fledged architect," he said, beaming.

"Chad, that's great! Why didn't you tell me? We should celebrate!" She took his arm and hugged it, her cheek pressing against the rough fabric of the coat. The coat smelled like him: sharp and clean, with just a hint of aftershave.

"We are," he said, blushing a little. "And I have better news."

"What?"

"They have an internship program at the firm. And no one has applied for next semester. I told them about you, and they want to hire you."

Linda released his arm, her falling mouth open. "But," she stuttered. "I don't have a college degree. I'm not even in school. I only had those two years of college."

"That doesn't matter. I told them how talented you are. Linda, you would make a fantastic architect."

Linda inhaled deeply. This couldn't be happening at a worse possible time. "But," she said carefully, "I don't even know when I'm going to be able to return to school. It might not be for another couple of years."

"I thought you were saving money to go back to school."

"I am, but these things take time. And there are other considerations. Like if this internship pays or not. If I'll be able to still work at my job while I'm doing the internship."

"I thought you hated your job."

"I do. But it pays the bills. I've been there almost seven years. For someone with only a high school diploma, I make quite a bit of money."

Chad stared straight ahead, half closing his dark brown eyes and straightening his lips into a thin line. Linda had seen that look before. Chad was frustrated.

"I don't understand you," he said, shaking his head. "Here's your chance to do something you've always wanted to do, to get out of the rut you've sunk into. And how do you respond? By thinking up excuses not to do it."

"Chad, this is a really bad time for me ..."

"When will be a good time?"

Linda closed her eyes. "Listen. I need to tell you something. It's about Elizabeth."

"Why are you changing the subject?"

"Chad, this is important. There are things going on that you don't know about."

Chad sighed. They passed beneath a streetlight and Linda glanced at him, struck as she always was by their resemblance to each other. Sometimes, when the light hit his face just right, Linda felt like she might as well be looking in a mirror. The same thick, dark, curly hair, the same large, dark brown eyes rimmed with the same thick, curly black lashes ... the high cheekbones, the sculptured face, the olive skin. With those eyes, and those delicate features, Chad was actually quite beautiful.

It never ceased to amaze her that those same features that made Chad beautiful could make Linda so plain-looking. Maybe hers weren't delicate enough, or her eyes large enough. Or maybe it was the expression in Chad's huge, brown, haunted eyes, sensitive and so full of pain.

Chad never should have been born to our family, Linda thought, not for the first time. Our family could never appreciate or understand him. Instead, they tried to destroy him.

And they had almost succeeded.

"Well," Chad said. "Are you going to tell me or do I have to read your mind?"

"Do you want me to tell you?"

"I wouldn't have asked if I didn't."

"It isn't a pretty story. I saw Steve Anderson the other day."

"Steve Anderson? From high school?"

"One and the same."

Chad frowned. "Why would you waste any time on Steve Anderson? He has a knack for bringing a lot of sorrow to our family."

Linda threw up her hands. "What are you talking about?"

He turned to look at her. "You know exactly what I'm talking about."

She looked away from Chad, studying the bare, dead-looking trees, the brown grass, and the shriveled bushes that lined the streets.

"One, Chad," she said softly. "One family tragedy out of thousands."

"That one family tragedy was more than enough. As I recall, you almost got yourself thrown out of the house."

"I almost got myself killed. You don't have to remind me. I was there. And thank you again for pulling Peter off me."

Chad made a wry face. "You know you don't have to thank me."

"I know. But I like to do it anyway. You're under-appreciated."

Chad ducked his head, but not before Linda detected a faint blush, barely visible under the street lights.

They passed a wrought iron bench by a bus stop that had what looked like a bundle of rags on the seat. On closer inspection, Linda realized the bundle of rags covered a dirty, unkempt man, his unshaven face resting against the metal armrest. She dropped her gaze. Although nobody liked to talk about it, much less admit it, Riverview, Wisconsin had its share of poverty and homeless. The difference seemed to be that, unlike bigger cities, most of the people in Riverview wanted to live their lives in happy denial of such issues. "That sort of thing simply couldn't happen in Riverview. Those kinds of problems don't exist," people said. "We especially don't have serial killers living in our precious little town."

Chad broke the silence. "So, what did you want to tell me about Elizabeth?"

She bit her lip. The trees waved their naked branches at her, mocking her. "Nothing."

Chad turned his head. "Nothing?"

She couldn't tell him. What good would it do? It would just upset him. She couldn't treat him as a sounding board, like she could Terri — he was too fragile for that.

"It's not important."

"If it has to do with Elizabeth, then it is important."

She didn't answer. Although she hadn't completely warmed up, the cold wasn't unbearable to her either. The night was still – chilly and windless. Her breath puffed out like little wisps of white steam. The full moon followed them on their journey, a chip of ice in the deep, black velvet sky.

Chad studied her, his eyes dark with a familiar pain, like an old wound that had never been allowed to heal.

"Why won't you talk to me?" His voice was filled with a strange combination of bewilderment, sadness and confusion — the way it was whenever he spoke of Elizabeth.

"So, what's up with those Packers?"

"What do you think Elizabeth did now?"

"Chad, stop this."

"What?"

"You know we will never agree on Elizabeth, so just stop it."

"But, Linda, we have to talk about it."

Linda looked at him, his face set and drawn. "Why?"

"Why what?"

"Why do we have to talk about it? We'll never agree, and all we end up doing is upsetting each other. So, why even start?"

Chad lifted his arms helplessly. "We've never spoken about her since the funeral. Never. And we have to."

"There's nothing to say. We don't know why she did what she did. We'll never know that, so all we can do is move on."

"How can we move on? Our sister killed herself and we did nothing about it. We didn't even know how much pain she was in. How could we have been so horrible?" His voice broke.

"Oh, Chad." Linda stopped walking and hugged him tight. "It was her choice. Hers alone. We can't second guess ourselves. She made the decision herself."

"I know, but ..."

"No buts." She squeezed him harder. "What does your therapist say?"

"Basically what you're saying, but ..."

"See? Then I'm right, so you should listen to me."

Chad laughed a little. He put an arm around her and hugged her back. For a few moments they stood there, drawing strength from each other, before resuming their walk.

Someone stumbled out of a bar in front of them, weaving heavily before collapsing on the sidewalk, giggling uncontrollably.

Chad stepped around the prone but happy figure, before breaking the silence. "Look, I know she wasn't nice to you when we were growing up."

Linda rolled her eyes. "That's certainly an understatement."

"And she did some mean things to you when we were teenagers. I know she even tried to pit me against you. But, we were only kids. Kids do mean things to each other. Look at how Peter, Mark and Mike treated me."

"And look how close the four of you are now."

Chad winced and dropped his head.

Linda immediately regretted her words. "I'm sorry."

"No, you're right."

"That doesn't matter. It wasn't called for. I'm just trying to tell you that just because we were kids, and maybe didn't know better, doesn't justify her behavior."

"I know. You're right. And I'm trying to forgive Peter, Mark, Mike, and even Father as part of my therapy right now. I guess what bothers me now about you and Elizabeth is that you honestly believe Elizabeth had it in for you. You don't think it was just kids being kids – kids being mean."

Linda didn't answer, because he was right and they both knew it. Chad touched her hood, turning her head so he could look her in the eye.

"Father was the one who used to beat you. Peter beat you, and nearly killed you. Yet you don't seem to carry the same feelings for them as you do for Elizabeth, who, to my knowledge, never laid a hand on you."

"That's because I think Elizabeth was the one who goaded them into it."

"Maybe she did some of the time. But she didn't mean anything malicious by it."

Linda winced. Oh, yes, she did. "Did you ever see Elizabeth get hit? Even once? By anyone?"

"What does that have to do with anything?"

"Just answer the question."

Chad thought for a moment. "I can't remember anything specific right now."

"That's because she never did. I did, you did, Peter, Mark and Mike did and even Mom got punched around from time to time. But Elizabeth, not even once. And why? Because she manipulated them."

"Even if she did, so what? What does that prove?"

"It proves that she could control them. She could control who they went after, and who they didn't."

"I think you're making more out of this than what it was. She was a little girl, when the worse of that was happening. How could a little girl be that calculating? How could she control people?"

"I don't know," Linda said, suddenly weary. They had finished walking around the block and she could see Antonio's Pizzeria in front of them, its neon red sign so cheerful and beckoning. Feeling her knotted up stomach tightening even more, she wondered if she could even swallow a single bite of food tonight.

"It wasn't all bad anyway," Chad said. "Our childhood, I mean. Remember that time we went to the zoo and Peter took turns carrying us on his back?"

"I remember. Father had bought us all hot dogs and cotton candy. We were so stuffed, we didn't eat any dinner."

"Yeah," he looked mournful. "Almost like a real family."

Linda signed. "Almost."

Chad turned to her, squeezing her arm. "I'm sorry Linny," he said, using his pet name for her. "I don't want to fight with you. That isn't why I asked to see you. Yet it seems we've been at each other's throats the entire evening."

Linda smiled at him. "I know. I'm sorry too. I haven't been myself lately."

He smiled slightly in return, but the smile never reached his eyes.

"Thanksgiving is going to be really hard this year," Chad said. "What with Elizabeth gone and all."

"I know."

"I haven't talked to anyone since the funeral. How about you?"

Linda shook her head. *She* was the reason he hadn't talked to anyone.

She'd never be able to repay Chad for everything he had sacrificed for her. Sometimes, she thought Chad would have been far better off if she had never been born. Her presence in their family had just made life even more difficult for him.

They reached Antonio's Pizzeria. Chad opened the door for her. "A stuffed pizza sounds awfully good, doesn't it? And now that we got all that unpleasant stuff out of the way, we can spend dinner talking about fun stuff." He smiled at her.

He had such an infectious smile, she couldn't help but smile back. "Deal."

Mirror Image

CHAPTER 11

By Saturday, Linda felt she had reached the end of her resources. She could barely stay awake at Marshall Fields. Somehow, she had no idea how, she managed to drag herself through the day without falling asleep. She drove home with the window open, the cold air blasting against her face keeping her awake. She bought a cheeseburger, fries and shake at a McDonald's drive-thru, before reaching her apartment.

Once there, she fed Felix, ate most of her food, took her medication with some milk and tumbled into bed. She could fight it no longer: the nightmares didn't matter, the fear didn't matter. Nothing mattered, except sleep.

She drifted off immediately, only to find herself in that dreadful old house again. Elizabeth was still calling her, her voice even louder than ever before.

Menacing, shapeless shadows stretched across her. One had a long arm, an impossibly long arm that wrapped across the ceiling, ending with five splayed out fingers. Another had just a head and body, the head round as a Halloween ghost. A third looked as if it had two horns, curling upward like a bull, tapering to smooth points.

Linda tried not to look. She concentrated on the hallway, on the doors. Most of them opened at her touch, revealing their bare, dilapidated contents. She had to find Elizabeth. She had to get her to stop calling her name.

She noticed the carpet — brown and very worn. The walls were brown too, three different shades of paint, from dark to light. Except the paint was peeling off in long sheets, tearing off, even as she watched, floating gently to the floor. Spiders crawled up and down the walls, trailing long milky-white webs. Sometimes the carpet seemed to move, but when she looked closer she saw that it was actually ants, covering the floor. Their black, thin bodies hard and shiny, with long antennae.

Linda shuddered and tried not to touch them, but all of a sudden they seemed to be everywhere, swarming along with the spiders, creeping up her legs, her arms, their whispery limbs brushing against her cheeks, her hair.

She wanted to scream but couldn't. Blindly, she reached out, pushing them away, slapping her arms, legs, face. But still they came, the spiders with their long webs and the ants with their antennae.

Her hand banged a doorknob, instantly bruising her palm. Ignoring the pain, she forced it to turn. The door swung open easily, so easily Linda lost her balance and fell to the floor. The door slammed shut behind her.

The insects disappeared.

The room was quiet, almost too quiet. She lifted her head and looked around.

She lay in a living room. Dark brown carpet lined the floor and old wooden panels plastered the walls. An old beige plaid couch stood against one wall. Next to it sat a stained, olive green chair that sagged to one side. Both pieces of furniture had seen better days. Directly opposite the couch stood two very large speakers. Various electronics lay on top of the speakers, along with yards of wires, and a large screen television stretched between them.

Beer cans littered the floor, along with textbooks, notebooks and an empty pizza box. A tiny kitchen opened up from the living room, the counters piled high with dirty dishes. More plates had been stacked on a round table. The plates were covered with crumbs and food stains. One plate had a dried red stain smeared all over it.

Linda stood. Obviously a college apartment. But she had never been in one exactly like this before.

She could see a tiny hallway, almost hidden by the green chair, with a light shining out from the far end. Slowly, she started to walk toward it.

When she reached the end of the hallway, she wasn't surprised to find a bedroom. The door stood open just a slit. Light poured out of that slit and fell onto the dirty carpet. Certain of the gruesome image that would greet her in the bedroom, but helpless to stop herself, she pushed open the door.

It was impossible to discern the actual size of the room. On one hand, it seemed huge, vast, its space spilling out over the entire world, into infinity. But on the other hand, it seemed contradictorily tiny: no bigger than a closet, barely able to contain the few pieces of furniture within – a desk, chair, bookcase and dresser.

And the bed.

That bed.

Although only a double, it seemed to fill the entire bedroom. It sagged to one side, tangled in a web of unwashed sheets and blankets. A thick quilt spilled onto the floor and trailed off. Blues and greens joined together in an old-fashioned dance on one side of the quilt, the other held the stillness of a plain unbroken blue. It was obviously handmade: a mother's gift to her son as a going-away present when he left for college, to make sure he would be warm on cold winter nights.

Drops of red scattered across the quilt, equally covering both sides, contrasting the blues and greens. Her eyes traveled up the quilt, noticing how the drops became thicker, the closer they came to the bed.

To the body in the bed.

He was naked, hands bound above his head, his body slashed. His face, untouched, looked oddly serene, like a man simply enjoying his sleep. How could he look so peaceful when his body bore the marks of such violence, such rage, such hate? It wasn't right — he looked more peaceful in his violent death than Linda had felt in her entire life.

Then, his eyes opened. Linda flinched, expecting silver. Instead, she found herself looking into a pair of incredibly blue, clear eyes.

Those eyes studied Linda for a moment. Then his face clouded over. His mouth opened.

"You," he whispered.

Suddenly, his eyes were bright red. Linda recoiled in horror. His mouth opened, and a thin, serpentine tongue slithered out of his mouth. Linda could feel its hot breath against her cheek, burning her face. She shuddered and fell backward, but didn't hit the floor. Instead she floated up into the air, slowly sinking again as she moved toward the bed, watching as it grew larger, puffing up like a balloon and rising over her. Hovering with the bed above her, she could see the man, no, the thing, moving. The bed creaked loudly, when it pulled itself to the side.

The head peered over, popping up like a fiendish jack-in-the-box, outstretched arms still tied to the bed. Blood dripped from his face. Eyes the same deep red as the blood. The mouth slowly stretched again, this time into an insane smile, exposing sharp, pointed teeth and that serpentine tongue.

Suddenly, a scream pierced the silence. The image shattered, breaking into a million fragments. Linda clapped her hands over her ears, but it did nothing to stop the icy pain whipping through them.

Then the distinct words, clear as day:

"Your brother's blood cries out to me from the ground!" the voice shrieked.

Linda awoke, gasping for breath. She was lying on her stomach, her face buried deeply in the pillows. She lifted her head, in desperate need of oxygen, the cold night air so refreshing against her sweating cheeks. Her mouth tasted like cotton balls and her head swam. What on earth did it mean?

"Your brother's blood cries out to me from the ground!" It sounded vaguely, eerily familiar, but she couldn't place it.

She quickly rolled over and flipped on a light. Felix was nowhere to be seen, and the bed was in tatters. The clock's red digits glowed; it was just after three o'clock.

She got up, pulling on a robe, and headed into the kitchen, reassuring herself that she at least didn't smell the perfume. First she drank a big glass of water, then poured herself some milk.

Oddly enough, she did feel better then — more rested than she had felt in a while. She turned on the TV and made herself comfortable on the couch.

There's been another murder. He had blue eyes, Linda thought.

A sharp scratching noise interrupted her thoughts. *Screech. Screech. Screech.* Startled, she choked back a scream. It was coming from the front door.

The murderer, coming to kill her too.

Panic bubbled up inside her and she fought to push it down. She had to get a hold of herself. She had to be rational. There wasn't any way the murderer could know she saw the killings in her dreams. It can't be her.

Screech. Screech. Screech.

She tried to jump off the couch, but instead became entangled in the blankets and fell headlong to the floor. Her head banged the edge of the coffee table and the pain temporarily obliterated her fear.

Who could be at the door?

Meow.

Linda sat up, holding her head. Felix?

She heard it again, another meow, followed by more scratching. How could Felix be outside?

She struggled to her feet, pulling off the blanket, hurried to the door and opened it. There sat Felix, looking quite offended. He pushed his way into the apartment, pointedly ignoring Linda, and began grooming himself.

Linda closed the door and locked it. She studied the cat.

"How on earth did you get out there?" she asked.

Felix didn't even acknowledge her presence.

"You aren't any help, you know that? I have a feeling that even if you could talk, you wouldn't. I should have gotten a dog."

Felix quit cleaning himself, gave her a very disgusted look, and stalked off, flicking his tail.

Linda sighed and sat down on the couch. How could Felix have gotten out? He never went outside the apartment. In fact, he had never shown any desire to get out. He seemed content, living his life in her tiny, one bedroom apartment. His life was neat and orderly, everything the same, day in and day out. Linda had read somewhere that pets, like children, thrive on routine. Felix certainly seemed to back that up.

She double-checked the windows, finding them all tightly shut. She remembered turning the deadbolt when she entered the apartment, so the front door was out. Unless Felix had recently developed the ability to walk through walls, someone must have let him out. And, since the front door had been deadbolted, that someone must have been Linda.

Did he slip out when she walked in? She had definitely been beyond exhausted. She may not have noticed an elephant strolling through her door, at that point. No, that couldn't be it. She remembered feeding him. Actually, to be completely accurate, she remembered watching him sit on the floor with his full food dish right in front of him, impatiently watching her eat. Such an exasperating cat. The moment she left the kitchen, she heard him munch his food.

Could she have let him out while she slept? Maybe she had been sleepwalking. In her nightmare, she was running through a house. Could she be acting out her nightmares? That would explain a lot of things, including her lost-time episode. Hadn't she read somewhere that people had been known to do very strange and elaborate things while sleepwalking? Even murder? Didn't she remember reading about a man actually being acquitted of murdering his wife while sleepwalking?

And if her lost-time episode *could* be attributed to sleepwalking, then she had also been sleep *driving*. Not a very comforting thought, to say the least. If she had received a ticket, or, even worse, been in an accident, what would the police have done? Would they have figured out she was asleep? Doubtful.

She brushed her hair back away from her face. None of that mattered now. The issue here had nothing to do with sleep driving, or the police. What mattered, and what she should be focused on, was how Felix got outside.

Felix had never once, in the six years she had him, left the apartment on his own accord. So even if she had unlocked the door and held it open, while fast asleep, he likely would not have just sauntered out.

Could she have thrown him out? If she could unlock doors in her sleep, and drive in her sleep, she supposed she could scoop up the cat and deposit him outside in her sleep as well.

Would Felix have left on his own? It dawned on Linda then that he *may* have, if he had been frightened. But what could have frightened him?

Linda? Possibly. She thrashed around quite a bit during her nightmares; perhaps he got scared. But usually, when that happened, he just hid.

Could there have been something else in the apartment with her?

Linda got off the couch abruptly. "Stop that," she said aloud. "Don't even think about that."

She also refused to let herself think about how much Elizabeth couldn't stand animals — especially cats.

She wouldn't think about the dogs that growled and the cats that hissed when Elizabeth walked by.

And she wouldn't think about that time Elizabeth showed up on her doorstep, forcing Linda to invite her in. And how Felix had actually attacked her, as Linda watched in shocked fascination.

"This is nonsense," Linda said aloud, pacing between the living room and kitchen. "What am I thinking? That Elizabeth's ghost may have been here?"

That was exactly what her mind was suggesting. Maybe Elizabeth was still haunting her. Her torture of her sister cut short by her death, perhaps now she continued from the grave.

"Elizabeth is not here. She is dead. And there is no such thing as ghosts," Linda muttered to herself.

But what about the funeral? the little voice asked. *What about what happened at the funeral? What you saw?*

"Nothing happened at the funeral," Linda retorted, silencing the voice. "There was nothing there."

She longed to call Terri, to hear a voice of reason amid the insanity. But it was the middle of the night. She would have to wait until morning.

And until then, she would have to endure the hours, long hours, trapped in her apartment, with only her overactive imagination – and Felix – to keep her company.

She moaned, her body dropping into a kitchen chair, her head sagging into her arms.

"I have to get my act together," she said aloud. "Elizabeth is not here. Besides, if Felix really sensed Elizabeth here, I doubt he would have been eager to come back inside."

That thought reassured her. Although the dreaded little voice in her head continued, suggesting maybe Felix knew Elizabeth had left.

She ignored the little voice, rocking her head in her arms. Elizabeth couldn't be here. Not if she was busy murdering someone else. She lifted her head and dropped her arms on the table.

She gazed at her white inner wrist, smooth and unbroken, glimmering in the faint light. There was no jagged scar breaking the surface … no evil snake slithering under her skin. There was no visible reminder of what childhood violence had done to her soul.

For a second, she thought about what it must have been like for Chad — how it must have felt, gripping a razor and slitting his own wrists. Did he do it slowly, torturously dragging it out, or had he made a quick, fast motion? She remembered finding him in the bathroom, collapsed like a rag doll on the floor, blood everywhere.

It had been a Saturday. She had awakened with an urge to see her brother. She grabbed her cell, started to call and hung up.

Instead, she instantly decided to pop in unexpectedly and surprise him.

At the time, she hadn't taken even a moment to analyze the fact that this was not her normal behavior. She never just dropped by unexpectedly on anyone, including her family. But today, she had promptly decided to do just that.

So she had taken a shower and dressed, moving faster than normal, but not with a sense of urgency. She had no sense of anything being wrong. She just wanted, needed, to see her brother.

She drove to his apartment building, parked, walked up the three flights of steps to his door and knocked. No one answered.

She turned to go. He obviously wasn't home — something she would have known if she had called before coming over. She took her first step back down the stairs, when the hairs on the back of her neck prickled.

She turned back to the door and tried it. Locked. She had a key, just like Chad had one to her apartment. Just in case.

She pulled the key out and looked at it. This isn't an emergency, she told herself. He just went out. She had no reason to go in.

Still …

She might as well. She had come all this way. Why not make sure everything is all right, just to be sure?

She knew the moment she opened the door that everything was *not* all right. In fact, something was terribly wrong.

Her first clue was the smell. A strong, musky, sweetish, metallic smell. She knew that smell, but couldn't place it. Instinctively she recoiled.

"Chad," she called out, forcing herself to walk further into it – that heavy, think scent. No answer. Just silence, and an ominous, distinct dripping noise.

She walked into the living room. Nothing. She glanced into the kitchen, seeing nothing unusual. It was spotlessly clean, as was the rest of the apartment. Chad had always been tidy.

She turned into the hallway and saw a stain in the rug. She frowned. Very unlike Chad. She touched it. It was wet. She pulled her hand away. Red liquid dripped from her fingers. Blood.

Her eyes followed the trail of blood, saw it seeping from beneath the bathroom door. She forced the door open.

Chad was unconscious, flopped on the floor, surrounded by a pool of his own blood. She couldn't see his face; it hung over his chest, his arms and legs splayed out, the blood dripping from his wrists into the pool on the floor.

"Oh, my God," she whispered, her hands clenching into fists, pressing them against her mouth, trying not to scream. "Help," she whispered hoarsely, biting down on her hands. It wasn't until later that she realized she had bit into her finger hard enough to draw blood.

He must be dead, she thought while she raced to the phone to call 911. No one could lose that much blood and still be alive.

But he lived. Even the doctors had been amazed.

The doctor's bald head gleamed, his glasses sparkled. He had introduced himself to her just moments before, but for the life of her, she couldn't remember his name. "Normally, when we see a suicide attempt, there are several cuts to the wrists — trial cuts, so to speak, while the person works up the nerve. And usually, the hand wavers somewhat, and the cuts are quite shallow. Not in your brother's case." He shook his head, and Linda could have sworn she had seen admiration in his eyes.

"Strong and steady. And deep. More like a surgical incision than a suicide attempt. Your brother is *very* lucky to be alive."

"But he is — he is going to live?" Linda asked.

"Yes, he's going to make it, this time," the doctor said. Linda let her breath out in a rush, her relief so great she missed the real meaning of the doctor's words.

"Can I see him?" she asked.

The doctor looked at her, his eyes serious and penetrating. "Miss, your brother wanted to kill himself. *He really wanted to kill himself.*"

She shook her head, uncomprehending.

The doctor sighed. "Some suicides, actually I would venture to say, most suicides, are a cry for help. The person really doesn't want to die; he wants someone to notice his pain and help him. Your brother is not in that category. He was serious. And if you don't get him help, he will do it again. And next time, there's a good chance he'll succeed."

Shocked, Linda's mouth dropped open. She had known, known for a long time, forever even, how damaged Chad was. Although all the siblings (except Elizabeth) had taken their share of beatings and abuse, because Chad had been more sensitive than her other brothers, he had taken even more, and was abused more severely than the others. Rage welled up inside her, rage she could not summon for her own plight, but that would boil for Chad's. Just because he had been interested in drawing, books and dreaming, he was targeted by her father and three other brothers. And now, he was paying for it again.

When she saw her brother, he had been furious with her. "Why did you call the ambulance?" he ranted. "Why didn't you just let me die?"

"Could you have let me die? If the situation had been reversed?"

"That's beside the point," he shouted, flinging his bandaged arms around, knocking over a glass of water from the table. "If I knew how much pain you were in ..."

"Then what?" Linda demanded. "You'd let me die? I don't think so."

"You *should* have, Linda. You should have let me die," he said again, but this time, he sounded a bit less angry.

"Do you think I want to live the rest of my life without you?" she asked, her voice frail, beginning to break.

He stared at her then, seeing her, really seeing her. "Oh, Linny," he said helplessly, falling back against the pillows.

He got better then. He stayed in the hospital and saw the hospital psychiatrist. Then, after his release, he started an intensive therapy program.

Although she could imagine the pain and demons that haunted Chad, and certainly empathized with him, she never fully understood his wish to end his life.

Until that moment, in her apartment.

Staring at her wrists, she wondered how it would feel. The blade, cold as it touched her skin, then burning hot, cutting through the delicate layers, kissing the veins beneath. The blood would pulse out, hot and gushing at first, then drip more slowly from her wrists, taking with it the pain, the demons, the guilt, the fear of insanity. And she would finally be at *peace*.

She shoved her hands back from her view. "That's enough of that," she said to herself. If she ever had any question of what suicide did to the living, she now knew exactly what hell it put the survivors through.

She couldn't do that to her friends and family. Especially not to Chad. It would destroy him.

"I'm tired," Linda said to herself as reasonably as possible. "I'm under a lot of emotional strain. I'm not thinking straight."

She got up from the kitchen table and curled up on the couch, preparing to spend the rest of the night not thinking about anything. Felix joined her, settling on her lap, forgiving her at least momentarily for having somehow ended up outside the apartment. While Linda half-listened to the drone from the television, her eyes flickering over the images, she allowed herself to slip into a trance-like, almost hypnotic, state.

Mirror Image

CHAPTER 12

"It's urgent," Steve said over the telephone. "I really need to see you after work."

It was Tuesday, two days before Thanksgiving. Two days before she would be forced to confront her two oldest friends, guilt and blame, head on. She was having enough trouble with her emotions. She really didn't need Steve making things worse.

"I really can't," Linda said again.

"Linda, you have to. It's about the murder on Saturday night."

"But Steve ..."

"I'll arrest you if I have to."

That stopped her. For a second she said nothing, just listened to the gentle buzzing of the phone lines between them. *What did he know?*

She broke the silence. "You don't mean that."

"Try me."

Linda sighed. "All right. Where do you want to meet?"

She knew where before he even said it. "At the police station. As soon as you can after work."

Linda placed the phone down gently. At the police station. This was serious.

She wondered what on earth they could have found. She thought about her dream Saturday night. She had been avoiding the papers, unwilling to find out if she had dreamed about the victim, convinced she really didn't want to know.

It seemed she was going to find out, whether she wanted to or not.

Oh, well, maybe the news won't be so bad, she said to herself. Maybe the police have discovered that Elizabeth really has come back from the dead.

The thought made her grin at its ridiculousness, even while a small chill ran up her spine.

She hadn't called Terri. The rising sun Sunday morning had done more than brighten the day; it had also made her feel foolish. Elizabeth was dead. Period. End of story. Any other explanation was just silly — an exercise in futility.

"I'm simply exhausted and stressed," she said quietly. "There's nothing wrong with me that a few days off and some sleep wouldn't cure." She felt better, saner, saying it out loud.

Maybe she would request some time off. She had over two weeks of paid time off to use at Bay Mutual before the end of the year, and Marshall Fields owed her a weekend, seeing as how she had worked every weekend straight for the past six months. Of course, now that Christmas shopping season had begun, they might not see it that way. Maybe she could take at least a week off from Bay Mutual in December.

Her supervisor came in with an armload of work, interrupting her musings. It kept her occupied until the end of the day, and she didn't even have time to wonder what Steve wanted now.

She arrived at the police station shortly after five. She asked the desk sergeant for Steve, and he immediately ushered her to Steve's desk.

It surprised her, how much the office looked like the sets used on TV cop shows. The detectives were in one big room filled with messy desks. The cinder block walls had been painted white at one point, but time and cigarette smoke had given them a yellowish cast. In fact, the whole place stunk of stale cigarettes, old coffee and sweaty, unwashed bodies. A gray tile floor and cheap chairs completed the picture.

She saw Steve huddled with two other people over one of the desks across the room. None of them noticed her right away, and she stayed in the doorway, taking deep breaths, filling her lungs with the foul air, trying to calm herself.

Steve had on a white shirt with the cuffs rolled up, a navy and red striped tie, and navy pants. The tie knot was pulled away from his collar, as if he had been yanking on it most of the day. His black, slightly mussed hair curled around his collar. She felt somewhat dizzy. Perhaps she shouldn't be taking such deep breaths. She forced herself to breathe shallower.

He looked up, noticing her, and waved her over. She began to walk toward him, grateful for whatever impulse had made her dress in one of the outfits Terri had picked out for her. Her black skirt was only a little loose, and the bluish-purple jacket brought out some color in her otherwise pale face. She was starting to wear concealer and foundation every day, attempting to hide the ever-darkening circles under her eyes, along with blush and lipstick.

Steve straightened his tie and ran his hand through his hair, messing it up more than straightening. "Thanks for coming, Linda."

"Like I had a choice," she said under her breath.

He smiled his half-smile at her. Gently, he pulled at the coat she carried in her arms. She had taken it off almost immediately, the station heated so warm, it was almost unbearable. *Nice to know where my tax dollars are going*, she thought.

"Let me take that for you," he said. She forced herself to relax her death grip on the jacket. "Coffee? Water?"

"Nothing, thanks."

He went to hang up her coat, leaving her momentarily alone with the other two detectives. Her eyes followed him briefly, his lean body moving in such a graceful, sensual way.

Inwardly, she shook her head and firmly turned her attention to the two others.

Both had their gaze fixed on her, openly studying her, with what felt like more than a little suspicion. Especially the woman. She broke the silence first.

"I'm Detective Karen Thomas," she said, extending her hand. Linda shook it. Her hand felt dry and a little calloused, but she gripped Linda's hand firmly, almost to the point of painfully. She was smaller than Linda and very skinny, all bones and no curves. Dressed in a beige, loose-fitting pants suit and white shirt, she had pulled her long dirty blond hair tightly away from her face, emphasizing small narrow eyes and a jutting chin. Her face matched the rest of her body: all angles and sharp points. She might actually be pretty, if she let her hair down, allowing it to soften the edges of her face. To Linda, she looked very severe, in her early to mid-thirties.

"This is my partner, Detective John Norton," she said, gesturing to the man next to her, who smiled and offered Linda his hand. He looked to be about the same age as Detective Thomas, but in all other respects he was completely opposite — soft and doughy, with a very round face, brown hair and gentle brown eyes. He was tall, taller than Steve even, but much heavier. His black pants and white shirt strained at the seams. His hand, when she shook it, felt moist and plump, but his grip was gentle.

"Shall we go into one of the interrogating rooms?" Detective Thomas asked after Steve had reappeared, gesturing with her arm. On the surface, her voice seemed smooth and professional, but underneath Linda could hear a slight edge.

The interrogation room. Great, this was all she needed. She turned to Steve. "Interrogation? Should I call a lawyer?"

"Why, do you have something to hide?" Detective Thomas jumped on her.

"What is it with police asking if I have something to hide?" Linda said, exasperated. "You're questioning me in an interrogation room. Doesn't that imply I need a lawyer?"

Detective Norton intervened smoothly. "You're not under arrest. If you want to have a lawyer, that's within your rights, but we just want to ask you a couple of questions, that's all."

Linda looked at the three of them, their faces devoid of emotion, except for Detective Thomas. The faint hostility in her eyes belied the bland expression across her face.

Linda had a bad feeling about this, but what lawyer would she call? Peter? Her father? She swallowed. "Let's get this over with. Lead the way."

Steve stayed close behind Linda while they walked down a gray and white corridor. She could feel his warm breath on her neck. He smelled faintly of smoke and stale coffee mingled with traces of aftershave.

The interrogation room could also have come straight out of a TV set — walls colored that same yellowish white, tiled floors, a cheap wooden table sporting a deep scar and four matching straight-back chairs placed around it. A large mirror covered one wall, Linda assumed it to be a one-way mirror. On the table lay a pile of various papers and folders along with a microphone, connected to the wall by a black cable.

Steve gestured to one of the chairs. Linda sat down, noting that the chair felt as uncomfortable as it looked. Steve and Detective Norton both pulled up chairs on the other side of the table. Detective Norton pulled out a notebook and pen. Detective Thomas stood by the mirror, her back to Linda.

Steve coughed. "You're probably wondering why I asked you here. It's about the murders."

"I figured that. But I really don't know how I can help you."

"You have a sister," Detective Thomas said. It was spoken flatly, a statement rather than a question. She didn't turn her head.

"Had," Linda corrected. "She's dead."

"So we've been told," Detective Thomas said.

Nobody spoke. Steve's expression was flat, unreadable. Detective Norton looked up from the note pad, his face a calm mask. The silence filled the room with tension so think, Linda could actually feel it breathing, pressuring her neck and head.

"What's going on?" Linda asked, unable to stand it any longer.

Detective Thomas turned away from the mirror to face Linda. Linda was shocked to see the clear suspicion in her eyes. "When did she die?"

"This year. May."

"How did she die?"

Linda glanced at Steve, but he had found something far more interesting and absorbing to study on the scarred table. "She drowned."

"You sure about that?"

"Yes."

Detective Thomas walked over to the table, standing between the two men. "Was her body found?"

Linda swallowed. "No."

"Then how can you be so sure?"

"There were witnesses."

"Witnesses?"

"Yes."

Detective Thomas turned away again. She walked over to the pile of papers and started to sort through them. Her movements were deliberate and slow. She selected a flat book, walked over to Linda, and lay the book open in front of her. "Is your sister's picture in this book?"

It was a high school yearbook, from the year Elizabeth graduated. The book was open to the senior pictures. Elizabeth's face stared up at Linda, remarkable among the sea of other faces. Her straight white-blond hair, parted perfectly in the center, framing her face, so long it reached past her shoulders. Her pale, almost white complexion. Those gray eyes, so large in her tiny face, a glimmer of silver hidden in their depths, full of secrets and betrayal. Her lips pulled up in that faint, sardonic smile. The photographer had placed Elizabeth in front of a black background, causing her white blouse and white coloring to appear even more pale and fragile in contrast. Linda had always hated that picture.

"Yes, Elizabeth's picture is in this book."

"Show me where."

Linda looked at her. "Don't you think I know my own sister?"

The detective shrugged. "Humor me."

Linda looked back down at the book and pointed to that smug, self-satisfying face. How odd it was that though the photographer had been clearly taken with Elizabeth, as men always seemed to be, sniffing around her like they would a dog in heat, the photographer still had managed to capture her personality, her true lying scheming nature, in that photo. It was an odd contrast, her breathtaking beauty hiding the soul of the monster that that peeked through, peering out from the depths of her eyes, her smile.

"And you say she's dead."

"I don't say she's dead, she *is* dead," Linda said, beginning to feel impatient.

To Linda's immense relief, Detective Thomas shoved the book to the side of the table. "Tell me how she died."

"I already did."

"Tell me the details."

Linda sighed. "You must have seen the police reports. Or the newspaper articles."

"I want to hear it from you."

Detective Thomas pulled up the remaining chair and sat down in front of Linda, her eyes boring into Linda's face. Was it hostility Linda saw in those cold eyes? Flatly, Linda began talking, her voice taking on the quality of recitation.

"Sometime in early May, Elizabeth drove her car to Massachusetts. I don't know when she actually arrived. I can only tell you that she checked into the Seaside Resort on May 5. It was a Monday. As far as I know, no one saw her that night. Tuesday and Wednesday during the day several people said they saw her on the beach, mostly standing and watching the waves. Wednesday evening, around dusk, two people saw her walk into the ocean. She never came out."

"How could they be sure?" Detective Thomas said. "It was beginning to get dark."

"One man went after her. Tried to save her. He couldn't find her or her body. He couldn't search long, because the water was so cold. When he couldn't stand it anymore, he called for help."

"Was he sure he saw Elizabeth walk into that ocean?"

"Yes."

"How could he be so sure?"

Linda licked her lips. "He must have been close enough to see. I don't know – maybe you should find him and ask. Look, is there a point to all this?"

"Just answer the questions."

"There was a full investigation in Massachusetts. I'm sure they would be happy to send you their files."

"I told you, just answer the question. How could he be so sure?"

"I don't know," Linda said, but she knew she was lying. Once men saw Elizabeth, really saw her, they never forgot her. Many became haunted, practically obsessed, by her. Like Steve.

But, this woman would never believe her. Unless people experienced Elizabeth's strange power for themselves, they didn't understand.

"What about the other witness? Did he recognize her?"

"According to what we were told, yes."

"How did *he* know it was her, for sure?"

"Look, I really don't know. They both must have been close enough to identify her face. You've seen her picture. She's very unusual looking."

"Yes, she is, isn't she." It wasn't a question.

Detective Thomas got up and began pacing the room again. Linda wondered about the hostility she was sensing from Detective Thomas. Was it real, or only in her head? Is this how people are normally questioned by the police? If it was real, where was it coming from? Could just seeing Elizabeth's picture provoke this kind of response? If so, why was it being directed at Linda? And why weren't the other two detectives saying anything?

"Elizabeth was a strong swimmer, wasn't she?"

"I guess so, though that's a bit subjective. She would never have won a gold medal."

"Would it have been possible for her to have eluded this witness who jumped in after her? Perhaps swam around him ... away from him?"

Linda shook her head. "No."

Detective Thomas continued as if she hadn't heard Linda. "Perhaps she swam around him and came back to shore somewhere else."

"That's impossible."

Detective Thomas's head whipped around. "Why impossible?"

"Because ..." Linda's voice faltered. She started again firmly. "Because her car was in the parking lot, her clothes in her room. There was cash in her purse, which was also left in her room."

Detective Thomas shrugged. "You have to leave that stuff behind if you want to make people think you're dead."

"But there's more. She walked into the ocean naked."

Detective Thomas's eyebrows arched. "Are you certain of that?"

"Positive. That's what both witnesses reported. And that's why the second one jumped in after her so quickly. He thought she was going to freeze to death."

"But she still could have swam ..."

"No, the water was too cold. Don't you get it? It was just barely spring. The ocean was just above freezing. Nobody could have survived in that temperature for very long. And besides that, even if she did manage to make it to shore, wouldn't she draw attention to herself, wandering around naked and frozen?"

"She could have stashed extra clothes somewhere."

"But she would have been soaking wet. And very cold. Massachusetts was pretty cold that night, according to the police. She would have had to find shelter somewhere or she would have died from hypothermia. And chances are, someone would have remembered a very wet, naked, seriously messed-up person that night if they had seen her."

"Look," Detective Norton broke in, his voice sounding more reasonable and friendly than Detective Thomas'. "All we're trying to do here is find out exactly what happened with your sister. We're facing a lot of tough questions that don't seem to have answers."

Good cop, bad cop? Was that what was going on here? She felt so out of her element, so out of control, sitting here in the middle of a police station surrounded by cops and their multitude of accusations.

"Detective Anderson, here," he nodded to Steve, "has filled us in on what he told you. That someone who allegedly bears a strong likeness to your sister has been seen at the bars where the victims allegedly picked up their killer. But after Saturday night's murder, we have more solid proof."

He took a moment to dig through the pile of papers in front of them. He pulled out a file folder, glanced at the contents, and handed it to Linda.

She opened it. A grainy, black-and-white picture of a woman walking out the door of an apartment lobby fell out. She wore an overcoat, the collar pulled up to her chin, a scarf wrapped around her head and dark glasses shading her eyes. Sunglasses? That didn't make sense. It looked dark outside. Nevertheless, there was something familiar about the woman, the curve of her cheek, the gleam of her hair against her coat.

Suddenly, Linda realized with shock that she was looking at Elizabeth. She was disguised, yes, but it was definitely Elizabeth.

Detective Thomas tapped the photo. "Is that your sister?"

Linda shook her head, just a quick shake, not much more than a twitch. "It can't be."

"Looks like her, doesn't it?"

Linda shrugged. "I don't know how I can tell. I can barely see her face. And I can't see her eyes at all."

Detective Thomas plucked the photo from the folder. She slid the yearbook out from under the folder and laid it next to Elizabeth's high school picture. "You don't see a pretty striking resemblance, here?"

A dull pounding started above Linda's right eye. The two pictures were similar, she had to admit, but they were strangely different, as well.

Oh God, this couldn't be. What was going on here?

"Elizabeth's dead." Linda met Detective Thomas's flat gaze. "Yes, there's a resemblance, but not enough for me to positively say that yes, that's her. Not enough for me to believe that Elizabeth is alive."

Detective Thomas sat back and crossed her arms across her chest. "There's more."

Linda eyed the two detectives suspiciously. All her instincts screamed that she was walking directly into a trap, but she couldn't see any way to avoid it. "More?"

"A witness," Detective Norton said. "One of the victim's friends saw the victim leave with *this* woman," he tapped the photograph, "or as close as he could tell, considering the poor quality of the photo. And his description of the woman matches Elizabeth's. Right down to her silver eyes."

"But maybe it's someone dressing up like her," Linda said.

Detective Thomas leaned forward. "Yes, maybe that's exactly what's going on." She stared directly into Linda's eyes. "Know anyone who would do such a thing?"

It seemed less of a question than a statement – more precisely, an accusation. She began to feel short of breath. "Of course I don't know anyone like that. Do you think I would deliberately hang around with someone who was a murderer, masquerading around as my dead sister?"

Detective Thomas shrugged. "I have no idea."

"Well, let me give you a hint. I wouldn't." Linda pushed the photos away from her. "I'm sorry, but I just can't help you."

The motion of her hand dislodged another photo from the file. It caught Linda's eye and she glanced at it.

It was of a living room: messy, beer cans and a leftover pizza box strewn about in the middle of the ugly brown carpet, brown paneled walls, sagging olive green chair, plaid couch.

She slowly reached for the picture. It lay sideways on the table, partially covered by another picture. She had seen that apartment before. It was the exact living room that was in her dream.

For a second, she was overwhelmed — in complete and utter shock. Her mouth felt instantly dry and papery. Her stomach cramped. Threatening clouds of black swirled across her vision, and she fought the dizziness that usually accompanied a fainting spell. What would they think if she did? If she passed out right then and there? It would practically be an admission of guilt, and she knew they would pounce on her.

The room had gone eerily silent. She blinked and forced herself back to the present. She had to act cool. A feeling – a knowing – swept through her: her entire future rested on how she handled the next few minutes.

As casually as she could, she dropped the photo on the table and forced herself to meet their gaze. "Since I can't help you, may I leave?" She couldn't believe how calm she sounded. She felt separate from her own voice, as if she were listening to another person speak.

Detective Thomas's eyes never wavered from her face. "For now."

Linda pushed her chair back from the table and stood, turning her body away from Detective Thomas and her flat, accusatory gaze. She couldn't rush through the door. She had to walk naturally. Calmly.

"Just one more thing," Detective Thomas called out, her voice an odd mixture of forced casualness and dark suspicion. "We received a phone call the other day. Probably a prank, but the caller said the oddest thing. 'Your brother's blood cries out to me from the ground.' Ring any bells?"

The room spun and turned white. Oh God, she really was going to faint. Linda stumbled and managed to grab the edge of the chair, fighting to keep herself upright. She half-turned to Detective Thomas, giving her head a quick shake, not trusting her voice enough to speak. She wanted to look unconcerned, but she knew she had failed miserably.

She knew Detective Thomas suspected Linda was hiding something now, for sure. But what could she do? None of it made any sense. Besides, if she told them about her dreams, her admission wouldn't help the investigation anyway.

Linda blinked and the room straightened itself out. Not loosening her grip on the chair at all, she turned to face the three impassive faces. "I'm afraid it means nothing to me. Now may I go?"

"Probably a prank," Detective Norton intervened. He smiled, but it was forced and unnatural. "That's all for now."

Linda nodded and turned toward the door. Her legs felt stiff and shaky. She forced herself to walk as normally as she could to the door.

"Let me walk you out," Steve said, his voice in her ear. Linda jumped slightly; she hadn't heard him approach. "Besides, I have to get your coat."

Her coat. Of course. Perhaps if she put that on, the numbness would go away.

"We're all under a little bit of strain," Steve said to her once they were in the hall. "It's tough when a case is this frustrating."

He sounded almost apologetic, and Linda distrusted that even more than the accusations. "It sounds like a difficult case," she said. "And you're probably under a lot of pressure from the public, too, I'm sure."

He smiled. "That's an understatement."

"You guys don't really believe it's Elizabeth, do you?" The words were out of her mouth before she could stop them.

Steve cocked his head. "I guess that means you don't."

"I thought we agreed — Elizabeth is dead."

"Yeah, I did say that once, didn't I?"

"Oh, has your opinion changed?"

He reached over and gently touched her nose. "Now, I can't compromise an investigation, can I?" His voice sounded almost teasing, as if he were flirting with her.

She tossed her head, deliberately moving away from his hand. "Why would telling me that compromise the investigation?"

He said nothing for a second, just studied her. "Let me get your coat."

Linda ground her teeth and followed him to the lobby. Lovely. Not only could she not get a straight answer out of Steve, but now she was feeling even more like a suspect.

But why? How could she be a suspect? No one could possibly think she could *murder* anyone, for goodness sake.

Thankfully, Steve broke her train of thought by handing over her coat. She quickly put it on, her entire body feeling like it had turned into a core of ice.

He studied her. "Are you going to be all right?" He actually sounded concerned. She stopped herself from congratulating him on his performance.

"Yes, I'll be fine."

"I can drive you home —"

"No. No, that won't be necessary." Linda turned away before he could say anything else, and hurried out the door. All she wanted to do was get home, crawl into her bed and fall into a deep, dark, dreamless sleep. Maybe by morning the last few hours would fade in intensity, and she could convince herself it was all part of yet another bad dream.

Mirror Image

CHAPTER 13 — ELIZABETH

When Elizabeth was eleven, she almost drowned.

The family was in Massachusetts on vacation. At least that's what Don Shimon assumed. A crew member aboard the *Windstar* cruise ship — if you could call a three-hour jaunt a "cruise" — he had seen so many tourists, he could always differentiate between the vacationers and the locals.

Don didn't have the most exciting job in the world, but it paid the bills. Plus, it allowed him to sail, which is something he always loved to do. This way, he didn't have to travel to do it, which meant that every night, he could go home and see his wife and little girl. Not many sailors could say that, and he was grateful.

Because his job bordered on humdrum, he became an avid tourist-watcher. All of them had stories, and as he studied them (covertly of course), he imagined their stories. Many times, he could figure them out easily – a honeymooning couple, family vacation, retirees traveling the world.

But this family in particular seemed different, and he had a harder time figuring them out. True, on the surface, it looked like a regular family vacation. But something was off — odd — about the Rossinis. They didn't seem … well, "right," together.

The parents, sons and one of the daughters all closely resembled each other — dark hair, dark eyes, dark complexion. But the one girl, the youngest he figured, looked nothing like the rest of them. Her hair virtually sparkled white-blond; his wife would die for that color, he mused. The girl's china-white skin set off her high cheekbones, delicate bone structure and light gray eyes — the color of the ocean on a clear summer's day. She held her body, slender and straight as a young willow, with a grace and dignity many women would envy.

At first, he didn't even think she belonged with the others, as different as she appeared from them. But apparently she did, judging by how the father and brothers doted on her.

She seemed apart – distant even – from them as well. She hung back from the family, finding her own space at the railing away from the others. Don noticed too how she would gently shift her position whenever anyone came close to her — always keeping a distance between herself and the others. She was delicate — looking, leaning against the railing and gazing into the ocean, and he found it difficult to take his eyes off her. She somehow seemed sad and alone. He felt strangely drawn to her, her gray eyes and dainty features. He wanted to protect her, hold her, quell her sadness, keep her safe from the outside world. He wanted to tell her father and brothers to stop handling her so roughly. She looked frail enough to fall over into the ocean with the slightest of breezes.

Don had never felt that way about a passenger. Especially one that young. It scared him a little, but it made him feel powerful, too. Several times he approached her, wanting to ask the family to be careful, be gentle with her. But each time, he held himself back, his own self-awareness kicking in, telling him it wasn't any of his business what her family did with her. Just as long as they didn't abuse her. He clenched his fists. The thought of her being hurt immediately raised the temperature of his blood. But, he couldn't get involved.

He positioned himself close enough so he could see her profile, yet distant enough to not crowd her. He felt the importance of allowing her the space she seemed to want, to need … to give her what her brothers and father refused to.

When he wasn't memorizing her profile, he studied the ocean. The way she did, as if that would somehow bring them closer. It was a beautiful, clear day — perfect for a cruise. The sun sparkled brightly, while puffy white clouds meandered their way across a deep, blue sky. The ocean itself was the deepest shade of blue, as it met the horizon of the sky. Only up close did it look gray, lapping gently against the boat. A clear gray, much like her eyes, he noticed. So clear.

She moved then, turning to face him, her hair the color of sun shining upon new snow as it whipped around her face in the wind. She lifted her hand, white and brittle, the fingers long and tapering, to brush the hair from her face, her eyes. Looking past him, she focused on something beyond his vision; turning his head in the same direction, he couldn't find whatever it was she studied. Again, he was struck by how sad she seemed. And alone – desperately alone.

She turned back to the ocean, feasting the site with her eyes, devouring it. It was clear that she loved it as much as he did. Again, he started to approach her, and again he forced himself to stop.

One of her brothers approached. "Elizabeth," he said. She turned slightly at the sound, and he leaned closer to her, putting his hand lightly, familiarly against her slim back. Her pale blue shirt was too big, and hung on her awkwardly. Although he strained to listen, he could only hear a murmur as her brother bent his head closer to hers. Her name was Elizabeth. *Elizabeth.*

Don found himself staring at Elizabeth's brother's hand, the touch so casual against her back. He felt bile and rage rising in his throat, and had to force it down. That hand seemed huge compared to her fragile, slender back. Didn't he know he could hurt her? His jaw ached from clenching his teeth, and his hands formed tight fists. But before he lost complete control over his emotions, the brother moved away, leaving Elizabeth alone again by the railing, gazing into the ocean's depths.

He watched with her for a while. It made him feel even more in tune with her, looking at what she did. The water lapped gently against the boat, a comforting sound. It reminded him of rocking in his mother's rocking chair when he was a child, the soft wood warm and mellow, the chair smelling of bread dough and lavender: scents that always reminded him of his mother. He felt sleepy and secure, watching the waves, near that delicate child, that beautiful girl, with those fascinating gray eyes.

Sometimes he would glance at her, noting the long, thin hands clutching the railing, so white against the black ... the slender, delicate neck ... her hair flying madly about. Sometimes she would lean forward, her body bending like a young birch twisting beneath a heavy wind.

The family returned then, crowding around the child. He saw her cringe, saw her flinch when she backed away from them. He didn't blame her. They were loud and boisterous. They destroyed the mood, the sleepy, contented feeling. He resented them and knew that she did, too.

Her brothers and sister seemed to be arguing about something — what, he didn't know. Snatches of their conversation drifted over to him but he couldn't grasp what they said, the words blown apart by the twisting breeze. Not that he wanted to understand them. He wanted to be alone with Elizabeth, away from those anxious, nervous people. He felt lightheaded, dizzy, his thoughts breaking apart much like waves on the ocean.

From the corner of his eye, he saw Elizabeth lean forward again, her body molding itself against the railing, her hair sweeping across her face. He leaned forward eagerly, too, trying to see what had captured her attention.

He saw a flash of silver, a fin. A fish swimming near the boat, he thought. Only it looked too big to be a fish — must be a dolphin or porpoise, he reasoned. Maybe even a small whale.

The streak of silver flashed by again, breaking the surface briefly. It resembled a tail of some sort. He also saw long strands of something, seaweed probably, breaking the surface at the same time. They reminded him of hair, as they tangled together.

Don heard a splash. He started, the confused, sleepy feeling in his head broken. Elizabeth was gone. Panicked, he looked down just in time to see her disappear beneath the waves.

He wasn't conscious of any thought — he simply reacted. Stripping off his shoes, he plunged into the ocean after her.

The water was cold, bitterly cold. He had to clench his jaw together to keep his teeth from chattering. The waves, peaceful and comforting from the deck, now tossed him about like a cork. He had to fight to keep his head above water, as the waves constantly threatened to pull him under, to hold him there, to welcome him to a watery death.

Don struggled hard against it, focusing on the fact that he was a good swimmer, a strong swimmer. He had trained to be a lifeguard and he knew he could save her. He swam to the spot where he thought Elizabeth went under, filled his lungs with air, and dove.

He couldn't see very well, in the murky water. It no longer even slightly resembled the clear gray it had appeared from the boat. Swirls of green filled his vision and the water fought him, clawing and biting like a wild animal, cornered and desperate.

He stayed under until his burning lungs forced him to the surface. He dove a second time, then a third, trying not to think, not to consider the possibility that he was too late.

Finally, on the fourth try, he saw something.

Elizabeth, her hair streaming out behind her, swimming toward something. A fish of some sort, a very big fish, but he couldn't see through the murky water to make out any distinct features. The fish appeared to be swimming upright, its tail thick and pulsating, wrapped in seaweed. While he watched, while he fought to reach Elizabeth, the seaweed strands parted, and an arm stretched out toward Elizabeth.

A human arm?

A mermaid?

For a second, he stopped swimming, his brain momentarily stunned. The water swirled around him, threatening to drag him to the surface. He closed his eyes and opened them again. A school of tiny fish darted behind the mermaid, disappearing into the murky water almost as quickly as they had appeared. But now, the mermaid image was gone. He saw only the large fish – which actually could have been a rock covered with seaweed, for how it looked to him then.

Lack of oxygen, that's all. A tiny hallucination brought on by holding his breath too long. He had to get Elizabeth, and get out of there.

He struggled toward her, as she continued swimming toward the fish, or rock, or whatever it was. Out of the corner of his eye, he saw the seaweed part again, and this time, he glimpsed a face. A beautiful face.

A cold, white, dead face.

He looked straight at it, this time.

It was nothing but a rock.

His chest began to hurt. He knew he had to get to the surface soon. He struggled harder to reach Elizabeth.

Her back faced him, long strands of her hair, now green and distorted, floated above her head.

It was as if she were communicating with the rock. Fish swam all around him, fins fluttering in the murky water, mouths gaping open and closing constantly, big bulbous eyes glaring at him. Cold, dead eyes. Eyes like the mermaid's.

"You're not wanted," the fish seemed to say. "This is our *domain*."

Don batted the fish aside, feeling their slimy bodies brushing his skin. His chest hurt worse than ever. Threatened by fish? He really was hallucinating. If he didn't get to the surface soon, he could very well drown.

He moved his arms and legs faster, trying to reach Elizabeth, but his limbs felt heavy and weighed down, as if he were swimming in molasses — trapped in a deadly nightmare.

He could see the face in the rock again in the corner of his vision. But he refused to look at it, refused to acknowledge that he even thought it was a face. And he especially couldn't admit – even to himself – that he had clearly seen its eyes.

Silver eyes.

Glowing.

No, it was nothing but a rock. A rock covered with seaweed. And Elizabeth.

The closer he got to Elizabeth, the darker the water seemed, filled with silt and sand. He could barely see anymore — the rock, or Elizabeth — who still seemed to be in deep communication with whatever it was in front of them.

Don felt spasms in his chest. He stretched out his arm as far as it could go, knowing that was his last chance. If he couldn't grab her right then, he would have to swim to the surface or drown.

His hand snagged her shirt, the pale blue shirt, floating around her body like a halo, a cloud. He grabbed it and yanked, managing to get an arm around her neck.

Voices echoed in his head. Voices filled with static. Cold voices. He tried to shrug them off while grasping Elizabeth even more firmly.

"*You must go back.*"

"*Don't leave me!*"

He started to haul her up, but she turned in his arms to look at him. What he saw in her face shocked him, and for a second time in the water, he couldn't move.

Her face was contorted: pain, anger, hatred, possibly a combination of all those emotions distorted her. She looked like a monster, a demon, her teeth tiny fangs glinting against her bright red lips ... red as blood.

And her eyes *glowed* silver.

He choked, his body contorting for air.

But then, the expression instantly disappeared — her eyes closed, and her face smoothed out. She was Elizabeth again, a child dying in water. A beautiful child.

He renewed his grip on her neck and hauled her up.

As they broke the surface, the air felt even colder than the water, if that was possible. He sucked it in, gasping and choking from the burning sensation in his lungs. Waves smacked his face, the salt water stinging his eyes, filling his mouth. Beside him now, Elizabeth cried out, her legs and arms twitching uncontrollably, and he fought to keep her head above water.

Even with her hair plastered to her face and neck, she was still beautiful. He held her close while tucking her safely into the life preserver someone had thrown from the ship. She opened her eyes, her gray eyes, and they were exactly as they had been, on the ship. They regarded him now with a terribly odd expression: a mixture of anguish, sorrow, cynicism and calculation, all rolled together. No longer did he see the eyes of a child. These eyes were old. Ancient.

Just like the mermaid's.

She turned her head away and closed them again. He finished securing her in the preserver, and signaled the deck hands to haul her up. When they pulled her from the water, he caught her scent, sweet and warm. Diluted maybe by the briny scent of the ocean, but there all the same. He was inexplicably reminded of cinnamon apples — the kind his grandmother used to make. He used to sit in her warm kitchen, the sunlight pouring through the windows, the worn yet meticulously clean linoleum and cheerful red potholders and towels scattered throughout the room.

Someone, he couldn't see who, threw down a second life preserver. He grabbed it, relief flooding over him, as he too was hauled onto the ship's deck.

Towels covered him as he shivered uncontrollably. Voices urged him to go down below to the cabins to change out of his icy clothes, before he caught cold, or worse, but he ignored them. He pushed away the kindly, helping hands to look for Elizabeth. He had to make sure she was fine, before he could care about himself.

Her family was clustered around her, rubbing her with towels. Her mother had been crying. She kept stroking her daughter's wet hair, murmuring her daughter's name over and over again. Elizabeth herself seemed completely untouched by the outpouring of love and affection. She stared listlessly out at the ocean.

"It's okay, you're okay now," one of the brother's said.

"No thanks to Linda," another brother growled.

Don glanced up, following the gaze of the other family members. The other girl stood apart from the others — the only family member not hovering around Elizabeth. While everyone stared at Linda, she seemed to collapse inward, shrinking into herself.

"She pushed her," the same brother accused.

"You don't know that, Peter," another brother said.

Peter glared at Linda and she seemed to deflate even further. "Yes, I do."

Why was her family treating this other little girl that way? She obviously didn't do it. Don had watched Elizabeth fall in on her own. But even if he hadn't, Elizabeth's sister's clear discomfort was convincing enough of her innocence.

Linda was pretty, with dark curly hair and big brown eyes. A bit on the plump side, maybe, but endearing. Next to Elizabeth, however, Linda paled to nothing. She was a blown-out candle, reduced to a thin trail of smoke next to a bonfire, the red and orange flames leaping high into the dark night sky. It hit him them; the brothers probably assumed Linda had pushed Elizabeth in, because there was likely a huge rivalry between the girls. How could Linda not be jealous of her younger sister?

Don felt profoundly sorry for the poor girl, huddled in the corner. He couldn't just sit there, letting them believe Linda had pushed Elizabeth. He stepped forward and opened his mouth to say something, to defend her, but Elizabeth stopped him. Elizabeth chose that moment to begin screaming.

"I want to go back," she shrieked, her voice shrill and piercing.

Her family, startled by her outburst, drew back. Elizabeth took advantage of her family's shock by throwing off the towels.

"Let me go back," she screamed. "Don't make me stay here with you. I want to go back." Her slender body, so delicate, flew past her family to the ship's railing. She scrambled over it, contorting while she struggled over the edge. She would have slid off and gone right back into the ocean, if her father hadn't grabbed her leg, jerking her back.

"I *must* go back," she howled, tears coursing down her face. "You don't understand. Let me go back." She collapsed on the deck, crying and hiccupping, her body twitching uncontrollably, the salt from her tears mixing with the salt of the ocean. Her family could only stare at her, shocked into silence, their faces white and uncomprehending. Finally, mercifully, she fell silent.

For weeks after, she lay unconscious, her body ravaged by fever. The doctors were concerned, sympathetic, but unable to find the cause. At times, her temperature rose to one hundred and eight. That's too hot, the doctors would say. No one could survive that temperature.

But Elizabeth did.

Don visited her while she stayed in the Massachusetts hospital, before her family transferred her back to Wisconsin. He brought flowers and candy with him, more for Elizabeth's mother, who cried most of the time, and for Linda, whose pinched face remained tortured. Neither seemed to enjoy his offerings much. Mostly, they watched Elizabeth.

It hurt him to see Elizabeth like that. Her body shook with seizures, blanketed with sweat and tears. She screamed and moaned constantly. The nurses struggled to keep her cool. "We must expect the worse," the doctors said. If she *did* somehow pull out of it, she'd more than likely suffer from severe brain damage.

Then, one day, the fever finally broke. She opened her eyes and looked at her family, who anxiously hovered around her. She showed no trace of brain damage.

The mother called Don that day to tell him the good news: Elizabeth was conscious. Nonetheless, perceptive as he was, he couldn't help but notice a strain in her voice, a new tone that hadn't been there during Elizabeth's illness.

He called several times over a month's period, after the family had returned home, but he was never given any additional information. He knew something was wrong, something they weren't telling him. He could hear it in the mother's voice, the worry and anxiety mounting each time he spoke with her.

It drove him frantic with worry. Was she brain-dead and they didn't want to tell him? Had she suffered partial brain damage that had left her mentally disabled? Or could it be something even worse, something he couldn't even imagine?

Mermaids masquerading as rocks?

"*Don't leave me.*"

He had almost convinced himself that he had seen nothing but a hallucination under the ocean, brought on by too little oxygen and too much worry and physical exhaustion. But it pricked at his brain — why had she wanted to go back?

"I *must* go back."

He brushed off that line of thinking completely. It had to be a medical problem.

He tried calling the hospital, but got nowhere. Patient records were confidential, they told him. He was just about ready to jump on a plane — to hell with what his wife thought – just to see Elizabeth with his own eyes. He wanted to confront the family, to find out exactly what was going on with her.

But then, when he called again, Linda answered. After a little prodding, she finally told him what he wanted to know. She told it like a story read aloud, her voice taking on that sort of sing-song lilt. She spoke it all in a hush, a whisper that he had to strain to hear. It was as if she were repeating a curse, not a story — and if she spoke the words too loudly, she would invoke the evil in it.

"We took Elizabeth home from the hospital soon after she opened her eyes," Linda whispered. "But she never spoke unless we asked her a direct question. And even then, her answers weren't much — a shake, a nod, a shrug.

"At first she didn't do anything. Simply stared out the window. The doctors told us to give her time. Then one day, she started painting."

Linda's voice began to tremble. She paused, and Don could hear her suck in her breath. But when she started speaking again, the tremble disappeared, her voice clear and steady.

Her parents encouraged Elizabeth at first, she told him. They brought her paints and paper. But her paintings frightened them. They frightened everyone, including Linda.

She fell silent until Don finally asked what the paintings looked like.

Her voice nearly a whisper, she told Don that they were dark and tormented. Swirls of brown and gray disappearing into a vortex, faces screaming in agony, black shadows stretching out claws and teeth, tearing apart bodies, red splashes of blood, so vivid, so intense.

Her parents hid them. They were confused by them. Her father forced everyone to swear that they would never reveal those paintings to anyone outside the family. Everyone swore, terrified of the pictures, terrified of Elizabeth.

Linda paused again. "But Father couldn't have meant you," she said, her voice slightly louder, more sure of herself. "You saved her, after all. It must be okay to tell you."

Don murmured his agreement, too shocked to say any more.

The nights were the worst, Linda continued. Elizabeth suffered from nightmares. Awful nightmares. Her screams, in the darkest hours, woke everyone up, and when they hurried to her side, they would usually find her curled in a ball, rocking herself soundlessly, her sweat-soaked nightgown plastered to her body, her hair stuck to her face and neck. She refused to speak of her dreams. In fact, she refused to speak at all, not even answering when someone asked her a question. She would simply shrug her shoulders, her eyes gazing past her family members, fixed on something no one else could see.

"Then one day that stopped, too."

A murmur of voices on the other end of phone interrupted her. He could hear Linda muffle the phone while she replied to them. He heard Linda say she was talking to Don, but he couldn't hear what followed. When she spoke again, she announced that she must get off the phone.

"But wait," Don said. "You haven't finished. What about now? Why did it all stop?"

"Elizabeth is fine," Linda answered, her voice curiously flat and unemotional. "There's nothing wrong. There never has been anything wrong."

But Don knew there was more to the story – much more. As bad as it had been before, it was worse now. He could hear it in her voice, how she had paused before speaking that last sentence, sucking in her breath, as if to gain strength before she could continue. Her voice had dropped to barely a murmur, then, as if there was something she couldn't bear to say out loud. Something she *needed* to say. He cursed whoever interrupted them, but before he could try to convince her to finish, he heard a rustling at the other end.

"This is Thomas Rossini," the voice said, and Don realized he was now talking to Elizabeth's father. "I want to thank you for your concern for Elizabeth's well-being, but she is fine now." His voice was clipped and even. "I do not wish to seem rude or ungrateful; we are very much indebted to you for saving Elizabeth's life. But I really would prefer if you did not call here again. We are trying to get on with our lives, and talking about the illness and accident is not productive. I'm sure you understand." Don heard a click at the other end, and the line went dead.

Three days later, Don received a check in the mail for five thousand dollars and a note that read:

Please accept this small token of appreciation for saving Elizabeth's life. We are indebted to you.

Thomas Rossini

***

Don never cashed the check. And he never called the Rossini household again.

He resolved to put the matter out of his mind. Although he almost succeeded in forgetting about the incident in the ocean — only in barely recalled nightmares did the mermaid/rock still haunt him — he couldn't forget about Elizabeth.

No matter how many years went by, he was never able to banish her image from his mind: the beautiful young girl standing by the railing and gazing out to sea, the ocean wind blowing her white-blond hair away from her face, the clear gray eyes. Sometimes he would see her in his dreams, standing like that, her face full of such sadness and longing, that he struggled not to take her into his arms.

But he would always wake up from those dreams, his arms empty and his heart aching, for a loss he barely understood.

CHAPTER 14

Linda gazed through the window of her parents' home. Clouds scudded across a gray sky, the wind mourned through bare trees, rattling the last few dead leaves that clung to their naked branches. On the ground, dry, crumbling leaves flew across the carpet of brown grass. Why didn't it snow? It was depressing when it didn't snow.

"Linda, would you like something to drink?"

Linda turned and faced her mother. She stood in the kitchen doorway, her white apron tied around last year's holiday dress — navy and white complemented by a string of pearls. Usually her mother bought a new dress every year. In fact, until this year, Linda couldn't remember a time her mother hadn't purchased at least one new dress for the holiday season.

Although her mother faced her now, her eyes never quite *saw* Linda. Instead, they gazed past her, her expression vague and uncertain. "It's okay, Mom," Linda said. "You don't have to wait on me. I can get it myself."

"It's all right; let me get it."

"It's really okay."

"Linda, quit arguing with your mother," her father said. "If she wants to bring you something to drink, then let her bring you something to drink. You always insist on making things as difficult as possible." Although he said it in his usual clipped voice, it sounded hollow and empty: a mere echo of the man she had known.

Linda swallowed. "Wine please," she said. Her mother disappeared into the kitchen.

Her father barely glanced at her. He too had aged, but unlike her mother who seemed to be disappearing into a vast space of nothingness, he was turning into a pale, blurry shadow of what he used to be. He took a sip of beer, his eyes sliding back to the television.

Linda swallowed the urge to apologize to her father. Why was it that whenever she was with her family, she reverted to age seven, instead of twenty-seven?

Chad sat on the floor, playing with their nieces and nephews. He shot Linda a sympathetic gaze. They had arrived last today, together. The others, Peter, Mark and Mike, along with their assorted wives and children, had already made themselves at home by the time Chad and Linda appeared.

Peter and Mark sat on the couch, next to their father, while Mike lounged on one of the recliners, all of them sipping on their beer. Their wives were apparently helping in the kitchen, and Linda supposed she should be in there, too, but she couldn't stand any of her trophy-wife sisters-in-law. None of them worked outside the home — all three were completely consumed with being wives and mothers. They always treated Linda like an unfortunate relative. After all, Linda couldn't even find herself a boyfriend, much less a husband.

Of course, Linda deserved everything she got, having always been so terribly mean to their dear departed sister-in-law, Elizabeth. Never mind that none of them could tolerate Elizabeth while she lived. They conveniently forgot that.

As long as she remained in the living room, Linda didn't have to endure their snooty looks and catty remarks. Not that being with her brothers was much better, but at least she had plenty of experience dealing with them.

Her mother handed her a glass of wine. Linda took it. "Thanks, Mom. The food smells great," she said, though it really didn't. Her mother must have burned some of the dishes.

With a vague smile, her mother wandered back into the kitchen. Linda drank almost half of the glass in a single swallow. This was going to be a long day.

The house itself reflected the same decay and deterioration she saw in her parents. Her mother used to be as meticulous about her house-keeping as she was about her appearance — her father had seen to that. But now, a thin layer of dust blanketed the expensive knick-knacks displayed throughout the living room. Flecks of dirt, hair and other debris littered the carpet. Streaks and smudges covered the windows. Newspapers lay scattered half-haphazardly on the floor and coffee table. A few neglected, discarded glasses remained on end tables, their insides coated with a pale, unwashed film.

Definitely not the home Linda remembered.

Even the smell had changed. Before, the house had smelled like Lysol and potpourri – now, it reeked of dust, dry and brittle, unwashed bodies, moist and hot, and something faintly salty, like tears. The whole house needed a good airing out, to chase away the stuffiness and shadows.

A football game was on, the sound turned low. Her father and brothers pretended to watch, but Linda knew they weren't. Even her nieces and nephews, four of them all under the age of five, were subdued. It was almost as if Elizabeth was there, casting a dark shadow over everything.

She'll never leave us alone, Linda thought.

Pictures of her sister hung everywhere — the entire house was plastered with them. Elizabeth as a baby, Elizabeth as a toddler, at seven, nine, thirteen ... Everywhere Linda turned, she saw Elizabeth, at every stage of her life, those strange silver-gray eyes peering out from the frames, cold and calculating. Even as an infant, her eyes had looked old. The family portrait taken just two years ago hung above the couch. But the crowning glory, Elizabeth's senior picture, had been blown up to a whopping seventeen by twenty, and placed strategically above the television. Now, no matter where Linda stood in the room, she could see Elizabeth's sardonic smile, her strange eyes, following her.

It was a shrine. The whole house. A literal shrine to Elizabeth. Her mother preserved Elizabeth's room, lovingly cared for her books, paying no attention to anything else. Even those god-awful paintings Elizabeth had done after she had almost drowned had been dragged out of the attic, dusted off, and hung around the house. Every picture her parents could find of Elizabeth, they had displayed and kept meticulously clean, while the rest of the house sunk into a morass of neglect.

The worst was the way her father and brothers kept staring at Elizabeth. Their eyes would slide away from the television to feast upon her picture before they would force them back to the screen. It bordered on a creepy obsession, and Linda still found it pathetic.

Linda knew that Peter kept pictures of Elizabeth next to his bed, in his wallet, and in his office. He had no pictures of his wife or children in his wallet, and only one small photo of his family in his office. Linda knew this only because she had heard his wife Cindy complain about it at the funeral, in hushed tones, of course. Apparently, after Elizabeth's death, he had increased the number of photos he kept around, just as her parents had done. He, too, had purchased an enlarged senior picture of Elizabeth, but Cindy had put her foot down on displaying it in the living room. Now it hung in his home office.

The wives of Mark and Mike also seemed to be fighting Cindy's battle against their husbands' efforts to make shrines out of their homes.

At least Chad didn't follow suit. He carried one picture of her, but that was it.

One of Peter's children, Anne, otherwise known as "Daddy's Little Princess" with long blond curls and big blue eyes, approached Peter, holding her doll.

"Daddy," Anne said. "Lu Lu is broke. Can you fix her?"

"Not now, sweetie," Peter said, his eyes never leaving Elizabeth's picture. "I'm watching the game." He had a sharp face, like a fox, narrow and pointed, yet strangely elegant. With his stylishly cut brown hair just slightly curled over his ears, he looked like a stereotypical lawyer. Shorter and thinner than his brothers, Peter was a bully who overcompensated for his smaller appearance by being mean. Mark and Mike, on the other hand had soft, round faces, soft, round bodies and features that sort of blurred all together.

"Please, Daddy." Anne said, her mouth beginning to pucker.

"Not now," Peter said again, not even looking at his daughter.

"I'll fix it," Chad said quickly, while Anne began to squish up her face.

"I want my daddy to do it," Anne said.

"Not now. Let Uncle Chad do it," Peter said.

Anne stared at him, her mouth open, her eyes damp. But the child obeyed, silently delivering her doll to Chad.

"Time to eat," Darlene, Mike's wife said, leaning into the living room. The men paid no attention.

"Hey, the game can wait. Let's eat. It's Thanksgiving," Darlene said impatiently.

"We'll be there in a second," Mike said without looking at her.

Linda made her way into the dining room.

***

Dinner was a quiet affair. Even the children refrained from fussing.

"So what have you been doing lately?" Cindy asked Linda, mostly to break the silence.

"Same old, same old," Linda said. "But I have some good news."

"Finally found a boyfriend?" Darlene asked, sweetly acidic.

Linda ignored her. "Chad passed the test. He's a full-fledged architect now." Linda beamed at Chad, who ducked his head a little. She could tell he was pleased, though.

"That's very nice," murmured their mother. "Congratulations, Chad."

Their father said nothing. He stared at his dinner, pushing turkey and cranberry sauce from side to side on his plate.

Linda glanced around the table. This was not normal behavior for her father. Usually, he would glare disapprovingly at Chad, his lips pursed into a thin line, his eyes like frozen daggers, until Chad looked away. Then he would say in his clipped, quiet, lawyer voice, something along the lines of, "I would have paid for law school. I cannot understand your insistence on following such a non-lucrative career."

If Chad tried to defend himself, her father would have shot him down with an icy stare none of his children, save Elizabeth, had any defense against. If Chad still attempted to founder on with an explanation, he would have been immediately silenced with the back of her father's hand — or worse.

But still they tried. Even though she knew her father's reaction so well she could have scripted it, she still carried that little flame of hope that one day he might actually approve of something one of his children did.

But this reaction — while not openly disapproving — still wasn't what Linda wanted either.

Her sisters-in-law looked surprised. Her brothers didn't seem to be paying attention, except Chad who caught Linda's eye. He shrugged and shook his head.

Linda cleared her throat. "Dad?"

He didn't respond, merely pushing the turkey and cranberry sauce faster and faster around his plate, the red leaving ugly streaks across the white and gold-edged china. Little beads of cranberry sauce dribbled off the plate, staining the white tablecloth.

Linda found herself starring at the tablecloth. The tablecloth her mother took such careful pains with, bleaching and starching and ironing after each use. The drops looked like blood: blood that marred the pristine white surface, soaking in, a stain her mother would never be able to get out, no matter how many times she washed and bleached it.

The blood soaked into the bed, staining the white sheets, staining hands, staining fingernails, never get it out, never be clean.

She tore her eyes away and stood up abruptly, jerking the tablecloth in her haste and rattling dishes. "Dad. You have to stop."

Her father didn't even raise his eyes. But Peter responded.

"Sit down," Peter said, bored, his small, narrow eyes looking somewhere beyond his plate.

Linda barely glanced at him. "Dad? Dad? Are you listening to me?" She felt if she didn't get him to respond in some fashion, he would disappear into some void right then and there, never to be seen again.

"Linda, I said sit down."

"Dad? Say something."

"Linda, sit down and shut up," Peter lunged across the table at her, knocking his wine glass over, the contents spilling across the tablecloth. Linda finally turned and faced Peter.

"I wasn't speaking to you. I was speaking to dad."

"Don't you talk back to me."

Linda gave a short bark of laughter. "Talk back to you? You're hardly the boss here and you know it."

Peter's face turned bright red. "You better watch it if you know what's good for you."

Linda continued as if Peter hadn't said anything, her words clipped and hard, like short, sharp daggers, in the manner her father would speak, if he had chosen to. "Peter, don't you care about dad? Look at him." She flung her arm out toward her father, who was still spinning his food around and around on his plate, oblivious to what was going on around him.

"Of course I care about him!" Peter yelled. "You're so stupid, Linda. You don't even know what's wrong with him."

"Oh, I'm stupid. That's a good one, coming from you."

Peter choked, his breath choppy and irregular. "I finished law school. You couldn't even make it through college. I'm definitely not the stupid one here."

"Yeah, with Father's money and at Father's alma mater. Of course you passed."

"You bitch." A vein puffed up then, pulsing at his temple.

"You can't even find a job on your own!" All the anger and violence poured out of her, her voice dripping acidic poison. Peter never could win a verbal argument with her, despite being a lawyer. The combination of Linda knowing exactly what buttons to push and how he considered her his inferior fused together, and she knew exactly how to get the best of him, heightening his anger to new levels. Once he reached that state of rage, he couldn't win an argument with a sponge.

But he still beat her in fights anyway, because sooner or later, he would resort to using his fists.

"Daddy gave you a job, at Daddy's law firm, because you couldn't make it as an assistant DA, could you? How much trial lawyering are you doing now?"

Peter slammed his fist against the table. The loud bang coupled with the light tinkling of the china and crystal striking against each other seemed to enrage him further. His mouth worked but nothing came out. The children clung to their mothers, who hugged them back, their attention never wavering from the violence unfolding before them. Out of the corner of her eye, Linda could see Chad shaking his head violently.

"Stop," he mouthed at her.

Linda couldn't stop. Everything that had happened to her the past few weeks, the lack of sleep, the nightmares, the accusations, it all bubbled up inside her, sweeping her away in a boiling hot rage she hadn't experienced in years.

Not since Elizabeth stole Steve away.

Peter finally caught his breath. "How dare you speak to me like that? You're a secretary for God's sake. I *employ* secretaries."

"At least I found my job without Daddy's help. Where would you be working if Daddy hadn't given you a job, I wonder? Garbage collector maybe? You sure generate enough trash. Or should I say shit?"

"You bitch."

"Just like this conversation. You keep ignoring the main point. You don't care about Dad at all."

"You don't know shit."

"Is that all you can think of? You, the smart, wise-ass lawyer? You with your high-and-mighty college degrees? You didn't even earn them! But again, we digress. You lawyers are so good at that, aren't you? Pray tell Peter, oh smart one, oh wise lawyer, enlighten me. What do you think we should do about our Father?"

"Nothing!" Peter exploded, spittle flying across the room. "For God's sake, he's mourning Elizabeth. Something you wouldn't know anything about, let alone understand. You stupid, selfish bitch. You never understood Elizabeth, you never mourned her. You're nothing but a cold-hearted witch."

"That's funny coming from you, Peter, since you never understood her either, or mourned her properly," Linda retorted. "All you ever saw in her was what she wanted you to see in her — a reflection of yourself."

Peter shrieked, a wordless noise. He yanked the tablecloth off the table, sending china, glasses, food, and candles tumbling to the floor. The sharp sound of breaking dinnerware blended with the screams from the sisters-in-law and the sobbing of the children. He lunged toward Linda, face purple, eyes nearly popping out of his head.

Chad tackled him from behind, before he could make contact with her, sending him sprawling against the wall as Mark blocked him from the front. Linda watched her brothers subdue Peter, the rage still boiling inside her, but without an outlet. Then, she felt cold fingers dig like claws into her arm.

Mike jerked her arm, whirling her around to face him. "You worthless piece of shit," he snapped, and slapped her hard across the face. "You've never belonged in this family."

Linda's head rocked back on her neck. She tasted blood in her mouth. It reminded her of Elizabeth's funeral ... of her entire childhood. Twenty years melted away as she stood there, instantly seven again, sucked right back into the violence and rage. Bursts of red exploded across her vision, as it dimmed. Her head pounded, and suddenly, she couldn't stand the fact that the blood in her mouth tasted like her childhood.

"I said it because it's true!" Linda screamed, her self-control gone. "She did it to all of you! And you know it's true, or you wouldn't have thought it such a terrible thing to say!" Her hand shot out on its own accord, and she punched Mike in the stomach, as hard as she could.

He doubled over and fell to the floor, without making a sound. Through a haze of red rage, she wondered if perhaps she had hit lower than she intended, but then again, she didn't care.

"Enough. All of you. Stop it right now."

The quiet voice echoed across the room, powerful in its softness, freezing each of them where they stood.

In shock, Linda turned her head to face not her father, whom she had expected to speak, but her mother.

"Enough," her mother repeated, standing straight and tall. The ambiguity Linda had noticed in her earlier was gone, having disappeared completely, as if it had been a nothing more than a mask she had worn. And now that the masquerade had ended, she had simply torn off the disguise.

"That's better," she said and treated each of her children to a direct, icy gaze. A part of Linda, the part not in shock at her mother's change of behavior, marveled at her mother's simple, powerful action. It was exactly what her father would have done. Before he started hitting them that is. She had learned well.

Mike dragged himself up from the floor. "But, Mom," he said, in a half-whimper, half-sob. Apparently, Linda had hurt him more than she intended. Or maybe she had hurt him *exactly* how she had intended. "What Linda said ... about Elizabeth ..."

"She defiled Elizabeth's memory," Peter added, his voice once again tight and controlled, despite still being laid out on the floor, half covered by Chad.

Her mother swiveled her head around to stare at Peter. "Linda did nothing of the sort and you know it. Now, I want everyone to pitch in and clean up this mess right now."

Her father suddenly stirred. "You heard your mother," he said, raising his head, but still not looking anyone in the face. "This is my house and I am still the boss here. You will respect me. I am sure you are all aware of what will happen if you don't."

Although it was her father's voice and her father's words, somehow, it didn't *feel* like her father speaking to them. No, this sounded like a hollow echo, from a shadow of a man. The threat of violence, the whisper of evil that imposed the fear that normally wove through his words had disappeared, leaving them empty, meaningless.

Her mother turned to Linda. "Linda, you're bleeding. Come with me to the bathroom."

Linda automatically followed. Her limbs felt clumsy and jerky — robotic. Her anger, totally drained now, left her exhausted. She felt the lingering pain that pressed against her temples, recognizing it as the gentle beginnings of a monster headache.

Her mother stepped aside, letting Linda walk through the swinging door that separated the kitchen from the dining room first. She heard her mother's voice again, saying, "Now what did I just tell you? Clean up this mess right now." Linda kept right on going.

Her mother stopped her from entering the downstairs bathroom. "No. Come up to our bathroom. It's more private." Linda followed her mother up the stairs, wondering if she had somewhere along the way fallen into a different dimension, an alternative reality where her house looked like her house, her family looked like her family, but no one *acted* like her family. Maybe she was still in her bed right now, dreaming, in anticipation of Thanksgiving at her parents' house.

"Sit down," her mother said, gesturing toward the closed the toilet. Linda sat. Her mother turned on the light and shut the door. She examined Linda's mouth.

"Nothing serious," she said and her mouth twisted. "I'm sure you've had worse." She turned to the bathroom cupboard and fetched a washcloth.

Linda finally found her voice. "What happened down there, Mom?"

Her mom turned on the water and bent over the sink. "I stopped you kids from killing each other, that's what."

Linda swallowed. "Yeah, but why? I mean, usually Father —" her voice trailed off, unsure of what to say next. She had never spoken to her mother about the beatings. They were always there, the threat of them always understood, hovering in the background like an uninvited, unwanted guest, but never directly acknowledged. Linda had no idea how – or where — to even start.

Her mother turned back to Linda, wet washcloth in hand, and began carefully wiping away the blood from her daughter's mouth. The coolness of the washcloth felt soothing to Linda's burning lip. Although her mother's movements were gentle, her eyes remained hard and cold.

"Losing a child is the worst thing that can ever happen to a parent. Even, or maybe especially, if that child was never really understood, in life." She sighed. "Your father had a nervous breakdown. And maybe I did, too, I'm not sure. But whatever breakdown I experienced is nothing compared to what your father was – is – going through.

"When you and Peter started arguing, I sort of woke up. I suddenly realized just how far from reality I had strayed. Living with your father all these months has really pushed me more and more into — I don't know, a dream state, perhaps. I didn't even remember Thanksgiving until Cindy called, asking if maybe the meal should be at her house this year." Her mother smiled briefly. "I refused. I thought it would be good for the family, if we all got together again in the same house. Anyway, when you started fighting, I saw that I had a reason to continue living. More than one, to be exact. I have five healthy children, and four grandbabies, who still need me," she sighed and backed away, leaning against the sink.

"I've made many mistakes in my life, lord knows," her mother continued, looking away, studying the closed door. "And so many of those mistakes I made with you, Linda," she turned back to her daughter then, fixing her cold, bright gaze on Linda's face. "I should have taken you kids and left your father years ago. That's probably my biggest regret in a whole line of regrets. I realize it may be a case of "too little, too late," at this point, but I'd like to try to make amends. If you'll let me." Her mother trailed off, cocking her head to the side as she watched for Linda's reaction.

Linda swallowed. Her head spun. This was turning into one of the strangest encounters she'd ever had with her mother. She looked at her mother's messy appearance, black mascara and navy eye shadow smeared into the folds around her eyes, foundation splotched across her face, lipstick blotched across her mouth, hair disheveled and falling out of its bun. She thought of the soft words her mother had just spoken, and the hard contrast of the expression in her eyes. It hadn't been easy for her mom. They had never been close — her father's violence had been a wall between them that both had been too terrified to climb. But her mother had taken the first step, just now, and Linda could meet her halfway.

"I'd like that, Mom," Linda said.

Her mother smiled briefly, and Linda saw a faint softening – a thawing — in her eyes, for the very first time.

"Thank you," her mother replied. She stood up and rubbed her hands briskly together. "Let's go down and make sure everyone cleaned up properly." She caught a glimpse of herself in the mirror. "Oh, my. Linda, would you mind going down ahead of me? I need to straighten myself out a bit."

"No problem," Linda said, leaving her mother rummaging in a drawer for a hairbrush.

CHAPTER 15

She was back in college, walking down a hallway in her dormitory. All the doors stood open. She could hear laughter, music.

Something cold stung her fingers. She looked down. In her hand, she held the black-and-white picture she had seen in the police station — the one of Elizabeth in the apartment lobby. As she looked at the picture, it began to warp and stretch.

Elizabeth's lips elongated into a smile, and her mouth opened, revealing several rows of sharp, pointed teeth. The smile continued to expand, the teeth growing longer, warping, mutating, until all the picture contained was that hideous, toothy smile.

"Your brother's blood cries out to me from the ground," the mouth whispered, teeth shining.

An ant crawled across the picture, and Linda dropped it. She watched as the mouth opened again, swallowing both the ant *and* the picture.

She looked up. A young woman with golden hair, smelling fresh as a summer breeze, stepped into the hallway. She turned her laughing face, glowing and full of light, toward Linda.

Suddenly a black shadow clouded her lovely features, darkness descending on her. Linda watched as the young woman screamed, turned and plunged through a window to her death.

Linda outside, standing near the dormitory, staring at the smashed remains of the woman. A young man suddenly bolted past her, his hands dripping with blood, his eyes wild, filled with horror. Two corpses, half woman, half skeleton, pursued him, their bony, claw-like hands stretched out to grab him. One of the dead looked directly at Linda as it passed, eyes bright red and filled with hatred.

Linda in a police station, crowded with officers and chained-up criminals, their eyes red and bloody. A woman clutched a blanket-wrapped bundle. She had a plain, "mousy" face, except for her eyes, which looked as wild as the young man's who had run by her moments before. The mousy woman screamed at a police officer, "Take my baby!

Please. Before I hurt her. She wants me to hurt my baby. Please! You must take my baby."

The blanket wriggled and writhed in her grasp. The being within struggled to free itself, clawing the blanket away from its face, head emerging like a terrible insect from a cocoon.

It raised its head and looked straight at Linda.

Silver eyes.

***

Linda sprang straight up in bed, a hoarse, terrible scream caught in her throat.

A pale light shone through the window. It must be morning.

Linda struggled to calm herself, her breathing fast and heavy. The clock read a little after five: too early to get ready for Marshall Fields.

She slid out of bed and walked into the kitchen to make coffee. *What a strange dream*, she thought. Another nightmare, yet this one had been unlike any she had before. Oddly enough, it didn't scare her the way the others had.

There was something about the events that had occurred in her dream, something she should know, some meaning to take away from it … but she couldn't figure it out. It puzzled her, bothered her, tantalized her.

She carried her coffee to the window and looked out. The sky had changed to light gray, but the sun hadn't actually begun to rise yet. She watched the sky slowly brighten, as she drank her coffee and contemplated.

What could be going on? She knew something important was eluding her. She could *feel* it, the meaning sitting right there in front of her, waiting for her to discover it … yet she couldn't grasp it.

Suddenly, a thick rush of anger burned through her. What right did Elizabeth have to be invading Linda's life like this, six months after her death? Elizabeth was dead. Dead. And yet she somehow had the nerve to continue to poison her sister's mind — her very soul. Nightmares, hallucinations, blackouts. What next? The dark mouth of insanity smiling up at her, mouth filled with teeth ready to devour, to crush?

Linda had had enough. This was going to stop. She was no longer willing to be the victim, the reactor. It was time for her to go on the offensive — to become the attacker.

Now if she could only figure out where to start.

***

"So what is all this about?" Terri asked, sitting down on Linda's couch and accepting a cup of coffee from her friend.

Linda plopped down next to her, sloshing the liquid in her cup. She clutched her mug to her like a life preserver, drawing comfort from its warmth.

She had called in sick to Marshall Fields. Her supervisor hadn't been very sympathetic — calling in sick on the biggest shopping day of the year, the day after Thanksgiving, was not what he wanted to hear. He subtly threatened Linda with her job, and Linda responded by hanging up the phone. She didn't care. So what if she lost this job? She'd find another one. Dealing with her situation – her own sanity – took priority right now.

She had made another pot of coffee, and called Terri. It was the only thing she could think to do. Right then, Linda needed a sounding board – a trusted friend.

While waiting for Terri to arrive, Linda focused on cleaning up her apartment. She washed a few dishes, organized mail and papers, thrust her dirty clothes in a laundry basket in the corner of her bedroom. Her efforts didn't much improve the overall appearance of her apartment, she knew.

During the process, she had almost endured another anxiety attack. She could have *sworn* that some of the various piles of mess in her bedroom had rearranged themselves – reassuring her that she had done the right thing by calling in sick. She *needed* this time off. After all, there she was, considering the possibility that maybe Felix had taken up interior decorating as his new hobby.

Either way, she was losing it, and she knew it.

Terri, in creased blue jeans, a crisp, white button-down shirt and a pale pink floral sweater vest, looked out-of-place on Linda's faded, mud-colored couch. She held her coffee mug carefully in front of her, revealing perfectly manicured nails.

"There's been some new developments," Linda began. "About the murders."

"Elizabeth's been caught red-handed, I suppose," Terri lightly joked.

"Close," Linda said. "There was a picture."

Terri sat up straighter. "You're kidding. Aren't you?"

Linda shook her head. "I wish I were. I saw the picture with my own eyes. It looked like Elizabeth."

But did it really? the little voice inside her asked.

An image of her dream popped into Linda's head, the picture transmogrifying until it became a giant, hungry mouth.

"And you're sure it wasn't an old picture? Taken before she died?" Terri asked, interrupting Linda's thoughts.

"Well, it was in the apartment building of the latest victim. There was a video camera in the lobby, and it recorded someone leaving who looked a lot like Elizabeth. But, I don't know, maybe it wasn't Elizabeth. Now that I think about it, maybe there *was* something wrong with the picture."

"Like what?" Terri took a sip of coffee and made a face. "Ugh. You make the strongest coffee. Do you have any cream or milk?"

"Milk." Linda started to stand up but Terri waved her down.

"You tell me about the picture. I can wait on myself." Terri moved into the kitchen, frowning at the stack of mail and newspapers that littered her friend's table.

"It just hit me. I had this really weird dream about that picture. I was holding it in my hand, and it literally transformed into a huge, gaping, smiling mouth, with tons of sharp teeth."

"Weird," Terri said, putting her coffee cup down on the counter. She began inspecting the clean glasses drying upside down in the dish rack. Linda sighed. She had forgotten how fastidious Terri could be.

"You'll have better luck finding the milk in the fridge."

"Linda, I don't understand how you can live this way. You're just one person. How can this place be such a mess?"

"You know, it's the weirdest thing. The apartment is immaculate before I leave for work. When I get back home, it's like this. Felix is such a messy cat. I can't even keep up with him."

"Humph," Terri made a face at her. "Just wait until you're married, and you have TWO people to pick up after."

"Don't forget Felix."

"Oh, Felix. How could I possibly forget about him and his messes?" Terri opened the refrigerator door. "Ok, back to the huge, smiling mouth. What does it have to do with Elizabeth?"

"I don't know what to think about any of it," Linda said. "I don't know anything anymore."

Terri pulled the milk out of the fridge. "What's going on with the police?"

"I'm not sure. One of the detectives, a woman, thinks Elizabeth is still alive. I have no idea what thoughts are going through Steve's mind."

"Okay, hang on for a sec. You said they caught the woman on film *leaving* the building. Did they get a picture of her entering as well?" She pulled the cap off the milk and sniffed it. "Whew. When did you buy this?"

"Just this past week. Why? And I have no idea if they got a picture of her entering."

Terri waved the milk under her nose like it was a bottle of good wine. "I don't know. Smells a little sour."

"I think you're imagining things. It smelled fine to me this morning. And why did you want to know if the police have a picture of her going into the building?"

Terri plucked a glass off the drying rack and poured some milk into it. "Just curious. Wondering if anyone actually saw her with the victim." She swirled the glass, sloshing milk around the interior, then held the glass up to the light. She frowned while she studied it.

"The police showed the still frame to some witnesses who had seen the victim leave with a woman. I guess they all said the same thing – that it was her. What exactly are you looking for in the milk?"

Terri tasted the milk and shrugged. "I guess it's fine. I'll ask the obvious: Did you see the woman's eyes in the picture? "

"No, she was wearing sunglasses. But the witnesses told the police the woman they had seen had silver eyes."

Terri dumped the milk into her coffee. Then, she continued to poke around the kitchen. "I still can't believe it's her. I can't believe she could still be alive."

Linda sighed. "Now what are you looking for?"

"A spoon."

"Upper drawer on your right. No, your other right. Then will you sit down? I really need to talk to you."

Terri plunged the spoon into her coffee mug and briskly began to stir. "You are talking to me. Besides, I listen better if I'm doing something. You know that." She surveyed the kitchen with a distasteful expression on her face. "And there's certainly a lot to be done here."

"This is serious."

Terri finally looked at her. Really looked at her. "What?"

Linda took a deep breath. "I think I've seen her. Elizabeth."

"When?"

Linda told her about seeing Elizabeth that night on the street. Finally, Terri moved around the counter, to sit at the table. "Why didn't you tell me this before?"

Linda sagged against the couch. "How could I tell you? How could I tell anyone? It sounds insane. Maybe I *am* insane! There's no way Elizabeth could have walked out of that ocean alive. Yet, I've seen her. The police have a picture of her. It doesn't make any sense."

Terri put her coffee cup on the table. "There must be another explanation. Because you're right. Elizabeth has to be dead. She couldn't have survived the Atlantic."

"Actually, that's just part of it. There's more."

The rest of the story poured out of Linda then – every last rotten detail.

Terri tapped her nails against her mug while she listened. "All right, all right. Let's look at this rationally," she said once Linda finished.

Linda howled. "Rationally? What's rational about any of this?"

Terri left the chair to sit next to Linda on the couch. "Linda, you have to listen to me. You have to trust me." With one hand, Terri grabbed Linda's coffee cup and put it on the table. With the other, she took Linda's hand and squeezed it. Terri's hand felt so warm, her own a block of ice.

"Okay," Terri said. "Let's take it one step at a time. First, your nightmares. Linda, you've been under intense emotional stress. It's not surprising you're having nightmares."

Linda covered her face with her free hand. "Maybe not, but when you add everything together ..."

"We don't need to add everything together, at least not yet," Terri said firmly. "Let's look at everything individually, one at a time. There has to be a logical explanation for all of this. Are your nightmares the same every time?"

"More or less. I'm lost in a mansion, trying to find Elizabeth, who keeps calling me, louder and louder."

"Maybe that's a good thing," Terri interjected. "Maybe when you find her, you'll resolve everything."

"I can only hope," Linda picked up her mug of rapidly cooling coffee. "I wish I would find her. I'd rather find her than the murder victims I always see."

"What happens when you don't find anything?"

Linda shrugged. "Nothing usually. The shadows on the wall get more intense, change shape more. I still wake up terrified. Last night was the exception."

"In what way?"

Linda sipped coffee. She felt calmer then, more in control. Talking about it certainly seemed to be helping. "I wasn't that scared when I woke up, for one thing. But the nightmare was different, completely different. The picture was only part of it."

"So what was the rest?"

Linda told her.

"Creepy," Terri said when Linda finished.

Linda put her empty mug on the table. "You could say that."

Terri leaned against the couch. "There's something about it though. Something ... familiar, almost."

Linda looked at her, astonished. "You feel it, too? I can't believe it; that's *exactly* how it felt to me, too!"

"Yes, there's something ..." Terri paused, gazing past her. She was silent for a moment, lost in some other world. Linda watched her, hoping her friend could put her finger on what it meant.

Terri shook her head, jerking herself out of her thoughts. "I can't think of it," she said.

Linda felt her heart sink back down to the pit of her stomach.

"And that statement," Terri continued. "'My brother's blood calls from the ground,' or whatever. That sounds familiar too."

"Oh, I didn't tell you the craziest part of that little detail," Linda said, sitting up straighter and pulling her old gray sweatshirt down. "The police heard it too."

"The police?"

"Yeah. Apparently someone called them, repeating the exact same phrase."

"Who?"

Linda shrugged. "The caller didn't leave a name, I guess."

Terri picked a piece of lint off her sweater. "Well, was it a man or a woman?"

"They didn't say."

"Hmmm. The plot thickens." Terri stood up and walked over to retrieve her coffee cup. She peered into its depths, brow furrowed, as if trying to read her fortune in it. "This is all very strange."

"Yeah. Imagine what it's been like to live it, day in, day out."

"Well, I can definitely understand why you're having so much trouble." She swallowed some coffee and made a face. "Cold." She moved around the counter to retrieve the pot. "It all makes much more sense to me now," Terri said, while she splashed fresh coffee into her mug.

"Good, I'm glad it makes sense to someone. It sure as hell doesn't to me." Linda stretched her legs out and leaned back on the couch.

"I'm serious." Terri sat back down at the kitchen table. "Here's my working theory: You've been receiving a LOT of suggestion that Elizabeth is alive. Therefore, you've created her."

Linda sat up. "What?"

"Now don't immediately dismiss this. Everything that's been happening to you can all be explained because it's been *suggested*, quite convincingly I might add, that Elizabeth is alive. So your mind has re-created your reality to fit the perception you've been hearing about. It's the power of suggestion."

Linda sat back, dejected. "I've already considered that possibility."

"And?"

"And what? I suppose that *could* be it. It's possible."

"You don't sound convinced."

Linda raised her hands helplessly. "I don't know what to think anymore."

"I know the feeling." Idly, Terri stretched out a long, graceful hand and began flicking through Linda's mail. "Have you considered you may have something physical going on?"

"Yes."

"Have you seen a doctor?"

"No."

Terri raised one eyebrow at her. "Maybe you should consider it."

"Maybe. You don't have to sort my mail, you know."

"Well, someone has to. Unless you think it'll magically sort itself."

"No, that's Felix's job."

Terri pushed the piles away. "Let's go get something to eat. I'm starving."

Linda suspected that Terri wasn't hungry at all; she just wanted Linda to eat. Oh well, maybe she would be able to swallow something. She got to her feet.

"And we won't talk about Elizabeth or the murders or anything else. Stress is bad for digestion," Terri said, winking at her while she pulled on her jacket.

Linda went to get her coat. "Deal."

Mirror Image

CHAPTER 16

The following day, Linda had just gotten home from Marshall Fields when her cell rang. It was Steve.

"Hi, did I catch you at a bad time?"

She dumped her purse and keys on the table. "That depends."

"On what?"

"On what you want."

He chuckled softly. "I just wanted to know if you have any plans tonight."

"Why, so you can take me back to the police station and grill me some more?"

"No, I thought I'd save that for Monday. Actually, I'd like your help."

Linda began stacking dirty dishes next to the sink. "I thought I *was* helping you. Isn't that what the interrogation was for?"

"Ouch. That hurts. No, seriously, I really would like your help. I thought I could come over, and we could go through old yearbooks together. You know, to see if anyone jumps out at you."

Linda cast a disparaging look around her apartment. He wanted to come here? To this dump? "Why don't I meet you somewhere?"

"Naw, it will be easier to do at your apartment. I'll even spring for pizza."

"Gee, how generous! I give up my Saturday night to look through yearbooks to help you with your investigation, and you buy me a pizza? You must be a super-fun date."

"I'm a cop; I don't have fun anymore."

"I've noticed."

"So, can I come over or what?"

"I suppose." She hung up the phone, then realized that she hadn't given him directions or even her address.

"He'll figure it out," she said. After all, he was a cop. He had managed to find her at work, he could find his way here.

She looked around sourly. Guess she better get to cleaning up some more. Luckily, she hadn't made much of a mess since Terri had been there the day before.

After stuffing a bunch of junk in the bedroom and shutting the door, she ran water in the sink and began washing dishes.

She had just put the last dish in the drying rack when the buzzer rang. After pushing the button to unlock the front door, she combed her hair, sticking her tongue out at herself in the mirror.

It certainly hadn't taken him long to reach her apartment. When she opened the door, she found herself staring at a pile of books.

"Hi," Steve said from behind the stack. Linda stepped back to let him in. This was going to be a long evening.

"So, I guess we're studying for finals tonight," she said after Steve heaved the books on her kitchen table.

"Looks that way." He glanced around her apartment. "Nice."

She started straightening the books. "For a cop, you lie like shit. It's a dump."

"Don't hold back, Linda! Why don't you tell me what you really think?" he fired back.

Linda looked at him sharply, mouth open to retort, but when she saw the corners of his mouth twitch upwards, she burst out laughing instead. Steve joined her.

It felt like a dam had exploded inside her. Laughter bubbled up, frothing like champagne, and she leaned against the table, helpless to stop, until she realized how dangerously close to hysteria she was.

Slowly, she got herself back under control, scrubbing the tears away from her cheeks. Steve watched her, an amazed expression on his face. "I don't think I've heard you laugh like that since high school."

She hiccupped slightly. "I don't think I *have* laughed like that since high school."

His gaze sharpened. "I hope that's not true."

She looked at him in exasperation. "Why would you care? Now, aren't you here because we have a job to do? These yearbooks aren't going to start looking through themselves."

He studied her for a second, an unreadable expression in his eyes. Then he turned away and bent to pick up a couple of books. "That's for sure," he said.

Somehow, Linda suspected he had wanted to say something else, but had changed his mind.

They each filled their arms with books and carried them to the couch. After going through a few of them, Steve ordered a pizza.

It was nearing ten when Steve stretched and stood up. Linda glanced at him, but didn't stop working. He paced around her match-book-sized living room.

"You know, I meant it when I said your place was nice," he said, studying the books on the shelf. Linda eyed him, not bothering to lift her head. He ran his finger lightly down the row of spines. "My place is much more of a dump. Levington Courts. Ever hear of it?"

She actually had, and it surprised her that he lived there. Chad had put himself through school while residing at Levington Courts. It did not resemble anything remotely like a court, and she had to agree that it likely *was* more of a dump than hers. She rubbed her eyes and continued studying photos.

He turned to face her. "This is when you're supposed to say something back. A yes or no would do."

Linda kept her head lowered. "Yes."

Linda finally looked at him. He was watching her, head cocked, a quirky expression on his face. "Is there a purpose to your question?"

Steve's eyes widened. "Why, yes. It's called having a conversation."

"You missed your calling; you should have been a comedian." Linda bent over the yearbook in her lap. "I still have a lot of work to do — work you assigned me, by the way."

"I know, but I felt it was time for a break."

Linda turned a page, glancing over the photos without registering a single one of them. "Well, you thought wrong."

He sat down on the coffee table right in front of her, and yanked the book out of her hands. "Why did I think wrong?"

Linda glared at him, frustrated. "Steve, ever since you came back into my life, dragging these murders along with you, you have questioned me, interrogated me, treated me with total suspicion, and practically had me arrested. Now, you want to have a friendly conversation? Why? Are you trying to get me to lower my guard, so you wrangle some sort of confession out of me, or what?" She tried to snatch the book back, but he held it out of her reach.

"Now wait a second. You sure are leaping to conclusions here."

Linda hooted. "Leaping to conclusions? I think I just summed up our entire relationship pretty accurately, don't you?"

"All right. Let me explain."

Linda sat back on the couch and crossed her arms in front of her. "I'm waiting."

Steve sighed and lowered the book to his lap. "I know this has been tough for you. It's been tough on me as well. This case ... well, there are just too many things that don't make any sense." His hands curled into fists, knuckles turning white. "And also much of it, one way or another, leads back to Elizabeth." His eyes shifted, locked onto Linda's. "And you."

Linda tried to suck in air, but couldn't. Her lungs felt as if they had just collapsed, like dead balloons, devoid of even a molecule of oxygen.

His eyes bored into hers, stripping away the secrets, the hidden truths. She opened her mouth to breathe, and found herself gasping like a fish. Oh God, he must know everything.

"Wh ... why do you say that?" she managed, struggling to sound calm, casual, normal.

Instead of answering, Steve stood up abruptly and began pacing back and forth. Linda watched him, attempting to take slow, deep breaths, without him noticing.

He continued to speak, his voice low, as though talking to himself – as if she weren't even in the room. "This case has bordered on the bizarre from the get-go. Everything about it. Then, when that description of the suspect came in, bearing a striking resemblance to Elizabeth, I simply followed up on it by talking to you. It seemed like such a natural move, to speak with her sister. After all, there was a chance you could shed some light on the whole mess." He stopped pacing in the center of the room, and whirled around to stare at her again, his eyes penetrating deeply. "What I didn't count on was how suspicious you would act. Or, how attracted I would be to you again."

Deep, slow breaths. How on earth did he expect a response to either, much less both of those shocking statements? On one hand, the cold grip of terror had started to tighten around her throat again, forcing her to practically choke on the air she so desperately needed. On the other hand, she felt a quick surge of elation. He was attracted to her, after all those years. She closed her eyes for a second. One statement at a time. Opening her eyes, she tried on a smile that felt way too tight. "Suspicious? Me? What would I have to be suspicious about?"

He swiftly moved in front of her. "I don't know. But you *are* acting suspicious. Why is that?"

She squirmed in her seat, his gaze hot and heavy, leaning as far back as she could, trying to put as much distance between them as possible. "I don't know. I didn't realize I was acting suspicious."

"Then why, during our very first conversation, did you ask me if anything else had been done to the victim's bodies? Why do you act guilty and defensive when I ask you questions?" He grabbed her shoulders, squaring her to him. "Why do I get such a strong feeling that you're hiding something?"

Linda couldn't focus, his grip too strong. "I don't know why. I don't know anything." She cried out.

He jerked her closer to him, so close she could feel his breath hot on her cheek, smelling of onions and garlic. "Dammit, tell me what you're hiding. I can't help you unless I know."

"What makes you think you could help me even if you did know?" Linda asked.

His breath caught in his throat. "So, there *is* something."

Instantly Linda realized her mistake. "No, there is not," she said, pushing him away and scrambling off the couch, cursing herself the entire time. "There's nothing."

Slowly, he advanced on her, his voice soft and persuasive. "Tell me."

Oh God, now what was she going to do? He wouldn't believe her, even if she confessed everything, right then. Seeing the murder victims in dreams, seeing Elizabeth on the streets, smelling her perfume … why not just hand him everything he would need to convict her? She forced a laugh. "Really, Steve. You're misinterpreting what I said. I don't know anything."

He kept approaching, coming closer and closer. "Then how did you mean it?"

She shrugged, sidestepping, moving farther away from him. "Exactly how I said it. Even if there was something, which there isn't, why would you assume you could help?"

"Tell me."

"There's nothing to tell."

He stopped moving and studied her. She refused to meet his eyes, staring at chip in the wall. "Why don't I believe you?" he finally asked.

She didn't answer, continuing her examination of the defect in the wall. Her father's voice echoed in her head: *a good defense is a strong offense* — one of the few useful things he had taught her. Slowly, deliberately, she turned her head toward Steve, to look him directly in the eye. "Why should I believe anything you say, ever?" she asked, her voice soft and clipped, like her father's.

His eyes narrowed. "What the hell is that supposed to mean?"

"What do you think it means? You, who chose my sister over me?"

"Oh, so that's what this is all about," he said, but he didn't seem nearly as sure of himself as before.

She advanced on him this time, her voice threatening. "Yes, that's exactly what this is all about. Did you really expect me to open up to you after what you've done to me?" Her words dripped sarcasm. "Did you really expect me to trust you now, or ever?"

"That was ten years ago. We were in high school for God's sake."

"And that's supposed to make it okay? Because we were in high school?"

"No, that's not what I meant." He reached up with both his hands and tugged his hair. "We were different people then. Besides, you refused to go out with me anyway."

"It didn't take you long to find a substitute, did it? And oh, what a choice you made," Linda said bitterly.

"Dammit, Linda. I never meant to hurt you."

"'The road to hell is paved with good intentions'... right?"

Steve glared at her. "I see this is going nowhere. I'll see you later."

Linda watched him stride over to get his coat, draped across a kitchen chair. Old hurts, old jealousies seethed inside her. She stalked across the living room and into the kitchen. "Don't you understand? I *had* to say no. If I didn't, she would have stolen you away. Refusing you was the only way I could think of to stop her. To keep her away from you."

Steve yanked his coat off the chair. "What the hell are you talking about? How would not dating me save me from Elizabeth? If we had been together, wouldn't that have done the trick?"

Linda hesitated, for the first time realizing how inane she sounded. "It's not as simple as that. She had a way with men. Don't you remember all those boyfriends she stole from other women? I couldn't risk her stealing you away from me."

"Give me a break." Disgusted, he stomped over to the coffee table and began piling up the books. "What you're really saying is that you respected me *so* little, you wouldn't have trusted me around your sister. Thanks a lot."

"How do you explain her power over men?"

He slammed the yearbooks together. "I don't know. She was easy." He scooped them up in his arms and stood to face her. "It doesn't matter anyway. It wouldn't have mattered if she was so irresistible, every damn male in the school slept with her. What matters is that if we had been together, *I wouldn't have.* And you didn't trust me."

She looked away, feeling her heart break all over inside her. "It wouldn't have been your fault," she whispered. "She ... had a way with men. You couldn't have helped yourself."

"Thanks for the vote of confidence," Steve said, moving toward the door. "I'll be in touch." Fumbling with the doorknob, he managed to wrestle it open without dropping any books. She expected him to slam the door, but instead, he closed it with a gentle click.

That quiet, tiny sound of the door closing was almost her undoing. She sank to the floor, her trembling knees unable to hold her up any longer.

Steve suspected her.

Steve was attracted to her.

Her head pounded and she felt nauseated, the greasy pizza sitting like a rock in her stomach. She had only been able to choke down one piece, but it felt as if she had eaten the entire pie. She curled up on her side in a fetal position.

To think, in just one night, she managed to not only make Steve more suspicious of her than he already was, but she also destroyed any hope she'd ever had of having a relationship with him. This felt like a record, even for her.

Suddenly, curled up on the floor as she was, her life failures rolled through her mind, one disaster after another. Dropping out of college, hating her job, her broken relationship with her family, her lack of love. Everything she had managed to screw up over the years was now running on repeat in her mind, and she felt like she was teetering on the brink of madness.

All this, because of Elizabeth.

Something stirred inside her. She had to do *something*. Even if all she accomplished was saving her own sanity, that was more than enough. The rest could come later. Right now, she needed to know the truth. The truth about the murders. And the truth about Elizabeth.

It was time to put these new demons to rest. Lord knew she had enough trouble with the old ones. And maybe, just maybe, the old demons would quiet down, if the new ones disappeared.

She had to try to solve the case herself. She knew the police wouldn't be of any help. Hell, she was probably their number one suspect now, thanks to her most recent performance. But, she couldn't let that stop her. She had to find the truth — she had no other choice.

CHAPTER 17

"I'm still not sure what we're supposed to accomplish here," Terri said.

They stood in front of The Green Room, the downtown campus bar where the second victim had met his killer. During the day, the bar looked harmless enough. But it didn't feel harmless. In fact, it felt downright spooky. Linda shivered. She had to stop giving herself the creeps. She told herself she was only jumpy because she knew what had happened there. It had nothing to do with how the dark interior seemed to beckon to her, its shadowy blackness winking evilly.

She forced herself to stop thinking, and turned to Terri. "We're here to get some answers."

"Don't you think that the police have already covered this ground?" Terri asked. "I mean, this isn't exactly brain surgery. They've surely questioned everyone who worked here pretty thoroughly."

"Maybe." Linda pushed open the door. "But it doesn't hurt to check."

Terri muttered something and followed her.

The bar gave an immediate impression of desolation. Broken chairs and tables, pushed to the side, circled a scuffed brown linoleum floor. Fake wooden walls, covered with scratches and discolored in some places by who knew what, looked even drearier decorated with several pathetic sprigs of holly and mistletoe.

And the cold. It felt almost as chilly inside the bar as out. Linda could see her breath.

A man who didn't look old enough to drink, much less work as a bartender, stood behind the counter polishing glasses with a bar towel. Another towel lay askew over his shoulder, partially covering his white button-down shirt. His cropped brown hair made him look like an ROTC student, but his scrawny beard and body belied that impression. Linda felt even colder looking at him.

He glanced up when they approached. "What can I get you?"

"Nothing for now."

The bartender nodded and went back to his work. Linda slid onto a barstool in front of him. "You ever work nights?"

The bartender nodded. "Usually. You know that. Just filling in for someone right now."

"You know that." The words rang in her ears. Her blood suddenly felt sluggish, freezing in her veins. "Why on earth would I know that?" Linda asked before she could stop herself.

"Cause I've seen you here before. At night."

"I've never been in here before."

He shrugged. "Not surprised you don't remember. Usually, you end up having a bit too much."

Linda could only stare at him in horror. She felt Terri tug on her coat. "We should go," Terri said, her breath warm on Linda's ear. She shook Terri off and fumbled in her pocket. She would do what she came here to do.

"Have you ever seen this woman here?" she asked, holding up the only picture she could find of Elizabeth — the horrid senior picture. She noticed her hand shaking. She knew it wasn't because of the temperature.

The bartender took the picture and studied it. He handed it back with another shrug. "Might have. She looks familiar. Hard to say. There's so many people in and out of here."

"But you remember me." Linda couldn't help herself.

The bartender laughed a little. "You make it easy."

Terri jerked her back and off the bar stool before Linda could open her mouth again. "Linda, we're going," she said firmly, pushing Linda out of the bar. She thanked the bartender over her shoulder when they reached the door.

Once outside, Linda's knees could no longer hold her up. She sank down on the sidewalk, the chill permeating her jeans. But that didn't even compare to the block of ice that had somehow lodged in the pit of her stomach. Pricks of pain whispered against her temples. Her brain felt shattered, blown apart into a million pieces.

"Linda, get a hold of yourself," Terri said, kneeling in front of her friend, her hands grasping her shoulders.

Linda closed her eyes. "My blackouts. Is this where I go during my blackouts?"

Terri shook her. "No. Linda, please, pull yourself together."

"It would sure explain a lot." Linda opened her eyes. The winter sun glared down on her. It was so strange, seeing the sun. It so rarely showed its face during the winter. Pain licked her temples, the backs of her eyes.

Terri stood up and looked wildly around. "This is no place to have a nervous breakdown. Besides I'm freezing. Look, The Student Grind is just down the block. Let's go get some coffee."

Linda shrugged; she had no will of her own. After all, her body seemed to be perfectly capable of going places all by itself, without letting her brain in on the ride. Terri hauled her up and half-dragged her down the street.

The rich aroma of coffee and damp heat hit Linda in the face the moment she walked through the door. Usually, The Student Grind made her feel warm and cozy with its old wooden beams and scarred floors, high ceilings and cramped, maze-like rooms. She had always loved old buildings. But even The Student Grind's old-fashioned charm could do nothing to warm the ice that still coursed through her veins. Scattered throughout, hiding in corners and alcoves, the little wooden and metal tables had seen better days. Uncomfortable black metal chairs surrounded the tables.

Terri bulldozed Linda up to the counter. "What do you want? Oh, never mind." She turned to look at the menu.

"I want two medium, no, make that large French Roasts," Terri said to the girl behind the counter. The girl nodded, reaching for two paper cups. She wore all black; her short, asymmetrically cut dark hair boasted streaks of bright red. A silver hoop dangled in her nose.

"Wait," Terri said suddenly. "Can you add some Irish Creme to both of them? Be generous, please."

The girl barely glanced at them. "I.D.?"

Terri opened her wallet. "God, I forgot what it's like being on campus." Linda stood motionless beside her. Shock had turned her body numb. She didn't think she could move, even if she wanted to. Her entire core being seemed to have disappeared into some silent, dark void.

Terri turned to her, opened her mouth as if to say something, then shut it and grabbed Linda's purse instead, pawing through it to locate her wallet.

The girl took the identification, her silver bracelets jangling on her wrist. She glanced at Linda.

"What's wrong with her?" she asked, gesturing with her head. The silver nose ring sparkled.

"She just got some terrible news," Terri answered without even looking at Linda. "She's in shock. That's why she needs the shot."

The girl handed back the identification. "Why do you need one?"

"Because I'm the designated driver," Terri said, her face cold and set.

The girl studied Terri for a moment, her eyes narrowing slightly. Then she turned and picked up the Irish Creme bottle from the back counter and poured two healthy shots into their cups.

"Go find a place to sit while I pay." Terri gave Linda a little shove. She obediently turned and walked, robot-like, toward one of the little alcoves.

The place was practically empty. Perched at one table was a thin, pale man dressed in black, reading a slim volume of poetry. A young, frazzled looking woman, presumably a student judging by the books and papers surrounding her, sat hunched over a scrawled notebook, chewing violently on her pen.

Linda stood, practically frozen, unable to make even the simplest decision. She had no idea where to sit.

"Linda, I told you to, oh never mind," Terri said at her elbow. "Come on." She walked to a table in the corner. Linda followed.

"Drink this." Terri thrust the cup into her hands. Linda swallowed a big draught. It burned all the way down her throat.

Terri watched her, her eyes intent, anxious. "Better?"

Linda nodded and swallowed some more. Her brain felt clearer then. The heat radiated from her stomach, warming her body. She wrapped her hands around her cup and leaned her elbows on the table. The table rocked beneath her, one leg shorter than the other, sloshing the coffee in the cup. Linda rearranged her position, to keep the table steady.

Terri drank out of her cup. "Linda, the guy made a mistake. It's nothing to get so worked up over."

Linda breathed in the rich scent of coffee, closing her eyes. She didn't want to talk about it. Numbness surrounded her, blanketing her in its soft, suffocating folds.

Terri continued. "Listen to me. I've been thinking about your blackout. You could have epilepsy. I saw it on a television show the other night. People with certain types of epilepsy can wake up in strange places with no memory of how they got there."

Linda opened her eyes. "I've never had epilepsy."

Terri shrugged. "People can develop it as adults."

"Yeah, but don't you need to be hit on the head or something? Suffer some sort of head injury? I've never had one."

"Well, maybe you've blocked that out, too. Maybe you're suffering from amnesia."

"Maybe," Linda rubbed her head. "Although I think I would remember if I hit my head that hard."

Terri gave her look. "Kind of goes against the whole definition of amnesia, doesn't it?"

Linda almost laughed. "You got a point."

She swallowed more coffee, glancing around the room. Linda had forgotten about the pictures on the walls. Starving art students plastered their work all over the coffee house, hoping to snag the attention (and the pocketbook) of a customer. Most of the paintings displayed leaned toward the strange and full of angst and deep meaning — certainly nothing Linda would want to display in her living room.

Terri's voice broke into her thoughts. "I've been thinking about your dream."

Linda turned her head to look at Terri. "Which one?"

"The last one. The one about the woman trying to give her baby to the police."

"What about it?"

"It finally occurred to me why it sounded so familiar. It really happened."

Linda stared at her.

"Don't you remember? A few years ago, some woman went to the cops and asked them to take her baby because she was afraid she would kill it. Said she kept hearing voices telling her to hurt it. It was all over the news."

The table rocked again, making a thumping noise as one leg hit the floor. "I guess it does sound vaguely familiar. Maybe that's what I was remembering, too. I wonder what happened to her."

Terri leaned back and gulped her coffee. "I think she was committed to an institution, and the baby given up for adoption. Now if I could just figure out why the other part sounded so familiar. You know, the stuff about the brother's blood calling from the ground."

"'Your brother's blood cries to me from the ground,'" Linda said, her voice taking on an eerily dreamy tone. One of the mounted paintings suddenly caught her eye. She turned to study it. Black-and-white paint swirled together in an angry vortex. Faces screamed in agony from within the swirls. Vivid splashes of red, dark as blood, streaked through. Linda shivered. It looked like one of those awful pictures Elizabeth painted after she almost drowned. She leaned forward trying to see the name of the painter. The first name started with an E.

"It so vaguely rings a bell, but I just can't place it. Linda, what are you doing?"

Linda ignored her, leaning forward in her seat, straining to make out the signature. The table thumped beneath her, and coffee splashed her hand. She barely felt the warm liquid dripping down her fingers. The black handwriting swirls blended together, refusing to give up its secrets. The last name started with R.

"Linda," Terri turned to see what had captivated Linda's attention. "Linda. What is it?"

Linda got up from the table and walked toward the painting. The handwriting swirls instantly clarified, and took on a familiar pattern: *Elizabeth Rossini.*

Linda gasped, her hands reaching up on their own accord to grasp the hair at her temples. The numbness she had felt since her chat with the bartender at The Green Room dissolved like aspirin on the tongue, bitter and chalky. Now, she was consumed by a horror so deep, its roots dug right into the tips of her fingers and the bottoms of her feet. The pain roared in her head. Dimly, she heard Terri call her name, but Linda had already turned away. She ran to the front of the coffee house, to the counter, to the strange girl with the silver nose ring.

"The painting," she gasped. The girl stared at her, backing up a little from the counter.

"What painting?" Her eyes wide and mistrustful, watched Linda carefully.

"The one in the back. The one by Elizabeth Rossini. How did you get it?"

The girl looked confused. "We don't have any paintings by Elizabeth Rossini."

Linda leaned forward, her hands splayed out on the counter. "Yes, you do. The one in the back."

"No, I've never heard of an Elizabeth Rossini. You're mistaken."

"No," Linda tried to argue but Terri had her by the arm.

"Linda, what's going on? What?!"

She turned to Terri. "That painting back there. It's Elizabeth's."

"No, it isn't," the girl insisted.

Linda glared at the girl. "Go look ..." she started, but Terri interrupted her.

"Show me."

Linda hesitated, looked at Terri, and then the girl, who returned her look with sullen hostility, before leading Terri to the picture.

It wasn't Elizabeth's. Clear as day, the signature read *Georgina Wilson*. Even more disconcerting, the painting looked nothing like Elizabeth's, any longer. Yes, it was still black, white and red, but it had a blocky, abstract look — strange, nightmarish staircases that led nowhere, no matter how many steps you took, or how long you climbed.

Linda stared at the painting, biting her lip in frustration. "I'm seriously losing it. Now I'm full-on hallucinating." Horror twisted inside her, weighing her down, transforming itself into a heavy, sick feeling. The numbness began to return then, creeping slowly through her body, oozing into her pores like a giant amoeba. Idly, she wondered how much more shock she could stand before the numbness simply took over, smothering her very being, leaving nothing but a shell of human.

"Linda, why don't you sit down?"

Linda didn't move. "She's everywhere, Terri. She's buried so deeply in my thoughts, I can't ever escape her. Why is she *still* haunting me? Why can't I let this go?"

"Probably because you don't want to," Terri answered, although Linda had asked rhetorically. "This notion of investigating yourself is clearly a bad idea. You need to drop it. For your own good."

Linda turned to look at Terri. "No. If there's one thing I know now, it's that I have no choice anymore. I'm going to get to the bottom of this, God help me, even if it kills me. I want my life back. I'm not stopping."

Terri studied Linda for a long moment. "So what's the next step? More bartenders?"

Linda turned back to the painting. The staircases climbed endlessly. Up, up, up. No place to go. No rest. No end destination.

"No," Linda said quietly. "No. Tonight, I'm going to stake out the bars."

Terri's eyes widened. "What?"

"I want to see this killer, this Elizabeth. I need to see her with my own eyes."

"You're crazy."

"Actually I've never felt saner in my entire life."

"You can't. Look at yourself. You're about to fall over with exhaustion and lack of food. You can't keep doing this to yourself. You're going to collapse."

"I have to try."

"You're going to make yourself sick, Linda."

Linda snorted. "I'm already sick! This is the only way I know to make myself better again. I have no choice. With you or without you, I'm doing it."

Terri turned her head. She shifted her weight from one leg to another. "You know this is a shot in the dark. We might not see anything at all. "

"I don't care."

"It'll be dangerous."

"I don't care."

Terri sighed. "Can we sit down? Ugh, my coffee's getting cold."

Linda nodded, and started to follow her back to the table. A subtle movement on the floor caught her eye. An ant, sluggish and slow.

An ant. Just an ant.

Icy fingers trailed down her back, lodging a sick feeling somewhere in her stomach. Suddenly, she was stomping uncontrollably on the insect, overwhelmed with hot rage and cold irrational fear.

"Good God, Linda. What are you doing?"

Linda looked up, completely disoriented. Where was she? Why was Terri here?

"I ... saw an ant." She blinked and looked around the coffee house, her memory finally returning.

"An ant?" Terri asked, disbelief on her face.

Other faces turned, staring at her. She looked away and tried to smile at Terri. "I'm sorry. I'm not sure what has gotten into me. Can we sit down now and finish our coffee?"

Terri studied her, a strange expression on her face. She followed Linda back to the table. "Are you sure you're okay?"

Linda tasted her coffee. It was lukewarm, but the alcohol retained its own heat. "Fine. I just don't like ants. You remember how much I don't like ants."

"I don't remember that at all."

Linda shrugged. "Well, I don't. With everything that's been happening ... I guess I just overreacted a bit."

"Yeah, just a bit." Terri watched her, drumming her fingers on the table. "Okay, back to the matter at hand. What about Steve?"

Linda inwardly winced. It hurt to hear his name, especially after what had just happened between them. "What about him?"

"Why don't you talk to him about this? They might have set up their own surveillance or something. He might be able to connect some of the dots for us."

Linda swallowed more coffee. "Steve and I aren't really on speaking terms."

"What?"

"We had a fight."

Terri sat up, leaning forward. "Oh God. When? What happened?"

Linda brushed the hair away from her face. "I ... I can't really talk about it right now. I'm still sorting it out myself. Especially since I'm dealing with all this other crap at the same time."

"I understand." Terri said. Her eyes, filled with a mixture of curiosity and pity, contradicted her words.

Suddenly, Linda couldn't stand it anymore. Poor Linda who couldn't find a boyfriend. Poor Linda who had a rough childhood. Poor Linda who had a sister she couldn't stand and who couldn't stand her. Poor Linda who was now borderline delusional.

She finished her coffee in one gulp. "I've got to go." She pushed her chair away from the table. "Especially since I'm going to the bars tonight." She couldn't meet Terri's eyes, didn't want to see the pity reflected there.

"Can I come, too?"

Linda shrugged. "Only if you want." She stood up and straightened her coat. "Thanks for coming today. I don't know what I would have done if you hadn't been here." She flashed a quick, forced smile to show her gratitude..

Terri stood. "That's what friends are for." She gently touched Linda's arm, squeezing it through the coat. "Call me about tonight."

"I will."

CHAPTER 18

Elizabeth's picture, the one taken by the surveillance cameras. Slowly, her mouth stretched into a smile, lips pulled back to reveal blood-stained teeth. Elongating, expanding into a monstrous grin. A tongue appeared, darting between the teeth, licking the blood away.

Linda awoke with a jerk. She blinked her eyes, the apartment slowly coming into focus. She was in the living room, sitting on the couch with the television blaring. She had obviously fallen asleep while waiting for it to get late enough to try the bars.

She yawned and stretched. Felix, who lay curled up next to her, raised his head to look at her reproachfully. She stroked his head, trying to remember the last time she had taken a nap. She couldn't.

Dragging herself off the couch, Linda headed to the bathroom to splash cold water on her face. The thick, heavy makeup slid off her face, like a layer of shedding skin. She picked up the soap, to scrub it off completely.

Toweling dry, she studied her clean, bare face in the mirror. Dark rings below her eyes, her skin a puffy, purplish black. The rest looked white and waxy, the color of a corpse. She sighed. Maybe she was dead. Dead and in hell. That would certainly explain everything.

Picking up her concealer, Linda dabbed the bruise-like darkness around her eyes. Would it ever end? Even if she learned the truth, would it be enough to save her?

Her hand shook, knocking a dot of concealer on her nose. She reached for a tissue. She had to keep digging. Had to figure this out, regardless of what happened to her in the end. She had already spent six months ignoring the problem, as best she could, and it certainly hadn't gone away on its own. If anything, it had gotten stronger and uglier, while she holed up and licked her wounds.

Taking a deep breath, she steadied her hand and continued to apply the concealer. *For once in your life*, she told herself, *look on the positive side*.

Maybe everything *would* actually be all right. Maybe it was time for an attitude adjustment.

After all, she had already experienced so much misery in her life. Hadn't she earned some good?

***

"Think maybe we should call it quits?" Terri asked, sipping her beer and wiping the foam from her chin.

Linda looked around the half-empty bar. Despite the lack of patrons, it seemed louder than it should be. "Sunday probably isn't the best day to do this, I guess."

They were in Rowdy's, their third stop of the night. Linda knew she couldn't tolerate any more of the cheap tap beer without throwing up. She liked beer, but it had to be the *good* kind: not this college-bar crap. Unfortunately, her pocketbook didn't match her tastes. If she wanted to have at least one beer at every bar, which she felt was important in order to fit in with the crowd, then she had to drink the kind she could afford — even if it made her gag.

"I've been meaning to ask you something," Terri said. "Why did you think Elizabeth had painted that picture? The one in The Student Grinder?"

Linda sipped her beer and shuddered. Disgusting. "Remember when we were kids, and Elizabeth almost died? After that Massachusetts vacation? While she was recovering, she started painting these really horrible paintings."

"I remember her being sick. I don't remember the paintings."

"That's because they were so weird, nobody in my family wanted to acknowledge their existence."

"So, how long did she paint these pictures?"

Linda swirled her beer around in her glass. "Not long. Maybe a few weeks. Then, one day, she just stopped. No explanation. Nothing. She seemed "fine," on the outside, but really, she became even crueler than she had been before the accident. She seemed to get a lot more pleasure out of hurting people. Whereas before that, it seemed like she manipulated people just to see if she could — not because she was getting any great enjoyment out of it."

"Strange."

Linda traced a carving in the table. It looked like someone had attempted to chisel a name into the fake wood, but it had ended up an unintelligible scrawl. "To say the least."

"Speaking of strange, I think I figured out something more about your dream."

"Which one?"

Terri fluffed her hair with her fingers. "The last one you had. The one with the baby the woman kept trying to give it away, and the skeletons chasing the guy."

"Oh? What did you figure out?"

Terri suddenly looked mysterious. "I can't tell you now."

"Why not?"

"Because I want to check out a few facts first. Want to meet me at the library tomorrow? After work?"

"I don't understand why you can't tell me now."

"Humor me."

Linda sighed and reluctantly nodded.

Terri laughed. "Don't sound so put-out. Trust me. There's a reason I'm asking you to do this."

Linda didn't answer, as she continued tracing the carving with her finger.

Terri adjusted her necklace. "I know you think these dreams are Elizabeth's way of tormenting you, but did you ever consider turning it around? Maybe these dreams are supposed to help you, not hinder you? Maybe Elizabeth is actually trying to help."

Linda didn't look up. "If she's trying to help, don't you think she'd show me the killer, instead of the victims?"

"Hmmm. I guess you have a point. I probably should have remembered that point, since I was the one who said it first!"

"Besides, it's hard for me to imagine Elizabeth ever trying to help anyone. Especially me."

"There's always a first."

Linda didn't answer. She picked at the carving. It reminded her of a scar — an old wound that had never been allowed to heal.

Something swirled around the back of her head: a nameless, grayish cloud, refusing to reveal itself.

She had theories: theories about what Elizabeth had really been, when she was alive. Those ideas had been born in the darkness of her nightmares, nursed with the sour milk of approaching madness.

But she wasn't ready to speak them aloud, yet. To speak of it, even think of it, might cause it to change shape, and become real.

She shook her head and gulped her beer, the flat taste jerking her out of her thoughts. No, she wouldn't allow herself to continue down that path. To admit what she suspected about the true identity of Elizabeth may well catapult her straight into the darkness of insanity. And what would others think? Terri? Chad? Steve? They'd think she *had* completely lost her mind, that's what.

Terri pointed to another room off to the side and asked if Linda wanted to check it out before leaving. Linda agreed, sliding off her bar stool and picking up her glass.

Terri led the way into the smoke-filled room. Linda held her glass in one hand, her purse in the other, trying to make sure she didn't drop or spill anything. Without warning, she nearly crashed into Terri, who had stopped abruptly in front of her.

"Well, this is certainly an unexpected turn of events," she said. Linda craned her neck to see around her friend.

"Oh, no," she moaned, wondering if her luck could get any worse. It was Steve, sitting at a table by himself, a glass of beer in front of him. Linda quickly ducked behind Terri, hoping he wouldn't look her way.

"I wonder what he's doing here, all alone," Terri said.

"I don't know and I don't care. Let's go."

"No, I think we should find out. After all, maybe he's casing the place as well. Maybe we could share information."

"No, Terri, don't," Linda said.

Terri was already striding toward Steve. Linda debated disappearing through the door, but it was too late. He had already seen them, and was half-heartedly waving them over.

She managed a weak smile and trudged toward his table. Of all the hundreds of bars to choose from, they end up at the same one. It must be fate. Or a truly stupid coincidence.

Terri was busy chatting already, mentioning how long it had been since she and Steve had seen each other. Linda sat down and drank her beer, trying to look interested. She needed another one – her distaste for crappy brews, aside.

Steve sat back in his chair. "So, what are you two doing here? I didn't think you were the type to hang out in college bars." It seemed to Linda that he took a lot of trouble not to look at her.

"We don't," Terri said. "At least not usually."

Steve's eyebrows went up. "Oh? Is today a special occasion?"

Terri glanced at Linda. "You could say that." She smoothed her hair.

"So what is it?"

"Guess."

"I haven't the faintest idea."

Terri smiled. "Oh, I think you do."

Steve stared at her. Then he looked at Linda. "You're not here to ... no, that'd be too dangerous. I know you know better than that."

Linda stared right back at him. His eyes were cold, foreboding, again making her feel like he was accusing her of something.

"Why? You're here." Even to her own ears, she sounded harsh and argumentative. She didn't want to, but somehow she had.

His voice grew colder. "That's different."

"Last I heard the killer was going after men. Single men. Not women."

"That doesn't matter."

"It seems to me that it does. Might actually be safer for me here, than for you."

"I'm a trained police officer."

"So you're here on official business then?"

His eyes narrowed, never leaving Linda's face. "Not exactly."

"Not exactly? What does that mean?"

"Means not exactly. Why are you asking all these questions? Why do you care?"

Terri bumped the table. "Whoops, sorry about that. This table is a bit wobbly. Hey, guys, wanna another beer? I sure could use one right now."

Steve swallowed the last of his and nodded.

Linda turned away from Steve. "Why not?" A group of college kids sitting at the next table lifted their glasses in an exaggerated toast. Beer streamed onto the table as the glasses clanked together, accompanied by shrieks and laughter.

She felt bills being pressed into her hands. "Linda, do you mind getting them? I want to catch up a little with Steve."

Linda looked at Terri. The expression on her face clearly said, "I want you out of here so you two don't kill each other." Linda rose from the table. Steve didn't look at her. She walked away.

In just the time they had been sitting with Steve, the bar had suddenly become crowded. She found herself being jostled around, while making her way to the bar.

Oh, why did they have to run into Steve? If she had harbored any hope about them working things out, it had just been dashed to pieces. He looked more infuriated with her now than he had at her apartment. Of course, she hadn't been exactly pleasant to him, either.

Tears pricked the back of her eyes. Angrily, she brushed her hand over her face. She would *not* cry. She hadn't cried in years, and refused to start now. The last time, she was ten. Her father had just beaten her severely. Elizabeth had blamed her for something — she couldn't even remember what. But what she did remember, quite clearly, was Elizabeth standing in the corner of the doorway peering in, a slight smile on her face, as her father hit her. It was so severe, Linda's whole body hurt, bruises on top of bruises. Suddenly, she couldn't stand the fact that Elizabeth hovered in the doorway, untouched, while she lay in a crumbled heap of pain at her father's feet. She screamed at the top of her lungs, "Get out of here! I can't stand to look at you!"

Her father grabbed her wrist roughly at that, and wrenched her around to slap her hard in the face. Linda heard a crack and a pop, followed by an agonizing sensation shooting through her shoulder and arm. It quite literally took her breath. She screamed, tears filling her eyes, blurring her vision.

She would discover later that her father had jerked her shoulder out of its socket, breaking the bone in two places. He then slapped her again, and promptly walked away, leaving Linda whimpering and sobbing on the floor. It would be almost an hour before they took her to the hospital, and only then because she wouldn't – couldn't — stop screaming.

Linda couldn't remember much of that hour. Time and shock blurred most of the memory. But she remembered Elizabeth clearly. As

Linda watched her through tear-blurred eyes, Elizabeth laughed. The entire hour. Linda could do nothing but lie on the floor and bawl.

That was the day she swore she would never cry again.

Now, standing in line at the bar, she wondered why the thought of what had passed between her and Steve would cause the threat of tears, after all these years. She must be more unstable than even she suspected.

The bartender asked her what she wanted, a welcome interruption from the awful memory. She told him, then let her eyes wander, while he tapped beer into glasses. Behind the bar hung a mirror. She studied her reflection. The dim light darkened her hair to near black, curls cascading down her shoulders, softly framing her face. She hadn't realized how it had grown. She should probably get it cut, she mused. The darkness of her hair sharply contrasted the paleness of her face, making her skin look so smooth and white, she could hardly believe it was hers. She looked almost attractive — just as long as one didn't notice the dark, haunted pools that were now her eyes.

She shrugged. The reflection shrugged back. *Leave it to bar lighting to make anyone look good*, she thought.

Her eyes skimmed over the other faces in the mirror. All young, attractive, all having a good time. In one corner, a blond hunk of a frat boy draped his arm casually over a slim, petite, dark-haired sorority snob next to him. A group of students burst into laughter while a brown-haired, sharp-faced girl with slanted eyes planted herself in the lap of a guy who looked vaguely like a young Ashton Kutcher.

A sudden puff of cigarette smoke clouded her vision. She coughed, waving her hand over her face, and turned away from the straggly-haired, mustached kid who had blown it her way.

Something in the mirror caught the corner of her eye. It took a second to sort out what she was seeing, reflected among the mass of bodies. It was Elizabeth. Elizabeth's face reflected in the corner of the mirror, standing by the door. Watching her.

Watching her.

She jerked around, knocking a beer out of the straggly-haired smoker next to her. The amber liquid sloshed over her green cashmere sweater, a gift from Chad, and one of her favorite pieces of clothing.

The cold liquid against her skin distracted her, and precious seconds were wasted before trying to find Elizabeth again.

The door of the bar stood open, cold wind rustling the hair and clothes of those standing nearby. The smoker said something to her, and tried to grab her arm. Linda wrenched free and pushed her way through the crowd, moving as fast as she could toward the open door.

Was she was back in her dream? Molasses weighing down her limbs, struggling to move while the forces of nature shoved her back, laughing at her efforts ...

Finally, she reached the now-closed door and threw it open. Nothing. She stood on the sidewalk biting her lip in frustration. Groups, couples moved through the night, opening bar doors, stumbling onto the street.

But no solitary figure with pale hair, anywhere.

Another illusion. Linda raked her hand through her hair, pulling her roots, wincing at the pain. How could this keep happening? Would these visions *ever* end?

She turned her head, searching the opposite direction. No one looked even remotely suspicious. If Elizabeth had been there, she had disappeared, again, either down a side street or into a different bar.

A different bar. Maybe Linda really *had* seen her. Maybe Linda hadn't been hallucinating, after all.

It was worth a shot. But if she wanted to search all of them, she needed help. And the best people to help her were sitting in Rowdy's, waiting for her to bring them their beer.

Linda hesitated. She really didn't want to ask for their help. But, why else would they be there, except to find Elizabeth?

Of course, neither Steve nor Terri really believed Elizabeth to be alive. Or did they? They were there, after all, scoping out the bars with her. Although they likely assumed Elizabeth existed only in Linda's head.

But what if they found her? If they could, they also might find a rational explanation for what'd been happening to Linda, all this time. A rational, concrete explanation rooted in reality.

That thought tipped the scales. She pushed the door open and made her way back to Steve and Terri.

"Linda, where did you go?" Terri asked. "All the way to the brewery?"

Linda shook her head and sat down.

"And what happened to our beers?" Steve asked, but Terri, who had been studying Linda's face, waved him off.

"What happened?" She leaned forward to peer more closely into Linda's face.

Linda swallowed. "I saw her."

Steve's eyes narrowed. He sat up. "Saw who?"

"Elizabeth."

"In the bar? In this bar?" Terri asked.

"Yes."

Steve's eyes never left her face, but something had changed. Barely perceptible, a sense of alertness had come over his features. He seemed all at once more aloof, more professional, more predatory. "Where?"

Linda told him. She barely finished her sentence before he was up and striding to the front of the bar. Linda hurried to catch up with him.

She felt Terri tug her arm. "Are you sure, Linda? Are you really sure?"

"Yes. Absolutely."

Steve asked Linda to walk him exactly what happened. Linda complied, hoping everyone was having too much fun to pay any attention to her.

After leading Steve and Terri outside, Steve glanced around quickly before disappearing back in the bar. Linda and Terri remained outside.

"I can't believe it," Terri said, briskly rubbing her arms. "Elizabeth is dead. She has to be dead. None of this makes any sense."

Linda didn't answer, just surveyed the street. Despite being outside, the air still reeked of cigarettes. She moved away from the door, stamping her feet to keep warm. Terri wanted to go back inside, but Linda didn't budge. She felt safer out there, anyhow. No one could sneak up on her out in the open.

Eventually, Steve found them again. "I contacted the other surveillance team members," he said. "They're combing the other bars."

Linda nodded and hugged her arms for warmth.

Steve studied her. "You should go back inside. It's cold out here."

Linda shook her head. "I'm fine."

"At least go get your coat."

"Steve, I'm fine."

Steve nodded and looked down. Linda waited, shuffling around. Terri moved closer, crossing her arms.

Finally he raised his head. "Just so you know, I've questioned the bartender and some of the patrons. No one saw anything."

"Does that mean it didn't happen?"

"No, that means no one saw anything."

Linda looked down, fighting the disappointment that was splashing over her like a wave in the ocean. The ocean where Elizabeth drowned. Or came back to life, born into a new existence, where she could quietly torment Linda. Forever and ever ...

Steve shoved his hands in his pocket. "We're still taking this seriously. We're searching the other bars."

Linda didn't answer, just hugged herself tighter.

She felt Terri wrapping her hands around her arm, reassuringly. "You started this you know," Terri said, her voice sharp.

Steve looked taken aback. "Me? Started what? What are you talking about?"

Terri waved her hand over Linda, before tucking it back into Linda's arm. "This. Everything was just fine, until you brought up the ridiculous notion that Elizabeth was alive and killing people."

"I just told her the facts. That's all."

"The facts." Sarcasm dripped from the two words. "What do you know about facts? What facts do you have that Elizabeth is alive?"

"I told Linda ..."

"You told her nothing. No facts. Just suspicions. You scared her half to death. What do you expect?" She tugged on Linda's arm. "Come on, Linda. Let's go home. Unless you still need us, *officer*."

Steve stepped back, his face blank. "No. I know where to reach you if I do." His voice had immediately taken on a professional tone, flat and careful. Revealing nothing, of course.

"Yeah, I bet you do. Let's go."

For the second time in days, Linda allowed Terri to lead her away, like a helpless, unresisting lamb ... a lamb being led to slaughter. She wondered who would end up being slaughtered in this case: the lamb or the butcher.

Mirror Image

CHAPTER 19

Linda rubbed her temples, her hands propping her face up on the library table. Her head throbbed with pain. Next to her, Terri excitedly searched the computer. Linda had tried to look over her shoulder at the screen, but it had made her head hurt worse.

"It's just as I thought. It's exactly as I thought," Terri said. Next to her, the printer hummed and spat articles out.

"What?"

"The time frames. It's exactly as I thought."

Linda sighed and rubbed her temples harder. She wished Terri would be more forthcoming with information, instead of all the cloak-and-dagger stuff. She didn't think she could take much more.

Last night had been particularly bad, her nightmares especially intense and bloody, although she couldn't remember all the details. Struggling through the day had completely drained her, and sitting in the library trying to second guess what Terri had figured out was not helping her state-of-mind.

Terri excitedly muttered under her breath as she busily clicked through the screens. The library smelled dry and dusty, of old books and old knowledge. It reminded her of happier times, curled up on a rainy day, sketching buildings out of books next to Chad. It also made her sleepy. She gave up fighting it and put her head on the table.

"What's wrong with you? Get your head up. This is exciting stuff."

"Then why don't you share it?" Linda said, her voice muffled in her arms.

She heard sheets of paper rustling. Terri's voice, exasperated, floated down to her. "I've been printing all this stuff out so you can look at it."

Linda raised her head and started shifting through the sheets. "Terri, I can't read all this. My head is killing me. Why don't you give me the condensed version?"

Terri leaned over and started rearranging the articles. "Okay. Remember your dream? Let's start with the woman and the baby. She's in the police station begging the police to take her baby, saying she hears voices telling her to hurt it." She leaned over and tapped the article with one perfectly manicured, bright red fingernail. Linda found herself mesmerized by the nail, so long and sharp and red. Like a knife. Linda dragged her eyes away and forced herself to look at the article.

"Then I thought about the girl jumping to her death in your dorm dream. And I remembered there was that one year four girls – not one, but FOUR – committed suicide by jumping from their dorm windows. But the part of your dream where the guy was being chased by two skeletons, that really threw me. Until I remembered this."

Terri paused dramatically. Out came a third article. "Some guy killed his girlfriend and another girl. And before he died, he told one of his friends he heard voices telling him to kill his girlfriend."

Linda stared at the articles, cloudy connections starting to form in her muddled brain. "These all happened the same year, didn't they?" she asked suddenly.

Terri looked surprised. "How did you figure that out so quickly?"

Linda leaned over the sheets. The same year. The year Elizabeth started college. "After the suicides, my father threatened to pull Elizabeth out of the dorm," Linda said, her voice dreamy and unfocused, while she faced the dredged up memories now flowing through her consciousness.

"One of the suicides was Elizabeth's roommate. Did you know that? Elizabeth talked my father into letting her stay, until that guy killed those two girls. Then he yanked her out and put her in her own apartment."

He wanted Elizabeth to move in with Linda, she remembered. No, he had insisted. Said it wasn't safe to live alone as a woman, and he didn't want anything to happen to his little angel. Linda refused. Her father, enraged, told her he wouldn't pay a dime more toward her college degree unless she agreed. Linda dropped out that day, found her job at Bay Mutual after a week, and moved into a smaller apartment before the end of the month.

Terri's voice broke into her thoughts. "I had forgotten about that, with your father. Anyway, though, the stories have other things in common, as well. None of the people involved had any prior history of mental illness themselves or in their families — even the suicides. And one of the girls who committed suicide talked about hearing voices telling her to do terrible things."

Linda went to pick up an article, but her arm moved too slowly, trapped in the underwater sleepiness of her dreams. She could almost feel Elizabeth's eyes watching her, cold and empty, filled with predatory cunning. Oh God, Elizabeth had never left. She was still there. She had always been there. She *would* always be there.

"Linda, what's going on?" Terri grabbed her wrists, which had started to shake uncontrollably. Terri's hands felt searing hot. She was so cold. She swallowed her nausea, fighting to get herself under control. "It's Elizabeth."

Terri snapped her head around. "What? Where? Do you see her again?"

Linda shook her head, barely able to speak. "No, no. Just ... She's here. Just not here."

Terri's eyes narrowed. "Linda, you aren't making any sense."

Swallowing another bout of nausea, Linda took a deep breath. "Elizabeth. She, she wasn't ... She isn't normal."

Terri spoke very slowly. "Okay. So she isn't normal. What is that supposed to mean?"

Shaking her head, Linda couldn't say it. What she had thought, what she had started to suspect about Elizabeth completely overwhelmed her. She felt like she was drowning in strange, bitter-tasting knowledge that somehow made so much sense. "It's insane. I know it is."

"What?"

"What I think Elizabeth is."

Terri shook her arm. "What? What do you think Elizabeth is? How can you think Elizabeth is anything? She's dead. Dead people can't be anything — other than dead."

Linda's lips felt so cold, so stiff, she could barely form the words. "I'm not sure I believe that anymore."

Terri stared at her and squeezed her hand. "You think Elizabeth is alive."

"No. Not really. Not in the traditional sense anyway."

Terri looked at the ceiling. She seemed to be choosing her words carefully. "I know you've been under a great deal of strain lately, thinking you've seen Elizabeth and all."

Linda snatched back her hand. "Don't patronize me. I know *exactly* what I sound like. I *know* it sounds insane. I told you it did. Don't act like I'm some raving lunatic who has no idea how I sound."

"All right. I'm sorry. I'm on your side here." Terri held up her hands. "Why don't you tell me what you're trying to get at?"

Linda took a deep breath. "Maybe Elizabeth wasn't human. Maybe she was a ..." She trailed off, unable to finish the thought, knowing how foolish it sounded, even to her.

"A what?" Terri prompted. "Come on here. You have to help me."

"A devil," Linda blurted out. "Or a demon."

Terri sat back in her chair. "A devil."

Oddly enough, now that she had said it, the gray, dreamlike confusion that had swamped her seemed to lighten, allowing her to focus more. "Well, more likely a demon. You know. A succubus or something."

"A succubus?"

"Yeah. You know, female demons who seduce men so they can suck out their life force."

"I know what a succubus is. The *legend*, that is."

Linda continued as if Terri hadn't interrupted her, her voice speeding up. She suddenly needed everything out – every word – and they tumbled out of her as if she had just finally unblocked the opening of a dam. "And maybe *that's* why all these terrible things happened to people around her. Remember her job after college? She worked for Mannifred Corporation — you know, the big clothing distributor? And they had a huge turnover during the year and a half she worked there. Tons of people quit. I remember reading about jobs opening up there practically every week. And Mannifred is supposed to be good to their employees."

"Okay, for the sake of argument, let's say Elizabeth *was* a demon. What then? She's gone now. How can what she was – whatever that was — and what's going on now have any connection?"

"But that's just it. She's not gone. I think she's just in a different form. Her spiritual form."

"And her spiritual form is doing ALL this?"

"Yes. No. I mean, what's probably happening is she's haunting different people, causing them to do those terrible things. Think … possession. Sort of like what she's been doing to me."

Terri studied Elizabeth. "You think Elizabeth is haunting you? Possessing you??"

"It would explain so much," Linda sat back and sighed. "It would also mean I'm not going crazy, that there is an explanation. I agree it's not very logical, but it *would* explain what's been happening to me."

"Have you seen a doctor?"

Linda rubbed her face. "No. I keep meaning to, but I keep forgetting to make the call."

"You probably should do that. The doctor might also be able to give you an explanation."

"I know, I know. Maybe my blackouts are from something physical. But what about the dreams? And the fact that there is someone wandering around this city who looks exactly like her? Silver eyes and all?"

"I told you before, maybe it's just someone who looks like her. You know, a doppelganger."

"But what about these?" Linda flung her arm at the copies of articles lying across the table. "Look at what happened to all these people who have one major thing in common: they all came into contact with her."

"Could be a coincidence, you know. Just because she had contact with those people doesn't mean anything," Terri said, rather unconvincingly.

Linda arched her eyebrows.

Terri sighed. "Oh, all right. You have a point. While Elizabeth was alive, she was vindictive and manipulative. And maybe she *did* have something to do with those people going crazy. That still doesn't mean she is — or ever was — a demon."

"But look at the control she had over people! And how cruel she was."

"There are plenty of cruel, controlling people in the world who aren't demons. Maybe there's a more logical explanation. Consider the suicides. Maybe Elizabeth stole their boyfriends or something. She was good at that, although Lord knows why that would make them jump out of a window to their deaths. I would think it would make them want to push their boyfriends out, instead. Or Elizabeth."

"You know," Linda said, only half-listening to Terri. "Maybe Elizabeth wasn't a demon but something else. A changeling? You know, the old legends. The fairies would steal a human baby and leave one of their own in its place. And the human parents would be forced to rear the baby as their own, although the changeling was evil and would ultimately destroy them."

"I don't know. I agree that there may be something to all this, but humans are plenty evil on their own."

A short, squat man wearing thick glasses and holding a book glared at them from one of the aisles. Terri shrugged and rolled her eyes at Linda. Linda half-smiled back.

The library was huge. Its cavernous ceiling strung with huge fluorescent lights seemed to dwarf everyone in it. Across the room, a spiral staircase led the way to the second floor. Despite the warm, reassuring smell of old books, Linda never felt entirely comfortable in this particular library. It was too big, too impersonal, not at all cozy the way a library should be.

An older woman slowly, painfully, dragged her way up the staircase. Linda wondered why she didn't take the elevator.

"Maybe what Elizabeth was is something so old, so ancient, you only hear about it in myths and legends," Linda said. "Like the stories of the original mermaids. They were thought to be evil because they lured sailors to their death. And what about Sirens? They did the same thing — sang beautiful songs to the sailors, who would jump overboard and be killed. Both of those stories would explain Elizabeth's fascination with the sea."

"Linda, those are myths, legends, stories. They're not real."

"But look how long those stories have survived. Some of them are thousands of years old. Why have they lasted so long?"

"I don't know. Why does anything last a long time? It certainly doesn't mean they're real."

"Or the story of Lillith. Do you remember Lillith?"

Terri sighed. "No, I don't know who you're talking about."

"I learned about her in my feminist literature class. It's a Jewish legend. She was the woman God created before Eve. But she refused to be submissive to Adam. She left Eden, and God created Eve out of Adam's rib bone so Eve would be submissive to him. And Lillith supposedly became the mother of demons and succubi. Succubi."

"These murders ... Linda ..."

"You know, she might not even pick those men," Linda said. "They may pick her. They're attracted to her, want a little fun, take her home and wham. That's the end."

"But succubi don't stab their partners. They have intercourse with them and suck up their energy."

"I know, I know. It's not perfect. But the basic premise works. Don't these descriptions fit Elizabeth? How can you account for the fact that she could always – always — seduce any man, any time she wanted?"

Terri paused and ran her hand through her hair. "Look, it doesn't matter what my personal experiences or feelings are about Elizabeth. I'm really not buying this 'Elizabeth as a demon' thing. What if we look at this another way? Maybe those old legends were based in some form of reality. And that reality could be that there are some who just have an uncanny affect on men — women just like Elizabeth. *Humans* like Elizabeth."

Linda moved the articles around the table. "I just don't believe it, Terri. I don't think Elizabeth was human. She never felt 'right' to me. Not even when we were kids. Not that I was ever close to Peter or the twins, but they at least always felt *human* to me. Elizabeth never did." Linda frowned. "Tell the truth, Terri. Did she ever feel *right* to you?"

"I saw her grow up and age like a human," Terri said flatly. "She got sick like a human. And, for all intents and purposes, she died. Just like a human."

Linda sat back in her chair. "That's not answering the question. I know you know what I'm talking about."

Terri leaned forward. "Linda, Elizabeth is dead. If she were alive, well maybe then your theory would make more sense. It's not that I think Elizabeth isn't capable of committing these murders; if she were alive I think she'd be the prime suspect. But she's dead."

"They never found her body."

Terri made a face at her. "You and I both know that doesn't mean anything."

"Maybe it's like I said before. She's still doing it — she's just in a different form."

Terri shook her head. "I don't know. I really, really don't know anything anymore."

"But it makes so much sense once you think about it! Didn't Sherlock Holmes say when you remove all the probable solutions, what's left is the impossible? Or something like that?"

Terri rolled her eyes. "I suppose it's fitting you quote a fictional character to back up your position."

Linda shrugged. "Whatever it takes."

CHAPTER 20

Lost in her nightmare, Linda again found herself approaching the bed where the hapless victim lay.

Would it never end?

While she floated above the bed, something seemed different, but she couldn't immediately figure out what. The man lay on sheets smooth and white, the sheets stark against his dark body. White.

He turned to look at her, his brown eyes wide and terrified. Suddenly, she realized with a shock that the man wasn't dead yet.

"Here, let me help you," she tried to say, but the words stuck in her throat. She noticed movement on the bed, and watched a swarm of ants marching across his body. She recoiled, not wanting to touch him or the insects. But his smooth, untouched body beckoned her, and she realized this might be her only chance to stop the murders.

Leaning over the bed, she tried to reach the knots, wanting to undo them. But the man became agitated, cowering away from her.

She tried to speak, to comfort him, but again, the words refused to come. She tried once more to move her hands toward the knots to untie them, but a glimpse of silver caught her eye, and she looked down.

She held a knife in her hand.

She stared at it. A long, thin knife, too big to cut the knots with any degree of finesse, but she could still try. She raised the knife to bring it toward the knots, but suddenly, her hand was no longer in her control. While she was a bit fascinated by what was happening – this game of puppeteer – she quickly became horrified, as her arm, completely on its own accord, began slashing the helpless man on the bed.

Blood splashed everywhere. The man thrashed in his bonds, trying to scream, but released only a thick gurgle. The ants danced and writhed on the bed. She tried to stop, but couldn't. She kept stabbing, and tearing, and killing.

The next thing she knew, her whole body convulsed, and she found herself back on her own bed, a scream gushing from her mouth. Her sweat-soaked body trembled. For a second, she lay still, listening to her own harsh, raspy breathing, desperately trying to pull herself back to the present.

Christ, her dreams were becoming far too realistic. She could even *smell* the blood, sweetly metallic, like the time she found Chad in his bathroom dying in a pool of his own. His red blood had stained the white tile, the way the blood in Linda's dream had stained the white sheets.

She reached over to turn on the light. *Enough*, she thought. Her hand slipped as she fumbled for the light. Sweat seemed to be oozing out of her every pore, despite the coolness of her apartment. She finally managed to snap the light on.

Red.

It was *everywhere.*

For a moment, she really thought she would faint. Her dream roared through her head: the terrible bed, the dying man, unable to control the killing knife.

Blood – not sweat – dripped from her hands. Her sheets, soaked in red. She sprang out of bed, shoving the bloody sheets away from her body, trying with all her might not to scream. She heard whimpering, as she raced to the bathroom, pulling the sticky nightgown off her body. It must be Felix, hiding, terrified, the smell of blood so thick, so coppery in the air.

She twisted the knobs of the faucet and plunged her hands into the icy water. The coldness made her gasp, bringing her back to reality. She stared at herself in the mirror and realized it was herself: she was the one whimpering. Red smudges decorated her face. She looked like a deranged clown. Blood streaked her entire body. She could even see it in her hair.

Where had it all come from?

The man from her dream raised his head in her subconscious, and smiled at her. She groaned and turned to get in the shower.

Running the shower as hot as she could stand it, she soaped up her hair and body, and during the process, discovered the source of the blood. Her arm had been cut, up near her shoulder, sometime during the night. A deep gash, nearly two inches long, stung from the soap and water.

Relief.

She was so overwhelmed with relief, it seemed to fill her, so sudden and sharp, she almost cried. Her body went limp, and she sagged against the cool shower wall. It was *her* blood. Only hers.

She became aware of the pain that was now pulsating around the wound, mixed with the stinging sensation of the soap. Blood continued to pour from it, and when she pressed a washcloth to it, she marveled at how fast it turned red.

This was quite a wound. How had she managed to cut herself so deeply? Maybe she had been sleepwalking again. She shook her head. She didn't care how she got it — only that the blood was her own.

It took some time to clean herself up, all the while trying to stop the bleeding. She couldn't get all the blood off, but she decided she'd take another shower before work, when she had gotten some of her strength back. At least most of it was gone.

She got out, dried herself and found some gauze to wrap around the area of the wound. She pulled it as tight as she possibly could, the pain sharp and intense. Finally, the wound felt contained. Harmless, even. She dressed in clean sweatpants and shirt, tore the sheets from the bed, and bundled of them up with her nightgown and used towels. She grabbed laundry soap and quarters, and carried the whole mess to the laundry room.

After starting the load, she went back up to her apartment and began cleaning. She washed the spots of blood from the floor, then scrubbed the bathroom. She refused to think about anything except making her apartment shine. After she finished the bathroom, she tackled the kitchen, then the living room. When she pulled the vacuum cleaner out of the closet, she finally paused to look at the time. Too early to vacuum. She'd wake the neighbors. Besides, it was time to get ready for work.

Linda took another shower and dressed. She made a pot of very strong coffee and drank it while putting on her make-up. The thought of food twisted her stomach, so she didn't even try to eat. She took several aspirin, and then, after a moment's thought, stuffed the bottle in her purse. It never hurt to be prepared.

Her desk, nearly groaning under the weight of the work piled on top of it, greeted her. In all its mundaneness, it was the most welcome sight in the world to her, at that moment.

Several cups of coffee later, she found herself staring at a mostly empty desk with the day only half over. She needed to slow down; otherwise, she would have nothing to do this afternoon.

"You sure got a lot done today," Carla said. "You're like a madwoman, or something."

Indeed. She was exactly like a madwoman, pursued by demons who wore her sister's face. She smiled at Carla.

Carla asked if she wanted to get some lunch. Linda almost declined, until she thought of spending her lunch hour alone.

She managed to choke down half of a ham and cheese sandwich and a cup of cream of broccoli soup while listening to Carla's chatter. Her stomach churned violently. She better watch it with the coffee, or she'd end up sick.

The afternoon crawled by. She stared at the computer and her arm ached. Absentmindedly rubbing it, she felt the bandage.

"Damn," she muttered. It felt damp. She pulled up her sleeve to look at it, and the gauze was bright red.

"Shit," she said, and headed for the bathroom. The wound had opened up again and she had nothing to change the dressing. Maybe she could find something in the first aid kit.

She was aware of the moist feeling of the cut. She could smell the blood as it oozed from the bandage. Then, her whole body felt wet and sticky, as if she were covered in blood … again.

She started retching just as she reached the bathroom door. She shoved it open, stumbled into the first stall, and barely made it to her knees before what was left of the ham and cheese sandwich, soup and coffee shot out of her mouth.

Acid burned her throat. Her face felt like it was on fire. She held her head, pressing her icy hands against her cheeks. How could her hands be so cold when her head felt so hot?

The world seemed to spin, completely out of focus. She closed her eyes, her stomach weakly shuddering. All her thoughts, all her memories, everything she had spent the day trying desperately not to think about, filled her mind all at once. Her head spun, and all she wanted at that moment was to die, right there on the tile floor in the bathroom of Bay Mutual.

She groaned and forced her eyes open. She lay in a fetal position curled around the base of the toilet. The cold floor felt refreshing against her face. She could feel the painful rush of blood through her temples. The monster in her head roared in its agony. Slowly, she pulled herself to a sitting position. Her stomach continued to weakly churn, but she could bear that. Her head, however, was a different story.

She flushed the toilet and dragged herself over to the sink. She splashed cold water on her face and rinsed out her mouth. Maybe now she could take some aspirin. Otherwise she wouldn't be able to drive home.

And she had to go home. Immediately.

Carla came in as she dried her face with a paper towel. "Oh, my God," she gasped. "Linda, are you okay?"

Linda glanced at herself in the mirror. Her make-up was all but gone, and the dark circles looked like deep, black bruises beneath her eyes. The rest of her face was stark white.

She tried to smile, and winced as a new pain shot across her temple. "I threw up."

"You're going home," Carla said.

Linda nodded. Carla left to get her purse and coat. Linda leaned against the counter and tried unsuccessfully to massage her temples.

Carla returned, coat and purse in hand, trailed by Rachel. Rachel took one look at her and insisted on driving her home.

"I'm fine, I'm fine," Linda said, terrified that she would be stranded in her apartment without her car.

"You're not fine. You look like you're going to fall over any second." Rachel stepped forward and tried to feel Linda's forehead.

Linda stepped back. "Really, I'm fine. I just need to go home and rest." She found her aspirin and swallowed several tablets. Her stomach rolled over again, threatening to heave, her body convulsed, but she managed to keep the pills down. She washed her mouth out with water and put her coat on.

"I'm not arguing that. I just don't think you should be driving."

"I can drive just fine."

"Really, it's no problem driving you home."

Linda put her hands against her temples. "Rachel, I'll be fine. Just let me go home."

Rachel finally gave in. "Okay, okay. You probably have that flu that's going around. Stay home and rest for a few days."

How Linda wished it was the flu. "Probably," she agreed, and headed out to her car.

It took ten minutes of sitting in her parked car before she felt comfortable driving. Her head still hurt, but at least the aspirin took the edge off the pain.

She needed to think. Needed her head to be clear.

Her bedroom. That was where she had first noticed her clothes and books rearranged. The day Terri came over. She would start there.

Even though she had no idea what she was searching for, she somehow knew she would find *something*. And that's exactly what she planned to do – she'd find it, no matter how long it took.

***

As it turned out, it didn't take long at all. Shoved far back in the closet, hidden by various papers and clothing, she found a small, blood-stained bundle.

Pulling it out, she stared at it. A white sheet or blanket decorated with dark splashes of dried blood had been wrapped around various items.

She sat for a long time before she could bring herself to unwrap the gruesome package. It was almost like opening a Christmas present … except this one, *she* knew she didn't want.

The knife fell out first. It lay on the carpet, winking evilly at her, the surface dull and streaked. Swallowing hard, she carefully moved it aside. She'd look at it later.

Next she found a white blond wig, a pair of white scuffed shoes, a balled-up pair of white nylons, a contact case, and some saline solution.

The contact case puzzled her the most. She didn't wear contacts. She didn't even know how to put them in. Why would she have contacts in her closet? She had no recollection of buying them.

For that matter, she had no recollection of buying any of those items, or hiding them in her closet. She studied the odd collection on the floor. What did it mean? What was she missing?

Her eyes fell on the white sheet. Actually, now that she had unwrapped it, it looked less like a sheet and more like a dress. She picked it up and shook out the folds. Indeed, it was a dress. In fact, she had seen this exact dress before. Elizabeth had one very much like it.

Elizabeth.

She swallowed hard and picked up the wig. That white blond hair, in a very similar style to Elizabeth's.

And the contacts?

Her fingers trembled so much, she could barely unbutton her blouse.

I could never look like Elizabeth, her mind kept saying over and over again. We don't look anything alike. She's small and delicate.

You've lost a lot of weight, a little voice said. *A lot of weight. Maybe you're not as small as she was, but you're definitely as thin. And delicate.*

Her complexion. She was so pale. And fragile.

You haven't been looking at yourself in the mirror lately, the voice answered. *All those nights of broken sleep have done their damage. You're as fair now as she was. Not to mention what light foundation can do for one's complexion.*

I don't have light foundation.

Yes you do, the voice said. *Remember. You accidentally bought the wrong shade just a few months ago. If you recall, it was right after Elizabeth's death.*

Oh, my God.

I don't think God can help you now.

Somehow she managed to get out of her clothes. The white dress, stiff from the blood, seemed to mock her. She could smell the tangy, slightly metallic scent of blood mixed with something else … something deep and rich with musky undertones. Linda breathed it in.

Elizabeth's perfume.

The blood made the dress stick together in places, and when she tugged it apart, it made a slight tearing noise. She pulled it over her head. Stiff as it was, it still fit her body perfectly — molding it, engulfing it like an amoeba devouring its prey.

She picked up the nylons, but couldn't bear to put them on. That same dark rich scent clung to them, too, and she dropped them quickly.

Scooping up the wig, saline solution and contact case, she headed for the bathroom.

The bright light hurt her eyes and she squinted against it. Her head began pounding again, so she took some more aspirin from the medicine cabinet, all without meeting her own eyes in the mirror.

Pulling her hair back, Linda put the wig on. The blond hair fell softly across her face, caressing her cheek. Her hands moved automatically, like she had done this many times before.

Last, the contact case. She opened it and slipped the contacts into her eyes. No fuss, no thinking. She blinked several times, waiting for the contacts to settle, staring at the counter. The blond hair swung just slightly inside her peripheral vision.

Her hands shook. She gripped the edge of the sink tightly, willing herself to raise her head. She needed to see, had to see, what would be looking back at her in the mirror.

Slowly, inch by agonizing inch, she raised her chin. *It will be nothing,* she told herself. *I look nothing like Elizabeth, even with the wig and contacts. My bone structure is completely different. My complexion is completely different. My face is completely different.*

She raised her head and met her eyes in the mirror. They stared back at her, silvery gray. Her gaze locked on them, frozen, staring, her mind screaming while her mouth hung slack and loose.

She was looking at the mirror image of her sister.

CHAPTER 21 — ELIZABETH

When Elizabeth was sixteen, Linda tried to kill her.

It had all started in Linda's junior year, when Elizabeth became a freshman. Linda didn't mind the first two years of high school so much, but that third year, everything had started to fall apart. That was also when Elizabeth had started wielding her power over men like a wickedly sharp dagger.

Elizabeth seduced everyone — seniors, sophomores, the captain of the football team, even married teachers. No man was safe from her deadly siren. She especially liked to target boys dating girls she wanted to hurt.

Linda, quickly realizing Elizabeth's intention, stopped showing any interest at all in the opposite sex. She didn't want to attract Elizabeth's attention. That worked for a while, at least until Linda's senior year.

One afternoon, while in the living room watching television with a couple of her brothers, Elizabeth slid next to Linda on the couch.

"Who's taking you to the winter dance?" she asked, her voice purring out the words.

Linda never let her eyes leave the television screen. "No one."

Elizabeth leaned closer. "But there must be someone — special."

The canned laughter from the television jarred Linda. Mike laughed with the show. "There's no one," she said.

"I don't believe that," Elizabeth said. "There must be someone you like. It isn't, well —"

Linda finally turned her head to look at Elizabeth. Her sister's face was close to her, so close she could feel Elizabeth's sour breath on her cheek. She could see Elizabeth's smooth complexion, the pores so tiny they were practically invisible. There was no acne to speak of. Her nose flared slightly as she breathed. Elizabeth was breathing way too hard for doing nothing. The light glinted off her white teeth, her mouth open as she sucked in breath. Linda began to feel like a rabbit, faced with the jaws of death, those jaws panting with the excitement, the taste of the kill.

Although her eyes remained a clear gray, Linda could see the silver flash hungrily in their depths. Linda wondered if Elizabeth really did want to eat her.

"Why must there be someone I like? Are you trying to say I'm not normal?"

"Shhh," shushed a couple of her brothers.

Elizabeth's lips curled into a smile. She had such tiny, even teeth, so very white and just slightly pointed. Her thoughts flashed back to the first time Elizabeth had gone to the dentist. The dentist had been surprised looking into Elizabeth's mouth.

"Human teeth normally aren't that pointed," he said. "But it isn't totally uncommon," he added hastily, seeing the look on their mother's face.

Linda had the distinct impression that wasn't the truth; he had simply said that to appease their mother. He had also talked about her having a few extra teeth. He said normally he would pull them, but they fit so nicely in her mouth he didn't think it necessary.

"Of course, you're normal," Elizabeth said, yanking Linda out of the past. "That's why I'm wondering who you like. I can't believe there isn't someone. Why don't you tell me who, dear sister?"

Linda winced, as she always did when Elizabeth said that. "I'm afraid I have to disappoint you, Elizabeth. Frankly, I'm not interested in high school boys. They're too immature for me." She smiled sweetly at Elizabeth.

The smile never left Elizabeth's face, but her eyes grew colder, the gleam of silver brighter still. "Too immature you say. We'll see about that." Elizabeth slipped off the couch and left the room.

A commercial was on, the music loud and jarring. Mike turned to her. "What did you say to Elizabeth?"

"Nothing."

Mike glared at her. "It must have been something or she wouldn't have left like that."

"It was nothing. Just girl talk," Linda got up and left the room.

"I don't believe you," Mike called out. Linda ignored him.

Unfortunately for Linda, there was someone she liked — Steve Anderson. Along with being in several classes together, they had been lab partners during their junior year.

At first, Linda had trouble talking to him, he was so cute. But, gradually conversation began to flow between them as they realized they shared quite a few things in common. Linda wanted nothing more than to date him, but she knew it could never be. Elizabeth would see to that.

Even that knowledge, and watching Elizabeth steal boy after boy, couldn't dim her feelings. If anything, it made them worse. At night, she would wake from dreams half-remembered, her chest filled with such longing it was almost unbearable. The fact that Steve never dated anyone, and at times seemed to reciprocate her feelings only made the situation worse. But she could do nothing except struggle against it. She had no other choice.

Until the day Steve asked her out the week after the winter dance. Steve had talked to her about it, almost like he was working his way up to asking her to it, but she had pooh-poohed the whole idea of high school dances in general and he hadn't breathed a word.

He didn't really ask her on a date — more of a study session. He had hinted about that before, but she always refused to give him a straight answer.

He came up to her while she stood by her locker. "That history exam is going to be a killer."

Linda dumped her books in her bag and slammed her locker shut. "I know. I'm going to be spending my entire weekend studying."

"Why don't we do it together?" he suggested, staring at the floor. Linda bit her lip, wondering how she should respond.

"We could quiz each other. Then, maybe, Saturday night we could take a break and get something to eat or go see a movie or something. You know it isn't good to study all the time. We'll need a break." He spoke very fast, the words tumbling out, breathless.

Linda remained silent. Steve raised his head and looked at her, his dark emerald green eyes staring into hers. Her breath caught in her throat when she looked into their depths and saw the emotions and confusions swirling in them. He was so beautiful. Why wasn't he dating anyone? Why did he put her through this agony? Part of her bubbled over with joy. Maybe he really did like her. The other part of her drowned in despair — even if he did, it wouldn't last long. Not before Elizabeth would get her claws into him.

She stood there, biting her lip, indecision slicing through her like a white-hot knife. He watched her for a few seconds before turning away. "It was just a suggestion," he said, misinterpreting her silence, her indecision. "It's no big deal."

He started to walk away, but she cried out his name in a strangled voice. He turned back, but didn't look at her, his eyes focusing on something behind her.

"Hello, Elizabeth," he said.

Linda whirled around, her insides empty, as if every organ had fallen to the ground. Elizabeth stood halfway down the hall in the doorway of a classroom, one hip resting against the wall, a male teacher draped over her, practically drooling. She took no notice of him, her clear gray eyes studying Linda and Steve instead.

"Why, hello, Steve. Hello, Linda," she said in a very bright voice.

Linda turned away without answering. She swung her bag over her shoulder and headed down the hall.

She had only shared that incident with Terri. Terri, who had already lost a boyfriend of almost three years to Elizabeth the previous month. Terri, whose only crime had been her friendship with Linda. Elizabeth had taken her time with Terri's boyfriend, drawing out the seduction, giving Terri opportunity after opportunity to try to win him back. When Terri failed, which, of course was inevitable, it sweetened Elizabeth's victory all the more.

"So she saw the two of you," Terri rubbed her chin with one graceful finger.

"Yes." Linda's misery filled the one word.

"But you aren't dating him. So maybe she won't bother. Just try to leave him alone for a few days."

"I don't think it matters. After all, she asked if there was anyone I liked. And if she thinks I like Steve, well, even if I'm not dating him she'll probably go after him."

They spoke in low voices, almost whispers. They were in the cafeteria eating lunch, surrounded by the indistinct, echoing voices of the other students milling around.

They had to be careful. Elizabeth had this uncanny way of knowing things she shouldn't. She also had most of the males she ever came across under her thumb. It didn't take a brain surgeon to figure out the rest.

Terri sighed. "I don't know, Linda. Elizabeth hasn't really been focused on you a whole lot since starting high school. Not the way she used to. Maybe she's found bigger and better people to torment."

Linda shook her head. Elizabeth had been her nemesis her entire life. She couldn't believe Elizabeth would decide to leave her alone at a crucial time like the present.

Linda was right.

That Saturday night, so long ago, while she studied in her bedroom, she heard the doorbell ring. Next, she heard the squeak of the door as it opened, and the low mutter of her family greeting their guest.

She lifted her head to listen. The person at the door could be there for one of her brothers – as opposed to yet another poor, unsuspecting wimp there to date Elizabeth. But somehow, Linda doubted it.

Her mother called her name. At first, Linda ignored her. She had a curious reluctance to go down and see whoever it was at the door. Her mother called her name a second time, adding that her father wanted to see her. Linda slid off the bed, opened the door to the bedroom and slunk out.

Words and phrases became clearer as she descended to the living room. Through the din of her family, one voice in particular stood out: male, oddly familiar, but not one of her family member's. At first, she could only see the living room, spread out in front of her like a movie set, and her family, all curiously still, standing uncomfortably like actors unfamiliar with the script. Elizabeth faced away from Linda, her long, white-blond hair hanging straight down the center of her back. She wore black, which made her hair look even more unearthly than usual.

Elizabeth blocked the door, so Linda didn't get a clear view of the visitor until she was almost at the bottom of the staircase. Then, Elizabeth tossed her head slightly, the rope of hair swinging against her back, and as if her movement flipped some invisible switch, the rest of the family came alive. They began talking, moving, awkwardly and jerky, like wind-up toys being released on the floor.

Elizabeth turned her head, and Linda could see her profile: the pale white skin, the fragile bone structure. "Oh, there you are, Linda." She took a step to her right, almost pirouetting, to face her.

Linda's eyes landed on the person at the door. His head was bent, dark hair thick with soft waves. Linda gulped, trying to steady herself, forcing away the emotions that threatened to reveal her. The man raised his head, his dark green eyes locking with hers.

Steve.

"Hello, Linda," he said, and dropped his eyes again, almost immediately. Clearly uncomfortable, Linda watched as he switched his weight from one foot to the other.

Elizabeth, her smile brilliant, beamed at both of them. A silver sheen sparkled in her eyes, and she waited. But Linda, long-schooled in manners relating to Elizabeth, merely nodded her head at both of them, her face a mask of neutrality.

Elizabeth's smile slipped a notch.

"Isn't this your friend, Linda?" she asked, her light voice, outwardly friendly, hid the sharp core of ice Linda knew was there.

"Yes, we're in several classes together," Linda said, her voice cool. "In fact, we have a big exam on Monday. I hope you're ready," she addressed Steve.

Steve smiled at her, a ghost of his usual warm smile. "Can't study all the time."

Linda barely managed to smile back, her own lacking the same warmth Steve's had. "Well, I still have a lot to do. You guys have fun." She turned to go back upstairs, ignoring her family who had watched the entire exchange in silence.

Over the next two weeks, Elizabeth and Steve dated several times.

For Linda, those two weeks were pure hell. Not only did she have to suffer the agony of watching someone she had liked for so long date her sister, but she also had to be constantly aware of how she presented herself – she dared not show any visible emotion. Elizabeth watched her closely, looking for a chink in her armor, a sign of weakness, but Linda remained passive, neutral.

Inside, she wanted to scream.

Steve tried to approach her, talk to her, on several occasions, but Linda would quickly walk away. She sat as far away from him as possible in their shared classes. She was afraid if she let her guard down, even a little, her emotions would burst out of her so violently that she'd never get herself under control again.

And if that happened, there was no telling what Elizabeth would do to Steve.

Linda didn't even talk to Terri about her heartbreak. She didn't have to, since Terri had gone through the exact same ordeal herself. Terri understood: the more emotion Linda showed, the longer Elizabeth would draw this out. That understanding – that knowing – is why when Terri first saw Steve and Elizabeth together, she said nothing. She simply squeezed her friend's arm, once. That squeeze almost became Linda's undoing. She shut her eyes and breathed deeply to keep from screaming, or bursting into tears.

Once she got herself back under control, she was grateful Terri had done it. "You're not alone," the squeeze seemed to say. "We'll get through this together." The blackness growing inside Linda dimmed, ever so slightly, like a tiny flash of light winking companionably in the darkness.

Three weeks after their first date, Elizabeth appeared to have lost interest in Steve. Linda was in the kitchen, and despite herself, was morbidly interested in Elizabeth's new conquest, who was picking her up that night. The new date had rung the doorbell a few minutes before, and the bright chiming sound relaxed the knot inside her. The relief was so sudden it felt almost painful, like the loosening of a leg cramp biting into muscle. She had no idea how tense her insides had been since Elizabeth had honed in on Steve until that very moment.

While Elizabeth introduced her new date to the males in the family, the doorbell rang again. Linda heard a pause, then the squeak as the door opened. "Why, hello, Steve," Elizabeth's light voice floated back to the kitchen. "Whatever are you doing here?"

Linda pushed open the kitchen door just in time to see Steve falter. All the blood drained from his face, making him look almost ghostly in the harsh living room light.

"I thought we had a date," he said, through lips clenched and white.

Elizabeth laughed softly. "I'm sorry, Steve. I thought I made it clear to you that I didn't want to see you again."

The blood rushed back then, staining his cheeks with a hot, red flame. Steve was embarrassed, Linda saw, and angry. In the same moment, she knew that Elizabeth had lied, that she hadn't told Steve a thing, but had orchestrated this moment so she could hurt Steve, and so Linda could witness his humiliation.

"You never ... could I talk to you for a second? Alone?" he asked, a hint of anger in his voice.

Elizabeth laughed again. "Whatever for?" She started to push past him, but he grasped her arm.

"Elizabeth."

She stopped dead, freezing in mid-stride, her head snapping down to fixate on his hand. Slowly, she raised her head, and in the harsh yellow light, her eyes glinted sliver.

"Let go of me," she said, her voice like ice crystals shattering on the sidewalk. Her eyes shone silver — cold and deadly, like daggers.

Immediately the men in Linda's family leaped to Elizabeth's defense.

"Hands off," Peter said loudly.

"Get away from her." Mark stood.

"You creep!" Mike also stood and started toward Steve.

Her father didn't shout. Instead, his voice dropped to a whisper, and that whisper cut across the cries of her brothers like a whip. "Let go of Elizabeth and leave this house at once."

Steve dropped Elizabeth's arm as if it had burned him. Perhaps he heard the violence in her father's voice, and sensed the cold danger crouched behind the civilized veneer. Without another word, Steve turned and strode off into the darkness.

Her father and brothers immediately surrounded Elizabeth, cooing over her, petting her, stroking her, but Linda had had enough. She turned and ran to her bedroom.

She didn't come out for the rest of the night. Instead she feasted on her anger, the black hatred rising within her. "How dare Elizabeth do that?" Linda repeated quietly, over and over. "How dare she?"

She slept little, burning with a blackness she barely recognized, her entire body tense, her nerves tingling. In the morning, she stole down to breakfast, hoping no one would notice her, or better yet, that everyone was still asleep.

The house was quiet and still — perhaps the morning would go her way after all. Although she lacked an appetite, she toasted two slices of bread. A big glass of orange juice completed her meal.

The warm, rosy light outside slanted through the window, making the kitchen feel golden and cheery. She picked at her breakfast, knowing it would be wise to finish quickly and escape back to her room, but the coziness of the kitchen, albeit illusionary, made her comfortable and lazy, and she dawdled. She had time, she reasoned. It was early, on a Sunday morning. It would take some time for the rest of her family to wake up.

She used to do this in her younger years, too: get up early to sit in the kitchen and fantasize. She would pretend that soon, her family would get up, and they would all have pancakes, together, for breakfast. Later, they'd go to the zoo, or have a picnic, like other families. And her father would smile — a real smile — one without any violence at all, lurking behind it.

Linda sighed and drank her juice. Pretending was useless — a complete waste of time. It didn't do anyone any good. If she didn't get that at this point in her life, she never would.

The kitchen door softly opened, with barely a whisper even, but it shattered the warm, golden silence of the morning more completely than an explosion ever could. Elizabeth stood in the doorway. "Good morning, Linda." Her lips parted slightly to reveal her sharp, white teeth.

Linda glared at her, the black emotions that had started to simmer down rushing back to a boiling mass inside her.

Elizabeth glided lazily across the kitchen, her white-blond hair a shimmering, straight mass against the deep blue of her bathrobe. No trace of sleep lurked anywhere on her face. But then, Elizabeth never looked sleepy. You could stand by her bed and shake her out of a deep sleep, and as soon as her eyes opened, she would look — and BE — completely awake. It just wasn't natural.

It just wasn't human.

Elizabeth opened the refrigerator and took out the juice. "You're up awfully early. Didn't you sleep well, dear?" She picked up a glass and poured some juice into it, all the while smiling directly at Linda. Her eyes had started to take on that all-too-familiar silver sheen. Elizabeth's eyes changed colors often, especially when she seemed to be feeling particularly pleased with herself. The rest of the family was careful never to mention it.

Linda gritted her teeth, refusing to acknowledge her sister. She picked up her orange juice and tried to swallow a mouthful, but the cool liquid refused to move past the lump in her throat. She put the glass down.

Elizabeth continued, smiling almost pleasantly at Linda, her eyes growing brighter and more silver with each passing moment. "Cat got your tongue?"

"Why do you care?"

Elizabeth pretended to look taken aback. "Why, dear, how could you ask such a thing of me? Of course I care, very deeply in fact." She tried to look hurt, but couldn't quite pull it off, a smug expression skulking on her face.

"I decided to get up early. I have homework I need to do. That's all."

"Of course. It was silly of me to think you might be upset about Steve, wasn't it? I mean, you don't even like him, do you?"

"We're friends," Linda said through lips stiff and cold.

Elizabeth nodded. "Of course."

She put the juice away, moving gracefully around the island to sit at the table. She blinked her silver eyes at Linda while she daintily sipped her orange juice, like a high society British lady or a Southern Belle of old, graciously sharing her time and space with one who was not an equal … one who should be honored by her sacrifice.

"You shouldn't have treated him the way you did," Linda said at last. "Even though he's just a friend, I don't like seeing him hurt. You treated him with such disrespect."

Elizabeth shrugged. "It wasn't my fault he misunderstood. I told him we were through, and he showed up on our doorstep. What was I supposed to do?" She raised one white hand, letting it flutter back down in a helpless gesture.

Suddenly, Linda couldn't stand it anymore — the pretense, the games. She leaned across the table, catching a whiff of the strange rotting smell, like sour milk, she had come to associate with Elizabeth.

"Okay, *dear*. Let's drop the crap. No one else is around, and you and I both know no one in the family would believe anything bad I ever said about you. So let's really talk."

Elizabeth narrowed her gleaming eyes, resembling an extremely content cat. Linda could tell she was enjoying her reaction immensely.

"I really don't know what you're talking about."

"Oh, yes, you do, you heartless bitch."

Elizabeth's face darkened slightly. A dart of pleasure shot through Linda's insides. "Really Linda," Elizabeth said coolly. "There's no need to call me names. That's very childish, you know."

"Childish? How childish is it to steal other girls' boyfriends because you're mad at them, or want to get back at them? Oh, no, that's not childish at all."

"It's not my fault those stupid boys are more attracted to me than their silly little girlfriends."

"And you do everything in your power to make sure they are."

"I have no idea what you're talking about," Elizabeth said, her gaze now as sharp as a silver knife.

Linda sat back against her chair. "Don't treat me like I'm one of the idiot men blinded by your – whatever the hell it is. Or like our imbecile father and brothers."

A low whistle escaped from Elizabeth, as if she had been holding her breath and had just let it out. She smiled at Linda, but it was a true smile — nothing predatory about it. "That's what I like about you, Linda. That's what I've always liked. My charms don't work on you. They never have."

"Excuse me?" Linda said, stunned by Elizabeth's words, Elizabeth's smile.

But Elizabeth continued her musing as though she hadn't heard a word. "It's like that with most women. They can see through it. But the difference between them and you is that I can still frighten other women. That means I still have control of them, too. But not you. You're not like anyone else. I've never been able to fool you, at least not for very long. You're such a challenge, sis."

"Why do you treat me so terribly?" Linda asked, her words rushing out. She hadn't meant to ask that question; it had practically asked itself.

"You must know that answer already, dear sister. Why, I've practically spelled it out for you."

Linda shook her head, a deep horror swelling inside her.

Elizabeth leaned forward fractionally, her hair spilling down and covering her cheek slightly, her luminous eyes boring deep into Linda's. "Everyone has an Achilles' heel, dear Linda. What's yours?"

It took a moment for Linda to comprehend the words mixing with the black emotions now swirling within her. But when she did, it was like a piece of ember falling into a pool of gasoline. Her insides burst into a hot, violent flame.

"You bitch! All these years, you've been trying to *break* me," Linda said evenly, deadly, each spoken word stoking the flame. Before she was even conscious of moving, she was on her feet, her chair falling behind her in a clatter, her hands clawing for Elizabeth's throat. They both fell to the floor, tangled in Elizabeth's chair.

True to the violence that permeated her house, the violence dealt out by her father and brothers, she reacted exactly as she had been taught. Without thinking, without planning, she found herself straddling Elizabeth, Elizabeth still in the chair, her hands clasped around that lovely white throat, squeezing, squeezing, squeezing ...

Squeezing the life out of her sister.

Elizabeth's eyes had darkened to a steely silver, the color of old nickels, and she actually looked *scared*. For the first time in Linda's life, she had the upper hand over Elizabeth. The pleasure that rushed through her body burned almost as brightly as the flames of violence, so sweet it was painful. She couldn't even feel Elizabeth ineffectually beating her chest, scratching the hands that were locked tight around her throat.

Her face was turning a blotchy red: her eyes the color of tarnished silver, darkened pools reflecting nothing. Linda smiled. Her sister was finally *ugly*.

Inside her, flames burned hot and wild. Mixed emotions permeated her every cell. She was surprised by how much she was enjoying this. She had never reacted with violence before, ever, and a part of her was terrified.

You're just like your father, a voice whispered inside her. *You're just like Peter. There's no difference between you and them.*

Her flames of hatred burned away that voice, and any remaining doubts, leaving nothing but clean, white ashes in their place.

In reality, the struggle didn't last long. Maybe a couple minutes, tops. Elizabeth was never *really* in danger of dying. It just felt like an eternity, the two locked together in that twisted embrace, born of pain and nurtured with violence.

Still, the inevitable was bound to happen. Really, Linda should have expected it. Elizabeth would always win, even on an early Sunday morning, while the rest of the family should have still been asleep. Elizabeth's lure, her power, was too strong. Eventually, although it might be longer than Elizabeth cared to wait, eventually the men of the family would save her.

And, like knights in shining armor, they did.

"Stop," a voice screamed from behind. Peter's? So high and feminine, it couldn't be. "Stop! You're killing her!"

Rough hands grabbed her arms, painfully squeezing her wrists. "Stop, Linda. Stop this minute," Peter commanded in her ear, his breath hot on her cheek. Now he sounded like Peter.

He tore her fingers away from Elizabeth's throat, breaking two of them in the process. In the moment, she felt no pain. Emotions were running far too high, and she felt far too violent to feel anything besides the awful realization that Peter was stopping her.

"Let go of me, you asshole!" Linda hissed, her jaws clenched. She was afraid if she loosened her mouth enough to speak, she would start screaming.

Peter's eyes gleamed, bright with hate. He jerked her toward him, his fingernails digging so deep into her wrist that blood ran down her arms. "Asshole?" He pushed his face so close to hers, she nearly gagged on his sour morning breath. "You bitch. Always picking on poor Elizabeth. Elizabeth who never does anything to you. You think I'm an asshole now? You ain't seen nothing yet." He shoved her to the ground, straddled her and locked his fingers around her throat.

Linda's vision swam. She had no doubt he firmly intended to kill her, and that he might very well succeed. She kicked and jerked, trying to dislodge his grip, but he just squeezed harder. She couldn't catch her breath. The pain in her ribs and throat was excruciating, worse than any of the beatings she had ever received. Out of the corner of her eye, she saw Elizabeth sit up, one hand daintily holding her throat, her eyes bright silver once more, sharp as silver bullets boring into her brain. Above her, Peter's face bobbed like an ugly red balloon.

Everything was getting hazy. Bright pinpoints of light flashed across her eyes, filling the room with a sort of macabre fireworks. A dull roaring sound, like waves, filled her ears. Linda clawed at Peter's hands to no avail. In her desperation, she raked her fingers across Peter's eyes. He screamed, both in surprise and in pain, and the pressure on her neck eased.

"You fucking bitch," Peter yelled, one hand clamped around her neck while the other covered his eyes. Only able to strangle her with his one hand now, Linda wormed one of her hands under Peter's, not breaking his hold entirely, but managing to ease it up enough that she could gasp hoarsely for breath.

The air hurt her throat, but the pressure in her chest receded and her vision slowly cleared. She started coughing, agony burning her throat. Peter's hand clamped down a little more tightly, making her coughing more wretched.

Then, from out of nowhere, a force barreled into Peter, flattening him, knocking over another kitchen chair in the process. Peter groaned, lying next to Linda, and the shape that had taken him down began pummeling him. "You almost killed her! Is that what you were trying to do? Are you trying to kill her?" Chad yelled.

Linda endured a new coughing fit, as the air rushed into her lungs, painful air. She tasted blood in her mouth. She turned on her side, away from Chad and Peter. Her hands fluttered near her neck, too sore to touch but wanting to anyway. She barely heard Chad beating on Peter next to her; it was all she could do, to just lie there and breathe.

Gentle movement caught her eye, white material drifting across her vision like a giant moth fluttering its wings. Elizabeth bent over her, her white nightgown and bathrobe settling into place, her eyes still silver, bright and pointed. Linda could see the faint bruises already forming on the pale white complexion of her neck.

Their eyes locked: Elizabeth's unnatural silver with Linda's ordinary brown. Then Elizabeth smiled, that same predatory smile, the sharp teeth merely a suggestion in her tiny, well-shaped mouth. Linda closed her eyes, too exhausted to battle Elizabeth any longer.

The kitchen door hit the wall with a bang, thrown open so hard Linda could hear the windowpanes shake. "What in God's name is going on down here?" A quiet, deadly voice shot through the chaos, stilling it as effectively as a bomb.

Linda scrambled to sit up. Beside her, Chad immediately rolled off Peter, banging the kitchen chair, the noise loud in the sudden silence. Peter forced himself to stand.

Her father filled the doorway. Not a big man by any standards, he nevertheless seemed gigantic, huge, a monster looming over them. Their mother stood, peeking around him, not much smaller than him physically, but somehow, completely dwarfed in comparison.

Her mother let out a short scream, but her father didn't seem to notice. Slowly his head turned, studying the scene in the kitchen, his eyes cold and hard, his brain ticking off each detail in his slow, methodical way. His eyes fell on Linda, studying her, dissecting her, leaving her feeling naked and worthless.

"Someone tell me, this instant, what this is all about," His voice dropped a notch.

Peter collected himself first. "Linda was trying to kill Elizabeth," he said, his voice thick and hoarse.

Her father's gaze swept over Linda, then Elizabeth.

"Is this true?" he asked Elizabeth softly, without a trace of the menace he reserved for his other children.

Linda closed her eyes briefly, the pain still throbbing in her throat and chest. She opened them a moment later, and risked a quick look at Elizabeth. Once her father saw her neck, her bruises — well, it wasn't worth thinking about too deeply. She knew without a doubt that what Peter had done to her would be like a trip to the beach compared to the thrashing she would receive at the hands of her father.

But somehow, Elizabeth's bathrobe was fastened securely, all the way up to her neck. Linda blinked. When did that happen? She hadn't had time to do that since their father had barged in, and Linda was sure she had seen it open, her bruises showing, just moments before. But now they had completely disappeared under the folds of the blue bathrobe, as if by magic.

Her eyes had faded to a silvery gray. She looked stricken. "No, Father," she said, her voice laced with reluctant sorrow, like she really hated parting with her information. "Peter misunderstood. It was very sweet for him to come to my rescue, but it wasn't necessary. Linda and I were simply having a sisterly chat."

It was all Linda could do to keep her mouth from falling open in amazement. Elizabeth lying to protect her? It was too shocking to be believed, especially when Elizabeth had Linda exactly where she wanted. Elizabeth had been tormenting her sister for her entire life. Why stop now?

Her father's eyes crawled over to Linda. "Is that true?"

Linda gulped and nodded. She didn't trust herself to speak.

Peter stared wildly at Elizabeth, at Linda, at their father. "No, no, that's *not* true. She was trying to kill Elizabeth! I saw it. I *stopped* it. I stopped it!" He buried his head in his hands.

"I'm so sorry you misunderstood, Peter." Elizabeth said softly.

Peter looked up. "But what about the bruises on your neck?" He turned to his father. "She has bruises on her neck."

Elizabeth shook her head. "I'm fine. Really. Thank you, Peter, for your help." She swept past her parents and left the kitchen. Peter buried his head in his hands again, incredulous.

Her father studied them. The silence stretched out, thin and brittle. Finally, he turned to their mother. "Shouldn't you be making breakfast?"

Linda slowly got to her feet, completely mystified at Elizabeth's behavior. And, just like so many other secrets in the Rossini household, Linda never did find out why Elizabeth did what she did.

Her throat would hurt her for the next week, forcing her to eat soft foods, like jello and ice cream. The blackish-purple bruises that looked suspiciously like handprints took longer to heal — she wore scarves or turtlenecks for nearly a month, not trusting make-up to fully cover them.

Elizabeth, on the other hand, showed not a single mark from the incident.

***

A few days later, at school, Steve approached Linda at her locker. "Can we talk?"

Linda shoved her books in her locker. "There's nothing to talk about."

"So, you're going to ignore me now?"

Linda slammed the door shut. "You made your choice. Live with it." She turned and walked away.

CHAPTER 22

"I killed those men."

The chant ran through Linda's head over and over, mantra-like. "I killed those men. I killed those men. Not in self-defense. Not in revenge. Not even in anger. But in cold, cold, icy cold blood."

"I stalked those men. I offered them sex. And I killed them."

"And I can't even remember it."

Huddled in the corner of the bathroom, hands wrapped around her knees, pressing them into her chest, she buried her head in her arms, the mantra within her brain pulsing. Pulling her arms and legs even closer to her body, she tried to disappear into a little ball, into nothingness, wishing she could simply erase her entire existence.

She must be mad.

That was the only explanation. All those years of repressing her feelings, her emotions, of lying about the beatings and the abuse, the pretending that Elizabeth wasn't who or *what* she really was. She had gone over the edge somewhere along the way, and now, she couldn't even remember when it had happened.

Still, people often suffered from breakdowns. Many mentally cracked, but didn't turn into pathological serial killers. What on earth had gone wrong with her? How could she have so completely lost her morals, her sense of right and wrong? Sure, she couldn't remember any of it. But that wasn't much of an excuse. She had read somewhere that even when someone was hypnotized, he could not be forced to do things that would prove unethical for them. So, deep down, she must not be *incapable* of murder.

Murder.

Murderer. Oh God… that was what she had become.

You must turn yourself in, a different voice, a sadder voice, said within her. Linda pulled her legs in tighter. Every muscle in her body screamed in protest, but she relished the pain, enjoyed it. Her head roared in agony.

Turn herself in? Yes, she should do that. She killed those men. She needed help. She couldn't allow herself to be free, on the streets, to kill again. Especially when she was completely helpless to control it. Or prevent it.

For the first time she looked, really looked, into the dark face of insanity. It terrified her. It smiled at her, teeth gleaming white, fangs barely visible against the red mouth. A clown's face with make-up streaked and smeared, cheeks and lips decorated with dried blood. And always, always smiling. Always revealing the sharp, bloody teeth that would devour her.

She jerked to her feet. Cramped muscles nearly toppled her, but she caught herself against the bathroom sink and steadied herself. Anything, anything was better than that face, than going insane in this apartment alone. A hospital would be better ... even a prison hospital. Somewhere with drugs, lots of drugs that would blur all that tortured her mind – that would make it go away.

The wig had slid down, covering her ear. Some of her own dark hair spilled out, shifting her appearance as if she were undergoing some strange metamorphosis ... a horrible movie-monster insect ... half Linda, half Elizabeth. She snatched the wig off her head and removed the contacts.

Relief rushed over her when she recognized her own face in the mirror again. She never thought she would take so much comfort in seeing her own unremarkable face.

But now what? Should she turn herself in right now, tonight, or wait for morning? Should she talk to someone first?

Terri? No, Terri would tell her there must be a "reasonable" explanation for all of it. She started to laugh. A reasonable explanation. Sure, Linda had lost her mind. Reasonable.

She grabbed the bathroom sink again to steady herself, her laughter beginning to sound shrill. She forced herself to stop. If she went into hysterics now, she'd never get herself under control again.

Though it took some gulping and hiccupping, she managed to swallow her hysteria. She mopped her face, damp with tears and sweat, and splashed cold water on her skin.

No, Terri wouldn't do. She wouldn't take Linda seriously. Nor could she go to Chad. It would only upset and confuse him. She'd spend half the night comforting him.

The police station. She should go to the police station. Turn herself in. That moment. While she still had some control of herself.

The thought, however, of that gray corridor, cement walls, and concrete floors repelled her. She'd be stuck there long enough. Why go one night sooner than she had to?

To stop herself from killing more innocent men.

All right, the sad voice inside her said. *You go to the police station. Who will you talk to?*

She thought about that. Who *would* she talk to? A stranger? A disinterested police officer used to dealing with drunks, prostitutes and druggies? Like he'd believe her. He'd probably send her to detox, not jail.

Steve. She could go to Steve.

No. Not Steve.

Why not? the voice asked. *He's perfect. He's a policeman. He would listen to you objectively. He could turn you in tomorrow, quietly and without a fuss. And he could …*

She tried to stop the thought before it could finish itself, but it formed anyway:

Protect himself. Protect himself from you, Linda. Linda, the mad killer.

Still she hesitated. She didn't want to see him. The memory of their last encounter was still fresh, still raw in her mind. She couldn't see him. She couldn't.

Who else? the voice asked.

Who else indeed?

She couldn't go to Steve, even if she felt compelled to. She didn't even know where he lived.

That wasn't true. She did. Chad's old apartment building.

She sighed. She left the bathroom and collected the rest of the Elizabeth costume. At the last minute, she decided to bring the light foundation, too. She went back in the bathroom and started rooting through the bottom cabinet drawer.

Buried behind her sanitary napkins and extra toilet paper she discovered the foundation. But it wasn't alone. Next to it sat a half-full bottle of Obsession. The perfume Elizabeth used to wear. Yet again, her memory failed her. When did she purchase it? Like a missing piece to

an awful puzzle, she had just found the source of her perfume hallucinations.

***

"I'm coming, I'm coming."

Linda could barely hear the voice, muffled and fuzzy, through the
door. She continued to bang on the wood anyway. She stood there,
pounding on his door, seemingly unable to make herself stop.

"All right, all right already," the voice on the other side of the door
said. She heard the dead bolt unlatch, and the door opened with a
squeak.

Steve stood in front of her, eyes half closed, sleep thick and heavy
on him, hair sticking up in little tuffs. He wore dark blue pajama bottoms and a light blue robe. The robe gaped, obviously just tossed on as
he made his way to the door.

He opened his eyes wider. "Linda?" he said, his voice hoarse with
sleep and questions. "What are you doing here?"

"I have to talk to you. Not out here. Please, let me in."

He held the door open and stepped aside. Linda hurried in, brushing past him so suddenly she nearly knocked him over. She apologized
distractedly.

He shut the door and belted his robe. "It's okay. What are you
doing here? It's the middle of the night. Oh my God." His eyes fell to
her clothes.

Linda glanced down, following his gaze. Her coat hung open. She
hadn't bothered to zip it up when she left the apartment. Underneath
she still wore the white dress. The blood-stained white dress.

"It's nothing."

"What do you mean it's nothing? Let me call the doctor." He started toward the phone.

She moved to intercept him. "No, no you don't understand. It's not
me. The blood isn't mine. It's dried. See, it's dried." She held it out to
him. He stared at it but made no move to touch it.

"What do you mean it's dried? Why are you wearing it? What's
going on?"

"I'm sorry, Steve. I really am. I didn't mean to dump this on you.
But I didn't know where else to turn."

Steve blinked several times. He rubbed his face and ran his hand through his hair.

"Hold it a second," he said. "I think I'm beginning to wake up. Let's sit down and you can start at the beginning. Tell me exactly what's going on here."

Linda nodded. He tilted his head, looked like he was going to say something, changed his mind, and moved toward the living room.

Like her apartment, the kitchen, dining and living area was combined into one room. A cluster containing a couch, two chairs and a large, flat screen television took up one corner of the large room. Steve led the way to the couch and sat down.

Linda perched herself on the edge of one of the chairs. She didn't want to sit, felt too emotional, too frazzled to sit. She stared at her hands, still clutching the paper bag. The bag with all the evidence. The bag that proved she was a murderer.

Steve waited.

Linda took a deep breath, then looked into his face. She said, in the most calm and rational voice that she could muster, "I killed those men."

Steve's face went blank. "Excuse me?"

"The men. The ones tied up in the beds. The ones everyone is talking about. The ones you think Elizabeth killed. I did it. I'm the killer."

Steve sat back on the couch. He looked at Linda. His face contorted into several different expressions, some at the same time. Finally, he took a deep breath. "Maybe you better start from the beginning."

She nodded, dropping her gaze, watching her fingers clench and unclench the bag, as if they were separate from her, under no control of her own. She spoke quietly, yet her voice seemed to scream in the emptiness of the apartment. She heard the howling of the wind against the window.

Beginning from when she had seen Elizabeth outside her apartment, she omitted nothing, letting the entire tale pour out of her.

Steve sat silently during her story, moving only to fetch a bottle of whisky and two glasses from the kitchen, handing her one and draining the other. Even after she finished her confession, he remained quiet, staring straight in front of him, his face drawn and pinched.

Linda, more exhausted than she ever felt in her life, studied a crack that ran down the wall, stretching from the ceiling to one of the windows.

Finally, he spoke. "What about the stuff you found?"

Linda's fingers clenched again, entirely of their own volition. Forcing herself to relax, she carried the bag to the coffee table. "It's here." She turned the bag over and dumped the contents out.

The collection of items crashed together in a jumble, loud in the stillness of the apartment. Only the wig remained silent, sliding off the table like a slinky toy.

Steve leaned forward but didn't touch anything. "So, you're trying to tell me that all this – you've used all this to look like Elizabeth?"

She nodded, not trusting herself to speak.

He reached for the whiskey and poured another shot in the glass. "The family resemblance isn't that strong."

"Does that mean you don't believe me?" Her voice started to rise.

"That's not what I said."

"Then, what?"

He lifted his hands helplessly. "This is all a little, well, far-fetched."

Abruptly, she stood up and snatched the items off the table. "Where is your bathroom?"

"Linda, what are you …"

Her voice dropped several notches, cutting through his protests louder than a scream. "I said, 'where is your bathroom?'"

Swallowing the last of his drink, he pointed. She turned and walked away.

Once in the bathroom she made up her face, slipped in the contacts and adjusted the wig. Her eyes, silvery gray now, gleamed back at her, so cold, so cruel. The eyes of a killer. She quickly dropped her gaze, took a deep breath, removed her coat and opened the door.

Steve was standing in the middle of the living room, holding his empty glass. He tried to say something, but then she stepped into the light.

At first he could do nothing. He simply stared at her, his expression frozen in a mixture of fascination and horror. He took two steps backward and fell against the couch. His mouth opened and closed several times before any words managed to escape. "Dear God."

"I told you." Linda moved closer. Steve pressed himself against the back of the couch.

"Don't come any closer."

Linda stopped. "Now, do you believe me?"

He covered his face with his hands. "Just take it off. Take it off."

Linda turned and went back to the bathroom. When she emerged, she found Steve pouring more whiskey into the glass. He glanced at her and winced. "Can't you put something else on?"

Linda looked down at herself. She still wore the stained white dress. "No, I didn't bring anything else."

Steve grunted. "Follow me." He led her to his bedroom. Except for the unmade bed, Linda could hardly believe how neat it was. After rummaging through his closet, he finally threw a pair of sweatpants and a Packer sweatshirt to her.

"Put those on. I can't look at that dress another second." He pushed past her and shut the bedroom door behind him.

The clothes were hopelessly big, but at least the pants had a drawstring. Even though she knew the clothes to be clean, they still smelled like him, the faint tang of his aftershave, the clean scent of his soap. She closed her eyes and breathed deeply, imagining for a second she was there in his bedroom under different circumstances. Romance instead of murder. She opened her eyes and shook her head. Those kinds of thoughts would get her nowhere. She left the room.

Steve sat on the couch, the bottle and the glass still in front of him on the coffee table. He said nothing. Linda seated herself on the chair and watched him, waiting.

Finally he spoke, although his eyes never reached Linda's. "I admit that I thought you knew something about this case. I'll even go so far as to say that I was beginning to suspect you knew who the killer was, and were protecting her for whatever reason. But I never, never thought it was you." Finally his eyes found Linda's. "I'm still not convinced."

"But the evidence ..."

"Doesn't all add up," he interrupted. "Besides you're not acting like the profile. This killer is cold-blooded, ruthless. It takes a certain kind of person to plunge a knife into someone. They don't, well, they don't act the way you do."

Linda shook her head. "It's the only answer that makes any sense."

Steve ran his hand through his hair. "Maybe. Maybe not." He sighed and rubbed his face. "Look, I can't think straight anymore. I think we should sort it out in the morning." He paused and studied her. "You probably should stay here tonight. It's the safest place for you. There's clean sheets in the cupboard. Why don't you take the bed? Try to get some sleep."

"Nonsense. I'm the one dumping this on you. The couch is fine. Go to bed." Linda wondered if he meant it was the safest place for her, or for everyone else.

Steve tried to protest, but Linda refused. "Go to bed. I insist."

Finally, he dragged himself up and went into the bedroom. Linda watched him go, before stretching out on the slightly lumpy sofa and adjusting the pillow behind her.

Steve cleared his throat. She sat up to see him standing in the hall, a blanket in one hand and handcuffs in the other. He gestured to the handcuffs, "I'm sorry, I hate to do this ..."

She sat up. "I understand," she said gently, and held her wrists out. He swallowed. "I'll make this as comfortable as possible for you."

Linda nodded. He yanked one of the chairs closer to her and reclined it back. One handcuff clicked over her wrist, the other on the metal part of the recliner. Then, he tossed the blanket to her. "Sleep well."

"Don't let the bed bugs bite." She smiled tiredly at him. He tried to smile back and failed, then turned and disappeared into his bedroom.

She spent the night studying the bumps in the ceiling. Oddly enough, now that she knew and had unburdened herself to someone, much of her hysteria had evaporated. Her fate lay in someone else's hands now. She was no longer in charge of her own destiny. She could do nothing more.

Something resembling peace filled her, relaxed her, and even though she never thought she'd be able to sleep, she finally drifted off, thinking to herself how the *not knowing* had been so much worse. Now that she knew, she could finally be at peace.

***

The light woke her. She blinked several times, confused by her surroundings. Had her living room rearranged itself during the night?

Then, she saw Steve leaning against the wall, the handcuffs in one hand, watching her, and she remembered everything.

Pulling herself into a seated position, she rubbed her face and attempted a smile.

"Good morning," she said, as brightly as she could muster. "Did you sleep well?"

He snorted and walked into the kitchen area. "Do you want coffee? I'm afraid I don't have much for breakfast. There might be a loaf of bread around here somewhere if you want toast."

Linda followed him. "Coffee's fine."

He opened and shut the cupboard, measuring coffee, filling the pot with water. "I'm not one for breakfast. Sorry."

Linda wondered what he was really trying to say. "Fine. I don't think I could eat anything anyway."

He plugged in the coffee maker and flipped the switch. The water gurgled. Steve stopped, put his hands on the counter and leaned forward, head bowed.

"I called Terri," he said, staring at the counter.

Linda leaned against the kitchen table. "Why did you do that?"

"Because I want her to bring you a change of clothes." He turned his head to face her. "I'm taking you in to the station. I have to. You know that."

"I understand." It shocked Linda to see him looking the way he did — unshaven, pale, his eyes blood-shot and weary. "I expected you to take me in last night."

He sighed and ran his hand through his hair. "I'm still not convinced you did it."

Reaching out, she squeezed his shoulder. "I know."

The buzzer sounded, startling them both. Linda jerked her hand away like she had been caught doing something wrong.

Steve muttered something about Terri at the door and brushed past her. Linda stayed in the kitchen, watching the pot fill with coffee, wishing she could have had some before facing Terri.

Once she heard her friend's voice at the door, that wish quickly changed: all she wanted was to simply vanish.

"This is ridiculous." Terri's voice cut across the stillness of the apartment, shredding it into knife-sized pieces that seemed to sink into

Linda's brain, starting yet another headache. "This is the most absurd notion I had ever heard in my entire life. Linda, a killer? Complete and utter nonsense. And you, Steve, of all people, you should know better."

"She came to me." Steve's voice, exhausted but reasonable. "What was I supposed to do?"

"Well, you were the one who started sticking these notions into her head in the first place. You should be ashamed of yourself."

"She's confessed to killing those men. She has what looks like evidence. I have to take her in."

"Ridiculous. I can't even believe we're having this conversation. Where is she? Maybe I can talk some sense into her."

"Here I am," Linda called, turning away from the coffee maker and heading into the living area. Terri stood at the door, coat on, clutching her gloves in one hand. Steve leaned against the wall opposite her, arms crossed. Although he still looked tired, he radiated something else as well, a calmness, a steadiness. Or maybe it was simple resignation.

Terri strode toward Linda. "Finally. There you are. Now maybe we can get to the bottom of this."

Steve met Linda's eyes. "Show her."

Terri whirled around. "Show me what? It won't matter. There isn't anything you can say or do that will change my mind. Linda, you're not a killer. Forget this nonsense. Let me take you home so you can get some sleep."

Linda stepped aside before Terri reached her, not wanting to be touched. "Let me show you something, okay? After that we'll talk."

Terri put her hands on her hips. "We can talk now because there isn't anything you can show me that'll make me change my mind."

"Terri, I really think you need to see this," Steve said. "I think it'll explain a lot."

"And if it doesn't?"

Steve shrugged. "Then you can take Linda home and I won't pursue any of this."

Terri looked at him in surprise. "Promise?"

Steve held up his hand. "Scout's honor."

Terri folded her arms across her chest. "All right then. Show me."

Linda nodded and disappeared into the bathroom. Everything was there, the wig, the dress, the contacts. She quickly changed, and re-emerged as Elizabeth.

Terri stood in the middle of the living room, tapping her foot impatiently and glowering at Steve. But when she saw Linda, she froze.

"Oh, my dear God," she whispered, raising her hands to her face, her eyes wide, disbelieving. She staggered backward, hitting the couch and losing her balance. She toppled sideways, her purse and gloves falling to the floor.

Linda slowly approached her, allowing it to fully sink in.

Terri stared at her from the floor in a tangled heap. "Dear God. Where on earth did you …"

"From my closet," Linda answered, continuing to walk forward relentlessly, as if by convincing Terri, she would finally convince everyone. "It was in my closet. Along with a knife. A bloodstained knife."

"Jesus." Terri squeezed her eyes shut and turned her face away. "Take it off."

"Now you see why I have to bring her in," Steve said, his voice so close to Linda it made her jump. "I don't understand it and I don't believe it, but I have to look into it."

Terri shook her head violently, keeping her eyes tightly shut. Then she seemed to change her mind and straightened up. She opened her eyes and looked at Linda.

"Give me your apartment keys. I'll go get you some clothes." She turned to Steve. "But I'm not buying this for a second, you got that."

Steve smiled faintly. "I know what you mean."

CHAPTER 23

Linda's arrest and booking on the charge of murder passed by in a complete blur.

Handcuffed, she was searched, photographed, and fingerprinted, all without any of it making any type of impact at all on her consciousness. Exhausted, it took all of her energy just to remain awake. Only after changing into the scratchy prison uniform and being thrust into a cell did the enormity of the situation finally sink in.

No way out. That's it. Now that they've got you, they'll throw away the key, the voice inside her said.

At least this will stop the killings, she thought, staring at the bars.

"You killed those people," she said out loud. "Never forget that. You deserve to be in here. You should be punished."

She sighed and laid down on the hard cot, trying to get accustomed to it. The blanket smelled stale, and its harsh roughness scratched her cheek.

It doesn't matter if you get used to it or not, the little voice said. *You should get a lot worse. Like the electric chair.*

But Wisconsin didn't have the death penalty, so the worst she'd get would be life. Could she argue temporary insanity? From the little she had gleaned from court cases on television, she knew temporary insanity didn't always work out so well. Still, at least in her case, it was accurate.

She remained absolutely clueless about what could have possibly happened to short-circuit her brain, causing her to commit the murders. She didn't even like killing spiders. How could it even be possible that she had taken human life? Plus, she hadn't just killed them, randomly. She stalked them first. She had become a predator, when she had always thought of herself as prey.

That line of thinking had to stop. She pressed her hands against her eyes. These were questions she needed to ask a psychiatrist. She wouldn't be able to answer them on her own, ever, and all she was doing was upsetting herself.

Uncovering her eyes, she stared at the gray concrete ceiling, and forced her mind to go blank. She focused on listening to the echoing footsteps, the jangling of keys, an occasional scream, and mutterings from the guards. She breathed in the scents of urine and fear mixed with must — the scent that belonged to rooms never allowed to feel the kiss of fresh air.

The guard banged on the bars. "Lawyer's here." The door made a clanging sound as he unlocked it.

Linda sat up slowly, her mind still lost in a black void of emptiness. No sense of time. No pain. Nothing. She felt so old. Old and dried out. Her life over before it could even properly start. "What do you mean, lawyer's here? I don't have a lawyer."

The door swung open with a creak. "Sure you do and he's waitin' for you. Come on, haven't got all day."

The guard handcuffed her wrists and led her to a small room that contained only a plain wooden table and several chairs. Someone was seated in one of the chairs, head hanging down, thick, dark hair so familiar. When he heard the door open, he looked up eagerly.

"Chad," Linda gasped, and ran to him. He quickly stood up and embraced her, before the guard interjected with "No touching." Chad squeezed her arm briefly before letting go. "I came as soon as I could."

"I know."

They sat down at the table, but not before Chad saw the handcuffs. His face tightened. "Are those really necessary?"

Linda shrugged. "I killed several men. I guess I *should* be considered dangerous."

"You're no killer."

Linda didn't want to argue with him. She changed the subject. "So, why did you tell them you were my lawyer? Wouldn't they let you see me otherwise?"

Chad looked away. "Actually, I found you a lawyer."

"You did? Who?"

He shifted uncomfortably in his chair, his hands twitching at the cuffs of his shirt, revealing the white scar on his wrists. He looked back and smiled at her, a quick, nervous, apologetic smile, before ducking his head.

Linda suddenly had a bad feeling. "Oh, no. You didn't."

Chad reached out to her, then stopped himself, remembering the guard, and placed his hands on the table. "He worked in the D.A.'s office. He has experience, criminal experience."

"No." Linda shook her head. "How could you even think to call him?"

"He is your brother."

Linda leaned forward. "He's your brother, too. That doesn't make him any less of an asshole."

The unlocking of the door stopped them both. Linda leaned back in her chair and tried to look civil. Chad gave her a glowering look. "Be nice," he mouthed. She stuck her tongue out at him.

Peter walked into the room carrying a briefcase, brown hair carefully combed and styled, navy blue pinstriped suit pressed, dotted yellow power tie in place. Yet his clothes hung on him, appearing too large and ill-fitting.

He put the briefcase on the table with a bang and shot Linda a cold look. "You've really done it now."

"Nice to see you too, big brother. I'd give you a hug but, well," she held up her handcuffed hands, "As you can see, I'm a little tied up right now."

Peter's look turned even colder. "Very funny. Jail hasn't made you any less of a comedian, I see. Jurors love comedians. Maybe they'll only give you twenty-five. " He sat at the table and spoke without turning his head. "Chad, you can go now."

Chad stood up, but Linda leaned forward quickly. "I want you to stay."

Peter continued to face Linda. "Lawyer-client confidentiality. Chad, go."

"But I'm the client and it's my confidentiality in question. I want him to stay."

Peter grimaced, but gestured for Chad to sit back down. He then opened his briefcase and started shuffling through papers. "I must say, Linda, this doesn't look good for you. Do you have any idea what you've done to the family? To our parents?"

"Is that what you ask all your clients? If they know what they've done to their families?"

Peter slammed the briefcase closed. "You always were selfish. Always thinking of yourself."

"What does being selfish have to do with being accused of murder?"

"Like I said, you don't think about anyone besides yourself! I mean, my God, Linda. Picking up men and killing them in their beds? Dressing like Elizabeth? What were you thinking?"

Linda pounded her hands against the table. "That's it. I want another lawyer."

Chad started to speak, but Peter interrupted him. "What? You think I can't defend you properly?"

Linda howled. "Defend me? All you've done since you walked into this room is accuse me. You'd probably make a better prosecutor than defense lawyer, in this case."

Chad leaned over the table and put a restraining hand on Peter, before he could react in anger. "Look. I thought we could work this out. We're family. Peter, you've got to know she didn't do this — it's horrible, what they're accusing her of."

Peter fixed his cold gaze on Chad. "I know of no such thing."

"Now I definitely want another lawyer," Linda said, but neither brother was listening to her.

"How can you say that?" Chad asked, his eyes wide with shock. "How can you possibly think that about your own sister?"

"It's *because* she's my sister that I have the doubt. I've seen her capacity for violence."

"What capacity for violence? She's usually fending OFF the violence."

Peter glared at Linda. "She tried to kill Elizabeth. I'd say that shows a capacity for violence."

"You don't know that she tried to kill Elizabeth."

"I walked in on her when she had her hands around Elizabeth's throat. Pretty obvious she was trying to kill her, don't you think?"

"That's stupid. She wasn't trying to kill Elizabeth any more than you were trying to kill her when you did the same. None of us assume that made YOU a murderer."

Peter banged his hand on top of his briefcase. "I'm not the one being accused of anything, either. Not to mention how much proof there is against her."

Chad looked at Linda. "Proof?"

Peter picked up his briefcase. "I can see this is going nowhere. I'll come back after you've had some time to think things over. I don't think you have any idea how grave your situation is." He walked to the door.

Linda leaned back in her chair. "Thanks for all your help, Peter. Maybe you could recommend a *good* lawyer?"

Peter swung around, his face tightening, the hand not holding the briefcase clenched tightly into a fist. Chad stepped forward and touched his arm, but Peter shook him off.

He forced his face to relax. "Considering the predicament you're in, I would be real careful what you say. You can't afford any more enemies. I'll be in touch." He walked back to the door and knocked rapidly. The guard opened it, and he left abruptly.

Chad collapsed into a chair. "I suppose I should have known that would happen."

Linda forced herself to smile. "Oh, Chad. You're such an idealist. A dreamer."

He looked at her sharply. "You sound like Father."

"I didn't mean it in a bad way. There's nothing wrong with being a dreamer or an idealist. You know that."

"Well, I guess there might be, if I do stupid things like this."

"You're only to blame for half of the stupidity. After all, he showed up."

Chad stood and started to pace around the room. "I just really thought this would bring us together. That he would rise to the occasion and try to do the good thing for once. Tragedy is supposed to bring people together."

"Like I said, an idealist."

"I should have thought it through, I guess. I was just so shocked, so scared, so helpless. I wanted to do something to help you and I thought maybe finding you a lawyer would be it."

Linda reached out to touch him, but her handcuffs got in the way. She folded her hands back in her lap. "I don't blame you. It's okay."

He stopped pacing and faced her. "What did Peter mean by all the proof?"

Of course he'd have to ask that. Linda couldn't bear to tell him, couldn't stand to see the confusion and pain swamping in his eyes. Her brother, who had always loved her. And who loved Elizabeth. It would crush him.

She started to frame several answers when the guard opened the door. "Time's up."

Chad looked like he wanted to stay longer, but Linda quickly stood. "Come see me again?"

"Of course."

She tried to give him a reassuring smile, but it felt fake and flat on her face. He smiled back, his eyes mirroring worry and fear.

She turned to go back to her cell.

***

Some time later, although Linda couldn't be sure how much later, being so disconnected from reality, Steve appeared at her cell.

He smiled when he saw her, but it didn't reach beyond his lips. A female guard accompanied him, along with a woman dressed in a white lab coat.

"Just want to run some tests," he said as the guard opened the door. "Take some blood, some urine. Here's the court order."

Linda approached the door and took the paper, but didn't look at it. The guard then waved her back, so the white-coated woman, presumably a lab technician, could enter the cell. The guard closed the door behind the technician. Linda saw she carried a tray table and a small case. She swiftly set up the table and began removing items from the case.

Linda looked questioningly at Steve, who remained standing on the other side of the cell, along with the guard, hands behind his back, his face tired and drawn.

He shrugged. "Standard procedure. Plus, Terri's been kicking up a storm. Put some ideas in people's heads. You should see her." He shook his head a little, an expression of admiration appearing and disappearing on his face so quickly, Linda wondered if she had imagined it. "She's one-hundred percent convinced of your innocence."

The technician bustled around her, drawing the shirt up from her arm, wrapping a tourniquet around her bicep, cleaning the skin with alcohol.

Linda watched her. "It's nice to hear *someone* is convinced of my innocence."

"She's not alone. Others are, too. "

Linda looked at him. "Are you?"

Steve dropped his gaze. "I find it nearly impossible to believe you'd do anything like this. That you'd even be capable. "

Linda nodded. The technician asked her if she wanted to sit down. "Do you faint at the sight of blood?"

In the corner of her eye, Linda saw Steve wince. She shook her head. The technician inserted the needle and began drawing blood.

Linda looked back at Steve. "What ideas does Terri have?"

He smiled slightly. "Let's just wait and see if anything comes of it."

The technician filled up four test tubes with blood before finally pulling the needle out. Linda held the gauze to her skin while flexing her muscle. "Four?"

"Just making sure we have enough."

The technician busied herself at the table. Linda walked up to Steve, standing close enough to almost touch the bars, almost touch him. "What's going on?"

Steve sighed and reached out like he was going to brush her cheek, but instead grasped the bars. "We're doing everything we can. Checking every possible lead."

"Why hasn't Detective What's-Her-Name been here yet? I thought for sure she'd jump at the chance to interrogate me again."

Steve stepped closer to the bars. "She'll be in tomorrow."

They were so close, Linda could feel his breath against her cheek. He leaned his forehead against the bars. "Are you going to be okay?" His eyes reflected a mixture of emotions, and utter turmoil.

Linda nodded, feeling almost dizzy, her own feelings swamping her in confusion. Too much had happened in one day. She had no ability to make sense out the bedlam of voices inside her.

The technician broke the spell. "I need a urine sample."

Steve closed his eyes briefly, then straightened. "Of course." He turned to go, motioning for the guard to stay. "I'll be back tomorrow. Try to get some rest."

Linda nodded. Steve attempted one more smile, then left. Linda listened while his footsteps echoed fainter and fainter, until they dissipated into nothingness.

CHAPTER 24

Back in the house of nightmares, lost in the hallways, surrounded by closed doors and black shadows. This time, she seemed to be descending, moving downward into the bowels of the mansion. Streaks of black stained the walls. Under her feet, the carpet made a squishy sound with each step she took. The light dimmed, turned green and murky. Cracks broke through the walls and ceilings, big chunks crumbling away into nothingness.

She could hear Elizabeth calling her. Louder. "Linda — in here."

Something green and slimy was growing, creeping up the walls. Moss? Maybe seaweed? She couldn't tell. Water ran down the cracks, dripping into the carpet. It even smelled wet. Wet, dank, and salty.

"Linda — in here."

Water splashed onto her shins. Broken pieces of rusted doorknobs and hinges littered the floor. The further she went, the higher the slimy green plant tendrils reached, until finally, they crept across the ceiling, like fingers splayed against a flat surface.

She turned a corner — dead end. She started to turn back, but then caught a glimpse of rusted metal, and realized she had finally found what she had been looking for the entire time.

Elizabeth.

The metal door, eroded to a blackish-red color, stood at the end of the hallway, its handle a huge circle, resembling a steering wheel. It reminded her of a door on a ship. She grasped the wheel. Bits of metal flecked off in her hands. At first it refused to turn, rusted shut, but finally it yielded with a low groan, dissolving in her hands.

She was in a cell then, much like her own in the jail. Except here, water dripped from the walls, and the bars crumbled with rust. She could smell the stench, powerful in its intensity.

A figure stood behind the bars, hidden in the murky glow. Linda stepped forward, straining to see, almost slipping on the green slimy plant that was now the floor.

The figure slowly came forward, the light turning the pale hair green, the face sickly and strained.

Elizabeth.

"You found me, at last." Her voice echoed eerily off the rocks. Linda could hear water dripping. She stepped closer, trying to get a better view of Elizabeth.

Her hair, soaking wet and entangled with seaweed, hung flat against her neck and body. Her face looked bloated, puffy around eyes that appeared greenish-gray, with the slightest hint of silver.

The lips curled in her slightly mocking, sardonic smile. "Go ahead. Gloat. See how far I've fallen?"

Still the same Elizabeth. "What happened to you?" Linda asked.

"I'm being punished."

"Punished? For what?"

She tilted her head. At one time it would have been a coquettish look, but now, it was slightly gruesome. "For failure."

"Failure?"

She turned away. "Drowning myself. Giving up."

"Then, you *are* dead?"

Elizabeth turned again, the mocking smile back, bigger then before. "Oh, yes. Quite dead."

Linda moved forward and clutched the bars of the cell, pieces crumbling to bits in her grasp. "Then why are you haunting me? Why won't you leave me alone?"

"Because you need help."

"Help?" Linda spat the word out. "*You're* trying to help *me*?"

She tilted her head again. "Don't sound so surprised, dear sister. I'm actually quite fond of you, all things considered. In fact, I'll probably be punished even more for bringing you here." She sighed, looking worried. "We don't have much time."

"Who are you?"

Elizabeth smiled. "You know who I am. I'm Elizabeth, your sister."

"No! There's more to this. There's something else going on. I know it. I've always known it!"

Elizabeth approached the bars, her eyes glowing. "What do you think is going on, Linda?"

Linda let go of the bars and backed away. "You're a demon, aren't you? You're Lillith, or a succubus, or … *something*!"

Elizabeth burst out laughing. The sound echoed and bounced off the walls, sounding surprisingly warm and friendly, and very human. "You humans are always wanting to put things into neat little boxes! It's both simpler - and more complicated - than that."

"So what are you?"

Elizabeth looked away. "An experiment." She sighed. "A failed experiment."

"Experiment?"

Elizabeth blew out a mouthful of air. She studied the ceiling. Linda noticed the dripping sound again. Was it getting louder?

"What's your earliest memory of violence?"

Linda stared at her. "What?"

Elizabeth's eyes gleamed. "How old were you when you first remember Father hitting … hurting someone?"

"I don't know, maybe five? What does this have to do with anything? "

Elizabeth smiled slightly. "Actually I think you were a bit older. Seven sound about right?"

"How on earth would you know that?" Linda snapped, getting irritated. "They're *my* memories. And besides, you're younger than me."

Elizabeth's smile widened. "I know because I caused it."

Linda gaped at her. "*You* were the cause? How? WHY? What did you blame me for?"

Elizabeth laughed again. "I'm not talking specifically about *you* getting hit, dear sister. I'm talking about the violence." She stepped forward and grasped the bars. "*All* the violence." She licked her lips, revealing a tiny glimmer of pointed, white teeth.

Linda took another step back. "What are you saying? That Father wouldn't have abused us, would never have hurt us, if you hadn't been born?"

"Ah, now you're catching on! But it's even bigger than that. I'm talking about ALL the violence."

Linda felt her knees begin to buckle. "You're talking about my dreams, aren't you? The suicides. That kid who murdered his girlfriend. The woman and her baby …" Linda's voice trailed off.

Elizabeth smiled, before letting go of the bars and backing up. "I never did a thing. Not one single thing. It's not my fault all that violence, all that anger, all that despair happened *around* me. It's not like I *instigated* it, or anything." She licked her lips again, an almost hungry expression on her face.

"But, you just said you caused it," Linda said. "Why are you talking in riddles?"

Elizabeth cocked her head. "I'm talking in contradictions. When can you both cause something and not do a thing? Just think about it, dear sis."

Linda shook her head. "You're giving me a headache. Why can't you just say what you mean?"

"That's where you're wrong. I always say *exactly* what I mean. It's not my fault you refuse to understand me. But enough of all that. As enjoyable as this little family reunion is, that's not the reason I brought you here. We don't have much time."

Linda stared at her in horror. "Who *are* you?"

Elizabeth began to pace. "I've already said too much. And it's really not important. I brought you here to warn you."

Linda wondered if she had heard right. "Warn me?"

"Yes."

"Me?"

Elizabeth whipped her head around. "Don't be so thick. You're smarter than that." Droplets of water grazed Linda's cheek. But they didn't feel like water, more like acid, burning a hole into her skin. She rubbed her face violently.

Elizabeth saw her and moved closer. "Nothing's wrong with your face."

Her voice, oddly gentle, seemed so out of character for Elizabeth that Linda stopped rubbing her cheek in surprise. The pain stopped. She touched her cheek. "How did you ..."

"Never mind. Things are happening here that are beyond your comprehension. You only need to be concerned with what's happening in your reality, not mine ..." Elizabeth trailed off, lifting her arms up, then letting them fall at her sides. The dripping water was definitely louder now, a booming noise that echoed off the rocks.

"What does that mean?"

Elizabeth began to pace again. "All you need to understand is that I failed."

"Failed? At what?"

"At my mission."

Linda moved closer to the bars. "I don't understand."

Elizabeth sighed. "I failed because I drowned myself."

"Why did you do that?"

Elizabeth stared directly into Linda's eyes. Linda could see the flicker of silver behind them. "Because of you."

Linda took a step back in surprise. "What?"

"You heard me."

"Me? That doesn't make any sense. All you ever did was torment me! And you won, every single time. Dad, Peter, Mark, Mike, even Chad. They all took your side against me."

Elizabeth jumped forward, her face twisted, her breath wheezing. "And you didn't break. Not once. You survived. I *targeted* you, and you didn't break. *You* won."

"What are you talking about? My life is a complete mess! I didn't finish college, I don't have love, I'm estranged from my family, I'm in jail for murder, for God's sake. How can you possibly say I won?"

Elizabeth grasped the bars again, pressing her face against them. Her eyes flashed silver, then immediately shifted back to the weird, grayish-green color. "If I had been successful, you *would* have committed those killings."

The pounding noise swelled to a roar. Water began pouring in from the walls, running down in streams. Linda detected a rotting, salty, brackish scent. The mixture of feelings inside her altered again – a mixture of horror and relief – horror around what might have really happened, relief around what she had just heard.

"You mean I didn't kill those men?"

Elizabeth let go of the bars and backed up. "Your brother's blood calls to me from the ground."

Linda's blood went cold. "Elizabeth, I don't understand."

"Don't you recognize it, Linda? It's from the Bible. Cain and Abel. The first murder. Brother murdering brother. It's the same here, now. Except it's not a body being murdered, but a soul."

Linda shook her head. "I'm so confused. You're talking in circles again."

"*You know who murdered those men.*"

"No I don't."

"You've known all along."

The din of the water almost swallowed Elizabeth's voice. She had to practically shout to be heard.

"My masterpiece. I destroyed a soul. But, then my masterpiece turned around and tried to do that to you. And almost succeeded. That's why I stepped in." Elizabeth smiled her sardonic smile again. "I couldn't let the one person who defeated me be defeated by *my* own creation. My pride, you know. Of course, the murderer was using artificial elements to break down your barriers. Not fair really. I know … funny for me to believe in fairness, huh? "

"Who is the murderer?"

Elizabeth smiled. "You already know."

Linda tried to protest, but Elizabeth held up her hand and turned away. "Stop asking me that. We're almost out of time."

Water was filling the cell. It already covered Linda's ankles. She sloshed forward. "But, wait. I still don't understand *anything*. How did I win?"

Elizabeth kept her back to Linda. "Remember when I threw myself overboard in Massachusetts? That was the first time I tried it. I was sent back and targeted you again. But I failed a second time." Elizabeth spun around, the water now at knee level. "Despair is a terrible thing for me. I know how to instigate it, but I had no idea how to live with it."

Linda tried to say something else, but the noise of the rushing water prevented her. The walls started cracking under its weight. Elizabeth cupped her hands around her mouth and shouted. "You're stronger than you think, Linda. You have the power to turn your life around. It's in you." Their eyes locked for a second, and for the first time in her life, Linda felt a connection with Elizabeth, a bond.

Then the walls broke open, and the water poured in.

A wave swept Elizabeth away, tossing her like a rag doll. Linda tried to turn around but found herself suddenly covered in water, fighting it, drowning in it. She struggled to push to the surface, water filling her nose, her throat. She choked and held her breath. Her hand banged a piece of metal — part of a cell bar. She pushed it away and frantically struggled toward the surface.

The water turned black, thick and sticky, like tar. From somewhere far away, she could hear a voice. "Hurry, Linda. Others are depending on you." It was Elizabeth. Faint, labored, but Elizabeth.

A pair of red, huge eyes, abruptly appeared in front of her. Suddenly, she was rushing toward them, helpless to stop. Then, there was a mouth, open, bright red with rows of teeth. Pointed teeth. Fangs. Rows and rows of fangs ready to devour her, and she was helpless to prevent it. The mouth smiled, opening even wider.

She struggled against the current, refusing to give in, to let herself disappear into that huge maw. "No," she shrieked and flung herself away. Black, sticky water filled her mouth, choking her, strangling her, beating her.

She awoke in her cell, on her cot, gasping for breath and twisted in the scratchy blanket. Sweat poured down her face, and she continued to thrash even though a part of her knew she was safe, knew she was no longer drowning. Somehow, she couldn't stop her limbs from jerking.

"Hey. Easy there. You havin' a fit or something?" She could hear the guard banging against the cell. She sucked in her breath and fought to get herself under control. Her body shook uncontrollably and she fell onto to the floor in a heap.

She could hear the guard talking and shaking her. She sucked in big gulps of air. Slowly, her body stopped shuddering.

"You gonna be okay?" Linda nodded and untangled herself from the blanket. "I came to release you. I'd hate to have to take you to the hospital instead."

Linda stood up. "Release me? What are you talking about?"

"You're free to go."

"What? Why?"

The guard shook her head. "They don't tell me that. All I know is you can go. Sure you're okay?"

Linda nodded, taking deep gulps of air. She could still smell the briny salt water, just a hint now, mixed with the jail's constant stench of urine, vomit and fear.

The guard handed her clothes to her. When she finished dressing, she held the door open and gestured for Linda to step in front of her.

Linda walked down the corridor, followed by the guard, listening to the sharp, slapping sound of her footsteps echoing off the concrete.

Your brother's blood calls to me from the ground.
You know who murdered those men. You've always known.

A mental image of Chad, lying in a heap in his bathroom, covered with his own blood, popped into her head. She could still smell the blood, feel the stickiness from when she had touched him. Other images seethed in her brain, just below the surface, but she couldn't grasp them. Only that picture of Chad.

But, it wasn't Chad. It couldn't be Chad. He couldn't kill anyone. There must be some other reason for those images, something else they had in common.

Blood. The smell of blood. Violence. And despair.

Despair is a terrible thing for me.

The images threatened to boil over in her consciousness.

Terri suddenly appeared at her elbow. "I knew all along you didn't do it," she crowed, taking Linda's arm and leading her to the lobby. Linda immediately felt something inside start to loosen.

"What do you mean?"

"The tests proved it. You didn't do it," a familiar, mocking voice interjected. Linda looked up. Detective Karen Thomas leaned against the wall, arms crossed over her chest, blocking their route to the lobby.

Terri glared at her. "What's wrong with you? Can't you admit when you're wrong?"

Linda squeezed Terri's arm to silence her. "What tests?"

Detective Thomas's eyes shifted from Terri to Linda. "You mean she didn't tell you yet?"

Terri tried to speak, but Linda shook her head and freed her arm. She approached the detective. "I want to hear it from you."

Detective Thomas shrugged. "The wig hair didn't match the hair we found at one of the scenes."

"What about the blood on the dress and the knife?"

Detective Thomas's eyes bored into Linda's. They were such a light blue, they appeared to be almost colorless, like chips of ice. "Apparently, that was your blood."

Linda swallowed. "My blood?"

The detective took a step forward. "Don't even try to tell me you didn't know that. You may have fooled Steve with your innocent act, but I know you're guilty. I don't care what the lab tests or the toxicology report say. You're in it, and you're in it up to your eyeballs."

Linda met her stare. "Then why didn't you interrogate me? You had your chance. I was right there in the cell the whole time."

The detective leaned forward. "You watch yourself. I'm keeping my eye on you." She turned away and marched down the hall.

"Worthless bitch," Terri muttered behind her. Linda turned to face her. "She was my worst adversary this whole time, you know that? As I was trying to build your case. I don't know why it's so stuck in her craw that you're guilty."

"What did she mean, toxicology report?"

Terri reached out to take her arm again. They continued walking into the lobby. "Drugs. Your system was loaded with drugs. Like that date-rape drug, the one that knocks you out and keeps you from remembering what happened. No wonder you had blackouts. Someone's been drugging you."

"Drugs?"

"Yeah. Lots of them. And different kinds, too. The technicians said they weren't a bit surprised that you thought you were having a nervous breakdown. You probably were."

Chad sat on a couch in the lobby, legs crossed, feet twitching rhythmically. When he saw them, he quickly got up and hurried over to give Linda a hug.

Terri stepped back. "The lab guys aren't exactly sure how you ingested so much. I know some was in your milk. I remembered how strange it tasted that day, so I had it tested. It had traces of drugs in it."

Chad squeezed her tighter, murmuring something into her hair. He smelled so comforting to her, a mixture of aftershave and soap. She never wanted him to let go.

Without warning, a face, distorted by rage, screamed at her in her head. So real, she could practically feel spittle land on her cheek.

Look what you did! How could you do such terrible things? You are an evil, evil person.

Linda stumbled, her legs turning to mush under her. Chad caught her gently by the arms. "Easy there."

Terri touched her gently. "You ok? The lab guys said it might take some time for the effects of the drugs to wear off. We need to get you to a doctor."

Black flowers bloomed at the corners of Linda's eyes. A roaring vacuum echoed in her head. "Maybe I should sit down, just for a minute."

Chad gently lowered her to a chair in the waiting room. Terri hovered over her. "Not only should we get you to a doctor, we should also get you some food. When was the last time you ate?"

The clamoring in her ears subsided a little. She tried to remember when she had last eaten something — nothing today, she knew. She couldn't even bear to look at the food presented to her in jail, let alone force herself to eat it. She remembered throwing up part of a ham and cheese sandwich at Bay Mutual yesterday ... God, was it only yesterday? It felt like a lifetime ago.

She smiled weakly at Terri. "You don't want to know."

"You're right. Let's get you to a doctor, then somewhere with food, *good* food."

You evil, evil person.

Linda closed her eyes and shook her head a little, trying to clear the fuzziness – and that voice – that clouded her brain. Chad wrapped his arm around her in a reassuring, protective hug. She looked up at him and struggled to smile.

"Okay, let's go."

CHAPTER 25

The doctor Terri and Chad had found for Linda was a woman with short dark hair, a soft round face and a comforting manner. Terri had the police station call her ahead of time, so when they arrived, she was already waiting for them, filling out paperwork.

She looked up and smiled when they walked in, introducing herself as Dr. Jacobs. "Come on back; everyone else has already gone home." Linda glanced at the clock. Almost six-thirty. Time sure flies when you're stuck behind bars. She smiled bitterly.

Terri and Chad started to walk with her toward the examination room, but Linda stopped them. "I'll be fine."

"You sure?" Terri asked.

Chad said nothing. He simply continued looking worried.

Linda gestured toward the doctor. "I highly doubt she's the one who's been drugging me." When they still didn't look convinced, she sighed loudly. "Don't worry. I'll be back before you know it."

Dr. Jacobs gave her a complete physical, including more blood and urine samples. "I have the toxicology report from the lab, but I'd like to run some of my own tests." She asked Linda a battery of questions, and Linda found herself revealing more of the story than she had intended. But the doctor just listened quietly, her manner warm and friendly, seeming without judgment.

"I don't see any indication of a brain tumor," Dr. Jacobs said, after Linda had poured out her story. "I suspect you're suffering from nervous exhaustion, malnourishment and shock. If your symptoms don't go away after a few weeks, we'll look at running some more tests."

The doctor ordered Linda to rest, eat and drink as much water as possible. "Your body needs to flush out those toxins, and it needs nourishment." She warned that Linda might also suffer from withdrawal symptoms, and wanted to see Linda again in a week.

Leaving the doctor's office, they drove directly to a restaurant, where they coaxed Linda into eating a large bowl of tomato soup, a tuna melt, cottage cheese and a chocolate shake. "No more coffee, at least until your system works these drugs out of your body," said Terri. "You promise me."

Linda nodded, feeling too drained, too exhausted to argue. The dizziness, the fuzziness, still had not gone completely away. Her body felt hollow, empty, and there was a constant buzzing in her ears. She kept dropping things — silverware, napkins — her hands weak and trembling.

Although she knew she had suffered a massive violation — someone had been sneaking into her apartment to drug her and do God-knows-what to her, and she didn't remember a thing — she only faintly comprehended the enormity of the horror.

It was as if she were standing at the brink of a black cesspool filled with rotting corpses and wiggling maggots … and she had this awful feeling, an inkling, that she hadn't even begun to discover how deep it went, or what dreadful things she might find at the bottom.

Chad picked at his own food, watching Linda carefully as she ate a piece of the tuna, her hand shaking slightly. "I think you should stay with me, at least until the drugs are out of your system and you've gained some weight. I don't think you should be alone."

"That's fine," Linda answered. She was in no hurry to return to her apartment — the scene of the crime. "What about Felix?"

"I'll take care of Felix," Terri quickly volunteered. "And, I'll bring you some clothes. I don't want you to worry about anything except getting better."

Ants crawling everywhere, swarming. Kill the ants. Kill the ants. The gray fog descended on Linda, the roaring grew louder, and she pressed her fingers against her temples.

"Are you okay?" Both Terri and Chad said at once.

Linda looked up at them, rubbing her temples. Why ants? What was it always ants? "Will you guys relax? I'm okay. You heard the doctor, I'm probably suffering from withdrawal symptoms."

"We should get you home, and in bed," Chad said.

Linda took her hands away from her head and picked up her fork. "As if I can sleep."

"You'll sleep," Terri said confidently. "Your body is exhausted, and now that the drugs are dissipating, you'll sleep like a baby. Besides, you're safe now."

Safe. Linda examined that word in her head like she would an interesting shell she found on the beach. Knowing what she did now, about everything that had happened to her, and how easily someone could take advantage of her, would she ever feel safe again? Really safe? She shook her head softly. *Safety is an illusion,* she thought to herself. Something we comfort ourselves with so we can get through our days without breaking down ... without losing our minds.

"Eat, Linda," Terri broke into her thoughts. "Just a few more bites and we'll take you home." Linda obediently picked up her fork again.

Although she had finished most of her meal, it did nothing to alleviate the weakness, the hollowness in her body. Her legs trembled as she stumbled to the car, black spots blooming at the corners of her eye again: an ever-present companion who seemed to show up every time she stood.

She couldn't believe how much she had deteriorated physically. Maybe because her entire focus had been on her mental breakdown, she had ignored her body's warning signs, and was now paying the price. Chad helped her into the car, carefully protecting her head so she wouldn't hit it.

Although Terri kept up a determined chatter all the way to Chad's apartment, Linda found herself unable to focus on her words. Instead, she stared out the window into the darkness, jumping at every figure that looked remotely like Elizabeth.

She knew Elizabeth was dead. Elizabeth had told her, herself. But she had also claimed she wasn't the killer.

If it wasn't Elizabeth, then who? Who was dressing up to look like her?

Ah, the question of the hour. Who is the killer? She hadn't a clue.

You know who murdered those men. You've always known.

But, she didn't.

Your brother's blood calls to me from the ground.

From the Bible?

Damn Elizabeth, and her riddles. She never could get a straight answer from her.

Chad pulled into his garage and parked. He and Terri helped Linda out of the car and into his apartment.

"You can have the spare bedroom," he said to Linda, after depositing her on the sofa. "There's clean sheets. I can lend you spare sweats and a tee shirt if you want to get some sleep."

Terri nodded. "Good idea."

Linda leaned back and closed her eyes. She felt dirty and grimy, like the prison's foul air had permeated her every pore. The idea of climbing into a clean bed was completely repugnant to her. She knew she'd contaminate both the bed and the sheets. "I need a shower first."

"Can you do it yourself?" Terri asked.

Linda sighed and slowly stood up from the couch. "Yes, Terri. I'll be fine. But I'll leave the door unlocked in case you hear a bang."

Terri made a face at her. "Very funny."

The hot shower soothed her. She relaxed, allowing the water to wash away the tension, along with all the prison scum. She desperately hoped she'd be able to fall asleep.

After dressing in Chad's clothes, she went back out to living room to find her brother and friend.

Terri had left. Chad sat alone at the kitchen table. "Terri went to get you some clothes and pick up some food."

Linda sat down in front of him. "That's nice of her."

He leaned over and brushed a strand of hair out of her face. "She loves you. She's a great friend. You should go to bed. We'll talk in the morning."

That face, distorted by rage, screamed at her again: *It's your fault those men are dead.* Linda gave her head a quick shake. "I'm not sure I can."

He gently touched her cheek. "Try?"

She studied him for a second before finally nodding. He was right, she desperately needed sleep. She hauled herself to her feet and went in search of the bedroom, convinced she'd never be able to turn her brain off. To be able to fall asleep. But she must have, because the next thing she remembered was waking up with a start, sweaty and sticky, heart racing, sheets twisted around her, a pounding noise in her head. *It's your fault those men are dead.*

She switched on the light. A little past two in the morning. What time had she gone to bed? She couldn't remember, but that seemed to be as much sleep as she was going to get that night.

The cool air gently kissed her sweat-drenched body. Even her hair was soaked. She made her way to the kitchen for a drink.

Out of habit, she opened the refrigerator and studied the contents. Milk, on the top shelf, so innocent and white. Who would have thought it to be loaded with drugs? She eyed it, shut the door and opted for a glass of water, instead.

The distorted face kept screaming at her, from somewhere deep within the shadows of her mind. It seemed so familiar, somehow. Why couldn't she place it? She shook her head, trying to bring the face into focus, to chase away the fogginess that blurred the edges. She knew that face was key. If she could just see who it was, she knew she could finally break the gray mass swirling in and out of her consciousness, pregnant with memories, memories of what had been done to her when she was drugged and helpless.

"Couldn't sleep?" a voice asked from behind her. She whirled around, almost dropping the glass in her shock. Chad stood at the door, rubbing the sleep from his eyes. "Sorry, I didn't mean to scare you."

She put the glass down on the counter. "That's okay. I'm sorry I woke you. I was trying to be quiet."

"I wasn't sleeping anyway." He came closer, peering at her through sleep-crusted eyes. "You're all wet. How did that happen?"

She shrugged. "Sometimes I wake up like this, all sweaty."

"Night sweats. Yeah, the doctor said that might be part of the withdrawal process."

"Or, a side effect of the nightmares."

He looked at her carefully. "I think it's withdrawal. That's too much for a simple nightmare."

"You don't know my nightmares."

He smiled a bit, then turned away. "I'll change the sheets. Why don't you change your clothes? Terri brought two suitcases full."

"Chad, you don't have to wait on me," she said, but he was already gone.

Picking up her glass, she drained it, then went in search of the suitcases. She didn't think she would sleep any more, but it would definitely be good to get out of those sticky clothes.

On her way back to the guest bedroom, she passed a hallway that led to the front door. Without knowing why, she found herself being pulled in that direction, down the hall, to stand in front of it.

It was locked — the chain securely in place. But of course it would be. Chad always locked the door.

Her thoughts traveled back to the milk, untouched, back in the fridge. She gently stroked the dead bolt, an almost furtive gesture. Could it really stop someone from getting in? She felt dreamy, nervous, unfocused.

"No one knows you're here," Chad said from behind her. She half turned to look at him. "Only me, Terri and Steve."

"Steve?"

"He called after you went to bed," he said, pressing his lips into a thin line.

She nodded and went back to studying the door, running her hand over the chain. Chad slowly approached her.

"My door didn't have a chain." She watched him out of the corner of her eye, never letting her hand leave the chain. "Would it have made a difference, do you think?"

"Linda ..."

"Or a dead bolt, like this," she said, pressing her cheek against the wood. "I wasn't always so diligent about locking it, although maybe that wouldn't have changed anything, either."

Chad reached the door and tenderly removed her hand from the chain. "No one knows you're here. Ok? I promise." He cupped her hand in his. "And besides, only two people have a key — you and me."

"Ah." Linda went back to studying the door. "The only two people who have a key to my place are you and me. How do you suppose he ... or she ... got in?"

He tightened his grip on her fingers, his warm, hers cold, almost as cold as death itself. He watched her the way one would a wild, cornered, completely unpredictable animal. "Don't do that to yourself."

"Do what? Wonder how he or she accessed my apartment? That's how it started, that's why I'm in this mess. If I could have kept that person out, none of this would have happened."

He gently pried her away from the door. "Not now. You're still recovering from everything that's happened. You need to give your body time to heal physically."

Linda snorted. "What about mentally? You and I both know those wounds take a lot longer to heal."

"All in good time. You need to get more sleep." He led her to the bedroom.

She protested. "I won't sleep. I never sleep after I wake from a nightmare."

"Try."

He let go of her arm in front of her bedroom, then disappeared down the hall. A moment later he returned, dragging two suitcases, and deposited them in her room. "Come on Linny," he said. "Just change, then try to get some sleep. It's just the drugs leaving your body. That's all the nightmares are."

He looked so worried about her that she agreed, albeit reluctantly. After he left, she stripped off her sweaty clothes, donned a clean nightshirt, and crawled back into bed, deciding she'd get up and watch television once Chad fell asleep.

Much to her surprise, she drifted off instead, and found herself in what Chad had called a withdrawal-induced nightmare, again.

This time, she was in a bedroom. A strange marionette-type figure danced, its shadow jerking menacingly along the wall. She could hear a clock ticking, somewhere in the distance, like the steady beating of a heart. A knife appeared out of nowhere, slashing through the shadow, leaving a trail of blood.

The blood formed itself into words: *Your brother's blood calls to me from the ground.*

The blood melted into a swarm of ants, writhing together, like a body on the ground. Then, they exploded in all different directions, leaving in their place a bed with a man latched to it.

He opened his eyes and smiled at Linda. "You know who's been murdering those men. You've always known." A wig manifested on his head, long white blond hair, and his eyes flashed silver. Suddenly, he was dancing around the room, whirling around like some insane wind-up doll.

She felt something in her hands and looked down at them. A dead chipmunk stared back at her, his fur matted and bloody. She flung it away, confused.

A disembodied voice whispered to her: "You killed them, Elizabeth. It's your fault those men are dead."

Suddenly, she was wearing the wig and the white dress and the contacts.

"You're beautiful, Elizabeth," the voice whispered. "Those men deserved to die. They didn't treat you the way you deserve." The clock ticked louder. The ants crawled over the walls, the floor.

She heard Elizabeth laughing at her. "You know who it is, Linda. It's so easy. You've always known."

A face filled with rage, wearing a wig and silver contacts screamed at her. "It's your fault those men are dead. All your fault."

Her own voice whispered back, "Yes, all my fault, all my fault."

Elizabeth laughed again. "Don't you recognize it, Linda? It's from the Bible. Cain and Abel. The first murder. Brother murdering brother. It's the same here, now. Except it's not a body being murdered, but a soul."

Not a body, but a soul.

The words reverberated throughout her mind. An image floated in front of her — Cain murdering Abel. *The one rejected killing the one chosen.*

Was that it? Was that the connection? The ants ran across the image, and it dissolved.

"Hurry Linda," a voice whispered in the night, the clock now booming in the stillness. "You must remember, and quickly. Steve's life is in danger."

The giant red mouth opened in front of Linda. It smiled, revealing the rows of teeth, then widened even more, as if to swallow her whole.

She gasped and opened her eyes. Sunlight poured in her room, and for a second she was completely disoriented. She couldn't even remember the last time she had slept until daylight.

She stared at the ceiling, feeling her heart pound.

Steve was in danger, but from what? From who?

She lay in sheets completely drenched again — so much for changing them in the middle of the night. Rubbing her hand across her sticky face, she tried to assess what kind of state her body was in. The dizziness seemed to have receded, further into the distance. It wasn't completely gone, but it felt further away. The food and sleep had actually helped.

But what about mentally? That strange dream, the obsession with ants? Maybe it wasn't a dream at all, but messages, to remind her of what she'd forgotten, or blocked out. Maybe it was all filtering through her subconscious, until all that was left were symbols. The ants … they must be symbols. But of what?

Hurry, Linda.

If only she could find the key. A sense of urgency filled her. What if she was already too late?

The smell of bacon and eggs broke through her thoughts. Chad might know.

Shuffling into the kitchen, Linda found Chad standing in front of the stove, humming a song and cooking up a storm. "To what do I owe this honor?"

Chad turned his head and smiled when he saw her. "Perfect timing. Sit right down. My famous omelet, coming right up."

"In a second."

Chad looked at her sharply. "What's wrong?"

"Nothing," Linda quickly reassured him. "I was just wondering if you had heard anything from Steve?" She tried to make her voice sound as casual as possible.

"Steve?" Chad frowned. "Didn't I tell you he called last night?"

"Yes, but what about today?"

"No. Why would he call again already?" Chad slid bacon dripping with grease onto a paper towel.

"Well, do you think we could call him?"

"Why?" Chad looked at her sharply. "Do you remember something?"

"No, no, nothing like that. I just want to make sure he's okay." Even to her, the words sounded lame.

Chad turned away from the stove and faced her. "Why wouldn't he be?"

"I don't know. It's just something from my dream last night."

"I told you, it's just the drugs leaving your body."

"I'm sure that's true. I just can't shake this feeling that something is very wrong."

"There is something wrong. Someone is out there murdering people, not to mention the fact that there's also someone out there who's been drugging you."

Linda made a sour face at him. "You know what I mean."

Chad deliberately turned back to the stove. "Is there something going on between you and Steve?"

"What?" Linda was so surprised, she stepped back and hit the back of her head against the wall. "Ouch. No. Why do you ask that?"

"Because of the way you're acting."

"Oh, for God's sake, Chad."

He made a point of not looking at her, and not answering.

She ran her hand through her hair, her sense of urgency growing stronger by the minute. "And even if there was something going on, why would you care?"

"I told you, he's brought a lot of tragedy to our family. He even had you arrested!"

"God, Chad, I went to *him*. Oh, never mind, I'll take care of it myself." She strode across the kitchen, picked up the phone, and dialed the police station.

It seemed to take forever before they located him. All the while, she chewed on her bottom lip. *It couldn't be too late. Oh, please, dear God, don't let it be too late.*

When his voice finally came on the line, full of concern, she nearly wept with relief. "Linda. Everything all right?"

Yes, yes. It was all right. "Yes. Everything is fine."

"Have you remembered anything yet?"

"No, not yet."

He paused, and in the silence, she listened to him breathe. "Take your time. We'll catch the bastard who's doing this. You just concentrate on getting better."

She closed her eyes. "I will."

"I gotta go. It's time for me to catch some bad guys."

"Wait, Steve."

He waited. She took a deep breath. There was so much she wanted to say, so much unsaid between them: how wrong she was, how much she wanted to go back and undo everything bad that had ever happened between them ... but she couldn't. The words didn't come. "Just ... be careful."

"I will." Then he was gone.

Gently, she replaced the receiver and turned around. Chad was standing by the table, glowering at her. "So, are you going to eat or what?"

"Chad ..."

"You really have to eat."

Silently, she walked over and sat down. He filled her plate — cheese and mushroom omelet, several strips of bacon, and a toasted, buttered English muffin. He poured orange juice into a tall glass. After setting it all in front of her, he seated himself across the table.

"I wish you wouldn't be like this."

He pressed his lips into a thin line. "I've never liked him, Linda. You know that. Ever since high school. I like him even less after what he's done to you. Harassing you, planting ideas in your head, making you think you committed those murders ..."

"The drugs did that."

He slammed his fork against his plate. "How do you know? Maybe the drugs made you more susceptible, but he's the one who swooped in with his accusations."

"Chad." Linda struck the table herself. "Did you look at the evidence against me? I'm the one who found things in my apartment — a wig, a blood-stained dress."

"I don't want to talk about this anymore," Chad covered his face with his hands. "Every time I think about what's been done to you, what you were going through, how you actually thought you could be a murderer ..." His chest heaved while he struggled to get himself under control. "I just can't stand it."

Linda sat back in her chair. "I know. I'm sorry. I wouldn't have been able to stand it either, if all this had happened to you."

He took a deep breath and uncovered his face. "All right, now that we've gotten that out of the way, will you please eat?"

Linda gave him a small smile. "Okay, 'Mom.'" She picked up her fork and cut a piece of omelet. "Mmm, delicious," she said, although it tasted like sand in her mouth. Sand dribbling down inside an hourglass, second-by-second, diminishing Steve's time. It wouldn't be long until the hourglass would be empty and Steve would be ...

Chad smiled back. "Told you."

She blinked, trying to stop her flow of thoughts. Steve was fine. She'd just talked to him. And besides, there was nothing else she could do. She struggled to finish her breakfast.

When she had eaten enough to satisfy Chad, she went to take a shower, since her brother absolutely refused to let her help clean up from breakfast. Dressing in old jeans and a sweatshirt, she lay on the couch and turned on some inane daytime television show. Chad kept coming in, asking her if she wanted tea, juice, water, until she told him to quit hovering. She was a big girl and could fetch her own drinks. All that did was change his location. He moved himself – and his worry – into the kitchen, where he peered out at her from time to time, asking her other questions. How was she feeling? Was she hungry yet? Did she remember what the doctor had told her about flushing toxins out of her system? Finally, she let him bring her some juice, just to keep him quiet.

Her dream haunted her. She couldn't get it out of her mind. There had to be *something* in it, some clue that would break through the cloudy, dreamy confusion hovering in her subconscious and unleash her memories.

Ants. Why did she keep thinking about ants?

If they were a symbol, what did they represent? She tried to remember everything she had been taught in school about ants, but none of it seemed applicable.

Your brother's blood calls to me from the ground.

It must be someone she knew. Someone she trusted. A member of her family, even.

Your brother.

Her mind instantly focused on Chad, banging pots and pans in the kitchen, making her lunch. Chad, always picked on, always misunderstood, her troubled brother who tried to kill himself ...

"No," Linda shouted, falling off the couch.

Not Chad. Not Chad. Not Chad.

He could never — would never hurt me.

Chad rushed in from the kitchen. "Linda, what is it? Are you okay?"

Linda looked at him, his dark hair falling across his forehead, his eyes full of concern. She sat up. "I'm fine. I think I just fell asleep and had another nightmare."

Chad smoothed back her hair. "I guess you did. You're sweating again."

Linda pulled away from him and heaved herself back on the couch. "Really, I'm fine ..." But he was already running off. She heard the water run, and he returned holding a wet washcloth. Tenderly, he pressed the cool cloth against her sticky forehead. "Lunch is ready. Do you want to go in the kitchen or should I bring it here?"

"I just finished breakfast," Linda protested. "I can't eat lunch already."

"Breakfast was over three hours ago, silly. It's time for lunch."

"Three hours?" Linda's eyes automatically sought a clock. She'd been lying on the couch, thinking horrible thoughts, unspeakable thoughts, for three hours? Where had the time gone?

Chad was not the killer. He *couldn't* be.

Although the washcloth felt cool and refreshing against her heated skin, she pushed it away, ashamed of what had been going through her mind. "I'll go in the kitchen to eat."

True to form, a huge lunch greeted her — soup, sandwich, fruit salad, water and a tall glass of milk. Linda eyed the milk suspiciously, then felt instantly ashamed again. Oh, God. Would this nightmare ever end?

She ate everything, but didn't touch the milk. If Chad noticed, he didn't say anything. Instead, she drank the water. After lunch, she escaped to her bedroom, claiming she needed a nap, but really her guilty conscience refused to let her be in the same room with him.

She lay on the bed and stared at the ceiling. If not Chad, then who? You have three other brothers. It could be one of them.

One of them, one of them. A swarm of ants covered the ceiling. The clock was still ticking. Why couldn't she find whatever it was that was eluding her? The key, to all of it?

Your brother's blood calls to me from the ground. The ants danced. The voice again: *Kill them! They're nothing but ants, nothing but ants, never treating you the way you deserve ..."*

A face, that face, distorted by rage, screamed at her. "It's your fault those men were murdered. Everything is your fault. It's all because of the ants! How can they possibly understand? They're so beneath us. All of them. Ants we step on, ants who should worship us. Because we are gods. We are gods, and they are nothing."

Linda's eyes flew open. Elizabeth was right. She knew who the murderer was. She had known it all along.

The ants had finally revealed it all.

She got off the bed and went into the kitchen. Terri and Chad were sitting at the kitchen table, quietly talking, but they stopped when they saw her.

"Hi, Linda," Terri said. "How are you feeling?"

"Did you sleep well?" Chad asked.

Linda looked at both of them. What would they say, what would they think?

"I know who murdered those men." Her voice was quiet, calm, the voice of reason. "I know who's been drugging me."

It amazed her, how composed she felt, although she knew she should be feeling anything but. She had looked right into the face of nightmares, and seen evil so pure it glistened. Yet all she felt now was a calmness. An odd sense of relief. No more secrets. Finally, no more secrets. She had, at last, broken his control. He would never be able to hurt her again.

Terri and Chad simply stared at her. "Who?" Terri asked after several long seconds.

Linda smiled a little. "You won't believe me."

"Who?" Terri said again. "Linda, come on, the suspense is killing us."

Linda ran her hand through her hair, taking a deep, cleansing breath. "Peter."

CHAPTER 26

"Peter?" Chad and Terri asked, at the exact same moment.

"Yes. Peter."

Terri shook her head. "Your brother, Peter."

Linda went to the sink, poured herself a glass of water. "I told you you wouldn't believe me."

Chad looked at her carefully. "Are you sure, Linda?"

She nodded. "I remember now. Not everything, but it's all starting to come back."

Chad got up from the table, gently took her arm and led her to a chair. He urged her to sit. "What do you remember?"

Slowly, haltingly, Linda pieced together the entire story as best she could for her brother and friend. Myriad memories jumbled together, now, like photographs jammed into a drawer. Peter slipping into her apartment at night, injecting her body with drugs, and her mind with poison.

"*You were always so selfish, so worthless.*" Giving her a wig and contact lenses. Forcing her to dress like Elizabeth.

"*Elizabeth, you're so beautiful. I'm so glad you're back. I missed you so. That terrible Linda, she never appreciated you. She never realized what a wonderful woman you are.*"

Peter, bringing her animals — dogs, cats, squirrels — all butchered. Placing their broken, bloody, lifeless bodies in her lap.

"*Look what you did to these animals, Elizabeth. I know they hated you. It's good you killed them. I would kill them for you if you wanted. I did before. Remember, I took such good care of you when we were children, and those awful animals would attack you. They deserved to die. It's good you killed them.*"

Peter's voice, high-pitched and childlike. Taking her hand and running it down the animals' body, their fur matted with blood, their bodies so cold, so cold. They smelled of death, of betrayal.

"*They can't hurt you now, Elizabeth. It was good you killed them.*" Linda's arm, heavy and complacent, doing what Peter wanted, obeying Peter's every wish. Her mind, so thick, she couldn't think, couldn't fight.

The perfect woman. Peter's dream woman.

Peter, ecstatic about her thinness, her paleness.

"You're beautiful. You look more like Elizabeth every day."

The drugs, the broken nights, doing their work and breaking her down. Their faces reflecting back at them in the bathroom mirror, his cheek pressed against hers.

"We look like twins."

His eyes dark and twisted, his face pale and sweaty. He panted, licked his lips.

"Take off the wig."

She obeyed, her hands stiff, swollen. He snatched it out of her hands and arranged it on his own head. He panted harder, the sweat dripping down his features. She could see that he was fully aroused.

"Contacts. Take them out."

She slowly removed them. He stood over her, barely able to contain his excitement, grabbing the contacts as soon as they were out of her eyes and putting them in his own. The smell of sweat so strong it nearly choked her. He stared at himself in the mirror, smiling.

"Elizabeth. So pleased you could be here. You're so beautiful."

He undid his pants, groaning, biting his lips until the blood flowed.

"You're so beautiful. I missed you so."

Telling her all about his business trips. Dressing as Elizabeth, then hitting the bars. Prancing about in her apartment, both of them … both Elizabeths.

"Men are stupid. They don't realize who we are. They don't feel our power. They can't possibly understand us, yet they try to pick us up anyway." Laughing gleefully. *"How can they possibly understand? They're so beneath us. All of them. Like ants we step on, ants who should worship us because we are gods. We are gods! And they are nothing."*

Peter bringing her a bloodstained dress, a bloodstained knife.

"We killed him. Remember."

His voice high and excited, like a child again. A demon child.

"We let him pick us up and take us to the hotel room. We were just playing around, wanting to see how far we could go, how long it would last. It took longer than we thought, remember? He was already undressed.

And he was so mad. So furious. But we took care of him, didn't we? Tried to beat us up, but we showed him a thing or two. Then we got the knife, didn't we?" Peter's voice cracking. Smiling and licking his lips. *"Much better than the animals, wasn't it? Much, much better."*

Groaning, biting his lips again, until the blood flowed, reaching for his pants.

Bringing her pictures. Of the apartments, of the bodies. *"Look what you did. You killed that man. Butchered him, didn't you? But he deserved it. Just an ant. Didn't worship you the way he should. Didn't treat you the way he should."*

Describing in detail exactly what happened. *"You remember, don't you?"*

Becoming "you." Gone was the "we." Always telling her she had done those terrible things. Her mind, so clouded with drugs, lack of sleep, lack of food, finally just gave in. She started to believe him. *"Yes, I do remember."*

Peter starting to kill in Riverview, not just on business trips, where he could easily slip away, undetected, unnoticed. The need growing, in him. Becoming so great. So powerful. *"You did this. How could you kill those men? You must be an evil, evil person."*

And Linda nodding, agreeing. She *must* be a terrible person, doing those things.

Too drugged to be terrified when he thrust his face, mottled with rage, into her own. Too drugged to even care if she were facing her own death, when he brandished the knife at her, holding it against her cheek, her eye. Even the night he stabbed it deep into her arm, still so full of rage that she had dared go to the bars without him – without being under his control. She had ruined that night for him, for Elizabeth. No way could they find a man – a new victim – with all those cops swarming around. No way could he satisfy his gnawing, growing, uncontrollable need.

Chad and Terri stared at her, their faces full of horror, horror Linda had never allowed herself to feel.

Terri put her hand up to her face. "Linda ..."

Chad's eyes appeared glassy, full of tears, tears Linda had never been able to shed for herself. "Linda, I'm so sorry. I can't ... I mean, we knew Peter was an asshole, but never, never this. Never *this*."

"A monster," Terri finished. "An absolute monster."

Linda sat back in her chair, feeling oddly cleansed. Confession *was* good for the soul. "At least I finally know. That's what's most important."

Terri reached over to grasp her hands. "We're here for you. We'll help you get through this."

Linda squeezed her hand back. "You've already been here for me, and I appreciate it more than you'll ever know."

Chad abruptly shot up from the table, his chair falling to the floor with a clatter. "I'll kill him," he muttered, clenching his fist. "I'll fucking kill him."

"No, Chad," Linda quickly stood up and hurried over to him, putting her hand on his shoulder. He flinched at her touch. "I would be just sick if anything happened to you."

"How do you think I feel?" he asked bitterly.

"It's a job for the police," Terri said from behind.

The police. Oh God, Steve. She had nearly forgotten.

Linda whirled around. "What time is it?"

Terri glanced at the clock. "Almost nine. Why?"

"Oh, no, it's that late?" Frantically, Linda scrambled for the phone.

"What is it? Linda, what?" Terri hurried to her side, while Linda tried to press down the numbers using fingers that had turned frozen and numb.

"It's Steve," she said, through lips equally cold. "He's in terrible danger. You saw him the other day, Chad. Steve ruined Peter's fun. There's no telling what Peter's capable of."

Chad pressed his lips together and turned away, pacing the length of the kitchen like a caged lion.

The phone rang and rang in her ear before finally being answered by a voice messaging system telling her to call back during normal business hours. She slammed the phone down, biting her lips in frustration.

"Call 9-1-1," Terri urged. Linda picked up the phone again and dialed.

After an excruciatingly long phone conversation trying to explain to the woman who answered that no, *she* was not in any immediate danger, but an officer was, she finally got transferred to a manager who patched her through to one of the detectives working the case.

"Why wouldn't they give you Steve?" Terri asked.

Linda shook her head.

"Detective Thomas," the voice on the other line said.

Linda rolled her eyes. Great, exactly the person she would get, right now. "Detective Thomas? It's Linda Rossini."

There was a long pause. "How did you get this number?"

"I called 9-1-1 and they patched me through."

"What do you want?" she said in a clipped voice.

"Steve. I need to talk to Steve."

"You can't. He's busy."

Linda felt her heart stop. "Busy? Busy doing what?"

"Trying to catch a killer," Detective Thomas's voice was scornful. "What did you think? Taking ballroom dance lessons?"

Linda wiped her forehead. She was starting to sweat again, like a dripping faucet. Would she ever feel normal again? "Can you get him for me? Please? It's urgent."

"So is what he's doing."

"Please, it's a matter of life and death." She could feel the clock ticking inside her, each second a little more death.

"If it's so important, why don't you tell me? I'll pass it on to Steve."

Fat chance, Linda thought. Out loud she said, "Look, if you can't get Steve, can you at least tell me what he's doing."

"Police business."

"Detective Thomas, *please*, I really need to know this."

Silence. Then she said, "He's doing undercover work."

"Oh, no."

"What do you mean, 'oh no'?"

Linda pushed the phone hard to her ear, squeezing her eyes shut. Sweat poured off her face, running down her arm and neck. "Has he talked to anyone? Has he left with anyone? Tell me." Her voice rose higher and higher, bordering on hysteria.

A murmur of voices on the other end, as if Detective Thomas were talking to someone else. Then she came back on the line. "A man. He was talking to a man. Happy? Now, will you tell me what this is all about?"

Linda took a deep breath and opened her eyes. "I remembered something. It could be important. I'd like to tell him as soon as possible."

"Tell me."

"I'd rather tell him myself if you don't mind. Could you tell me where you are?"

Detective Thomas grunted. "Yeah, right." The phone went dead.

Linda turned away from the wall to look at Terri and Chad. "He's doing undercover work. They last saw him talking to a man." She tried to let go of the phone and found she couldn't; she had been clutching the receiver so tightly.

Terri frowned. "A man. Well, at least he's safe for now."

"Maybe." Linda reached for a paper towel to wipe her face and arm. Something didn't feel right, the ticking in her head growing louder and louder, until it was practically booming.

Chad continued to pace. "Did she say who?"

Linda snorted. "Are you kidding? I'm lucky I got that much out of her."

He paced slower, then, his hands clenching and unclenching. "I know you don't think too much of Peter's intellect, but he did make it through law school."

Linda made a face and continued to mop her face. "Meaning?"

"Meaning, do you really think he's stupid enough to go after Steve dressed as Elizabeth?"

Linda froze. Time screeched to a halt. Silence draped itself like a shroud over the kitchen, muffling everything except for the ticking of the clock, counting off the seconds left in Steve's life, as it hit her: of course he wouldn't.

Terri first broke the silence. "But how could he entice Steve back to Steve's apartment? It doesn't make sense." Her gaze darted from Linda to Chad.

"He wouldn't have to," Chad said quietly.

"Drugs," Linda moaned. "He could just drug him and slip him out. The way he did me." She covered her face in her hands.

Terri still kept trying to explain everything away. "But, you weren't watched by a whole bunch of cops. Wouldn't they notice something?"

"Not if he walked out with Peter on his own accord," Chad theorized. "Maybe Peter told Steve he had something to show him, but they had to go out to his car. Then, once they're away from the police and any potential witnesses ..." His voice trailed off, and he drew his finger across his throat in a slashing motion.

"Oh, God." Linda ran out the room. She could hear Terri calling her from the kitchen, but she ignored her. Her purse. She had to find her purse.

Running into the bedroom, she skidded to a halt by her suitcases and started tossing clothes out of them.

"Linda, what are you doing?" Terri stood by the door.

"My purse. I've got to find it." She shoved the suitcases out of the way, in a complete frenzy.

"Here it is, Linda. By your coat." Terri held it out to her.

Linda dove for it, tripping over suitcases, and swiped it out of Terri's hand. She immediately dumped the contents on the floor and began to paw through it frantically. "It has to be here somewhere," she muttered anxiously, the clock continuing to tick loudly inside her, raising her blood pressure with every beat. It had been ages since she cleaned out her purse. It had to be here somewhere, it just had to. Finally she found it and snapped it up.

"What, what?" Terri peered over her shoulder to see.

"Steve's card," Linda gasped, moping the sweat from her forehead. "It has his home phone number on it." Standing up, she raced to the phone, brushing by Chad who still stood in the middle of the kitchen floor.

Just when her hand touched the receiver, the phone rang. Linda jumped, suddenly convinced it was Peter calling to mock her. Shaking that thought off, she snatched it off the hook. "Hello."

"Linda." Detective Thomas. "We may have a problem."

Linda sank to her knees and squeezed her eyes shut for a second. Not Steve. Oh, God, not Steve.

She could barely hear Detective Thomas through the roaring in her ears. "We can't find him. Last anyone saw he was talking to a man, but now we can't locate him." Dimly, Linda recognized strains of concern cracking through the detective's professional voice. "Someone here thought he might have been talking to your brother, Peter, but that shouldn't be ..."

"It's him," Linda interrupted, her face numb and cold, sweat continuing to drip from her forehead. "Peter. He's the killer. He's the one who was drugging me. You must find him. He's probably got Steve drugged ..."

"Whoa, wait a second," Detective Thomas's voice sounded incredulous. "Your brother is the killer? Peter, the former Assistant District Attorney? There must be some mistake."

"There's no mistake. He's the one. He's been drugging me for months and showing me the details of the murders. He's killed in more places than Riverview. It started when he took his business trips."

Detective Thomas said something to someone off the phone before speaking into the receiver again. "Where do you think he would have taken him?"

Linda gasped in relief. "Steve's apartment. You must hurry."

"We're going now. Don't worry." The phone went dead a second time.

Linda leaned her head back against the cabinet, the phone dangling limply from her fingers. "It was Peter they saw with Steve. And now, he *has* him."

Terri crouched in front of her. "Do the police believe you?"

"I think so. I don't know." She lifted her head and looked at Terri. "But we've got to do something. We can't just sit here."

"Do something? Do what?" Terri exclaimed when Linda got to her feet. "Linda, this is a matter for the police, not us."

"I don't care. I'm going to Steve's apartment."

"What?" Terri nearly shrieked.

"I'm going with you." Chad's face was cold and set. "I have to look Peter in the face."

"But, you can't kill him." Linda carefully watched him.

Terri looked at each of them. "I can't believe this. You're both crazy."

Chad stared back at her. "I won't kill him."

"Then let's go." Linda dashed out of the kitchen in search of shoes and a jacket, followed closely by Chad. Terri brought up the rear, muttering to herself the entire time.

***

The ride to Steve's apartment seemed to take forever.

Linda sat in the front, perched on the edge of the seat, hardly daring to breath. They can't be too late. They can't be too late. Please, God, don't let them be too late. Every passing second brought new fear that it had been his last. She could see the lifeblood draining from him, darkening the white sheets, his hands helplessly latched to the headboard, Peter watching him die, laughing and laughing.

The police had beaten them there. When they rounded the corner, Linda could see the flashing blue and red lights brightening the night sky, almost festive. Chad didn't even have the car in park before Linda opened the door. She could hear Chad and Terri both calling to her, but she ignored them, flying across the street as fast as she could.

"Hold on, you can't go in there." One of the police officers tried to block her, but she ducked under his arm and dashed to the door.

Someone snagged her arm, jerking her back. "You can't go in there, official police business," a low male voice said in her ear.

Linda struggled to free herself. "You don't understand. My brother is in there."

The hold on her never slackened. "Which apartment is he in?"

Linda turned on him exasperated. "He doesn't live here. He's the killer, he's trying to kill Steve! Now let me go."

The cop looked down at her, heavy brows framing dark brown eyes that showed a tinge of surprise. "How do you know that?"

"Where's Detective Thomas? She can vouch for me. I'm the one who sent her here. Where is she?"

"You have to let us do our job ..." the cop started to say, but Linda stopped listening to him, seeing movement by the door. Detective Thomas walked out first. Weary. She looked weary. A sick feeling bubbled inside Linda, mesmerized by the detective's exhausted expression. With a twist and a jerk, she managed to free herself from the cop and run to the door.

"Where's Steve? Where's Steve?" she screamed, running toward Detective Thomas.

Detective Thomas looked up and saw Linda. "You're not supposed to be here," she started.

Linda grabbed her arm. "Where's Steve? Is he all right?"

She started to push past the detective, but Detective Thomas blocked her way. "He's fine. They're bringing him down now. We got here just in time. It's over."

Linda fought the detective a few seconds longer before her words finally sank in. She stopped struggling and turned to her. "And Peter?"

Detective Thomas nodded, pushing her hair back in a tired gesture. "You were right. We got him."

A high-pitched squeal sliced through the commotion like a hot knife slicing through ice. "You think you've got me! Ha! You don't know anything. You're just ants before a god! Bow down before me, you ant." It was Peter, but it wasn't Peter. He spoke in a high falsetto, a voice that sounded eerily like Elizabeth's.

Linda felt chills run down her back.

A gruff voice answered back. "Yeah, and I'm Elvis. Come on let's go."

Detective Thomas grasped Linda's elbow and pulled her to one side when two officers, dragging Peter, burst from the door.

"Good God," Linda heard a voice behind her. Chad. But she didn't turn to him; she was practically entranced … staring at Peter, paralyzed by a sea of emotions.

He wore a white dress, the white-blond wig and the silver contacts. Make-up smeared his face, lipstick and blush running grotesquely together. The wig hung askew on his head, allowing tuffs of his brown hair to poke through, making him look like some sort of mutated monster — half Elizabeth, half Peter.

"He really does look like Elizabeth," Chad muttered. "If I hadn't seen it for myself I never would have believed it."

Peter hadn't stopped screaming, a foul stream of words spewed from his mouth like venom.

"He even sounds a little like Elizabeth." Terri's eyes widened, astonished at the sight.

"Yeah, but Elizabeth would never have talked like that," Chad quickly answered back. Linda couldn't stop her eyes from rolling. Trust Chad to defend Elizabeth to the last, even under these circumstances.

She looked back at Peter, a complicated brew of horror, terror, revulsion and rage swirling inside her. She had trouble breathing.

It's your fault those men are dead.

How could he have done such horrible things to her? How could she have allowed him to do them? The more she thought about it, the more the rage started to take over, bubbling over all the other emotions.

Peter turned his head toward her at that exact moment. His white-hot, silver eyes blazing with madness burned straight into hers. "Fucking bitch!" he screamed. "There's the killer, not me. Arrest that whore! She's the one."

Linda shook off Detective Thomas's arm and approached Peter. *"Do you have any idea how much trouble you're in?"* she asked, her voice deceptively soft.

"Arrest her. Arrest her!" Peter shrieked, madly.

From behind, Detective Thomas motioned, and the policemen stopped. Linda continued to walk toward Peter, her steps slow and measured, rage frothing and boiling. *"Do you have any idea what you've done to the family? To Mother and Father?"*

"She's the killer! Not me."

"But you were always selfish that way, weren't you?" She had almost reached Peter now. She could see patches on his skin where his make-up had rubbed off.

"Why don't you *do* something?" Peter yelled to his captors. "She's the killer. Not me."

Linda leaned closer to him. Dangerously close. She could smell Elizabeth's perfume on him, thick and strong, and something else — the smell of sour, rotting milk. "I remember everything," she said softly. "And I *will* testify against you. It's over. All of it. They'll lock you up and throw away the key, counselor."

A flash of sanity, of understanding, flared through the madness in his eyes. "I don't know what you're talking about," he muttered, leaning away from her. *"You're* the killer."

Linda smiled — cold, predatory. "Elizabeth would have been very disappointed in you. She never would have allowed herself to be caught." She turned and walked away. Behind her, Peter let out a howl of utter despair. "You bitch. You whore!" he cried. "How dare you say such a thing to me? You never understood her. Never, never, never."

Linda kept walking, not turning around, the bitter cold air sweeping over her cheeks like a dead lover's kiss. Police and spectators quietly stepped aside when she passed, head held high, eyes straight ahead.

The rage still burned within, but it was now more of a cleansing flame, igniting the evil and turning it to ash, so it could be blown away on a winter breeze, disappearing forever.

CHAPTER 27

Linda drank her coffee and watched the snow fall from the sky. Just in time for a white Christmas — how perfect.

It had been three weeks exactly since Peter had been arrested for murdering all those men. Although he was going to be tried in Wisconsin, other states were in the process of collecting evidence against him as well, thanks to Linda's testimony, albeit incomplete.

Chances were he would never again see the light of day.

Linda had not seen Peter since that fateful night. Chad had gone once, but he refused to tell her what had transpired between them. Instead, he had simply pressed his lips together and made an appointment to see his therapist.

Linda smiled grimly. It was difficult to accept the fact that they were related to such pure evil, that his blood ran through their veins as well. She knew they were wondering what happened to make him turn out like that.

And would it happen to them as well?

She took another sip of coffee while continuing to gaze at the snow, big fluffy flakes, falling from an almost entirely gray sky. According to Chad, her family had not taken the news of Peter's arrest very well. Cindy, his wife, had first staunchly denied all charges. Once she had seen Peter for herself, however, she had immediately filed for divorce, packed up their two children, and moved out of state to live with her sister.

Like Cindy, Mark and Mike had also refused to believe any of it in beginning, claiming Linda to be a liar. A bad seed. After speaking to Peter, Mark had collapsed on the spot and had to be hospitalized. Mike had fallen into a deep depression, and was now being carefully monitored by several doctors. Both wives had followed in Cindy's footsteps — quietly filing for divorce and leaving the state.

Her father, once understanding the enormity of the situation, had a nervous breakdown and was committed to a private hospital, broken in mind and spirit. Her mother, on the other hand, had pulled herself together. She was now the only person holding the shreds of the family together, and doing it with a quiet dignity Linda would never have believed her capable of, in such a situation.

Irony. Who would have thought that when the chips came tumbling down, tumbling at breakneck speed, the ones left standing would be the "weak" ones — her, Chad and their mother? Who would have ever guessed? Linda had first thought she would be happy to see her childhood tormentors reduced to such a destroyed, helpless state, but oddly enough, she felt nothing at all.

She swallowed the last of her coffee and went into the kitchen for more, although she had sworn to Terri, Chad, God, her doctors and anyone else they could think of that she would only drink one cup a day. She would compromise — just a half cup more. They were small cups anyway.

Weaving around boxes in the hallway, she made her way into Chad's kitchen, stopping for a moment to pet Felix who lay on one of them. Her eyes fell to a slim, cardboard mailing tube tucked in the corner.

It had arrived in the mail for her the day before yesterday. No return address, her name had been written in bold, block letters. Opening it, she found a rolled-up painting — one of Elizabeth's — swirls of blacks and grays disappearing into a void, slashes of angry red streaked across the black. Oddly, a yellow sun peered out from the corner, bright and cheery, such an incongruous mark to the rest of the work. She had never seen this painting before.

When she had first opened it, she immediately thought someone in her family had mailed it to her. But, as she studied it, she knew that wasn't the case.

Despair is a terrible thing. I know how to instigate it, but I have no idea how to live with it.

Elizabeth had sent it to her. As a reminder. As a curse.

What was it she had said?

"When can you both cause something and not do a thing?"

Was it possible that, whoever or whatever Elizabeth was, there were others out there like her? Those who could instigate killing – evil – without physically getting their own hands dirty?

Were those "people" human?

And what made Elizabeth change her mind about Linda? Would Linda ever know? Did it matter?

It still surprised Linda that Elizabeth would reach out to her, of all people. To sacrifice herself for Linda? She ran her finger down the painting. It felt like a kiss, a real kiss from a real sister, sent beyond the grave as a gift of hope.

Linda thought a lot about what Elizabeth had told her, that she was the reason why her childhood was full of violence. At first, Linda felt vindicated — she had been right all along. Then it moved to resentment — how dare Elizabeth put the family through all of that. How dare Elizabeth destroy her childhood.

But now, she had moved to acceptance. The past was the past. It couldn't be changed. It could only be accepted.

It was time to stop being a victim. To stop blaming Elizabeth for all that had gone wrong in Linda's life. It was time to grow up, and start taking responsibility.

The buzzer rang, causing her to jump several feet in the air, jerking her from her thoughts.

Would she ever be her old self again? She felt like one of those Victorian women, suffering from a case of "vapors." If she didn't get her act together soon, her doctor would probably end up wanting to prescribe something to her. Valium, she guessed. As if she needed more drugs.

The buzzer rang again. Obviously someone very persistent, Linda thought, and made her way to the intercom. It was Steve.

"Can I come up?"

Her mouth suddenly felt dry and hot, as if it had filled with sand, but she pushed the button to unlock the front door. She had only seen Steve once during the past three weeks, in the hospital. Drugged and beaten, the police had taken him immediately to the emergency room. They hadn't allowed Linda to see him that night, so she had returned the next day.

Chad drove her. He hadn't said a word, but the expression on his face told Linda he still was not entirely comfortable with the relationship. Without explanation, he chose to sit in the waiting room while she visited Steve.

His appearance shocked her. He lay on the white sheets, his face a mass of swelling bruises. A white bandage had been wrapped around his neck. Linda swallowed when she saw it, wondering just how close he had come to not surviving that night … if death had looked into his face, breathed into his lips and bent for a kiss.

Steve opened his puffy eyes. It took a second for him to focus on Linda, but when he did, he tried to smile through cracked and bleeding lips. "Linda, I'm so glad you're here. Please, sit down." He held out one bandaged arm to her. Linda took it and seated herself in the chair next to the bed.

He started to struggle to sit up, but Linda gently pushed him back. "You're fine. You don't have to sit up for me."

He made some sort of face, Linda couldn't really tell what it meant, since it took on an entirely gruesome appearance because of all the damage. "Looks worse than it is."

"I have no doubt."

He stopped struggling and leaned back, wincing slightly. "I owe you my life."

Linda shrugged. "It's nothing. Really. Besides, I owe you as well. If it weren't for you, I might still be in that jail cell thinking I was the murderer."

"The lab tests did that for you, really."

Linda frowned. "Maybe, maybe not. I've seen plenty of television shows where the framed person gets the book thrown at him. Or her."

"That doesn't happen in real life."

"Gee, why doesn't that make me feel better?"

Steve laughed a little. "Ouch, don't make me laugh. It hurts too much."

Linda looked down. "Sorry."

Neither spoke. The silence stretched between them, taunt and brittle. Finally, Linda lifted her eyes to his. "Tell me," she said, through lips that barely moved. "Tell me what happened that night."

Steve shifted on the bed. "Peter approached me in the bar. Said he had been to your apartment and had found something he wanted to show me. Wouldn't tell me what it was, but said it was very important. It was in his car, which was just parked around back. "Just take a second," he said. I agreed and got up to follow him. He had been acting strange, almost jumpy, his eyes darting all around the bar. At the time, I thought it was just stress over everything that had happened. Some detective I turned out to be, huh?" He said the last sentence in a voice filled with scorn and self-loathing.

"He fooled a lot of people," Linda replied, her voice soft and gentle. "Don't blame yourself. I of all people should have known, and I didn't."

"That's because he kept you higher than a kite most of the time. Anyway, he hit me with something from behind, once we were near his car, because the next thing I remember is being tied to my own bed and Peter dancing around me, dressed as Elizabeth."

He swallowed, closed his eyes, then opened them. "I still can't believe it, even though I saw it with my own eyes. I was pretty hazy from the drugs he injected, but Peter wanted me awake. He wanted me to watch my own death." He winced and his hand unconsciously touched his throat. "He almost succeeded, too."

Linda gulped. "I'm sorry you had to go through all of this."

He dropped his hand and looked at her. "Why? It's not your fault."

You evil, evil person. It's your fault those men are dead.

She rubbed her face with her hand. Beads of sweat dribbled down her face. She tried to smile. "I know. But somehow I still feel responsible."

Steve squeezed her hand. "Don't. You saved my life. Don't you ever forget that."

Linda nodded, then looked away. She had come here to say other things, things that really needed to be said, but found her voice had dissolved. She glanced at the clock. "Goodness. I have to be going." She stood up. "You take care of yourself, you hear?"

Steve watched her, his eyes unreadable in his distorted face. "You too. You need to get better as well."

"I am. I am." She slipped through the door.

***

A sharp rap startled her out of her thoughts for the second time that day. She made her way to the door and opened it.

He stood there, the swelling down, but faint outlines of yellowing bruises still harsh on his features. A smaller bandage covered his neck. "Hi, Linda. You're looking well."

Linda swallowed and held the door open. "So are you."

He stepped into the hallway and immediately let his gaze fall on the boxes. "Moving?"

Linda closed the door and stepped around him. "In. I'm moving in. With Chad."

He nodded. She cast her gaze around and noticed her empty coffee cup still clutched in her hand. "Would you like some coffee? I was about to get some."

"Sure." He followed her into the kitchen. "I heard you're not working at Bay Mutual anymore."

She waved at the table, then went to the cupboard to find another cup. "Yeah, I quit. Finally." She poured his coffee before sitting down at the table with him. "They were actually pretty good about it, all things considered. I was going to work two more weeks, but they told me not to — gave me two weeks of paid sick time and all my vacation. Couldn't believe it."

Steve rolled his coffee mug between his hands. "So, now what are you going to do?"

"Go back to school. Get my degree. Be an architect." She brought the mug to her lips but didn't immediately drink. "It was too late to get in this spring, but I'm set for summer. Instead, I picked up a few more hours at Marshall Fields and will be doing an internship at Chad's firm." She sipped her coffee.

Steve looked around the kitchen. "And living here to save expenses."

Linda smiled. "You got it. Between tuition, therapy and doctor's bills, I've got to do what it takes. But, I figured it out. With what I saved over the years plus working at Marshall Fields and the internship, which is paid, I'll be able to cover everything and not take out any loans."

"That's good, Linda." He studied his cup. "It sounds like things are starting to work out for you. I'm glad."

Linda shrugged. "It took me awhile, but I finally figured out that I was never going to get what I wanted unless I actually did something about it. It won't be easy, but it's worth it." She cocked her head. "But, you didn't come all the way here to listen to me blather on. What is it?"

"Actually I did. I wanted to check up on you and see that you were all right."

"I see." Linda dropped her gaze to the table. A smear stretched across it. Obviously, she hadn't cleaned it very well after breakfast. The silence stretched. So much still unsaid. Could she tell him how sorry she was? That she now understood she had never given him a chance in high school, yet held the fact he dated Elizabeth over his head anyway? That it wasn't fair of her?

Steve cleared his throat. "I also wanted to ... I don't know. Apologize, I guess."

Linda looked at him in shock. "Apologize? For what?"

Steve laughed a little. "For dating your sister back in high school. For never looking you up all these years. For suspecting you in this murder case."

Linda played with her coffee cup. "It's not necessary. I have a lot to be sorry for myself. I should have trusted you in high school. The phone goes both ways; I could have looked you up as well. And, I thought I was guilty, so it was no wonder I *acted* guilty."

He ran his finger around the rim of the mug. "This may be too little too late, but I was wondering if we could start over. Maybe get to know each other all over again."

She ran her hands through her hair. "I don't think we can ever start over. There's too much that's happened between us. But, as for getting to know each other again, I'd like that."

Steve looked up, his dark green eyes warm, his smile brilliant. "Perfect."

Linda smiled back, the knot inside her finally relaxing.

Outside, the snow continued to fall, covering the brown, cracked earth and turning Riverview into a winter wonderland.

THE END

Michele Pariza Wacek (also known as Michele PW) taught herself to read at three years old because she so badly wanted to write fiction. As an adult, she became a professional copywriter (copywriters write promotional materials for businesses, nothing to do with protecting intellectual property or putting a copyright on something) and eventually founded a copywriting and marketing company.

She grew up in Madison, Wisconsin and currently lives with her husband and dogs in the mountains of Arizona. You can reach her at MicheleParizaWacek.com. *Mirror Image* is her second novel; the first, *The Stolen Twin*, was published in 2015.

Made in the USA
Coppell, TX
04 September 2020